Once Upon a

To Mary my mother for everything, and to Gwen my partner for everything else

Once Upon a Time Traveller

Charles Bevons

CHAPTER 1

I was falling into darkness, my parted lips locked in a silent scream, and my arms and legs flailing but failing to halt my drop into oblivion.

Yet such is the nature of dreams, I seemed to sense the moment of approaching impact. And when that moment arrived my eyes snapped open, and the faint resonance of a muffled scream bounced off the walls and echoed distantly in my sleep-soaked half-conscious mind. The cold grey light of a new day spilled through carelessly closed curtains, as I half listened to the dull groan of early morning traffic, and the piercing call of shrill birdsong. I was cold and turned to wrap my arms around her, but she too was cold, very cold, and quite dead.

The sheets seemed to ensnare me as I released her deathly chill and pulled away, tumbling to the floor, and dragging my prone body across the carpet until my back met resistance against the chest of drawers. Shoulders rising and falling as I struggled for air. And when that moment passed, I whispered the word 'no'. Faintly at first, and then repeating the word over and over again. I stayed like that for some time, rocking backwards and forwards, until my rapid breathing abated. Slowly I raised my head to the god's and silently cursed them all. Particularly the so-called one God and his son Jesus. Because I had once loved and believed in both of them in another life, another time.

And then an almost primeval scream tore through my lips, and a deep red mist rose quickly. I felt a sort of rage that I have never felt before or since. Shafts of sunlight fingered across the carpet, and after a time I crawled back into our bed and wrapped my arms around her. Hoping that I could somehow absorb her deathly chill, and we could journey on together, as we had always done. I remember spilling hot tears and cold snot into the gentle curve of her slender neck like a child. Until I was too exhausted to cry any more. But I did continue to repeat her name, over and over again. Like some long lost Eastern mystic chant for the safe passage of lost souls.

The phone rang, shrill, insistent, and then clicked into message mode. 'Morning Fay, I'm running a bit late love, so can we meet at one thirty instead. Give me a call if there's a problem.'

The sun rose higher before the phone rang again. 'Jimmy boy, if you are going to Harrogate this morning I would really appreciate a lift, call me.'

I hoped that was it, and they would leave us alone. Leave us in peace, to lie here, to die here. The doorbell chimed over and over. ' Hello, it's the police, can you open the door please.' Then I heard another voice, it was Ammo. ' Can I help you officer?'

'We received a call from a neighbour, they heard loud screaming coming from this flat.'

There was another more urgent hammering at the door.

'Jimmy, the police are here, please open the door.'

I realised then that it was time, time to leave. Reluctantly I unravelled myself from her cold embrace and padded naked to the door.

'Ammo,' I croaked.

'Yes, it's me Jimmy, please open the door.'

' Fay is dead Ammo, she died in her sleep.'

I walked over to the kitchen and slid a carving knife from the pine rack. The first cut was deep, opening veins and severing tendons. I felt no pain, but my legs began to tremble, and the knife somehow slipped through my fingers and clattered as it hit the tiled floor. Ammo hammered on the door as another officer arrived, carrying a circular iron battering ram, affectionately known in the force as 'the enforcer' or 'the big red key'. He swung the enforcer once and hit the lock.

I dropped to my knees in a state of panic, scrambling to retrieve the knife, slipping clumsily in the gathering pool of blood. I heard a sound like the crashing of waves in my ears, and then a much louder sound, an explosion

of splintering wood. I almost had it, the knife was just a fingertip away, when a large black boot came out of nowhere. Sliding across the bloodied tiles, and kicking the knife beyond my reach.

Ammo's voice was loud, full of reproachful anger and distress. 'Oh, my good God Jimmy, what have you done?'

***

14 months later.

Dave Berry was singing 'The Crying Game' on the radio when I pulled up at the house. A distant rumble of thunder sounded and it started to rain.

'Watch your step in there,' the agent had warned, 'the place has been empty for years. The security screens have been removed, but there is no power, so I would suggest you take a big torch.' He paused and scratched his thinly bearded chin, making a soft clicking sound, like a man with ill-fitting dentures.

' Apparently, when they opened the old place up, it was fully furnished.'

'You're Kidding.'

'I kid you not, the house was completely undisturbed.' He slid the mouse beneath a large computer screen. 'It seems that not only was it fully furnished, but there was unopened mail on the kitchen table, next to a half-eaten breakfast.' He looked up and grinned. 'Sounds a bit like the Mary Celeste, it looks like whoever lived there just walked out of the door and never came back. It's empty now though, all the contents were assigned to auction.'

The solid Victorian door was half glazed, with thick textured glass that revealed nothing beyond. The lock was new, as were the keys. A cold grey light filtered down a long hallway, with two open doors on the right, and a staircase on the left. At the far end of the hall there was another door, with two upper glazed panels, leading, I presumed, to the kitchen and rear of the house. The first room was large, with an imposing but quite plain black slate fire surround, decorated with fine floral swags picked out in gold paint. My footfalls echoed loudly on the bare floorboards. An ornate plaster ceiling rose took centre stage, from which a solitary light bulb hung. The floral wallpaper was faded, but there was evidence of its original colour in square and oval patches where pictures and mirrors had once adorned the walls.

I stepped over to the large bay window, jutting out into a jungle, that had, no doubt, been a very pleasant garden in times past. One thing struck me in particular, somehow the house had escaped the attentions of the brain dead, the crack heads and thieves. The second room was slightly smaller, with a similar slate fire surround and a sash window looking out into a small rear yard, and solid Victorian red brick back -to- back houses across the road. The staircase protested loudly as I climbed to the first floor. A small landing area invited me up two more steps and I was in the bathroom. A huge free-standing roll top enamelled bath stood on impressive ball and claw feet. The off-white enamel stained brown from overflow to plug hole. A grey zinc water tank was set at ceiling height next to the door, and a large pedestal wash basin next to another sash window, with the same textured glass that decorated the front door. The battery in my torch flickered, so I continued my exploration of the upper rooms at a brisker pace.

Finally, I entered the kitchen. On the right, there was an old four panelled door, no doubt original to the house. A large cast iron Yorkshire range on my left dominated the room, facing another old sash window. I was about to leave when I noticed what had to be the door leading to the cellar. The rain returned, chattering against the window. I checked my watch, it was 4.15. Logic told me that I shouldn't bother, it's only a cellar after all, forget it.

The first thing that struck me was the rank smell of damp and decay as I gingerly made my way down, sweeping the beam of light before me, and picking out a narrow room ahead.

There was a bank of ancient off-white ceramic fuse boxes above a narrow shelf on my left, and an eye level shelf to my right, heaving with years of accumulated junk. Tins of paint, old rusting tools, fuse wire, tins of metal polish, tins of grease, light bulbs, baking trays and pots and pans. Even a one-eyed dolls head stared back at me, with a rather unnerving startled expression. It was as if she had woken suddenly from a wonderful dream, where she had possessed everything that was now missing, and found herself in a spooky spartan cellar with only a knackered bicycle pump for a neighbour.

At the far end of the room there was a waist high stone shelf, with an antique enamelled bread bin in one corner. The word ' Bread' in bold blue letters on one side. It brought a smile to my lips, as I recalled a heated but good-natured debate with Fay. We had met at a rural market town auction house, bidding on the same painting. I lost that particular battle, but I did win her heart. She had a penchant for objects that stated the obvious. Letter boxes stamped 'letters', porcelain toilet handles bearing the word 'pull', brass coal boxes pressed with the word 'coal,' the list was endless. My argument was that they had taken the patently obvious a trifle too far. Her response was, it was sweet. Needless to say, she won that debate hands down, and I had to grudgingly admit that it was illogical, but 'sweet.' Turning the beam away from the bread bin, the light suddenly flickered and died. I cursed softly, so as not to disturb any resident ghosts, and gave the torch a reprimanding slap, and it responded admirably with a bright new beam of light. I left the narrow room and noticed a crude wooden latticed door on my right, furnished with a simple spoon style rusting latch. It revealed nothing more than a primitive low-ceilinged room with an earthen floor. I was looking at part of the base foundations of the house. It was full of discarded junk, so I closed the door and moved on. Three steps down and I was in a narrow passage, emerging into the main part of the cellar. There was another older Yorkshire range in line with the one above, but it looked like it had last been used when pigs' trotters on toast was the flavour of the day. Facing the range was an old sash window, I played a beam of light through grimy glass. Above me I could see the bars of a large cast iron grate. The void beneath the grate was deep enough for a man to stand up in and doff his cap, and it amplified the sound of the falling rain.

Beneath the window there was a small access door, through which one could crawl to maintain the drain, but only on a really good day. I moved on, peering into the coal cellar It was small, as one would expect, but with a neat mountain of coal, which one would not. A quick check on the outer wall revealed a square of later brickwork where the original cast iron coal grate had been.

A sudden sharp clap of thunder made me jump, it was time to leave. However the cellar had other plans, had to show me something before I left. Blue lightning flickered through glass, revealing long abandoned dusty traces of spider dwellings. I closed my eyes and started to count, as I did when I was a child. It was a sure method my father had told me, used by Meteorologists and weathermen to ascertain how close the storm was. I got to twelve, when a distant rumble sounded. It was no longer an angry god, but simply a reproachful father.

My eyes were half open, when warm sunlight caressed my face, causing me to stagger back and cry out in alarm and confusion. Then my ears were assaulted by an angry noise, like a dying neon light strip running out of gas and attempting to ignite, resisting the inevitable lights out. I was in a dream as I stared around me. No storm, no darkness, just sunlight, making the cellar appear to be almost a pleasant place. I glanced to the ceiling, as the neon buzz faded. Searching for the source, but there was nothing, but a solitary silent and very dead light bulb.

I stepped over to the window and touched the glass peering up through the bars of the grate. I saw summer clouds hanging like candy floss in a pale blue sky. I saw a bird emerge from nowhere. Watched it hover for a heartbeat, and then swoop out of sight. I pressed my face and hands against the glass, and stared up, my eyes wide with wonder, like a child at an ice cream parlour. Mouth wide open, I listened to the thump of my runaway heart, as the sun slid into view from behind a cloud and winked at me. The alarming sound returned, but louder, more piercing. I covered my ears, shaking my head, eyes shut.

And then silence. I was kneeling, like a penitent priest. The rain echoed in the void and I was shrouded in darkness once more. Distant thunder brought me back as I swept the cellar floor with an outstretched hand, searching for the torch. Somehow, I managed to stumble from that place, and emerge into the garden. The rain beat a drumbeat on my head as I unlocked the car and drove away

The storm had passed when I let myself into the flat. Leaning on the open fridge door, I looked for evidence of edible food when the phone rang. I had to pull it sharply away from my ear as Gordon's loud, jovial voice rose above the pubs background noise.

'Jimmy, where are you?'

I checked my watch, 'I got caught in the storm.'

'No shit, well there's a pint with your name on it, and it’s getting warm.'

Staring forlornly into my wasteland of a fridge, I slammed the door and

stepped over to the
window. I could see the pub, lights glowing enticingly in the wet bright moonlight- kissed
street.

It was busy and noisy, but I still heard Gordon over the din. ' Jimmy, over here!' I caught sight of him, his muscular arms waving in tandem to his long blond hair. He looked like a Viking warrior who had just won the lottery. I pointed at the bar, but he shook his head, indicating an empty chair and a pint of lager waiting for me.

'Strength and honour,' I said, raising the glass to my lips. We clinked glasses like some gay gladiatorial society. ' Strength and honour,' was the cheerful response. Gordon sat on my right. A natural blue-eyed blond-haired Glaswegian who sounded more like an old Oxbridge fellow, but actually went to the same school as me. Ammo, real name Shane, sat on my left. A well rounded, balding, going to seed fast thirty-year-old. According to legend I peered into his pram and quite generously gave him my 'everlasting' gob stopper. It was only when his Mother, who was otherwise distracted by urgent gossip, smiled down at her little pink treasure and was alarmed to see he had turned a brighter shade of blue. She screamed so loud that he responded in kind by bawling his head off, and in doing so, cannoned the gob stopper back into my grubby grateful mitt.

Ammo had always loathed his 'real' name, Shane. So he had adopted the middle letters of his surname, which unsurprisingly was Hammond.

Sitting facing me was Suzie, long-time girlfriend of Gordon. A lovely girl with the patience of a saint. Her short auburn hair framed a full face that was very easy to look at. Her blue eyes radiated intelligence and warmth, and a quick ready smile was never far away.

'So how did the viewing go today,' she asked.

Ammo's pint was raised and then placed back on the table. ' Oh yea man, you were checking out that old pile of a house today, so what's the story?'

I stretched my legs under the table and took a slow theatrical sip of beer.

'In your own time old chap,' drawled Gordon. 'I know we are all living longer, but not that long for goodness sake.'

'It's a big old place,' I said. 'Five bedrooms on two upper floors, and a bathroom and separate toilet. There are two large rooms and a kitchen on the ground floor, but the really interesting thing is what they found when they opened the old place up.'

All attention was now focused on me as I pressed my back into the chair. It was time to tell them the Mary Celeste story, and they listened in complete silence.

'Wow,' said Ammo, 'so he or she just walked out of the door and never came back...far out!'

I smiled, 'that's about the measure of it.'

Suzie cut in, 'but he or she must have had family or friends, someone must have filed a missing person report or something, surely.'

'I agree, absolutely, they should have, but plainly didn't, and that's all I know.'

Ammo shook his head, 'it all sounds a bit spooky to me Jimmy, are you still going to bid on
the joint?'

'I don't know, but I would like to learn more. I may do some digging around.'

The rain was just a memory as we left the pub, and we shook hands and hugged in between some banter and laughs. But Suzie hung back and leaned into me. ' There was something else, something you are not telling us.'

In the time following Fay's death, my friends had held on to me while I raged like a madman. They had listened patiently when I had long rambling and nonsensical conversations with my dead wife. And they still do, even now. I looked urgently into her eyes, desperately wanting to share what I had seen, but something held me back.

CHAPTER 2

The following morning, I handed the keys back. ' Have there been many viewings on this property?'

She clicked the mouse, ' forty-seven so far, keen are you?

I shrugged, ' just curious, and has anyone said anything?'

'Like what?'

'Like, anything unusual, did anyone report seeing anything out of the ordinary.'

She frowned, and spun her chair to face me. ' I don't understand.'

I was floundering, and realised how odd my questions sounded, even to myself. I half opened my mouth to make some lame apology and leave.

'Oh you mean the hauntings and weird noises, yes we get them all the time. People talking about good vibrations and bad vibrations.' Her eyes seemed to glaze over as she peered at some distant horizon. ' Reminds me of that song by the Beach Boys, yes we get all sorts in here,' she said dreamily.

I smiled, ' I'm sure you do.'

'Especially with the older properties like this one,' she sighed. ' Of the forty-seven who have viewed the property so far, approximately seven will be prospective buyers.' She paused and pointed an upturned palm at me, ' like yourself. At least ten will be regulars who never buy anything, and have absolutely no intention of buying anything, but have such a huge vacuous hole in their lives, they spend most of their waking hours poking around houses they don't want and probably cannot afford. There will be at least three professional ghost hunters who only want to view at night.'

'Really?'

'Oh yes, complete with sound equipment, machines for measuring room temperature, night vision goggles, flasks of tea and packs of biscuits.'

I cranked her up, ' I never realised.'

She was in full flow now. 'As for the rest, we call them dreamers. People who see the property for it's potential as a temple for some obscure religious sect, or a women's only centre for photographic excellence, or, even as one candid customer suggested, a brothel.'

'Is that legal,' I enquired.

'Not quite sure,' she answered thoughtfully, ' but apparently some local councils are exploring the possibilities. They are keen to see working girls not working on the street, so long as the premises meet the right criteria.'

I was mesmerised, ' which are?'

She started counting on her fingers, ' one, that they meet all the health and hygiene laws, two, that the business is run on a strictly legal footing with all taxes and VAT paid.'

' Interesting, is shagging subject to VAT?

She nodded, ' apparently so, it comes under luxury items.'

I left a more informed individual than the one who had entered.

It was a cold but bright morning as I pulled up at the house again, and somehow it seemed less sinister and foreboding. There was a gap in the huge wild hedgerow, where a garden gate had been, and a concrete path leading to the front door. My attention was drawn to an old stone wall situated to the left of the path. I stepped over and ran my hands over its course surface. It was much earlier than the house, possibly the last remnants of a long forgotten farm. So why was it still here, how had it been overlooked during the Victorian house building boom? Then I heard a sound drifting over the wall, not unlike a boxer hitting a punch bag. I peered over and a vision of awfulness greeted my sad eyes. There before me was a ghetto of 1960s council houses. Built no doubt with good intentions from some quarters, and at the cheapest possible quote from others, with plenty of left over cash to slip into greasy palms. The source of the sound was easy to locate, and not surprisingly it was not a boxer working out at all. The garden was a mess, an old sofa, sodden sagging and bursting at the seams. Car body parts rusting in long unkempt grass. Bursting bin bags spewing filth into the hidden soil, and cheap plastic children's toys abandoned and unloved. It occurred to me that if this had been a Tracy Emmin creation, then it would have won the Turner prize outright.

In the middle of all this mire, a young man bounced upon a circular child's trampoline. He was probably no older than his mid-twenties, a good time in life. A time when anything is possible, and dreams can be realised with good health and determination. Sadly, it appeared that each of these had deserted him as he bounced barefoot, arms hanging loosely by his side. His hollow unshaven face revealed no pleasure in his activity, as he stared into oblivion. It seemed to me that he was old before his time and all dreams had been snuffed out, extinguished even before they had become dreams. He bounced with little effort and even less of a future.

With a heavy heart, I left him to it.

The sun slid behind a cloud as I walked up the street, and I zipped up the collar of my fleece. I counted seven houses in all, each diminishing slightly in size. They faced a tall relatively new brick wall, which surrounded a large squat square glass and more glass university campus building. I turned left and then left again, and was suddenly transported back to another age. I was surrounded by an island of old red brick back to back houses, isolated and forgotten in a time of desperate modernism. I imagined that once upon a time, they were clean and well kept, and that generations of families had taken some pride in their homes. But now it was just student bedsit land, and it showed. The houses were poorly maintained, with peeling paintwork and rotting woodwork.

Impoverished student cars jockeyed for space with ugly multi coloured wheelie bins. There was a depressing feeling of loss and neglect. It was now a place where families had long since packed their bags, and departed without leaving a forwarding address. The house looked even larger from the back, I stepped into the modest yard and looked up at the steps leading to the back door. At my feet was the cast iron cellar grate. I stared down into the void and imagined seeing a grainy, almost ghost like familiar face, peering upwards through filthy glass. His expression was quite haunting: a mixture of wonder and fear, and as the memories came flooding back, I retreated and crossed the road.

She seemed to appear from nowhere, pulling a rattling shopping trolley behind her. I stepped to edge of the pavement and waved her through, lighting a cigarette. She stopped to rest against the low brick wall behind me, her breathing loud and laboured, like a pair of leaky old bellows. I turned and looked down at her. ' Are you okay?

She held on to the wall for support, gazing down at the pavement. '

Never mind me,' she wheezed, ' what about you?'

I smiled, she was a formidable West Indian lady, well advanced in years. ' I'm fine if your fine,' I replied, turning my attention back to the house and drawing on my cigarette.

' You thinking of buying that ol' place?

' I was, but I'm not sure any more.'

' It be needing a whole lot of work.'

'A whole lot of money too.'

' Are you a rich man?'

' Absolutely,' I replied solemnly.

She laughed out loud then, ' why I bin looking for you all my life,' she declared like an old preacher woman, and we both burst into laughter. Her joyful smile was a treat to behold as I turned to look at her. So I was barely prepared for what happened next. The smile drained from her face as quickly as it had appeared, and she staggered back against the wall. A low moan escaped through her lips and she started to tremble. Stepping forward I took her arm but she pulled away and produced an inhaler from her coat pocket. Her eyes never left me as she held the inhaler to her lips

' You're not well, should I call an ambulance?'

She shook her head and mutely pointed down the narrow cobbled street behind her, so I let her take me by the arm and lead me to her home, with me pulling the bone shaker shopping trolley. Her hands were still trembling as she tried and failed to place the key in the lock. I gently removed the keys from her hand and opened the door, leading her to the nearest chair. Filling a glass with water from her matchbox sized kitchen, I placed it on the table beside her.

She pulled a man sized linen hankie from her sleeve, removed her glasses and dabbed her eyes.

'You should drink some water,' I said.

She took a tentative sip and pulled a face. ' Tea,' she said, her voice sounding stronger. I headed back to the kitchen and found an old fashioned kettle, complete with whistle, the sort you fill and set on a gas ring. I then rummaged through cupboards looking for the tea bags.

' Where do you keep the tea bags? I called.

' Tea bags,' she scolded, making me jump as she stood in the doorway. ' There ain't no tea bags in this house, never has been an' never will be.

Best you sit down an' let ol' Beatie make the tea boy.'

I did as I was told and soon she returned with a tin tray advertising the delights of Tetley's bitter. There was a brown earthenware tea pot, a chrome tea strainer, two blue and white china cups and saucers, a matching bowl of sugar lumps, a matching milk jug, and a plate of plain digestive biscuits.

' My guess is that you swilled the tea pot with hot water before adding the tea and boiling water.'

She smiled and stirred the tea in the pot, ' of course, is there any other way to make a proper brew. I know all you young folks are in such a hurry, but you miss the point, the ceremony of making the tea is as important as drinking it.' She looked at me, her big brown saucer eyes suddenly serious. ' There is something I have to tell you Jimmy.'

I was suddenly on red alert; how did she know my name?

She played mother and poured the tea as I stared at her, ' I'm sorry but have we met before.?'

' Oh yes,' she said softly, ' a long time ago.'

'I think you must be confusing me with someone else.'

'Names I forget,' she answered shaking her head, ' but faces I never forget, especially important faces.' She studied her cup of tea and seemed afraid or reluctant to continue.

'So,' I said brightly,' your name is Beatie, short for Beatrice I presume.'

She frowned, ' I always hate that name, it sound so...so.'

'Wet?' I offered.

She let out a loud whooping noise and punched the air, ' that's it, wet as a fish!'

I smiled, 'so here I am Beatie, in your house, and you don't know me from Adam, why I could be a womanising playboy or worse.'

She covered her mouth and giggled like a schoolgirl, ' give me worse any day.'

I glanced around at my surroundings: the walls were smothered in paintings and prints of a bygone age. There were groups of photographs, some in colour, but most in sepia or black and white. More photos were prominent on a long teak sideboard. One in particular caught my attention, and I stood and picked it up. It was a black and white image of Beaty as a young woman, posing with a tall distinctive looking chap with a pencil thin moustache and large rather serious eyes.

' That me Cleveland,' she sighed.

' Your husband?'

She nodded, ' He went to sleep an' never wake up again, that be nearly fifteen years ago.'

' I'm sorry.'

' Me too,' she sighed.

I looked at the photo again, ' you were a bit of a stunner.'

She roared with laughter and raised her arms in the air. ' You is a womanising playboy after all, but there ain't nothing wrong with your eyesight boy. I was a stunner, an' that's the truth.'

We laughed, and there was a moments silence as we sipped our tea.

'What I am going to say to you Jimmy, may sound like the ramblings of a crazy ol' woman.' She checked her tear stained eyes with the hankie. ' An' I'm not sure how to put it into words that make any kind of sense.' Then the words spilled out of her, as if she had nurtured and kept them close over many years. ' It was the fifteenth of January nineteen fifty seven, an' cold, very cold, not like Jamaica at all, an' we wondered if we had made a big mistake.' Her expression told me she was in another time, another place. 'We had nothing, just our beat up old suitcases, and the kind of dreams that young folk have' She waved expansively at the floor 'We slept on the bare floorboards, but we had each other, and that was the most important thing. Cleveland soon found a job on the railways and I cleaned at the factory down the road.' She paused, and a smile off fond memories creasing her careworn face. 'As I recall, we woke up that first morning and stared at the empty room and everything was real quiet like'. She looked at me, her eyes wide with wonder. 'No traffic, no voices, nothing but silence'. She raised her hands to her cheeks and smiled at the memory. 'We peered through the net curtains like children, and there was a thick blanket of snow everywhere. For us it was a magical landscape, our eyes and mouths wide open. I remember that even the clothes line was transformed into a beautiful necklace of God's glistening feathers.' She paused and produced the big hankie again. Dabbing at her eyes and blowing her nose loudly.

'I'm guessing that was the first time the two of you had ever seen snow.'

'Oh yes Jimmy, we had seen it in the old black and white films of course, and pictures in books, but this was a very special day for us I can tell you' Her eyes widened as she recalled the wonder of it all. 'We threw the door open and there was a wall of snow. I swear it was five feet high. Cleveland let out a whoop an' walked straight through the wall, him taking me by the hand an' leading me out in me good slippers, an' we touched an' tasted an' sniffed like mongrel dogs, an' then we danced'.

She rocked in her chair and then suddenly reached out and took my hand. 'We danced with joy in our hearts, it was so exciting. Cleveland hummed a tune as we waltzed.' She paused, and self-consciously pulled her hand away. 'He was a good hummer' she said as her voice trailed away into a mist of memories.

I absently pulled out a pack of cigarettes without thinking, but then slipped them back into my pocket. Nothing, I soon learned got past Beatie, and she was on her feet fetching an ashtray.

'Are you sure?'

'Sure I'm sure, Cleveland smoke a pipe an' I grew to love the smell. So much so that I sneak a puff on his ol' pipe from time to time, just to remind me'.

I lit up and proffered the pack but she declined.

'The dancing soon stop when a door open across the street. A man stood there with his hands on his hips. I clearly remember that he wore a collarless shirt, and that his braces hung down by his side. Out of sight a woman's harsh voice shattered the serenity of the moment.'

'What's all that bloody racket Cecil! She shrieked'

Beatie shook her head. 'The gormless looking excuse of a man removed his glasses and
polished them on his grubby vest before placing them back on the bridge of his thin crooked nose.

'There's two niggers dancing in't snow,' he said.

'We had a lot of that in the early years, folk calling us rude unchristian names. Some of the children were even worse, following us around shouting thins like 'ave you 'ad your bananas today or making silly monkey noises and then running away'

She picked up her hankie and shook her head sadly.

I was lost for words, and instead of remaining lost and wisely saying nothing, I heard myself mumbling something about the good old days not being so good after all.

Her response was immediate and extremely loud. She raised her considerable arm and brought the palm of her hand crashing on the table. 'Wrong, wrong, wrong, wrong!' She declared in a powerful and passionate voice. 'They were the best of days. Yes, we had problems with a few, but Cleve tell me that the few were just curious and frightened of change an' we should just turn the other cheek an' pity them, as the Lord Jesus Christ tell us. We learned to accept that there will always be sad frightened folk, an' in time we made a whole lot more friends than enemies. Good, God fearing' people an' neighbours'.

There was a moments silence as she paused for breath.

'What about the fools across the road, did you continue to have problems with them?'

She toyed with her tea cup, slipping it round and round in the saucer and for a moment her lips trembled and formed a sound, but none was forthcoming. I was about to say something when she raised her hand for silence and I obeyed without question. A moment passed until she had regained her composure, then almost in a whisper she said. 'All that stopped after he called'

'What? The fool knocked on your door and apologised?'

Beaty did her leaky bellows routine again, as she wheezed and laughed at the same time. 'Why that foolish man was so thick, he would need a whole gang of guide dogs just to cross the road.' She continued to turn the empty cup on the saucer. I could see that she was troubled. Perhaps, I thought, it was time to make my excuses and leave her in peace.

She raised a hand as if reading my thoughts and looked up with that big Beaty smile. 'We were only here a week when he come knocking at the door. He was a young man, probably in his mid-thirties. He was tall an' slim an' wore a long black coat with the collar turned up against the winter chill. He wore no hat, an' his dark brown hair matched his eyes. I was shy and nervous to see a stranger on our doorstep but his affable lopsided smile put me at my ease.

'Sorry to bother you,' he said, 'my name is Jimmy and me mam lives in the next street. She heard that you had just moved in and sent me round with this stand pie, as a sort of house warming gift, to welcome you as a neighbour."

I let out a short burst of laughter, 'brilliant'. Now it was my turn to slap the table 'I bet that made your day'.

She raised both arms in the air, 'I was flabbergasted, so I call out to Cleve an' he come pretty quick.'

'Hang on a minute, you said his name was Jimmy?'

She nodded, a strange look in her eyes.

'Well there we go, he had to be a messenger of good tidings with a name like that'.

She dabbed the corner of her eyes again, her gaze focused on the tea cup. 'This poor young man is still holding the pie an' had to repeat the message to Cleve'. She paused, wheezed and shook her head. 'I felt such a shy ninny when Cleve come. He looks at the young man slowly, then he looks at the pie. 'Your Mama bought that for us?' he said quiet like.

The young man smiled an' handed Cleve the pie. I have never forgotten what that young man say. It has stayed with me for all these years. He say, 'me mam heard that some people were making your life a misery. Well, we are not all like that, as you will discover in time, so please accept this small gift and welcome'.

Cleve shake the young man by the hand, 'Be sure to thank your Mama,' he said, 'an' tell her she is welcome in our home come rain or shine. Then we sit here, at this very table an' place the pie on a plate, pride of place in the middle like. We stare at it, an' then at each other, an' then we laughed till we cried because we had finally arrived at a place we could call home'.

She picked up a table mat and worked it like a fan across her face, tiny beads of sweat formed on her forehead like tears which she dabbed away.

'Are you okay.'

She nodded, 'Just old Jimmy; a fat ol' black bird who talk too much, an' is getting seriously tired'.

'Maybe I should go, you need some rest'

She shook her head, 'don't you like my story?'

'Of course, I like it a lot'

'Then let me finish, where was I?'

'You were admiring the pie on the table'.

She nodded slowly and the smile reintroduced itself. 'Suddenly Cleve was on his feet so fast that he knock the chair almost into the kitchen. I never asked him in he cried. The first real human being to bring a gift to our home.'

She shook her head and exhaled deeply, her lips trembling. 'He rush out into the snow without even taking his hat, so I follow an' look up the street, but he's gone. Just leaving a mad swathe of a path in the snow. Then Mr Creepy appear at his door an' I'm waiting for the usual tirade of abuse'. She looked at me, her eyes mirrored with tears kept prisoner for too long. 'But you know what, he keep his big fat mouth shut for a change, he pretend he don't see me, an' closes the door.' She sat back in her chair, hands resting in her lap and murmured, 'may the lord forgive me.'

I frowned, and then smiled, she looked so happy and content. 'What, what did you do.?'

'It's not what I do, but what I think. When he close the door, I can hear the witch screaming an' him shouting, shut up you old bag, followed by the sound of breaking glass. Even when I close the door I can hear it, an' it goes on for hours'. She nodded silently at the memory 'I'm ashamed to say that I felt a comforting warm glow inside knowing that two wretched people who brought such wickedness and sadness to others should be so unhappy themselves'.

I tutted like a vicar and shook my head in mock horror 'I expect more from you woman, these are not the thoughts of a Christian soul'.

She rocked in her chair and laughed so loudly my teeth rattled.

'You is a tease Jimmy, an' no mistake, but it felt like a revelation from the good book, I confessed my sins the following week, an' they were forgiven after three Hail Mary's and four Our Fathers.' She sipped her tea and looked me in the eye. ' I'm ashamed to say that the barren winter of their union has been a comfort to me ever since.'

I lit a cigarette and smiled, ' so did Cleve catch up with the mysterious stranger.'

'He come back an' say nothing, he didn't have to, it took some soothing words to bring him around. We'll see him again, I said, why his mama lives in the next street, we're bound to bump into them sometime.'

I inhaled and waited with smoking breath, ' and did you?'

A sadness shimmered in the pools of her eyes. ' The short answer is no, we never did see him again, or meet his saintly mama. We make many good friends over the years, an' we search the streets, talking to folk as you do, but the answer was always the same. A shrug of the shoulders here or a shake of the head there, it was like they had never existed.'

A sharp knock at the door made both of us jump. Beaty hauled herself out of the chair as a second louder knock shook the door. ' All right, I'm coming, who do you think I am, Linford Christie.'

'Hi Beatie, how are you love.' His voice was quite high pitched but carried a resonance of real concern.

She answered in the only way she knew how, ' I'm fine Darren, how are you.'

'I just got in from work and Megan said she saw a man follow you into the house, someone she never saw before.'

She waved him in with a chuckle, ' Jimmy's an old friend.'

A blip came up on my radar as I rose to my feet, an old friend?

He was a short sturdy looking man in his mid-twenties. His muscular tattooed arms curved out from his side, as if he was carrying an invisible small cask of ale under each arm. His closely cropped fair hair already showed signs of receding, and he wore a deep look of suspicion as we shook hands.

‘Darren an' Megan live across the street,' she said beaming. ' They keep an eye out for me, they are true Christian neighbours.'

Darren coloured and visibly relaxed, ' we do our best.'

' You do more than that, will you have a cup of tea with us.'

He was already moving to the door, ' no, me dinners on the table.' He glanced at me quickly and gave a curt nod. ' Give us a shout if you need anything.' And then he was gone to his dinner on the table.

I got to my feet, 'I think it is time I was making a move.'

'Before you make a move Jimmy,' she said quietly, ' the boy who knock on our door, the boy with the pie...'

' What about him, you said you never saw him again.'

' It's true, we never did see him again.' She picked up her glasses from the table and started to polish the lens with her hankie.

'Beatie?'

She put her glasses on and blinked at me, ' it was you Jimmy, you is the boy with the pie.'

CHAPTER 3

I immediately regretted the short laugh that burst through my lips. ' Look at me Beatie, how old am I?'

' I know it sound crazy.'

' I was born in 1989, it is now 2019, so if I am not mistaken that puts me at thirty years of age. Now as I recall this chap knocked on your door in the winter of 1957, looking just like me, as I am now.'

She smiled, ' just like you are right now, yes.'

'So, let's fast forward, the pie man would now be a pensioner.'

She nodded her head vigorously. ' That's the truth, you've aged well Jimmy.'

My sigh of exasperation was deep and heartfelt, ' so it could not possibly have been me.'

She shrugged her shoulders and pulled a face. ' The good Lord gave me eyes to see an' ears to hear. First I hear your voice an' something tell me that I have heard that voice before. An' then I see your face an' bingo! I recognise you straight away.'

We were seated once more and she leaned forward and patted my hand. Now what, I thought. Is she going to read my tea leaves? I was almost right.

'I sense a great sadness in you,' she said, ' I can feel your sorrow.' How long is it since your wife passed Jimmy?'

'What are you, some kind of witch doctor?'

'I've been called a witch a few times in my life, but never a doctor.'

'Not long, I answered in a monotone voice. ' Just over a year.'

'An' you still talk to her don't you.'

'She calls me up from time to time; on the Radio or TV. But more often than not she is just there.' It was a hollow laugh that followed. ' And I thought you were crazy.'

'It ain't crazy boy, why I talk to my Cleveland all the time, 'specially when I'm feeling low. An' it has been a great comfort to me in the empty years that followed, I can tell you.'

'The problem is Beatie, when we are talking I really believe that she is there, still alive.'

'Course you do, you is still grieving Jimmy. Time takes away some of the pain, but never the memory. Believe me when I say I have been there, read the book, an 'eaten the pie.'

I smiled, ' somehow I thought the pie would enter our conversation again.'

She tipped back her head and laughed so loud I thought I detected delicate china figures dancing on the mantel piece. And I imagined birds taking to the wing, and street wise stray cats seeking refuge behind wheelie bins or beneath parked cars.

'In my church some folk call me a healer, but they get the wrong idea. They think that I can just lay my hands on them an' they will be cured of all the diseases an' ailments visited upon mankind. But it ain't like that at all. A true healer is someone who just knows when another soul is in distress. I can shake someone by the hand and instantly know that they is weeping inside. That they is crying in the dark, an' I just reach out to them an' listen, real careful like. The healing is in the listening Jimmy, letting folk spill out their pain.

I drove away on a promise to call again and continue our conversation. Spots of rain hit the windscreen and I flicked the wipers. The weather was foul but I was feeling better. My chat with Beatie had raised my spirits and I had discarded a few dark shadows along the way. I almost jumped a traffic light and rubber squealed in protest as I hit the brakes. The windscreen wipers clicked like a lazy Metronome, and headlights glittered through rain and steamed-up glass as I glanced at my rear-view mirror. Probably the cops, I thought, knowing my luck, but when I went for green, the car peeled off in another direction.

Effin Elsie's Chinese takeaway beckoned. Its real name was 'Beautiful View'; and considering that it faced a brick wall surrounding a dog food processing plant, it was certainly a name to conjure with. But the old girl who took the orders always finished with the line 'effin else?', and the nickname became a local byword for just passable Chinese cuisine.

That night I dreamt I was standing close to a lonely cliff edge, with only a large all-embracing moon and an angry sea for company. It was a time and place that seemed vaguely familiar to me. Seagulls slept in silence, but the raging sound from the incoming tide would have smothered their sharp hysterical screams. I stepped back as the wind buffeted me closer to the edge; when she emerged from darkness, pushing an old butcher's delivery bike. It had a large woven basket hanging from the handlebars, laden with rotten fruit and dead flowers. She wore a long black coat, with the hood pulled up to protect her from the elements. Yet somehow; even above the rush of noise below, I detected a soft wheezing sound, and instinctively knew that it was Beatie.

She paused by my side and looked up at me with that big smile. The bicycle fell into long grass as she shook her hooded head. 'If you are going to jump Jimmy, then fucking jump!' For an old lady, she was quick and strong, her hands pummelling me in the back. My slithering feet tried and failed to pull me from the edge on the wet grass,
until I was kicking thin air. I reached out and tried to grab the moon as my body arched and fell to the rocky beach far below.

The sudden startled cry was real as I woke with the sort of heart stopping violence that I had almost grown accustomed to. The next time I opened my eyes, it was a new day, the day of the auction.

It was busy, but not buzzing, and the bidding was steady, but by no means frantic. Finally we came to the house of special interest. It had an auction estimate of eighty to one hundred thousand, but I knew this was just a 'bird call'. A method used by auctioneers to draw people in with a low estimate. Then later, they could pat themselves on the back, on how spectacularly well they had done. My ceiling bid was firmly fixed at one hundred and sixty
thousand. Not a penny more, and hopefully a few pennies less. The auctioneer was good, waxing lyrical. ' Lot twenty-one ladies and gentlemen, a fine and substantial Victorian through terrace property, requiring some sympathetic modernisation. Consisting of five bedrooms; a large bathroom with separate toilet, a large lounge and parlour. The kitchen has a small walk-in larder, and extensive cellars. The property is well within walking distance of a fine school, university, and the city

centre. This ideally situated house has a front garden, and a handy yard at the rear.'

He looked around the room, his eyes quick and searching, gavel in hand. 'Where do we start?' There was a pause.' One hundred thousand...ninety...seventy surely?'

Someone came in at seventy and the bidding climbed steadily in fives. It staggered to a halt at one hundred and thirty. ' Are we all done?' His gavel was poised when I joined the party.

'New bidder!' he cried, ' one hundred and thirty-five.' I thought it was mine, but I was wrong as late bids pushed it up to one eighty, and I was gone, staring around the room to watch the bidders.

'One eighty-five, and I am selling, going once, going twice...' The gavel came crashing down. Again I scanned the room, trying to spot the clueless bidder'

'Your paddle number sir?'

Still no sign of movement from the winning bidder.

'Excuse me sir, but may I see your paddle number please.'

What a numpty, I thought, turning with a grin to look at the auctioneer, who in turn was looking at me with a furrowed brow. A ding dong resonated within the vacant confines of my skull, and it wasn't the Avon lady calling. My arm was still reaching for the sky, like I was asking permission to go to the wee boy's room. When all I really deserved was to piss my pants and stand in the dunce's corner.

The auctioneer raised his eyebrows as I sheepishly raised my bidders' number. ' Forty-two,' he said brusquely, ' thank you sir.'

I was trembling and leaking sweat from every pore of my skin, as I realised that I had become the proud owner of a very strange house. That evening my rabble were already gathered and waiting when I entered the pub. Sally smiled from behind the bar.

' Hi Jimmy, the usual?'

'A round for that lot,' I said, peeling a brace of twenties. ' How are you Sally?'

She shook her head as she pulled, ' I'm having the mother of all periods, chances are I'll need a blood transfusion before the night is out.'

' I'm sorry to hear it, buy yourself a bloody Mary.'

' Thanks, I'll bring them over.'

Barely had I time to slide into my chair when Suzie hushed for silence.
' Well?' she said.
' Well what?'
' You know very well well what.'
' Ah, the auction, did I buy the spooky house or did I not.'
I looked at each one of them in turn, ' and the answer is...' I paused and settled back in my seat. As I had been taught to do by watching all those sad, cheap TV shows that I loathed and loved in equal measure, and perversely continued to watch as my poor excuse of a brain was bubbling, and evolving into a bile flavoured blancmange. They in turn were equally brainwashed and more than familiar with the format, and waited patiently without question.
' The answer is...yes!'
Our table was transformed into a micro Wembley stadium, as pint pots and knuckles rapped the beaten copper surface, and joyful cheers almost raised the rafters of our humble inn. Gordon reached over and shook me by the hand. 'Well done James.'
Ammo beamed as only he could beam, ' a man of property, good on yer mate. I always knew you would go far...'
'But not far enough!' they all chimed in chorus, having heard his well-worn and cliqued lines before. Suzie smiled, but I detected a questioning look in her eyes. While Ammo slipped easily into hippy mode. ' Hey Jimmy, I don't want to burst your balloon or drag you back to realityville.' He shifted his considerable arse in his chair. A place that might appear to the casual observer, to be somewhere where young boys fight in a bag for a bet.
You bought the creepy house?'
I nodded, ' the very same.'
' Oh wow, far out man, I mean after that thing about someone just disappearing, didn't that kind of put you off.'
I shrugged, ' It's just a house with a lot of potential. Sure, it's got a history, but everyone and everything has a history. I spread my arms and emotionally embraced them all, speaking in my best Godfather voice. ' It's just business.'
Ammo shook his head. ' I'm not sure any more Jimmy; when you told us the story of the man or woman, who left their breakfast in a hurry, and

they just got up out of the chair and
walked out the door, never to be seen again...' He looked troubled and traced a circle on the rim of his beer glass with his forefinger. 'I've been thinking about it, and it gives me the willies.'

'There's more isn't there?' said Suzie.

I caught her eye and nodded, ' oh yes.'

Sally arrived with our tray of drinks.

'Jimmy bought the house Sal,' she said.

Sally placed the drinks on the table and smiled. ' I thought as much when I heard the racket from you lot,'

Suzie nodded, ' and there's more, you had better sit down.'

I thought for a moment that Sally was gazing fondly at someone over my shoulder, but knew deep down I knew that she was looking at me. She was a lovely girl, but I was still strictly a one-woman man. I clasped my hands together as if in prayer; took a deep breath, and told them the tale of my chance meeting with Beatie.

The silence that followed was quite deafening. It was Gordon who chimed in first. ' So, let me be clear on this, the old biddy was convinced that the chap with the pie, was you?'

I smiled, ' absolutely.'

'She immediately recognised your voice, and the moment she clapped eyes on you, she was convinced you were the pie man. And you looked then as you do now, but remind me of the date?'

'The 28th of February nineteen fifty-seven,' I said.

' This is really deep Jimmy,' said Ammo.

Gordon raised his glass and peered into it, as if searching for a sign. ' The old girl is obviously gaga, confusing you with someone else. I mean, for goodness sake, we are talking about fifty odd years ago.'

I smiled but said nothing.

Sally shook her head, ' she sounds like a lovely lady.'

'She is a lovely lady, very interesting and still of sound mind,' I replied, looking directly at Gordon, who then shifted uncomfortably in his chair.

'Something happened when you viewed the house,' said Suzie quietly, ' something you are holding back.'

It was not a question, but a statement of fact. I knew then with complete certainty, that the moment had arrived to tell all. If I could not confide in my friends, then I was floating down diarrhoea river, with only my hands for oars. So I told them everything; from the first crack of thunder and the buzzing sound in my head, to the warm embrace of summer sunlight in the depths of winter. I told them about the acrobatic flight of a lone songbird emerging from bright billowing lazy cotton clouds hanging in a bright blue sky, and when I was finished, there was silence.

'I know it all sounds completely bonkers, and you are all thinking that I am slipping back down the slippery slope to bedlam once again, but it all seemed so real, and still does.'

'Jimmy,' Gordon paused and looked at me nervously, ' are you still talking to Fay?'

You could hear a pint drop; the whole pub seemed to be on the pause button. It was Sally who came to my rescue.

' Really Gordon,' she chastised, ' how could you be such an insensitive arse!'

I smiled and shook my head, ' thanks for that Sally, but really it's okay, and the short answer is yes. She calls me up from time to time and we chat, and yes, I am aware that she is dead, and like a fool I am really just talking to myself...but it helps. It gives me a little comfort when comfort is a stranger, and I almost feel alive again. After all we constantly talk to ourselves, we chastise and praise ourselves out loud when no one is listening. So, what am I supposed to say when my nearest and dearest come calling, piss off I don't talk to dead people?'

Sally reached out and held my hand. ' There are people who can help, people who listen without making judgements.'

I looked around at their glum faces. ' I know, they are called mates. Maybe you all believe that I have lost the plot entirely, and my next port of call is a comfortable padded cell, but what I have just told you was not a dream or a nightmare. It was real; something happened in that strange house, and I intend to find out what that was.'

Many days followed as I got stuck into licking the house into shape. Sometimes on my lonesome, but more often than not, with more than a little help from my friends. We pulled smashed and hammered, and filled many skips. We played loud music; laughed, joked, and ate fast food from boxes. Three months passed, and a few favours were called in. The roofers had finished their days on the tiles, the sparkies worked at an electrifying pace, and the plasterers had soberly completed their work. It was the day of the final inspection as I walked with Sean from room to room, before handing over the cheque. Our feet clattered on bare boards as we entered the last attic room. ' It's a job well done Sean.'

'Aye, and on time, which is no mean feat when you're a man down.'

I turned and looked at him curiously, ' how so?'

He shook his head and pocketed the cheque. ' One of our young lads walked off the job, he were a good worker an' all.'

' Did he say why?'

He lit a cigarette and the smoke snaked from his nostrils as he breathed a short laugh. ' We were working Saturday morning to reach our target like. He was in the bathroom and I was finishing off in the front room. When suddenly I hear him crashing down the stairs, calling my name. Poor lad were in a right state, looking all wide eyed and shaking like a hooked dab.'

'It's Saturday morning Sean,' he says, pointing a shaking finger at the bay window. 'Well it didn't seem like the right time to take the piss like, so I just nodded like.'

'So why is it fucking night time up there Sean, tell me that!'

Sean looked at me and shook his head. 'And then he was gone before I could open me gob.'

I could feel a knot tightening in my stomach.

'Course I went upstairs and had a gander.' He shrugged and took another pull on his cigarette. ' There was nowt to see out of the ordinary, and the lad had done a very neat job. But for one small section above the sink, where his trowel had raked the wall. He still lives with his mam, so I went round with his wages. He wasn't in, and she apologised for his behaviour, and I said think nothing of it, and promised to put him on another job on Monday.'

We walked out into the garden, and he paused to stub out his cigarette on the side of an
overflowing skip. I smiled and slapped him on the back. ' You're a soft touch really, aren't you Sean.'

'Well I felt sorry for the lad; he's had it tough recently. His Nan died a few weeks ago, so obviously I gave him some time off. They were really close and he took it bad.'

I was now on familiar ground, ' poor kid.'

'His Mam was a bit alarmed to see the state of him when he arrived home early like. She fussed over him as they do, and after a hot brew and a bacon butty, he starts to tell her what happened. He said that he was just about finished skimming the wall, when he heard this strange sound.'

My heart skipped a beat.

‘ He said it were like an odd buzzing sound, and he spun around, dropping his trowel. And the room was plunged into darkness in an instant, illuminated only by the light of a full moon.' He looked at me uneasily. ' I'll tell you what Jimmy, if that had happened to me, then I would have been out of there faster than a vegan in an abattoir.'

He held out his hand, ' all the best.'

'Look after the kid,' I said.

He grinned and nodded, and the pickup whined as he reversed away from me. I slipped my hands into my pockets and leaned against the skip. I looked at the large bay window, the glass glinting brightly in the sharp sunlight. Then at the old front door, wide open, and shaded from the sunlight by the small arched porch. It was time to call on Beatie again.

CHAPTER 4

She was hanging washing on a line when I approached, her beaming welcome immediately brought a smile to my lips. ' Jimmy! She cried; her arms raised as if she was about to break out into a rousing gospel song. 'I knew you would come back to see old Beatie...come in, come in.' She disappeared into the kitchen while I pulled up a chair at the plain pine table, and a delightful aroma drifted delectably from the kitchen.

' You bin baking Jamaica cake woman?'

I heard a laugh and a snort of derision. Then her head burst through the bead curtain with a light jingle. ' What's wrong with you boy, is your nose so blocked up with soot an' cement you don't smell a home-grown Yorkshire pudding?'

Now size matters when it comes to a Yorkshire pudding, and this was big enough to sit in and row across the Channel. Crisp on the outside, but with a soft and textured inner core, and the rich beef and onion gravy made me realise just how much I missed proper home cooking with fresh ingredients.

'Beaty,' I said between mouthfuls, ' this is by far the finest Yorkshire pudding that I have tasted in...' I paused and grinned, ' well, ever.'

She nodded, ' don't talk, eat.'

So I ate, and as I ate I detected a warm and very pleasant after taste. ' There's something else going on here, something ever so slightly spicy?'

She tilted her head back and laughed as only she could laugh. 'That be a little Jamaica sunshine I sprinkle in there, a touch of black magic; it's not too hot is it?'

I placed knife and fork onto an empty plate, ' there's your answer,' I said. And there was more. Tender medium roast beef with mashed and roast potatoes; green beans, carrots and tartar sauce. I was content, full of food and bursting with questions.

'You've been busy on the house I see.'

I smiled, ' word gets around I suppose, so you heard I bought the old place.'

She shook her head, 'I heard nothing, I saw men working an' just knew it had to be you.' Her big saucer eyes looked troubled, as she searched for the right words before proceeding. ' The boy who bring us the welcome pie was you Jimmy, make no mistake about that. You looked then as you do now, does that suggest anything to you?'

Surprisingly it did, and somewhere within the shaded corners of my subconscious mind, I accepted what she said without question. She removed her glasses and dabbed her eyes with the ever-present hankie. ' You will be going on a journey soon, a journey that will take you to another time. The house you bought is not any old house. It hides a secret, a doorway that only a very few will ever see, let alone enter.' As she spoke, I drifted back to that brief moment in the cellar. The warm kiss of sunlight, and a lone bird soaring high in a sky that had no right to be there.

She reached out and touched my hand. ' I believe you have seen it; you have heard that abominable sound before the revelation.'

I looked into her eyes and nodded like a deranged puppet on a string, and then she smiled and beat the table top with the open palm of her hand, making cups rattle nervously in their saucers.

'Lordy lordy!' she cried, slapping the already distressed table once more. ' I tell you now that sleep became a stranger when I saw you looking at that old place. Then I put two an' two together. This calls for something a bit stronger than tea.' She stood with surprisingly agility, and retrieved a bottle from a cupboard in the sideboard.

' French brandy Jimmy,' she assured me, ' it beat Jamaica rum into a tin hat.'

'Cocked hat,' I replied, ' the phrase is cocked hat, not tin hat.'

' Oh, an' what does that mean, cocked hat?'

I shrugged lazily and sipped my Cognac laced tea. ' I have absolutely no idea, sounds like an old Navy saying, are we celebrating something?'

'Oh yes,' she raised her cup.' The beginning of a great adventure for you, an' the end of a great adventure for me.'

We clinked tea cups, but surprisingly the brandy did little to raise my spirits, so to speak. ' This all sounds a bit crazy Beaty, like something you might see in a film, a good yarn perhaps, but you have to leave your credibility boots at the door.'

She nodded and then captivated me with those big brown eyes. ' I know, it sound more than crazy.'

I smiled, ' there is no mystery here, that old house is just a house. Whatever I imagined that I saw in there was

probably just a dream. I have officially been diagnosed as clinically depressed, an official term for not quite right in the head since Fay died. So, a touch of loopy loo in the cellar of an old empty house is really just par for the course. I am in fact quiet frequently mad in my more lucid moments.'

'So, what happened to the boy?'

I frowned, ' the boy?'

'The boy who walked off the job.'

'You heard about that?' Or did you see it in a dream, or the tea leaves perhaps. Honestly Beaty, time was when you would have been burned as a witch.'

She rocked so far back in her chair I was afraid that she might topple over. ' Don't be silly boy, why I talk to Sean all the time. I know his mam an' we have been good friends for many years.'

' You are a wicked women, you knew all along I had bought the house, but instead of coming right out and telling me, you played your mystic Beatie trick.'

She roared with laughter and waived her hankie in the air like a flag of truce. She then tipped some more brandy into our tea cups, and I made no effort to stop her. I decided there and then to tell her my story. To describe the strange events that had occurred in the cellar of the house. She listened intently, simply nodding from time to time, and when I had finished, she was looking down at her hands. They were clasped in her lap, and very still.

'When you heard about the boy, what did you think then?'

I stared at her and struggled to find an answer. ' Well I had sort of convinced myself that I had imagined it all. That it was simply a symptom of my mental breakdown.' I touched my forehead as a trickle of sweat touched my skin. ' Then he threw a spanner in the works, and logic flew bird-like out of the window. His experience was so close to mine, I had to concede that what happened, really happened, whatever that was.'

' An' what do you think happen Jimmy?'

I ran a hand through my hair and looked desperately at her for help. '

My mind is all over the place, I can't sleep and when I do...'

Memories of this lovely old lady casually pushing me over the edge of a cliff came into focus. 'When I do, I have very bad dreams...nightmares.'

She smiled, ' what if I told you there was someone else who had seen the light, so to speak.'.

I was catching flies again.

' We're only talking about time travel Jimmy, not the second coming of the messiah. His name was Professor Michael Kennedy,' she said. ' He owned the house at that time.' She mopped her brow with the hankie. ' I did a little cleaning for him.' She screwed up her eyes and went in search of memories. ' It was the summer of '94 I think, I was retired by then of course.'

Curiosity may have killed the cat, but I was no pussy. ' Retired from what exactly?'

' I was a nurse,' she said quickly. ' First in Jamaica an' then here in Leeds. Thirty-eight years I worked, twenty-nine of them as a matron, an' I love every minute. It was a sorry day when I had to retire, I can tell you. Cleveland work on the railway for a few more years.'

She paused and sipped her bran tea.

'I became more involved with work in my church; cleaning an' flower arranging an' the like. When he earwigged a conversation in the greengrocer's shop, 'bout my prowess with a mop an' a bucket of soapy water. When I leave, I hear him call after me, anyway I turn around an' he lifts his hat as gentlemen did in those days. He asks me if I might consider doing a few hours a week for him, cleaning an' tidying like. It's a big house as you know Jimmy, an' I wondered why this intelligent but single man had bought the old place.'

' So, he had no family?'

She sighed deeply and applied the hankie to her eyes. ' Turned out he had a wife an' daughter. They lived in Edinburgh where he had worked at a place called Fettes Collage. He was then offered a place here, at Leeds University. He could lecture for a few hours a week, an' pursue his own research in whatever hours remained, which were plenty. So, he embraced the move, an' his wife an' daughter were to follow as soon as the Edinburgh house was sold.'

'They died didn't they,' I said flatly.

She nodded in silence and dabbed at her eyes. 'There was a fire; they both died asleep in their beds, it was a terrible time.' She toyed with her cup, absently turning it round in the saucer. 'When he returned, he was a changed man. Still civil an' composed like, but there was a darkness about him, an' I never did see him smile for many a year.'

' What was he like?' I asked softly.

' He was a tall man, probably six two in his stockinged feet, an' quite slim. A softly spoken slightly reserved man, with a pencil thin moustache an' a ready smile as I recall. He was not always an easy man to get along with, sometimes he would let fly some cutting words if you disturbed him when he was working.'

He had a temper then,' I said.

She paused to formulate the correct description. ' Well yes, he could be very abrupt and dismissive on occasions, but most of the time he was old school charming. A gentleman is how I would describe him. He was a shy man, who only seemed to prefer silence an' his own company.'

She frowned,' there's a word for it.'

'Reclusive,' I offered.

'That's it Jimmy, you are a bright boy. He became a reclusive man, lost in his own thoughts. He was no longer employed by the University, an' he hardly ever step outside the house. He never saw no one, 'cept me and Cleve. I cooked him meals an' sometimes he ate, an' sometimes he just pushed it around the plate. Days would pass when he would sit in his library, seemingly engrossed upon some paper he was writing. An' I tell you now, that I enter that room at my peril, he would always apologise later, but I noticed that his eyes were ever so slightly bloodshot. Then I started to find the empty Gin bottles, so he was venturing out, but under the cover of darkness. One thing remained constant in those troubled times, me an' Cleve were still welcome.'

The big white hankie made an entrance once more, as she dabbed at her eyes. 'Then one evening Cleve return from one of their regular meetings an' he looked troubled.

'Has he been drinking again? I say.

'Cleve sit down in his favourite chair an' smile his handsome smile. ' He was in a good mood, better than I have seen him since his loss.'

' So why the long face?

' He was acting kinda strange, agitated like. One minute we were talking local politics, when all of a sudden, he goes all quiet like, and I'm thinking maybe I should leave him to his own thoughts. Then out of the blue he looks me in the eye and says, do you think it is possible to travel through time Cleve?'

'Can't say I have given it much thought,' I says, but it's a real interesting question,' and then he smiles.'

' He smiled, you telling me that man is smiling again?'

She chuckled softly at the memory. ' Well Cleve slap the arm of his chair.'

'As God is my witness, why he was almost like the professor of old. He seemed somehow rejuvenated, like a man reborn."

'So he has been drinking,' I said, but Cleve shake his head.

'It wasn't like that Beaty, he just looked me in the eyes and said, well my friend, you are now talking to someone who has stepped through a doorway into the past, and it was absolutely fascinating."

'You check the room for hidden bottles, right?'

'Course I did woman, what you take me for. I not only check but he watch me check with a wide grin on his face, then he starts laughing out loud. 'This is not the booze talking Cleve, it is me. And I tell you that yesterday morning I walked out of my front door, and into the year nineteen twenty four.'

Beaty looked at me with bright shimmering moist eyes. 'Well you could have knocked me down with a feather. I have heard some crazy things in my long-life Jimmy, but this was way up there with the best of them. Cleveland then tell me the whole tale. How the professor heard a loud buzzing sound an' saw the light flickering beyond the net curtains, and the moment he stepped down into his garden.'

She nodded and smiled, ' then I see that Cleve is holding a book, an' he hand it to me.'

'He gave it to me and said, this wonderful book is simply a novel. A tale of a man who builds a machine that can propel him through time, but the truth is Cleve, one does not require a machine at all.'

'What was the title of this book Beaty?'

She frowned and pondered for a moment, and then slapped the poor table. 'It was called 'The Time Machine.'

'By H. G .Wells,' I whispered.

' That's the one, why you is a clever boy Jimmy

I lit another cigarette in a vain attempt to calm the rhythm of my beating heart.

' Is he going crazy?' I say, ' but my Cleve just shake his head. 'We will have to keep a close eye on him Beaty, an' see that he don't come to no harm, it's the Christian thing to do.'

'He then takes the book, settles back in his chair an' starts to read.'

She topped up her cup up but I placed a hand over mine. 'I'm driving,' I said, and she nodded and continued. ' So we did, we kept our ears an' eyes wide open, an' everything seemed just dandy. He was coping well, but even when he smile you could still see that look in his eyes. An' when he was sad, I swear he was back in that smoke-filled burning house with his poor wife an' daughter. Then one evening Cleve went over for a chat, but returned shortly afterwards.'

'He ain't there,' he said, ' I knock on the back door and no answer, so I stroll around to the front and the door is wide open. The lights are all blazing and the wireless is playing some jazz, but no professor.'

Beaty worked the place mat so fast that even I felt the draught. She looked a little drained or drunk, it was hard to tell. I had been so mesmerised by her tale, that time had passed in a blur. I glanced at the clock; it was five thirty.

'Beatie, look at the time?

She glanced lazily in the direction of the clock and hiccupped, ' I was supposed to be singing, oh well it's too late now.'

I was confused, ' you're a singer?

She nodded, grinning like a half-cut Cheshire cat after sniffing a line of Charlie. 'In the church choir, an' here I am getting drunk as a sunk, whatever will the vicar say.'

I smiled. ' I think he would say that the word is skunk.'

She shrugged and waived a regal wave, ' skunk, stink, who cares.'

I stood and swayed a little. ' I care lady.' I sounded like my mother, and was afraid, very afraid.

' I'm going to leave you in peace.'

She slapped the completely innocent table and shook her head. ' No you ain't Jimmy, you're gonna sit back down an' let me finish my story.' She gestured to my empty chair. 'Are you afraid that this little old lady might drink you under the table?'

I sat.

She studied me closely and silently, and then raised her cup. ' To absent friends, I'm an old woman Jimmy, an' I don't know when the good lord will come for me...'

I started to protest, but she raised a hand. ' I ain't complaining. I've had a good long life, an' I'm hoping soon that I will feel Cleve's hand in mine once more.'

She sipped her bran tea and laughed softly, ' hopefully sober.'

'Are you ill Beaty? I said.

' Hell no, but I've been waiting so long to tell this tale.'

' Were you waiting for me, waiting to tell me the story?'

She nodded, ' I didn't know it at the time, but yes, I was waiting for the boy time traveller to show his face. The boy who make such a big difference to our life here in England.'

She paused and frowned, as if she was searching for a long-lost memory.

'Where was I?'

'The professor disappeared,' I said.

' He sure did, he walk out the door with the wireless an' the lights on, an' the front door wide open for anyone to enter. Cleveland went back later, an' it was late. 'Bout one in the morning, but he just shake his head when he returned. We was mighty worried I can tell you. Did you switch off the wireless?' I says.

'Course I did, I switch off the wireless and the lights, 'cept the one in the hall, what you take me for woman?"

' Did you lock the door?'

'With what, am I gonna stick my pinkie in the lock. I don't have no keys, do you?"

She laughed softly at the memory. 'Neither of us slept well that night, an' when Cleve leave for work, I headed straight over there an' knock on the door. There is no answer an' I turned to leave, when I hear the key in the lock an' the door opens. He looked tired, but bright eyed an' alert. He stands aside as I enter. 'Good morning Beaty, and how are you this fine morning.'.

Never mind fine morning, it's the fine nights I'm worried about. We've been worried sick about you.'

'Really?'

'Yes really, Cleveland come over last night an' you had disappeared.'

'Ah yes, I popped out to stretch my legs,' he says.

' So how come you ain't ten feet tall, 'cos you must have done a whole lot of leg stretching. Cleve came back 'bout midnight an' you was still out a leg stretching. Leaving the front door wide open an' the wireless blaring. In my book that is a stretch too far.'

' Ah, yes, shall I make us a cup of tea?'

' I make the tea 'round here,' I says, taking my coat off. Then he sits at the kitchen table, opening his mail while I boil some eggs an' toast some toast.'

' That was extremely careless of me, leaving the wireless on and the door wide open. I will have to be more careful next time.'

' Next time,' I says, ' do you mean the next time you stretch your long legs, or the next time you go a time travelling?' The teaspoon slipped through his fingers and clattered upon the plate. He sat straight backed in his chair an' looked at me sternly. Then his face softened an' he smiled. 'Naturally Cleve would tell you about my little adventure, I should not have expected anything less.'

' My Cleve tell me everything, we ain't got no secrets.'

He nodded, picked up his spoon and cracked his egg. ' I suppose you think I am a madman?'

' Don't think nothing of the sort, you seen some very bad things, things that can send sensible folk crazy.'

' This egg is perfect by the way.'

' Good, I'm glad it's perfect, that's what I do.'

' So, what you are saying is that I am not insane after all?'

She paused to mop her brow, ' that man could talk the talk Jimmy, make no mistake.'

'Well,' I said, 'he was a lecturer at the University, that would give him a head start.'

She smiled, ' that's true.'

'But the man would have to be a fully paid up member of the witch doctors and dancers club to silence you.'

She rocked back in her chair with laughter, ' I think there must be some black blood in you boy.'

This time we both roared with laughter, and it was my time to pull a tissue and dab my eyes.

'So in the end he say to me, what if I promise never to mention the subject of time travel again.'

'That would suite me just fine,' I says, an' we shook hands on it.'

She looked at me sadly, ' he was as good as his word, but his recently acquired interest in popping out for some fresh air became a regular occurrence. Sometimes he was gone for a week or more. Finally I turn to Cleve an' say, where has that man gone to now?'

She shook her head and mopped her brow. ' Cleve just shrug his shoulders, ' he's a grown man Beaty, he can come and go as he pleases."

I was catching flies again, ' so Cleve knew that he was time travelling?'

She gazed into her past life and nodded. ' My Cleveland was always a quiet sober man, but he always say to me, it is better to listen than to speak. Folk don't listen no more, 'cept when they hear the sound of their own voices. It's only when you listen, real careful like that you hear the truth, or the clever demonic overtures of the devil his self. He then tell me how the professor had been taken in by a family, and how he returned, time an' time again.' She smiled, but it was the mixed smile of fond memories, tinged with irreconcilable loss and deep sorrow. ' Cleve was sat where you are sitting now. He is silent for a moment, an' then he looks at me an' says. 'We were talking quiet like, 'bout the poetry of Dylan Thomas, when all of a sudden he leaps out of his chair and says, did you hear that old friend? Well my Cleve stare as he rushes out of the room, only to pause at the door with a big smile on his face. I have to change Cleve, he says, won't be a tick. Then he returns wearing a different suite and smiles. He caught Cleve by the arm an' said, I have something quite amazing to show you. They hurry down the hallway an' the professor throw open the front door, turning with the gleeful laugh of a child. Isn't it just bloody marvellous Cleve?'

She paused, wafted the table mat, and sipped what remained of her bran tea. ' Cleve say that he stepped forward and looked out into the garden. He saw nothing, it was just the front garden in darkness. Then the most extraordinary thing happened. The professor stepped into the porch an' paused to look fleetingly back, his face a picture of joy. Come on Cleve, no time to dawdle.'

Beatie blinked and dabbed at her eyes. ' Cleveland looked at me an' shake his head. That's what the man say to me, no time to dawdle, and then he was gone in the blink of an eye. He stepped into the garden and just disappeared. I was mighty fearful as you can imagine, but I run into the garden any way's, calling and bawling. But he had just disappeared into thin air before my very eyes. I just knew there and then that he was a time travelling man.'

Beaty scraped back her chair and swayed to her feet. ' Now it is way past my bed time.'

I stumbled to my feet, still in a state of shock. She looked at me with those big saucer eyes and held out her arms. ' Now you give old Beaty a hug before you go.'

It was an order and I readily complied. She looked me up and down and wiped away a stray tear or two. ' You're going on a long journey Jimmy, to a place where no one can follow. It will be a great adventure, an' when you come back. You come an' tell me all about it, you hear?'

I could only nod dumbly.

' Can't hear you boy?'

' Yes,' I whispered, ' of course I will.'

'Oh, an' one more thing Jimmy.'

I turned at the open door.

' Don't forget my pie,' she said.

CHAPTER 5

It started to rain as I pulled the car away, my mind was all over the place, and when I reached the flat, I had absolutely no recollection of the journey. I could have jumped a light or three; squashed a puppy dog or two, run. But I didn't, though I still gave the car a cursory once-over for tell-tale splashes of blood, or the shattered remains of a cute puppy dog smeared to the bumper, a toilet roll still clamped in its jaws.

I opened the fridge door, and was surprised to see that it was still doing its job, refrigerating sod all. Except for a matching pair of overripe tomatoes, that now resembled dead man's bollocks, a carton of yoghurt that claimed to be milk, and a six pack of beers. It occurred to me that I should do a big shop tomorrow, if buying for one could ever be described as big. As things were, it looked like a trip to effing elsie's, and the six pack in front of the telly. I clicked open a can, and tried to make sense of my conversation with Beaty, when my mobile phone rang. It was Fay, when she died it never occurred to me to delete her from my phone. Silly I know, but that final act was simply a nonstarter.

Hello sweetheart.'

'Jimmy, what a day you've had.'

I grinned like the fool that I was, the sound of her voice was like the sound of life itself'. 'Tell me about it, I've just bought a house that doubles as Dr Who's Tardis.'

'Amazing, I told you to buy it, I just knew that it was special.'

The phone crackled, and then silence.

' Fay...are you still there?'

' Still here Jim, the line seems to be breaking up, I don't think she can take much more of this captain.'

I grinned, ' Scotty from Star Trek right.'

She laughed her girlish laugh, ' was it that bad?'

' So bad it was good.'

There was a moments silence before she whispered, ' I miss you.' I tried to reply but a rock lodged in my throat prevented me from doing so.

'Anyway,' she said briskly, ' one of the reasons I called was to tell you that my credit is running low.'

'What?'

'Yes, I have only got so much call time, and when it runs out it runs out.'

'What in heavens name are you talking about?'

'It really doesn't matter Jimmy, I will be out of range soon anyway.'

Suddenly I was in panic mode. ' I don't get it, when you die you have to hang around a bit, but they give you a mobile phone?'

'Sort of, it's hard to explain.' Suddenly the phone hissed and crackled, and I cried out loud as it slipped through my fingers and dropped to the floor. I fell to my knees and snatched it up, but it was as dead as the woman I still loved.

I slept without dreaming; did not awake in the early hours and slide my hand over the empty space beside me. Did not stare into the empty darkness and scrunch up my eyes in a vain attempt to rediscover sleep. Did not listen for the soft sigh of her regular breathing, or the amusing sounds and farts she made when she was dreaming. Or even the sudden sharp blow to my kidneys from her elbow. Sometimes I wondered if she was really sleeping when that happened. I awoke to a bright morning, feeling sharp and refreshed. Fleetingly I thought about my brief conversation with her, over a cup of builder's tea and a cigarette.

'You have to get a grip Jimmy boy,' I said out loud to a silent room. ' Beaty is right, you're only talking to yourself. I stubbed out the fag and drained my cup. 'A bit like now.'

An hour later and I was admiring the contents of my newly stocked fridge. There was bacon, sausages, eggs (free range) butter (Irish) A bottle of Italian virgin olive oil. A bottle of Vodka, two bottles of tonic and another six pack of beer. There was salad in a bag, fruit in a tin, chocolate in foil, sardines in a can. Three pizzas, one Italian and two German, and severable microwavable complete meals for one.

Job done!

As I showered and shaved, unable to avoid my face in the clouded mirror, I saw flecks of blood floating in my eyes. I saw lines, none of them laughing, and early spring grey hairs sprouting from my nostrils. Some fine scissors banished the offending growth, but only until the next time. Otherwise I was just dandy, picked up my keys and headed for the house.

The first of many skips had gone, but the garden still resembled a grisly corner of the Somme. I spent the morning applying an undercoat to woodwork in the front room, when my mobile phone rang. It was Ammo.

' Jimmy, are you at the house?'

' I am up to my armpit in emulsion mate, why.'

' Stick the kettle on, we'll be over in five.'

He was as good as his word, and came clumping over the bare floorboards as the kettle started to sing. When I looked up from my labours I was pleased to see that Jackie Tanaka (better known as Elvis) was with him.

'Grab a box chaps,' I said, and laid the paint brush aside.

Jackie grinned and held out his hand as if we had just been introduced. ' Nice house Jimmy, spooky but nice.'

I looked at Ammo and he shrugged. ' Okay, I told him, it's a great story.'

Mugs of tea were passed around and I instantly spotted the carrier bag that Elvis placed on the floor.

' I hope that is not what I think it is.'

'What are you saying Jimmy, you don't like my sushi?' He looked at Ammo for support and Ammo shook his head sadly. ' That's not very nice Jimmy, Elvis makes the best sushi in Leeds.'

'I know, but I am a hardworking man right now. I'm tuned into radio one, I have a copy of the Daily Mirror, I pause for lunch with my mates and then we all sit down and eat sushi for god's sake. It's just not the done thing around here.'

Elvis grinned and reached into his carrier bag. ' Cod and chips with scraps mushy peas is okay then.'

'Now you are talking,' I replied, reaching out in earnest.

We laughed and ate and chatted over our meal and mugs of tea, and I recalled with fondness the time that Elvis had become a fully- fledged member of the not very politically correct society. We had been out on the sauce, celebrating something or another, when we fell into this bar. It was karaoke night and we were so blitzed, we thought that everyone was absolutely fab. Then Jackie took the mike and we were blown away by his Elvis impersonation. We agreed unanimously that it was by far the worst performance we had ever heard. Consequently, we invited him over for a drink and some questions about the drugs he was on. He openly admitted it was not a career move, and that his real job was making sushi at a restaurant in town. After a couple or more pints of real ale, we staggered behind him to sample the delights of his restaurant. As it turned out we discovered that raw fish and too much beer were neighbours from hell. But he was such a charmer, he was unanimously voted into our private members club without hesitation.

'So Jimmy,' said Elvis chewing a chip. ' We the family have discussed your situation, and we have come to the conclusion that at your present work rate, the house will be completely refurbished in approximately one hundred and thirteen years.'

'Give or take,' added Ammo helpfully.

Elvis nodded sombrely, 'So we have all voted to help you whenever we can without pay.'

'The beer,' said Ammo earnestly, ' you forgot about the beer.'

'Ah yes, we do however expect standard union breaks, with free liquid refreshment, namely, beer.'

A sizeable chunk of crispy cod was arching its way to my open orifice, when the angry neon tube returned so loud that my ears hurt. I saw light flickering beyond the old net curtains hanging in the bay window, and I leaped to my feet, spilling fish and chips in every direction.

'So soon?' I cried.

Ammo and Elvis were also on their feet, mouths agape.

'Easy Jimmy, you're just having one of your panic attacks,' said Ammo.

But I was having none of it and grinned like the proverbial Cheshire cat. ' Do you hear that boys, now do you believe me?'

I stormed out of the room and threw open the front door. ' Follow me and be amazed.' The garden still looked a mess and it started to rain again. I felt Ammos hand on my shoulder as we peered out. Elvis spoke softly in my ear, ' It's okay Jimmy, let's go back inside.'

I reached out and felt the rain on my arm, and then the dying neon buzz returned, and the garden was suddenly transformed from the Somme into a riot of colour. Bright summer flowers beckoned in well ordered beds. Green grass lawns appeared on either side of the path, and red and white roses clung to an old stone wall on my right. Then in an instant, it was gone.

' He's having one of his turns,' said Ammo.

The angry neon tube returned, and I clamped my hands over my ears. Then my eyes opened wide as the garden invited me to enter. I could smell summer, could hear the busy hum of bees as they moved from flower to flower. I could feel the warmth of the morning sun on my outstretched arm. I turned to look at my friends, ' Isn't it just fantastic!'

As I stepped into the garden, I briefly felt a restraining hand on my shoulder. But there was no stopping me as I easily shrugged away his grip, and stepped into another time. I was suddenly embraced by the sun and lifted my head and raised my arms triumphantly.

'Come on chaps,' I said, turning back to face the porch. The door was ajar and now painted green. I saw a plush multicoloured carpet with black painted floorboards on either side. I saw an old gilt framed landscape oil painting hanging from a white painted picture rail, I saw a large brass lamp hanging in the porch. But my friends I did not see.

I was alone.

Suddenly I was very aware that I had travelled back to a time before I was born; and I did the most natural thing in the world, I panicked. I stepped backwards, feet brushing through flower beds, as my mind struggled to accept the situation I found myself in. The house seemed somehow incomplete as I swayed on the newly mown lawn, and the intoxicating smell of freshly cut grass was almost overwhelming. The bay window shimmered in the sunlight as a complex spiders' web appeared through the glass, loose strands hanging untidily.

The buzzing dying call of the neon tube returned, but distant, almost spent. My heart leapt as the spider's web began to spin itself into a fine pair of delicate net curtains. Then, without warning a white painted plant stand appeared; topped with a large decorative jardinière, complete with an aspidistra. To my befuddled mind the transformation seemed to be complete, but I was wrong. Peeling paint fluttered from the window frames like confetti, replaced in an instant by a glowing coat of pristine white gloss. At this point I was feeling
distinctly unwell; and I stepped forward, placing my hands on the brick wall. It was reassuringly solid, cold to the touch, and very real. The sharp intake of breath that followed was mine, as I pulled my hands away as if I had been burned. Like a drunken man, I staggered back onto the lawn. When a flap of wings caught my attention. The Magpie eyed me from the

lower branches of next doors tree.

'Hello,' I said, ' where is everybody?'

The Magpie stared at me contemptuously and then flew away. I stood and watched as it soared over neighbouring chimney pots, and disappeared from view. Suddenly my legs buckled and I fell to my knees in the grass. I puked more than once, and remained in my prayer like posture as wave after wave of nausea gripped me. As my laboured breathing levelled out, I heard the horse before I saw it, as its metal shoes rang out against the cobblestones.

When I swayed to my feet, I didn't know who was the more surprised. The horse eyed me wildly, curling its lips and tossing its head from side to side. Looking back, I must have appeared threatening and quite mad to the poor beast. Rising as I did from nowhere; a pale sweating confused countenance, with snail- like trails of puke dripping from my chin. The spooked horse reared up and tossed its main; which heralded in a melodic sound of jingles from the assorted brass chains and horse brasses that he wore like a chain of office.

The old man in charge of the horse reigned it in gently. ' Easy old girl, easy now,' he said, pulling on the reigns. The 'old girl' settled, but still glanced nervously in my direction, but not making eye contact. The old man leaned forward from his seat on the bench of his cart and looked at me curiously. His face was so lined it was impossible to tell where the lines began or ended, and a greasy flat cap shaded kindly blue eyes. 'By 'eck young 'un, thi fair give me a start. Why's tha been laiking in't garden?' He paused, no doubt waiting for some kind of response, but I was still hovering between two worlds.

He frowned and puckered his lips. ' Tha dunt look too clever tha knows, a bit green aroun't gills like. I reckon tha should get thissen indoors, out of t'sun like.'

I nodded dumbly and he appeared to accept that as an apology and a sign of agreement. 'Ah well, can't sit around 'ere chewing the fat all day.' He looked me up and down one more time and grinned toothily. ' An' I'd forget about the fancy dress ball if I was thee.' He slapped the reigns on the horses back and moved away with a jingle. I saw that his open cart was half full of old junk, and a large hairy unmade dog of indeterminate breed, sound asleep in the back.

'Hello, can I help you?'

My heart missed a beat and an overwhelming surge of panic gripped me as I turned to face her. My scrambled egg of a brain suggested that maybe now was a good time to scarper. I was, after all, trespassing in someone else's garden now. Yet any attempt to leg it was a non -starter. I could barely stand, never mind run.

She was standing in the porch, her right hand raised above her eyes, to shield them from the sharp early morning sunlight. She was a young woman, probably in her late twenties. Her chestnut brown hair was tied back with a thin blue ribbon, and she wore a calf length cotton summer dress that moved gently in the breeze.

'I am sorry, this is your garden now, I should leave.' At least I think that's what I said, but my voice sounded somewhat akin to a frog with a very sore throat.

'Yes, I think you jolly well should,' she replied indignantly.

I made a poor attempt to step over the flower bed, but as I raised one leg the other started to do an Elvis. I stepped onto a lovely bunch of daffodils, crushing them under my size nines.

'Sorry.'

I fully expected anger and dismay, but her voice softened, ' are you unwell?'

'I'm just a little shaky on my pins right now.'

She had one clenched hand raised to her lips, and a concerned and startled look in her eyes.

'I'm sorry,' I repeated, and was thankful that my voice sounded almost human again. 'I didn't mean to alarm you, I am leaving now.'

Then something quite extraordinary happened. Her expression changed from one of alarm, to one of recognition. She seemed to be appraising me, like someone in an art gallery studying a painting. Her gaze started at my feet, and I felt that she was studying my sartorial but casual mode of dress. I shifted uncomfortably, aware I was not looking my man of the world, cut above the rest persona right now.

'You are a traveller, aren't you.'?

I didn't quite meet her eyes and nodded to confirm my status.

' You are a time traveller?'

Somehow, I made that giant step for mankind, and found myself retreating down the path in a daze, alarm bells ringing. A full moon of blood crashed in tidal waves in my ears as I staggered back. I felt that this was the time I should leave, it was now or never, time to go. How could she know? The blood tide rose higher, filtering into my eyes, and a dark crimson mist rose like a veil.'

I heard her call to me then, ' No, please, please don't go!'

The garden gate pressed into my lower back as I fumbled for the latch. Somehow, I knew that if I could make it out into the street, then all would be well. I found the latch and burst out into the street. Her voice seemed to come from a faraway place now, seemed to echo down a very long tunnel.

' I'm sorry, I didn't mean to frighten you, please don't go!'

I stumbled, saw the hard-paving stones rushing up to greet me, felt the shocking pain as we collided, and then nothing.

The first sensation to return was sound.

' So, she says, mother in law is coming to stay, and I says, not on your Nellie, (laughter) If she comes then I go's. Then I thinks about it, better still, if she comes then we go (more laughter) Then I thinks about it again and says, better still, if she comes and I stay and she leaves with you, then everybody's 'apply.'

I opened my eyes and found myself staring at a cream painted ceiling. The room was dark, and I was lying on a chesterfield sofa, my head propped upon a pillow, and a large patchwork quilt draped over me. Then silence, and I heard deep murmurings of a man's voice. I swung my legs off the sofa and groaned. Memories came flooding back as I placed a hand on my forehead. I found a bandage wrapped around my head, and stared at my surroundings. Recognition was instant, I was in the ground floor front room.

It was pleasant but cluttered. A large Victorian mahogany mirror backed sideboard stood imposingly against the wall nearest the door. It was fully laden with framed photos, numerous ornaments and a matching pair of classical bronzed spelter figures; one at each end. A large cut-glass bowl took centre stage, filled with improbably lurid coloured fruit.

My eyes were drawn towards the door, it was slightly ajar and a light shone through the crack. I could still hear voices, but they were muted, and it was impossible to hear what was being said.

I climbed to my feet and swayed gently like a man who had just disembarked from a ship after a stormy passage. The nausea had passed, but my head felt like someone was tapping a toffee hammer on my temple. I cast a glance around the room. The black slate fire surround was familiar to me, but the large Victorian oil painting above; of a stag in a Scottish highland landscape was not. The fireplace was flanked by two alcoves. A tall oak astragal glazed bureau bookcase in one, and a floor standing cabinet gramophone in the other. I gently lifted the lid and peered at the 78' record waiting silently to be played. The label showed a seated dog, its head cocked towards a horned gramophone. ' His Masters Voice,' it read, and the music was provided by ' Charlie Kunz and his band. I stepped over to a floor standing cast iron treadle sewing machine standing idle. But the half-spent cotton reels told me that it was just resting. I brushed aside the net curtains. It was dark; but a solitary gas lamp- post threw some light upon a very familiar scene. The sturdy old door with worn steps leading down into the yard. The kitchen window with light spilling through net curtains, and below, the dark cellar window, where I had once caught a fleeting glance of another time.

Across the street, two young women appeared beneath the gas light. Both wearing almost identical head scarves tied at the throat. They each wore similar knee length coats and matching hand bags. They chatted for a brief moment, and then went their separate ways. My eyes followed the one who headed down Beatie’s street. I held my breath as she entered her yard and pulled a bunch of keys from her pocket. She then flicked the light switch and closed the door. So, I had arrived, but another question remained unanswered. Would I ever be able to return to my own time.

CHAPTER 6

It was time to meet my hosts, but I was beaten to it as I heard a gentle tap on the door. A man entered, then paused as he saw my shadowy silhouette framed in the window.

'Ah good, you are awake, you must be hungry after your long journey.'

I nodded in the dark, which seemed like the logical thing to do at the time. He switched on the light, and I blinked. I was looking at a smaller, younger man than me. With a mop of red hair and a smile so bright it would have lit up the national grid.

'My name is Sandy,' he said, moving quickly across the room, his hand outstretched, 'welcome Nicky.'

Nicky?

We shook hands. ' You fainted in the street,' he said with a soft Scottish brogue, 'we carried you in here, we could'na carry you upstairs you understand.'

' Absolutely, that was very kind of you, I'm sorry to be such a nuisance.'

' No trouble, no trouble at all. We are about to eat, and hope that you will share a simple meal with us.'

I followed Sandy, but the layout was so familiar, I could have led the way. I could not resist pausing to look down the hall. It was the same front door, half glazed with textured glass. Old fashioned floral wallpaper covered the upper part of the walls, down to about waist height. While the lower section was painted in a cream gloss. The two divided by a white painted dado rail. Paintings and prints hung from white painted picture rails, and the theme continued up the stairs. The stair carpet runner was older than the one in the hall, and slightly worn and threadbare. It was held into position by burnished brass stair rods. The exposed floorboards on each side were painted gloss black, as was the hall.

Immediately above my head, was the ceiling light. A large cloudy looking coloured glass bowl, suspended on three brass chains. Dominating the hall was a large carved oak hall-stand situated near the front door. It had a small central mirror flanked by an array of ornate brass hooks. A small central drawer, and two tin umbrella trays at the base. Most of the stand was hidden behind an array of hats and overcoats. On my left there was a small carved Gothic oak occasional table, standing on tripod legs. Laden with papers, keys, and a tall spidery pot plant.

They stood side by side as I entered the kitchen, and I felt a rush of blood to my face ' I'm so sorry, it's just, well everything looks so...' I was lost for words.

Sandy smiled.' This is my better half, Mary, but I think you two have met already.' We shook hands and she smiled warmly. ' Hello again,' I said, 'sorry about, well, earlier.'

'Not at all,' she replied laughing, and gestured to a chair at the kitchen table. We all sat but I was restless and full of questions. Mary poured tea from a brown teapot, reminding me of my conversations with Beaty. She placed a chrome tea strainer over each cup as she poured, catching stray tea leaves, and I became aware that Sandy was studying me.

' I'm a plain-speaking man Nicky, and as a Yorkshire man I don't doubt that you will appreciate that.'

I stirred my tea, ' certainly, It's the first rule of Yorkshire law.'

'Aye, and Scottish law too,' he replied. He pulled a pack of cigarettes from a waistcoat pocket, offering me one, which I gladly accepted. The pack was unfamiliar to me, but I could see the words 'Senior Service'. He then produced a box of matches from another pocket, and struck the match, offering me a light. I coughed, it was my first introduction to cigarettes minus a filter. Sandy then placed two cigarettes between his lips, lighting them with the same match, and handed one to his wife. ' Before we eat, there are some questions that need to be addressed. First, we know that you are a time travelling man.'

I was in fly catching mode again, and looked at Mary as she pushed the sugar bowl in my direction. She smiled and nodded. ' There was a moment when I didn't realize who you were. Then I saw those big white pumps with Nicky written on the sides...' She covered her mouth and laughed softly, ' we thought it was a bit strange that a grown man should wear such pumps, if you don't mind me saying.'

' Then there is the small matter of your hair,' said Sandy behind a haze of smoke.

' My hair?'

' Aye, well it's a bit spiky, Mary said you looked a bit like 'Dennis the

Menace.'

I laughed out loud, looking at her as she coloured and apologised.

' Why?' I replied, ' everyone loves 'Dennis the Menace.'

I looked down at my old Nike trainers, and raised a leg. ' These pumps are called trainers where I come from, and Nike is the name of the company that manufactures them.'

Sandy glanced quickly at his wife, ' it's a bit like the sandwich board man.'

She raised her eyebrows and nodded knowingly.

I frowned, ' the sandwich board man?'

'Aye, he gets paid for walking around with a sandwich board, advertising what folk are selling.'

I shook my head, ' no, it doesn't work like that at all. In fact, I pay more to show the world that I am wearing expensive designer shoes.'

The canny Scot spluttered in his teacup, and stared at me in disbelief. ' So, you pay them to advertise their goods?'

I broke into a grin and pulled on my cigarette. ' It does sound a bit odd when you put it like that, anything else?'

'Your vest is a little unusual,' added Mary.

I looked down at my old paint spattered black tea shirt; emblazoned with the legend 'Led Zeppelin', and decorated with mock human skulls and lightning bolts. It occurred to me that fortune had decreed that I did not sling on my ' Too Pissed to Shag' tea shirt that morning.

' And the cowboy trousers and gun belt are not quite the latest fashion either,' she said with a wide grin.

I looked down at my black jeans and broad leather belt. ' I was painting, this is my painting gear.'

Sandy smiled, ' painting gear? Now there's a turn of phrase. Och, we're only jesting man, times and fashions change, we know that. Now drink up, you need to get some fluids inside you.'

I drained the cup in one, and Mary wasted no time as she picked up the teapot and topped me up. 'This is proper tea, absolutely delicious.' I smiled at Mary, ' I'll bet you warm the teapot beforehand as well.'

She looked surprised, ' of course, doesn't everyone!'

'Not where I come from, teapots are history, it's all teabags now.'

She leaned forward and frowned, ' tea bags?'

'The tea is sealed into small porous paper bags; you just pop one into your cup, pour on boiling water and bingo, you have tea.'

Sandy laughed aloud, ' away man, now you're having a laugh, why the paper would just dissolve.'

'I know, you would think so wouldn't you, but it doesn't, it's a modern miracle.'

Mary looked incredulous, ' it sounds horrible.'

I shrugged, 'we don't know any better. If you offered anyone loose tea in my time, they would probably try to smoke it.'

They broke out into a fit of giggles, so I waited before asking the one-hundred-dollar question. 'I understand that my clothing may look a little odd, but how did you know that...?' I paused, unable to complete the sentence.

'That you were a time traveller', said. Mary.

Sandy reached across the table and took her hand. ' Because my darling' wife here was also a time traveller, is that no' right sweetheart.'

She fought back tears and lost, as they welled up and ran down her cheeks. Her chair made a scraping sound as she stood and rushed from the room. I looked at Sandy, ' I'm sorry.'

He placed a reassuring hand on my shoulder. ' There is no need to apologise, I'm listening to time travellers meeting for the first time, and I must say that I envy you.' He nodded in the direction of the hall. ' I must go to her.'

' Of course,' I answered, and he left the room. I stepped over to the Yorkshire range and stood with my back to the heat of the coal fire, arms folded behind my back, when I heard a loud hissing noise from the pantry. A large pan was boiling over, spewing its contents onto the gas ring. I turned it off and removed the pan, opening a small window at the far end. The escaping clouds of steam snaked past my head, out into the night.

Out of sight I heard young girls playing with a skipping rope, as they chanted an old rhythm in monosyllabic tones. It suddenly occurred to me that there were no cars, and then right on cue one swept into view, coming to a halt across the street. It was black of course, and reminiscent of models I had seen in my favourite Ealing comedy films. I held my breath as the driver's door swung open from the front, and Humphrey Bogart stepped out, locking the door and glancing around warily. He wore a long trench type coat, and pulled the brim of his hat over one eye.

' My god,' I whispered, ' it's that private dick, Philip Marlow.' I smiled as he let himself in, the pool of light picked out his silhouette perfectly. The scene could quite easily have been a book cover for ' The Big Sleep,' by Raymond Chandler. I imagined that memorable Bogie line as he closed the door behind him. ' I'm 'ome love, what's for tea?'

I heard them return and closed the window as I returned to my seat in the kitchen. Mary bustled past me to rescue what was left on the cooker. I caught Sandy's eye, and he just smiled and placed a finger to his lips.

' Is she okay?' I whispered.

' She's fine, it just brought some sad memories back, that's all. Now that we have established that your name is not Nicky after all...'

' Jimmy,' I said quickly, ' my name is Jimmy.'

' Why that's a lovely name,' Mary remarked as she placed the pan into the centre of the table. 'Don't you think Sandy?'

He was about to reply when she returned with three warm bowls and a large ladle 'Help yourselves boys.' She paused and looked down at me, as if she could not believe her eyes. 'Welcome to our home Jimmy, in our time there will always be a roof over your head and food in your belly. This is just a simple Irish stew, if I had known you were coming...'

'She'd have baked a cake,' said Sandy with a wink, and he was rewarded by a quick clip around the ear. She returned with a dish of freshly baked bread, and I ate until I was fat and content. I wiped my dish clean with the remaining bread, and then asked the burning question.

'What time have I returned to?'

It was Mary who answered, ' today is Friday the third of June Nineteen Fifty-Six.'

They were silent as I absorbed the information.

Then it was Sandy's turn. ' What time have you come from Jimmy?'

I found the question difficult to answer, it all seemed so unreal and dreamlike, but eventually I blurted it out.

' February the third, twenty nineteen,' I whispered.

A moment passed as we all pondered upon the impossible.

It was Mary who broke the silence. ' You have travelled back through time Jimmy; your room is prepared and you are welcome to come and go as you please.'

'My room, you have a room prepared for me?'

She smiled, ' of course.'

'You were expecting me?'

She laughed and shook her head, ' we were expecting someone at some time.'

Sandy produced some keys from his pocket, and rattled them theatrically before sliding them across the table.

' The keys to our home,' he said.

I stared at the keys, at their smiling faces, at the empty bowls and the large pan that had once contained a delicious Irish stew. ' I think I need a stiff drink.'

Mary was out of her chair in an instant and opened a cupboard set into the wall by the fire place. ' We have some sweet sherry here somewhere.'

Sandy looked at me and shook his head in exasperation. ' Will you stop your blethering about sweet sherry woman, can't you see that Jimmy's in need of a proper drink. There's some wee bottles of Babycham in there if I'm not mistaken.'

' Babycham?' I said weakly.

'Aye, left over from Christmas as I recall.' He stroked his chin thoughtfully, ' or was it the Christmas before? We keep a dry house here, generally speaking, except for Christmas and Hogmanay. Do you remember who brought the Babycham Mary, because I would dearly love to return their generosity one day.'

To say that my heart merely sank at the news, was akin to expressing 'disappointment' that my left leg had fallen off. So, it did not sink at all, but plunged torpedo-like until it reached the sole of my trainer, and upon impact it broke in two.

'Very commendable,' I replied with little conviction.

Mary was still rummaging in the cupboard, bottles clinked and I must confess that I was shocked to hear her mutter a curse. Sandy smiled and I acknowledged his smile, but I squirmed a little in my seat, wishing that I had not bothered to bring the subject of booze up in the first place.

' Ah here it is!' she called out triumphantly, and placed a bottle on the table. ' I found this bottle of eight year old malt behind the Babycham.'

'Oh well,' remarked Sandy with a deep sigh, ' it looks like the Babycham will just have to wait another year.'

'Which is a shame really,' said Mary as she placed three cut glass tumblers on the table, 'because they do say that the older it gets the worse it becomes.'

I looked at the two of them as Sandy played mothers ruin. ' I think I am going to have to keep a very close eye on you two.'

Laughter filled the kitchen as we clinked glasses in a toast. It was a moment in time that stayed with me until the end of my time.

Mary's story

'It was a new year, we had celebrated Hogmanay with Sandy's parents in Perth, and then we moved down here in January 1952.'

' Any particular reason?' I asked.

She paused to add some water to her whisky. ' I'm a Leeds lass and grew up in a house very like this one, but not as grand. My dad passed away some years ago, leaving mam on her own. So, we talked, didn't we Sandy.'

'We did indeed,' he replied, ' and decided it was best all round if we upped sticks and moved down here.'

' Sandy is an engineer by trade, and we knew he could walk into a job anywhere in the country,' she paused and looked at her husband.

' It was the war Jimmy,' he looked pensively down at his glass and turned it gently between his fingers. ' After the war there was a desperate shortage of skilled workers, a shortage of men, and that's the truth. So we found this house; it was larger than the ones we were looking at, but the rent was reasonable and we had a bairn on the way.'

I froze, somehow I knew what was coming next.

'I was seven months gone when my baby died.' She said it quickly, attempting to disguise emotion, which made it all the more painful for me. I pulled out my depleted pack of cigarettes, and she accepted one with a trembling hand as Sandy struck a light from his box of matches.

He, on the other hand, was less than impressed when he saw that they were filtered. ' I'll stick to my own, I canna do with those ladies' cocktail cigarettes.'

Mary composed herself after several puffs on her cigarette. ' We had been here about three months when I heard a strange sound.' She looked at me then, ' do you know what I mean Jimmy?'

I lit my own cigarette, ' oh yes,' I answered.

' It is a bit difficult to describe, it sounded like a bee in a bottle.'

' Perfect,' I murmured, ' that is a perfect description.'

She smiled at me hesitantly. ' I was hanging out some washing on the line in the back yard. It was a fine morning, warm with a gentle breeze, and I remember leaving the door open as I continued to wring out the washing on my mangle. I remember glancing over to the window, thinking some big old bumble bee had lost its way, and was trapped between the glass and the net curtain.' She stubbed out her cigarette and reached for Sandy's hand, which he readily took. ' Then chaos entered the kitchen, the infernal sound grew so loud I had to clap my hands over my ears. Sunlight flickered out like a spent light bulb, and suddenly I was plunged into darkness. A strong cold wind blew into the kitchen and the hallway door slammed shut.'

'You must have been petrified,' I said.

She shook her head at the memory. ' I was confused, and the noise was so loud I thought my ears would bleed. But more than that I was angry, angry that this sudden storm would ruin the washing on my line.'

I smiled, ' you were worried about the washing?'

She caught my smile and colour rose to her cheeks, eyes moist and bright. ' So I rushed out; down into the yard, when suddenly the most extraordinary thing happened. First my best frock disappeared before my very eyes. It was blowing in the wind as I reached for the pegs, and then it was gone. Sandy's vest and socks were next, followed by two pillow cases, my best tablecloth, and two pinny's, all gone. Now I was beside myself with fear and ran up the steps, slamming the door behind me.'

Mary paused and sipped her Scotch and water. ' I remember feeling quite sickly, my breathing was laboured. And then something else, the sound of footsteps coming down the stairs. Nausea gripped me and I could feel myself falling, as if into a deep abyss. I heard a voice then, but it seemed so far away, and then the sound of breaking glass. I was sprawled on the kitchen floor, my back against the wall, and when I looked up I saw that it was not my kitchen at all. And to make matters worse; I felt that I was not alone, that someone was watching me.'

I sat in stunned silence as I listened to her tale. Sandy must have heard this more than once, but I noticed he was very pale as he held her hand.

Mary seemed remarkably calm and composed.

' You just described my symptoms when I fell into your garden.'

She smiled, ' as I understand it, travelling through time does have its side effects.'

'Well it makes sense to me,' said Sandy, ' folk suffer with travel sickness on a coach to Scarborough, so a wee bit of travelling back in time may have that effect, wouldn't you say Jimmy?'

'Absolutely,' I replied, it's probably the most natural thing in the world. I really should have bought some time travelling pills from the Pharmacist before I left...silly me.'

Sandy frowned, ' Pharmacist?'

' Chemist,' I said quickly.

Sandy replenished our glasses and looked at his wife. ' Are you okay darling?'

She smiled, ' I am now that Jimmy is here, there were times when I thought I was going quite mad.' She squeezed his hand, and smiled at me across the table. ' Poor Sandy here has been my rock.'

Sandy turned a delightful shade of pink, ' away with you woman, ' I have only done what any good husband would do.'

'Please continue,' I said.

'Well I was very weak, but somehow found the strength to find the edge of the sink over there.' She nodded to the old ceramic Belfast sink in the corner. ' I pulled with all my remaining strength and found my feet. The next thing I recall is opening my eyes. I was looking at the flames dancing in the coal fire, glowing deep red and radiating flickering shadows on the walls. I was sitting in a red velvet covered armchair, and the warmth of the fire wrapped me in a comforting blanket. I saw his feet first, small and adorned with unusual Persian-looking slippers, slightly turned up at the toe. Then my eyes rested upon the man seated opposite. He was slightly built, and in his mid to late sixties I would say. He wore an oriental style silk dressing gown, over grey flannel trousers. A white shirt with a starched high collar; a bright yellow and black polka dot dickey bow, and a floppy rather absurd nightcap. His voice however was far from absurd, deep, rich and intelligent.'

'How are you feeling my dear,' he said.

Mary shook her head and smiled fondly at the memory. ' I must have looked like a trapped wild animal, trying and failing to make sense of my predicament. He held a small briar pipe to his lips, and a rich sweet aroma permeated the room. His dark brown slightly hooded eyes were kindly and steady as he studied me. He then pointed to my left with his pipe.' The brandy should be warm by now,' he said, ‘it will help calm your nerves and confusion.'

There was a small occasional table set between myself and the fire, and the brandy glowed like liquid gold in the light of the burning coals. The surface rippled as I raised it to my lips with a trembling hand.'

'You have travelled far young lady,' he said, ‘and judging by your attire I would suggest your journey cannot be measured in miles, but in years. You are by no means the first to enter this house unannounced and in such an unexpected manner, nor, I suspect will you be the last.'

'I am sorry,' I said, I do not understand what is happening, am I dreaming, am I trespassing?' He laughed then, a soft musical chant of laughter. 'How could you possibly be trespassing in your own kitchen. Admittedly it is our kitchen now, but undoubtedly it will be your domain in the future.'

I was mesmerised by her tale, yet still found myself fighting to keep my eyes open. I felt Sandy's hand on my shoulder and jolted to an upright sitting position.

'Jimmy,' he said, ' are you still with us man?'

'Sorry, but I am absolutely bushed.'

Mary pushed back her chair and stood. ' Of course you are, show Jimmy up to his room Sandy.' I half turned at the door and looked back at her. ' I really need to hear the rest of your story.'

She smiled, ' all in good time, goodnight Jimmy.'

I followed Sandy up to the first floor, turning right and passing the three steps on my left that led to the loo and bathroom. Four steps up and we entered the first room on the left. Sandy flicked the light switch and stepped aside.

' Sleep well Jimmy.'

' Oh I will, see you in the morning.'

CHAPTER 7

I awoke, not to the sound of birdsong, but to the sound of music. A big brass band played a foot tapping melody in my head. It made me smile inside, made me feel good to be alive. I peeled back my eyelids with some difficulty, it was like pulling open a difficult Velcro pocket, but soon I was wide eyed and ready for my brave new world. The music changed and I recognised ' In the Mood' immediately. The music was well before my time on this planet, but I had always nurtured a fondness for the old big band sound.

The room was quite dark until I pulled back the heavy brocade curtains, and it was a fine morning that greeted me. I saw a pair of pigeon's flutter from nowhere and settle in the yard below. They strutted their stuff close to the cellar window; the same window I had peered through a lifetime ago it seemed.

Suddenly I was a man in a hurry, dressing at formula one speed and taking the stairs three at a time. I was halted in my tracks at the foot of the stairs, the front door was wide open and the garden beyond looked absolutely beautiful. The temptation to rush out into the sunlight was almost irresistible, but the smell of crispy grilled bacon won the day, so I followed my nose.

Sandy was setting plates on the plain deal table, he grinned and gestured to a chair.

' How are you this morning?'

' Better, much better,' I answered, yawning and scratching my head, ' but a bit dopey, how long have I been asleep?'

He shrugged and glanced at the wall clock, ' about twelve hours, give or take.'

'Twelve hours!'

He laughed, ' there's fresh tea in the pot, so help yourself; I was about to wake you anyway.'

We ate in silence, the bacon was perfectly crisp, the eggs soft and runny, and the toast was done on one side. Sandy pushed the toast rack in my direction.

'Well there's nothing wrong with your appetite, I'll say that much.'

I scraped another layer of butter on yet another slice of toast. 'Gordon Ramsay would have been proud of you.'

He lit a cigarette and shrugged. ' It's just a wee fry up Jimmy, not afternoon tea at the Ritz.' He frowned then, ' who is this Gordon Ramsay fellah?'

I joined him in the smoking department, ' forget it, is Mary working?'

' Aye she is, but I decided to take the day off.'

' I hope you didn't call in sick on my behalf.'

' I didn't call in sick at all, I just took the day off. We could'na have you waking up to an empty house on your first proper day. Besides, we need to get down to Uncles and see a man about a suit.'

I raised my eyebrows above the cloud of smoke. ' We are going to your Uncle's for a suit?'

He roared with laughter, ' not my uncle man, that's what we call the pawn shop around these parts. We need to kit you out, so you can step outside without people laughing at you.'

I drummed the table with my fingers, 'the outside world awaits, lead on Macduff.'

Sandy smiled,' I will lead on when you have changed your clothes. You can't go out dressed like that, so I have laid out some of my clothes on our bed, so you had best go and change.'

I paused and turned at the door, ' hang on a minute, how tall are you?'

He pulled a face, ' about five seven.'

'Well I am five ten, so how is that going to work?'

'You worry too much,' he said, and waved me out.

We both fell about laughing when I returned. I just stood there, hands on hips, with a silly grin on my face. Sandy scratched a day's growth of beard on his chin. Meanwhile I discovered that each time I breathed in, the trousers rose a bit higher. They had now climbed to upper sock level, and the shirt and jacket were no better. The jacket sleeves were tight and came to a halt half way up my arms. At this point I could not resist doing a silly walk and almost tripping. Sandy laughed again, slapping his knee. ' Norman Wisdom, very good, have you ever thought of playing the music halls Jimmy, you and Charlie Chaplin would make a great team.'

At this point the relatively simple act of breathing was becoming an issue, so I peeled the jacket off and draped it over a chair. ' What about a raincoat, you must have a raincoat.'

He was on his feet in an instant and swept passed me, down the hallway. I watched and waited as he rummaged through a number of coats hanging on the hall stand.

'Aha!' I heard him cry, and he returned clutching a large overcoat, ' try that on for size.' He handed it to me with both hands, and I mistakenly reached out and took it with my right arm. Sheer weight and gravity did the rest, and I almost fell over.

'Good god Sandy, what is it made of, is that a silk lining I see, or lead lining?'

His eyes twinkled, ' is that no' a heavy coat.'

'Heavy does not even begin to describe it. If we had a pole and some tent pegs, a family of five and the dog could happily live in here.'

It appeared to be made up of military type blue serge, with a thick padded silk lining. Disappointingly there was no makers label, and the solid brass hanging chain was tarnished with age, old and very substantial. I pulled the coat on and disappeared, with only my head showing. My arms, legs and feet were completely smothered from view, as the coat folded on the floor.

' Where did you get it?'

' It was here when we moved in, hanging on the old hall stand.'

I looked down at the spot where my feet should have been, and felt beads of sweat forming on my forehead.

' He must have been six and a half feet, and big with it.'

' More like seven I would say,' he said dramatically. ' We did'na have the heart to throw it out or give it to the rag and bone man.'

I handed it back, feeling a great weight lifted off my shoulders.

'I'm with you Sandy; imagine him looming in the doorway, and you having to explain that his coat is now in the possession of the rag and bone man, well, it doesn't bear thinking about.'

I followed him along the hall as he placed the coat back on its rightful hook.

'Exactly,' he replied with feeling, ' we did ask around, chat to the neighbours like, but no one recalled seeing a giant of a man minus his coat. So we just leave it there...just in case.'

'Very commendable, and wise,' I replied, mopping my brow with a tissue.
Sandy handed me one of his own coats and I was pleased to see that it was a Humphrey Bogart affair. A light summer gabardine with a wide belt and buckle. It was a little tight on the shoulders and chest, but otherwise fine.
'So far so good 'I said, pulling up the collar and admiring myself in the tiny hall stand mirror.
Sandy looked less than convinced and scratched his head. ' Aye well, I suppose so, but what about the shoes.'
I looked down at his feet, and then mine. ' Do you have any wellies?'
' Aye, and they are a size larger to allow for winter socks.'
They were tight, and my feet were already complaining before I had taken a step. I tucked the short trousers into my boots. ' Well, how do I look?'
Sandy scratched his chin again, ' you look fine,' he lied.
'Fine for what, the annual scarecrows ball?'
'Stop your blethering, the pawn shop is only five minutes down the road, all the bairns are in school, and the factories are working, trust me,' he said reassuringly, 'the streets will be quiet.'
Sandy locked the front door and we left by the back. I couldn't help myself as I paused to look down through the grate to the cellar below, and I was barely prepared for the shock as I stepped out into the street. Everything seemed so ancient; it was if I had stepped back into the nineteenth century. The main road was black, smooth and unmarked, and the smell of newly laid tarmacadam still hung in the air. But every street leading off was cobbled, a sea of smooth shiny misshapen stones glistening in the bright morning sunlight. Green painted cast iron gas lamps stood like sentinels, and red brick houses huddled closely together, as if expecting a sudden tropical storm.
Sandy watched me, a curious smile playing on his lips. ' Is it so different Jimmy?'
I paused before answering, 'well yes and no, all of these houses are still here in my time, but there is something else. I feel that I am in another time, there are obvious reminders like that car,' I said, pointing at an old Ford Prefect parked across the road. And that advertising hoarding,' I said, pointing at a large sign on one of the gable ends, promoting 'Biles Beans.'

But there is something else, something telling me that I should not be here, and it feels quite scary.'

' Well you should not feel afraid, a time will come when the bee in the bottle will return, and you will step back into your own time once more.'

' Will I Sandy?'

He smiled, ' oh yes, you will understand when you hear the end of Mary's story.'

I fell into step beside him, my feet muttering mutiny. He glanced at me quickly. 'You're limping, why are you walking like that.'

' Because my size ten feet are being crushed by your size eight wellies,' I hissed between clenched teeth. ' And as my right foot is marginally larger than my left, it feels like it is trapped within a rapidly closing vice.'

' Why didn't you say something?'

' About what?'

' That you have two odd feet.'

' I didn't say that I have odd feet, but one is marginally bigger than the other, we all have odd feet.'

' I don't,' he replied with conviction.

As we reached the end of the road, I noticed an old bakers' shop on the corner. Sandy took the lead as I limped in his slipstream. Suddenly he almost collided with two ladies leaving the shop. ' Whoopsadaisy,' he said, pausing to raise his hat, old school style. ' Why Mrs Broadhead, how are you on this lovely morning?'

' I'm fine Mr Mackintosh, you are not working today?'

' Och no, we have a guest staying for a wee while, and I thought I would show him around.' He turned to introduce me, I was sweating as the sun beat down on my shrink-wrap overcoat, tight waistcoat, even tighter collarless shirt, and the Wellington boots from hell. My limp had become even more pronounced, and I was slightly breathless.

'This is my friend, Jimmy.'

Beads of sweat trickled into my eyes, blurring my vision. I blinked and nodded like the village idiot. Mrs Broadbent smiled warmly, ' hello,' she said. I wiped my dripping nose with my sleeve without thinking.

' This is Gwendoline,' said Sandy, looking at me with a frown, 'Mrs Broadbent's daughter.'

I heard a chorus of angels sing as Gwendoline, Mrs Broadbent's daughter, came into focus. Such a vision of loveliness simply took my breath away, and in a trice, I had become Igor, staring stupidly and ringing bells for Esmerelda. Without a doubt I fell in love with her eyes first. Deep lustrous pools of warmth and kindness; quick and intelligent oval orbs of perfection. Her long auburn hair framed a classical face, with high cheek bones and full ruby red lips that were smiling at me. She wore a light floral summer dress, tied with a thin blue silk belt, to reveal the tiniest of waists. And to top it all she held a small brown loaf of unsliced bread.

She was, to me, perfection personified.

However, I was in so much pain, I wasn't sure if it was safe for me to speak, so I just nodded and wondered if she had spotted the hump on my back. Then I detected something else, a look in her eyes that was all too familiar to me. I had seen it before and recognised it immediately, it was sorrow and pity, and the engagement was off.

I limped across the connecting street, listening as Sandy bid them good morning, and found myself standing on the brow of a grassy hill. Wide stone steps swept down to a cobbled street below. On my right a huge factory, topped with tall chimneys fitted with large aluminium extraction filters. Sandy joined me and pulled out his cigarettes. As we smoked he glanced at his depleted box of matches.

' Remind me to buy a box.' he said.

I nodded and turned to look at the factory, ' what happens in there?'

' Engineering,' he said flatly, ' munitions during the war.' I sensed an edge to his voice. ' You were very rude back there. '

I was stung by his rebuke. ' I'm sorry, it was something in her eyes, I don't do pity.'

Sandy inhaled deeply and released the smoke slowly. ' Aye, well you're in my street now, and you would do well to remember what year it is.'

I turned and looked at him, ' I don't understand.'

'The war is long over Jimmy, but there are many men of your age, and much younger, who still carry the scars of that awful time. You see pity in a young lassie's eyes, but what you don't see are the countless number of men who limp because part of their knee cap has been blown away, or they have lost a foot. Men who are still too shell shocked to speak of the abominations they have witnessed.'

I hung my head like an errant schoolboy, ' I'm beginning to realise how complicated this time travelling lark really is.'

He touched me on the arm and pointed, and I followed his gaze. More streets peeled off from left to right. I saw an old man sitting on a Windsor armchair, smoking a pipe and catching the morning sun. Neighbours passed the time of day in conversation, and some were kneeling, dipping scrubbing brushes into zinc buckets and scrubbing the steps to their home. Everywhere washing hung on lines across the streets.

'Do you see the wee shop at the end of the street Jimmy, the one with the three golden balls hanging outside?'

I raised a hand and peered into the distance, like the captain of a ship. An occasional breeze made the myriad of bed sheets billow and flap, like the sails of an Armada awaiting orders.

' Is that it?'

'Aye, I told you it was'na far.'

A bell tinkled as we entered, not by the main shop door, but an unassuming side door. The room was quite dark, with a large wooden counter, fitted with a gate and lift up flap. Blankets and sheets were stacked neatly upon rows of stained pine shelving, each bearing a cardboard tag tied with string. A pale hollow faced man of indeterminate age peered at us through gold wire rimmed circular spectacles. His glasses glinting in the light of a single gas wall light, burning above the counter. He had about him the air of a man who had heard it all, seen it all, and he probably had.

However, when Sandy explained my urgent need for suitable attire, he became quite animated, rubbing large rheumatic hands together in anticipation. We were led into a back room. Two sash windows let in some natural light, each window fitted with cast iron bars, painted green. Long racks of clothes filled the room, and he flicked a hand through a row of suits, and then cast an expert eye over me.

' Five ten?'

' Correct,' I replied.

He nodded, almost purring with pleasure.

' Forty-inch chest?'

'You're a magician,' I replied.

He raised an arched eyebrow. ' I am, but when I weave my magic, does anyone appreciate it.'

He lifted three suits off the rack, 'try these,' he said, pointing to a cubicle draped with a heavy velvet curtain.

I settled for a light grey fine pinstripe suit, with turn-ups on the trousers. Two white shirts with separate collars, and a dashing pair of bright red braces to keep my pants up. Shoes were more of a challenge.

' Um,' he murmured, looking at my stocking feet...size nine?'

'Ten,' I corrected; he looked crestfallen, but even magicians have their off days I concluded. Eventually I found a pair of black leather brogues, they were comfortable but one insisted on creaking. The choice of hat was a much simpler affair, all I had to do was find a Humphrey Bogart hat, and there were plenty to choose from. My ensemble was now complete, but the magician was not quite finished, producing an array of ties. I chose a red stripe to go with my braces.

'Will sir require any undergarments,' he said, plunging his hand into an old tea chest. He fished out a faded white pair of underpants; they appeared to have been the property of an incontinent Sumo wrestler.

‘No thanks, I'll stick to my boxers, if you'll forgive the pun.'

No one laughed, least of all Sandy, who shook his head, pulled a face, and looked at the ceiling in exasperation. I realised my foot in mouth mistake immediately, but it was too late.

'Boxers,' he murmured, dropping the offending hammock back where it belonged. 'So you practice the noble art.'

Sandy was standing behind him and made a cutting motion to his throat, a sure sign that I was doing just fine.

'Sorry, yes I do a little work out at the gym.'

'Really, how interesting,' he studied me for a moment. ' You must be a remarkably able boxer. You have a very fresh face, if I may say so. There are certainly no signs of punishment and defeat in your countenance, or even the suggestion of a scar.'

I was in a hole and still digging, so I just shrugged. ' I float like a butterfly and sting like a bee.'

At this point Sandy appeared to be experiencing some sort of a seizure. The man smiled thinly,' that would explain the lack of cranial damage.'

I looked to Sandy for an escape route.

'You see, I too did a little boxing in the army.'

My knees weakened and I felt a warm rush of blood to my face. And then I noticed how his nose pointed oddly to the west, and the fine skin beneath his eyes carried a countless number of permanent scars.

'In fact, I was Yorkshire Lightweight champion two years running.'

I raised my eyebrows and tried to look suitably impressed, ' really...excellent, well, what a small world.'

Sandy came to my rescue, ' right Jimmy, we can't stand here blethering all day.' As he settled the bill the man held out his hand to me. His grip was firm and I saw that his knuckles were swollen and calloused. His hand easily smothered my lily white, never done a proper day's work, marigold hand.

' Float like a butterfly and sting like a bee,' he said. His face cracked into a surprising smile for the first time, ' I will have to remember that.'

Sandy stared at me as we stepped out into the street. ' What was all that about? You are going to have to think before you speak Jimmy.'

I offered him a cigarette, which he accepted, snapping off the filter and patting his pockets.

' You need to buy some matches.'

' Aye, thanks for reminding me.'

He led me to a small corner shop and soon we were puffing away like a pair of steam engines as we headed for the back door.

She's a fine looking woman isn't she,' I remarked.

Sandy paused and looked at me, ' who are we talking about?'

I smiled and said nothing.

He stroked his chin and pondered for the briefest of moments. ' Oh aye, Mrs Broadbent is a good looking woman, but a wee bit advanced in years for you I would have thought.'

I sighed patiently and crossed my arms in silence.

'Ah, you mean the lovely Gwendoline.'

I shook my head as he released a short laugh. ' You're not wrong there Jimmy, she's a bonny lassie and that's for sure. Her husband certainly thinks so I believe.'

CHAPTER 8

It was late afternoon and I was relaxing in a Lloyd Loom basket chair, enjoying the cooling shade beneath next doors tree, when the click of the gate made me tip my Bogie hat back. Mary was back, standing in the drive and smiling down at me sweetly. I stood, bowed formally, and gave her a twirl. She laughed and clapped her hands. I then whisked my jacket draped over the back of the chair, and threw it over my shoulder, Italian gigolo style.

'My, you boys have been busy, you look quite the gent now.'

I grinned, slipping on the jacket and hat; not forgetting to flip the rim over my right eye. 'Me and the boys need a joint to lie low in sister, we just done a bank job see. Now we ain't here to hurt no one see, so you and your old man back there just carry on playing happy families, and we'll get along just fine. Any funny business and the dog gets it, I don't care either way.'

When Mary laughed, she leaned so far backwards I feared that she would fall over. 'Humphrey Bogart, how clever.'

I grinned and removed the hat and jacket. ' Sandy's making dinner.'

Her smile instantly turned into a look of alarm, ' Sandy is cooking?' she said with an element of panic in her voice. She turned and hurried up the steps.

'Ham salad,' I called after her, ' I believe that ham salad requires little skill in the cooking department.' I dropped back into my chair and tipped the Bogie over my eyes. 'Unless you are having new potatoes with it,' I murmured to no one in particular, 'or chips,' I closed my eyes.

'What did 'e say?'

It was a child's voice.

'Dunno, something about chips.'

I decided to play possum and listen.

'I don't like it,' said the younger squeaky voice, ' him sitting there with his 'at over his face, talking about chips, it's not natural.'

' Shurrup an' let me think.'

' He might be dead, he looks dead.'

I heard the older one sigh. ' Dead folk don't go around talking' about chips stupid. Of course, he could be a madman.'

'A madman,' echoed squeaky in a trembling voice.'

'Oh aye, sitting in the sun all day melts the brain, an' that's a fact.'

'I wanna go home Billy.'

Thing is,' said the older boy, ' madmen don't know they're mad. Why 'e could leap out of that chair any minute an' chop yer 'ead off with a chopper, an' then go back to sleep again without a care in the world. That's what madmen are like, they don't know any better...where yer going Albert?'

' Home, I'm going home.'

' Scardy cat!'

' Not.'

' Well bugger off home then, see if I care.'

It was at this point that I decided it was time for Lazarus to rise. I tipped the hat back with a finger. He was a lad of nine or ten, wearing a school uniform of sorts. A cheeky looking nipper with a round face filled with freckles. His tie was pulled to one side and he wore a peaked cap with a silk badge. He was hanging onto the gate, but looking away from me, presumably at his retreating brother.

'Hello,' I said. The gate could have been electrified, such was his reaction as he leapt back a couple of feet.

' Sorry, did I startle you?'

He stared at me, his eyes and mouth competing in a 'who could be the widest' contest. And then he almost composed himself immediately, shaking his head and pushing both hands into the pockets of his grey flannel short trousers.

'Nah,' he said with some bravado, ' we thought you was asleep, that's all.'

I smiled, ' so what's your name.'

'Billy,' he said, kicking the pavement.

Suddenly another boy appeared, much younger and smaller, his wide eyes peering through the slats of the gate.

'This is me brother, Albert.'

'Hello Albert,' I said, and the eyes blinked. Billy's confidence returned, as he stepped forward and leaned on the gate like an old farmer.

' We 'avent seen you round 'ere before mister.'

' No, I'm just visiting my friends.'

' You're not from around 'ere then, you sound a bit posh like.'

' Sorry about that, where do you think I come from?'

' Dunno,' he replied with a shrug.

' Doncaster,' whispered squeaky, ' tell 'im he's from Doncaster.'

I suppressed a laugh, ' why Doncaster Albert?'

Billy sighed deeply, as though he carried all the troubles of the world on his young slender shoulders.

' Don't mind 'im mister, he's an idiot.'

' Not!'

'You are!'

' Not!'

Aware that this intellectual debate could go on for some considerable time, I decided to intervene.

' Why Doncaster Albert?'

' Because Margaret Midgley's from Doncaster, an' when we 'ave our dinner at dinnertime, she 'as her tea, an' when we 'ave our tea at teatime, she 'as her dinner...so there.'

'Can't argue with that Billy,' I said, ' that is posh.'

He just shrugged and pointed a finger at his temple, making a circular motion, suggesting that a screw was loose somewhere.

' So, what can I do for you boys.'

' Ave you got any sterilised milk bottles?' said Billy.

I frowned, ' sterilised milk bottles?'

He nodded, his world-weary eyes viewing me with some curiosity and more than a little pity. I checked my trouser and waistcoat pockets, and even looked beneath my chair.

'Nope, it seems I'm clean out of sterilised bottles right now.'

He frowned, and a sadness crept into his world-weary eyes. 'The lady sometimes gives us sterilised bottles to tek back t'shop like.'

' Ah, right!' I hauled myself out of the chair and headed for the door.

' What was he doing?' said squeaky to his brother.

' Looking in 'is pockets for sterilised bottles,' he replied.

' So 'e is a madman then.'

'Oh aye, madder than that old biddy with the 'tash down Kingston

Avenue I'd say.'

I grinned as I walked down the hall, listening to their animated laughter. There was more laughter as I entered the kitchen, instantly stifled as I made my appearance. Mary had her mouth covered with a raised hand, and Sandy retreated to the pantry, whistling.

'Sandy was just telling me about your past exploits in the boxing ring.' She could contain herself no longer and giggled, setting Sandy off again.

I smiled, ' while you two are amusing yourselves at my expense, there's two young lads out there looking for sterilised milk bottles.'

She dabbed at her eyes, reaching for a bottle on the draining board. ' That will be Billy and Albert, here, give them this.'

They were still waiting patiently at the gate. ' Thanks mister,' they said in chorus, and ran off down the street.

'Thanks Mr Chips!' called squeaky, before disappearing into a shop.

The food was set on the table when I returned, and as I took my seat Mary looked across at me. ' No offence Jimmy, it was such a funny story.'

'None taken,' I replied, and sliced into a new potato. ' The odd thing is, I don't think he believed a word I said.'

Sandy snorted, ' aye well it's no sup...' He paused, fork and ham hovering between plate and mouth. ' How do you mean?'

The buttered potato melted in my mouth. ' Well,' I said slowly,' had I the time to explain, then I could have informed him that I was Inter school featherweight champion at thirteen. Lightweight champion at fifteen, and was even considered a possible England and Commonwealth prospect at age sixteen. But then I discovered girls and alcohol, and the rest, as they say, is history.'

They sat staring at me, food forgotten.

'Tell me you are having us on,' said Sandy with a frown.

I gave them my really serious look and skewered a slice of boiled egg. ' Yes,' I answered, 'I am having you on.'

It was time to give the food our undivided attention. They both laughed and Mary raised her tea cup, ' touché' she said.

Later we adjourned to the garden. ' It's such a lovely evening,' I said, ' we should have eaten out here.'

'Here, in the garden?' Mary looked visibly shocked. ' I couldn't eat my dinner in the garden with folk gawping on.'

It was my turn to look surprised, ' you never eat in the garden?'

Sandy shook his head, ' dinner is a private affair Jimmy, you canna have folk looking on. I know that some foreigners like the French and Italians do that sort of thing, but not here in old blighty thank goodness.'

' You still eat out though, go for picnics, that sort of thing.'

' Oh aye, a picnic is very acceptable, but no' your dinner.'

' It seems I have a lot to learn, so what's the story behind the sterilised bottles.'

Mary smiled, 'occasionally we buy a bottle of sterilised milk, especially in the summer months when fresh milk is prone to go off, even when we keep it next to the meat safe in the cellar. The shopkeeper gives you a penny for every bottle returned.'

'Interesting, an early form of re-cycling.'

Their expressions said it all, ' forget I said that.'

That evening we walked out for the first time. Mary had suggested that as it was such a fine evening, we should take a stroll up to Woodhouse Moor.

'You can tell us what has changed on the way,' she said. As we crossed the street, I looked back at the house and garden, with the old stone wall on the left. Next to the wall there was a tall and wide wooden gate, painted green, with a latched door set into the right side.

' Is that a garage?' I said pointing.

' No,' Mary replied, it leads to a cobbled yard and a row of tiny back to back houses hidden from sight and sunlight.'

I looked down the street, at the shiny cobblestones, the red brick houses, some connected by washing lines, held high by wooden poles.

' In my time, all you see below your home has gone, demolished in the seventies to make way for new housing.' I turned to look at the houses on our side of the street. ' All of these have gone, in fact we are standing facing a brick wall in my time, and beyond that there is now another University block.' I paused and peered at possibly the worlds tiniest shop. It leaned in a drunken manner, resting upon the gable end of a house. It was much older than the Victorian property that held it up.

I stepped forward and peered through the tiny latticed window, where rusted tins lived. Lined up in neat rows, their labels lost and faded from years of exposure to sunlight. I Did however make out a label for Whopper peas. Beyond the tins, lined up side by side like toy soldiers, the interior consisted of plain whitewashed walls, a large white marble slab, and an array of knives hanging on brass hooks. I turned and looked at them in surprise.

' It's so tiny, why two people would constitute a crowd in there.'

Mary smiled, ' when we first moved here we thought it was just a tiny abandoned shop. Then we discovered that the lady who owns it, takes delivery of fresh fish and ice from a van. She opens at midday and closes at three, leaving the ice to melt on the pavement. Apparently, the same family have plied their trade in this little shop for as long as anyone cares to remember.'

' Mainly finny haddock, Pollock and cod,' said Sandy.' There are many shops like this dotted around the city. You would have to trail into town otherwise, and who would dream of doing that for a piece of finny haddock?'

' Who indeed,' I murmured, and we moved on.

I soon realised that I was seeing not just the nineteen fifties, but the end of Victorian England. Everywhere there were reminders of another age. Colourful enamel advertising signs were in abundance. Promoting everything from 'Lyons Tea', ' Fry's Chocolate to ' Black Cat Tobacco.' The list was endless, and the most amusing was a sign depicting a slick waiter holding a silver salver, a packet of cigarettes lying in the centre. The caption read ' For Your Throats Sake, Smoke ' Craven A,' as if they were positively good for you. 'All the houses on this side of the road have gone in my time,' I said. ' All the houses on your side still remain, but only from your house upwards.'

' How odd,' remarked Mary, 'perhaps the council ran out of money.'

We reached the main road, leading down into town, or up to our destination. This was a main thoroughfare, and it was busy. Students sat in groups upon the university steps across the road, and I had to smile at how conservative they looked. Wearing the same drab clothing as their parents. Others hurried past clutching folders and books, and some simply watched the world go by in a haze of cigarette smoke. A family group passed immediately in front of me. Father, daughter, and mother pushing a large coach pram with the words ' silver cross' in chrome letters on the side.

Tram lines snaked up and down the road, while overhead a canopy of cables cast shadows onto the road below. The occasional car passed, straddling the tram lines. Someone brushed past me and I blinked rapidly, feeling quite overawed and anxious in equal measures.

Suddenly a tram rattled past, and a sharp crack pulled my gaze to the overhead power cables, as a blue light flashed. Another tram came to a humming halt across the street, and I stared as people disembarked, hurrying in all directions.

It started as a dull ache in the pit of my stomach, and then a chill wind blew from nowhere and made me shiver. I recall that my hand brushed against a low stone wall, and I stopped and leaned against it for support. I was freezing now, my body shaking violently in uncontrollable spasms.

The voice was gruff, but gentle. ' Better sit down before you fall down mate,' he said, and I felt a helping hand on my arm as I nodded and sat. The sound of a match rasping against matchbox sounded sharp, and louder than it should.

'Here,' he said, handing me the cigarette.

'Thank you,' I whispered.

'Jimmy!' it was Mary's voice, and she sounded distressed. ' I'm so sorry we were just chatting and...'

'He'll be fine love, just had a bit of a turn, didn't you soldier.'

I drew deeply on the cigarette, and became embarrassingly aware of a gathering throng of curious people.

He was perhaps around my age. Smartly dressed with a peaked flat cap pulled halfway down his forehead. I was immediately struck by his piercing blue eyes. Yet his gentle smile seemed to cloud a deep sorrow. He had a strong proud face, ravaged by numerous livid scars, running from the corner of his right eye, and spreading like a spider's web over his face, back down to his left ear and a section of obliterated lip.

' Thank you kindly,' said Sandy, ' he's not been himself recently.'

The man tipped his hat back and smiled. ' Aye, well he's not looking so green around the gills now.' He then turned his attention to the gathering throng of onlookers. ' And you lot, on your way, there is nothing for you to see here.' His commanding presence and ravaged features had the required effect, and the crowd drifted away.

I felt stronger, and stood and held out my hand. ' Thank you,' I said. We shook hands and he grinned, ' think nothing of it, we old soldiers have to look out for one another.' And then he was gone, disappearing into a sea of bodies heading into town. They hooked their arms in mine and we headed back the way we had come.

' I frowned, ' hang on a minute, where are we going?'

' Home,' said Mary firmly.

Sandy smiled at his wife, ' you've had a busy day Jimmy, plenty of time for exploring tomorrow.'

I felt much better, but let them lead me back anyway. Suddenly Sandy broke the human chain as we approached the house. ' Just popping down to the shop,' he said cheerfully.

Mary pointed at one of the basket chairs, and I obeyed as she disappeared into the house, returning with a tray of glasses and three bottles of beer. I smiled and picked up a bottle, reading the label.

' Nut brown ale?'

' It's Sandy's favourite,' she said.

The gate clicked and he stepped over the flower bed and dropped into his chair, placing three packs of cigarettes on the table. He slid a pack to each of us and grinned.

'I saw that you were running low Jimmy.'

Suddenly I was consumed by guilt. ' I'm costing you money.'

He dismissed my words with a flourish, ' away with you man, it's nothing.'

'It's not just the cigarettes, but the food and clothing you bought me today.'

He laughed aloud and poured beer into his glass, 'while you are here, you are our guest and owe us nothing.'

'While I am here?' I echoed, ' but what if I am unable to return to my own time.'

Sandy picked up his glass and sipped his warm beer, looking quickly at Mary.

She reached across the table and cradled her hand in mine. 'You just had a panic attack, I know, it happened to me. Suddenly you are transported back into a time before you were born, and the first thing to hit you is, am I trapped here forever. You will return to your own time Jimmy,' she said softly. ' In fact, you will journey back and forth as you please, as long as the door is open. But as I understand it, a time will come when the door closes for good. You will know when that time approaches, as the bee in the bottle takes longer to call. At the start it will be just days, then weeks, then months, and then not at all.'

I reached for my fresh pack of cigarettes, hands trembling as I fumbled for my nicotine fix. 'Are you sure?'

She nodded, 'absolutely, you will return to your own time whenever you please, but you should know that the door is always closing. And when it finally snaps shut, you are no longer free to travel, no matter where you are.'

I felt calmer and sipped my warm beer. My thoughts drifting back to the man with the pale blue eyes and ravaged face.

'He thought I was a soldier.'

'Aye,' said Sandy softly, ' he did.' He probably thought you were still suffering from shell shock.'

' I feel such a fake.'

'A fake,' said Mary indignantly, ' why if he knew that you were a time travelling Yorkshireman, he would probably pin a medal on you himself.'

Sandy leaned forward and struck a match and I inhaled too quickly, and coughed. I shook the beer in my glass and raised my head to the dying rays of the evening sun, as it slowly dipped down a chimney pot across the street.

' Will you finish your story Mary?'

' What, now?'

I smiled and squeezed her hand, ' now seems like as good a time as any, but only if you feel comfortable with it.'

She looked across at her husband, who in turn nodded slowly.

She frowned, ' now where was I?'

'He said you were sitting in his kitchen,' I reminded her, ' but it would be your kitchen in the future.'

'You have a good memory Jimmy.'

'Well it's not the kind of story I would forget in a hurry,' I replied.

She lowered her head for a moment, collecting distant, almost buried memories.

'He introduced himself as William, and as he did so his twin brother entered and pulled up a chair.' She smiled at the memory, 'it was almost impossible to tell them apart.'

'This is my brother Neville,' said William as he pulled a silver pocket watch from his waistcoat pocket, 'who, I am sorry to say, is quite unpunctual this evening.'

' My sincere apologies dear brother,' he replied with a merry twinkle in his eyes, the tepid temperature of the water made for difficult and quite challenging ablutions.' His well-scrubbed countenance beamed at me brightly.

' So welcome traveller,' said William, ' your room is prepared and we are your servants.'

' Indeed,' added Neville beaming, ' we shall of course endeavour to answer any questions you may have, but alas Emily is out purchasing provisions as we speak.'

William nodded soberly, 'she will be along shortly.'

'Indeed she will,' echoed Neville, as they smiled at me in the flickering fire light.'

Mary paused and sipped her beer. I watched as a starling settled on the stone wall behind her with a flap of wings, it was still warm and light, with just a whisper of a light breeze.

'The brothers were dispensing chemists, and owned their own shop, established by their late father. They spoke in hushed terms about their life and work, because the two were inextricably linked. Everything seemed to revolve around their desire to help the sick and infirm, their only complaint was the constant challenge in deciphering the doctors' illegible scrawl on prescription forms. I was still frightened and confused, when suddenly I heard someone enter the front door. The brothers turned and faced one another smiling.

'That will be Emily,' they chanted in union.

'It's only me my dears, goodness me but everything is becoming so expensive these days, why I...'

'She ignored the brothers completely, her eyes widening as she laid eyes on me. The brothers seemed to sense that she might faint, or drop the shopping. They leapt to her side and relieved her of the bulging brown linen bags. The brothers smiling, and Emily wearing a wide-eyed look of disbelief.'

CHAPTER 9

' Oh my!' She whispered, raising her hands to her chubby cheeks. ' Oh my goodness, we have a visitor...a traveller.'

'Indeed we do,' the brothers chimed as one.

She moved quickly for a large woman, and cupped her hands in mine. 'You're cold and shaking child.' She looked sharply at the brothers. 'She is unwell and has the traveller's sickness; I will take her to her room, she needs rest.'

Mary tilted her head back and watched the scudding clouds.

'So, you must have felt the nausea that I experienced,' I said. The sickness and fear that I have felt.'

She nodded, ' yes Jimmy, the very same.'

'Did you travel more than once?'

She shook her head, ' why would I? I just wanted to get back to my time and Sandy.'

'The call came on regular occasions,' said Sandy, ' but Mary had no reason to return, she wanted to be here with me.'

She looked at me and smiled, ' eventually it ceased to call altogether; but we knew that a time would come when another traveller would appear, so we prepared a room.'

I shot out of my chair and paced the lawn. ' This is perfect, don't you see.'

They didn't, but laughed along with this madman anyway.

' It means that I will indeed go back to my own time at some point, and when I return I will be better prepared.'

' In what way?' said Sandy.

I stopped pacing but my mind was still racing. ' I could bring some cash back for a start.'

Sandy shook his head, ' your money would be no good here Jimmy.'

I started pacing again, then stopped and pointed a finger at him. ' Good point Sandy, I will have to buy some vintage cash.'

'Can you do that?,' said Mary.

' Of course; no problem at all, there are people I know in the antique trade who deal in old gold and vintage banknotes. It will cost of course, but so what. And I will need to pay you back of course; for the food, the suit, the hat, the shirts, the shoes, the booze, the cigarettes...'

Mary was almost doubled up with laughter. ' Whoa Jimmy!' she cried, slow down and sit down, you are making me dizzy.'

Sandy leaned back in his chair, ' you owe us nothing, it was just a cheap second-hand suit. It's no' like we went to Montague Burton's.'

I sat as ordered, but a sudden cool evening breeze drove us indoors to the welcoming warmth of the kitchen.

Mary's Story (continued)

'As the heavy velvet curtains were drawn, daylight spilled onto my bed, and I was aware of someone moving across the room.

'Where am I?'

' You have been travelling dear, and now you should eat.'

I became aware of a breakfast tray fixed across the bed, as I pushed myself into a sitting position. There was a rack of toast, two boiled eggs, a cup of tea, and Emily sitting on the end of the bed. She was a large woman, with a kindly round face, framed by silvery hair tied back beneath a white linen mop cap. She wore a plain cream apron over a long black ankle length skirt, and I saw the golden glint of a fine crucifix and chain around her neck. She looked at me steadily.

' How are you feeling?'

I was so familiar with this room, it was the second floor back bedroom, but in essence it was transformed almost beyond recognition. It was much darker, with large dark oil paintings adorning the walls, and furniture that seemed to have taken root and grown there. A large wall clock hung in one of the alcoves. The glass panelled door below revealing a brass pendulum, cast in the form of a smiling sun, swinging ponderously from side to side.

'Please eat,' she said, rising to her feet, ' and I will explain more when you feel that you are ready to join me downstairs.'

Mary sipped her tea and smiled fondly at the memory. ' She was a lovely woman, caring, intelligent and very organised. She told me that she had been housekeeper to the brothers for over twenty two years. A post she had taken after answering an advertisement in the Leeds Mercury. She was forty-eight years of age, and in her own words, content. She had been betrothed to a young man when she was a lass of seventeen, but he died in an accident at a cotton mill. She found the work agreeable, and the attic rooms were her domain. A comfortable retreat from the hurly burly of the outside world. The brothers were kindly, if a little eccentric, but she soon warmed to them and they in turn treated her more like a sister than a housekeeper.'

I interrupted, ' what year was this?'

' It was September the fourth, 1886.'

I looked at Sandy and he nodded, ' I know, it still gives me the willies.'

Mary smiled, ' it was all so familiar, but old. You can feel time Jimmy, don't you agree. You can feel and smell the time you have arrived in. It's difficult to explain, but very real nevertheless...do you feel it Jimmy?'

I nodded, a lump in my throat, I had felt it the moment I had arrived.

'Emily told me that the brothers had lived in the family home all of their lives. Neither had travelled, or heard the bee in the bottle. However, it transpired that their father had travelled back to a point in time, when this house did not exist. It was said that when he returned he was a changed man, a gentler more considerate soul. He told them that he had been met with considerable kindness by some farming folk. He said they took him in and cared for him during the sickness. They had, it was said, been expecting someone for some time, and a room had been prepared. When he returned he had many tales to tell, and he had a room prepared for any future traveller.'

My mind was in racing mode again as I listened, engrossed in her story. ' So it’s not the house then?'

'Correct Jimmy,' said Sandy, ' it’s no' the house, but the ground it stands upon. 'It was said that some parts of the farm dated back to the sixteenth century, but the Standing Stone was much older.'

I looked at him frowning, ' Standing Stone?'

He nodded, 'do you know anything about them?'

I let my brain Google 'Standing Stone' for a moment. ' Only what I have seen on the telly.'

Their expressions said it all. ' Forget I said that, I have read a little about them of course. There are many ancient Standing Stones throughout the British Isles, but their original meaning or purpose have been lost in the mists of time.'

'Aye, he's right,' said Sandy lighting a cigarette. ' We have a fair few in Scotland, and some folk believe that they were simply erected as boundary markers. Others are less convinced, and believe such labour intensive activity was to mark a special or holy place.'

I shrugged and smiled at her, ' as you can see, it is not really our field of expertise.'

Mary toyed with her tea cup. ' All I remember is that Emily told me that the twin's father was proudly shown around the farm. Apparently, it was no more than a smallholding; with a few head of cattle, a small herd of sheep, some geese and chickens, and an acre or two of wheat. But as they turned the corner of a small stone barn, he recognised the stone immediately. In fact, he had clung to it in the howling wind and dagger point rain upon his arrival. It offered some refuge, he said, as the sickness raged within him. He said that he felt so sick, cold and lost, that he howled like an animal in pain.

Fortunately, his cries were heard above the din of the storm, and he was led to shelter, care and warmth. The stone stood in a large hollow, taller than a man. A solid needle, tapering slightly from its huge base. Much of it was buried deep within the earth he was told. Travellers and pilgrims would arrive unannounced and ask permission to rest within its long shadow. It seemed to be a place of tranquillity for troubled souls, a magnate for the lost and bereaved. Many of these pilgrims had travelled far, he was told, and they must be welcomed as you would your own flesh and blood.'

There was a moments silence as she paused to sip her tea.

'I wonder what happened to the stone,' I mused, talking to myself. ' I suppose over time it just toppled over, and was forgotten.'

Sandy grinned, ' now there you would be wrong Jimmy, the stone is still here, out in the garden. Still standing after goodness knows how many centuries.'

I stared at him, waiting for the punchline that never arrived, and then looked at Mary, dabbing a tear away from her cheek. 'Come, she said, standing and holding out her hand, ' I will show you.'

It was now dusk as they led me to a corner, where the stone wall met the red brickwork of the house. She placed my hand on its rough uneven surface, and stepped back. I don't know why, but I half expected something dramatic to occur as I placed both hands on the surface. Like some old hippie looking for a sign, but only an icy chill entered my hands and ran shivering up my arms.

The following morning, I rose early, and found myself in the garden once more. People were beginning to stir, a car rumbled over the cobbles, a crunch of gear, a puff of smoke, as it disappeared up the hill. I heard someone cough in the distance, the air was cool and fresh, and the grass damp as I studied the stone in my bare feet. How could I have missed it, it must still be there in my time. It was a couple of inches shorter than me, but it had once stood in a hollow, so much of it was now buried deep within the soil. I stood back, my eyes following the line of the wall. I could only assume that when the wall was built, they used the Standing Stone to butt it up against. Filling in the hollow and levelling it off. Presumably the people who did this, had no knowledge of its significance. Or perhaps it was an attempt by them to ensure the stone's survival.

Well survive it had, even when the Victorians rolled out their plans, and decided to leave the old wall as a feature for the garden. It was, after all, in line with the houses and gardens on the plan. I stepped forward and laid my hand upon it again, it was undoubtedly of a great age. Belonging not simply to another time, but another age. An age of darkness and light, of mystery, ignorance and enlightenment, a time of brooding danger and a harsh windswept moorland.

I tried to imagine the leap of faith that had driven people to cut and dress the stone, and then to haul it over rough terrain for goodness knows how many miles. And then to dig deep within a copse or hollow, and bury it deep and upright, standing like a giant finger, pointing to the stars for all to see...but why?

I breathed in the early morning air, it was a good feeling. I was alive, alert, and finally I felt strong again. It was time to step out, time to explore my brave new world. The fire was lit; the tea brewing, the bacon sizzling in the frying pan, and I was dangling another slice of toast on the end of the toasting fork before the glowing coals of the fire.

Mary surfaced first, yawning and scratching her sleep tousled hair.

'There's tea in the pot milady,' I said, blowing on my fingers as I dropped a slice of toast onto a warm plate. ' Bacon and eggs are imminent, where's his Lordship?'

She poured some tea and smiled. ' You have been busy, I could get used to this, having my own personal slave around the house.'

I stood and curtsied, raising my pinny, ' yes milady, we who are about to dine salute you.'

It was mid-morning when we retraced our steps to the moor. Mary had packed a picnic hamper, which I insisted on carrying as we linked arms on our stroll. I informed them about the changes that had taken place over the years. It was busy, with many heading in the same direction as us, but I now felt completely relaxed, and more like a time tourist.

I paused before an elaborate Victorian building, very familiar to me.

'That's the library,' said Sandy.

I nodded and moved on.

'Is it still there Jimmy, in your time?'

'Absolutely, but now it's a pub.'

'A pub! Well blow me down. Some changes have been for the better then.'

I looked at Mary as she raised her eyes to the heavens, and we laughed. As we entered the park, Sandy pointed a finger. 'What about the old lass, is she still there?'

We paused before a huge off-white granite statue of Queen Victoria in all her regal splendour. Seated upon a throne and peering off into the distance, with a less than amused expression.

'Oh yes, she is still there, but that has gone.' I pointed at a pretty picture post card house, standing on a gentle slope. It reminded me of a traditional Swiss alpine lodge, with an immaculate gently sloping lawn, surrounded by a white painted picket fence. To the left of the front door, a tangled web of Wisteria clung to the wall, snaking upward to reach the second story windows, creating a sea of glorious blue. Flowers bloomed in abundance in flower beds edged with terracotta tiles. Several mature Rhododendron bushes marked the garden perimeter. Their large shamelessly show- time blooms now fading and falling to lie in glorious splendour upon plush green grass. We joined a number of people by the picket fence, to admire this little picture of paradise.

'This is beautiful,' I said.

'It's the park keepers lodge house,' said Mary. People travel from all over to enjoy the park, and admire this house and garden.

'I'm not surprised, it's absolutely charming.'

Sandy lit a cigarette, 'aye you're no wrong there, his name is Ned O'Brien, and generations of his family have tended this park.'

We walked on, when a young lad collided with me as he chased a football bouncing ahead He paused and looked up at me, ' sorry mister.'

He appeared to be no more than ten years of age, with worn badly scuffed shoes, long grey woollen socks pulled to the knee with a band of colour at the top. Grey short trousers held up with a belt and buckle in the form of a snake with red ruby eyes, and a tartan shirt, that was obviously a hand me down, but something that he would grow into in time.

'No problem kid,' I said smiling.

He nodded, and then raised a hand to his eyes, as if to study me more closely in the bright sunlight. 'Are you a yank?'. The question caught me off guard, and he left us to retrieve his football.

I could hear them laughing softly behind me.

'What, do I sound like a yank?'

'Actually,' Mary replied with one hand over her mouth,' you do sometimes.'

'So what do I call the little buggers?'

'Young 'un, we call them young 'un around these parts.'

I shook my head and turned my attention to the decorative wrought iron archways we passed under, each set with a large hanging lamp.

'These are lovely, they must look a picture after dark.'

'Aye, they light the path well enough, I'm guessing that they are no longer here in your own time.'

'Correct Sandy, these lovely old lamps have long gone, and after dark you would not choose to walk with your sweetheart in this place.' I paused to watch, as a little girl stepped up to an old marble drinking fountain. She pressed a brass button set into the outer lip of the bowl, releasing a gentle fountain of water, from which she drank.

'They have gone too, no more public drinking fountains I'm afraid.'

We walked on.

'You'll be telling me there's no brass band next.' Sandy joked.

I paused to light a cigarette, picnic basket cradled on my left arm. ' No brass band, no bandstand, all gone.'

Mary shook her head sadly, 'such a shame, you make it all sound quite bleak.'

I inhaled and released a thin spiral of smoke. 'Not at all, the park is still loved, kids play football, or ride a bike. Lovers lie in one another's arms, it's still a place where dogs take their owners for a walk, a place to sit and read a book or go for a run.' I raised my head and looked around. 'But right now, at this precise moment in time, the park has never been more beautiful.'

Right on cue the band began to play. We chose a spot beneath an old elm tree. It's soft canopy of leaves allowing only a dappling of sunlight on the grass beneath. We were far enough away for conversation, but close enough to appreciate the music. The afternoon passed in a delightful summer haze, of good simple food, stirring music from the brass band, and fine company and conversation. Just occasionally they would look at each other in that special way, and I felt like an intruder. It reminded me of another time, another place, another life. The lazy afternoon drifted towards evening, as we packed up the picnic things, and walked leisurely from the park. Sandy took my arm as we passed a pub, ' do you fancy a pint Jimmy?'

I beamed and nodded, probably a little too quickly. 'I thought you'd never ask.'

Mary smiled and shook her head, ' make it just a pint or two,' she said, waving a finger at her husband. ' I don't want you boys rolling in drunk, do you hear me?'

Sandy grinned, ' now don't you be cooking darlin', I'll bring us home a fish supper.'

'Well you mind what I said, or it will be your last supper.' We stood and watched as she walked on, the hem of her light summer dress fluttering in the soft evening breeze.

'You've got a very special lady there Sandy.'

' I count my blessings every day. Sometimes I have to pinch myself when I realise that she is my wife. I'm a lucky bugger, and that's the truth.'

It was busy as we entered, on my left, the tap room. A long narrow space occupied by a noisy and motley assortment of men only. Flat caps were in abundance, as were the cigarettes and pipes, it was a hazy picture at best. It was to my mind, a proper local boozer, and had probably not seen a lick of paint or wallpaper since Dick's day. The ceiling and walls were stained a nicotine brown, a colour that many interior designers and fakers have tried and failed to emulate. The few pictures that hung on the walls, appeared to be of local sporting heroes or past landlords. The main bar was in the tap room. We however had entered the snug. There was no bar in the snug, just a serving hatch with a flip up counter and gate.

Sandy leaned on the counter and waited. Without warning a huge head appeared, it seemed to completely fill the hatch. It was hairy too, with a jet black full beard, and deep set eyes flecked with blood spots. A large avalanche of a nose that seemed to be held together by a network of blood red thread veins, that disappeared and reappeared amongst the wrinkled surface of his slightly jaundiced parchment skin. There was no smile or greeting from mine host, simply a nod.

'The usual Sandy?'

He nodded and looked at me.

'Oh, a pint of lager please.'

The gargoyle shifted his gaze and looked deeply into my troubled soul. He appeared to be weighing up his options. Should he kill me now, outright. Or just tap me on the head and eat me later.

'He'll have the same as me,' said Sandy.

The gargoyle stared at me balefully and moved away to pull our pints, and I could breathe again.

We found a table and I sipped my beer. 'This is good, what is it?'

'It's a pint of mixed, half bitter and half mild, and both from the brewery of Colonel Tetley.'

'Asking for lager was a mistake wasn't it.'

He smiled, wiping beer froth from his top lip. 'It was, but no damage done.'

'So what's the story about the landlord? I wouldn't like to meet him in a dark alley.'

Sandy laughed softly, 'Walters no' a bad man, he just drinks too much.'

'Is there a Mrs Walter?'

'There was, but it was said she was so sour- faced. that when she pulled the perfect pint, with a lovely creamy head, it turned flat as soon as she looked at it.' We burst into laughter, and Sandy rubbed a tear away from his eye. I noticed two old lady's sitting at a table near the door. The moment we laughed, they looked across in alarm and some dismay. As if laughter in a pub should be outlawed.

'So anyway, one day she ups sticks and runs off with the dray man.'

'She can't have been that ugly then?'

'Well, there's the rub, it was before my time mind, but I heard that the dray man was no' a bad looking fellah. He could have had his pick of many a lassie, but apparently his most distinguishing feature were the glasses he wore. It was said that the lens of his glasses were so thick, that folk were amazed that he found his way to the pub, never mind the cellars.'

'Is that when he started drinking heavily.'

'It was, but not to drown his sorrows, it was in fact the longest celebratory drink that anyone can remember.' Again we laughed, and I saw an old chap sitting with the hag sisters. He climbed to his feet and sauntered over.

'By 'eck lads, it sounds like you're 'aving a reet good time.'

'We are indeed,' I said smiling, 'and you are welcome to join us sir.'

'I wish I could but I'm with the wife an' 'er sister, so the good times will have to wait. They think that laughter is the sound of Satan at work, 'specially on a Sunday.'

'My apologies,' I said. 'We did not mean to offend anyone.'

'Nay lad,' said the old man with a lopsided grin, 'tha's not offended me.' He glanced back at the table where the witches were otherwise engaged in deep conversation.'Tha's offended me missus an' her witch of a sister.' He tapped the side of his nose with a finger, and winked. 'So I thought I would just pop over on me way to the gents, and say thank you.'

He swayed on the spot, a little worse for drink, 'don't let on mind, as far as they are concerned I am reminding you lads about the sanctity of the Sabbath.' He raised a hand and shook a finger at us, before heading to the wee boy's room. We grinned at one another, and then Sandy reached into his pocket and peeled two notes from his wallet, sliding them across the table, one green and one red.'

'You'll be out and about on your own tomorrow Jimmy, and you can't do that with empty pockets. We have our jobs to go to you understand.'

I nodded dumbly, ' are you quite sure you can afford it?'

'Away man, you can pay me back next time.'

I picked up the notes and stared at them, 'one pound ten shillings,' I said. He nodded and pointed at his near empty glass, 'your round I think, but no lager.'

The gargoyle swayed over to the hatch, and peered down at me with his satanic red eyes. 'We have no foreign beers in this establishment,' he boomed, ' nor will we ever serve foreign beers, not while I am the landlord.' I stepped back as an invisible toxic cloud of stale beer and halitosis assaulted my nostrils.

'I'll have two pints of your mixed together beer then please.'

He glared at me, 'you're not from around these parts are you.' It sounded more like an accusation than a general enquiry.

No, I'm just visiting friends...Sandy and Mary.'

He nodded, 'I know Sandy and Mary, good people,' he frowned, 'and they are friends of yours?'

'Absolutely, any chance of getting a drink?'

' Aye two pints of mixed,' he said, and swayed towards the pumps like a nine-force gale was blowing and he was on a slippery deck.

As I waited, I peered through the smoke at the 'clientele' in the tap room. Most appeared to be on the wrong side of forty, but it was hard to distinguish the younger element, as they were dressed very much like their fathers, and probably grandfathers. One chap caught my eyes as he raised a glass and smiled. I don't know why, but I grinned and waved at him like a girl. Then another old gent caught my attention. He sat on the long faded red leather bench, facing the bar. He seemed to be alone, but there was a freshly pulled pint and a half on the table. Intrigued, I watched as he sipped his pint contentedly. He then took hold of the half pint and placed it beneath the bench at his feet. The tiny terrier dog lapped his beer like it was the most natural thing in the world. The grin on my face was gone as mien host filled the hatch, placing two foaming pints before me. I handed him my ten-shilling note, and as he rang it into the till I said, 'oh, and one for yourself landlord.'

The draw of the old brass till shot open. I then became aware of faces turning to look at me curiously, and conversation levels died. The gargoyle stared at me, almost in alarm.

'What?'

'I said have one yourself.'

The silence was now almost complete, save for the dog lapping his half, and an old soak killing 'Danny Boy' at the far end of the bar. The landlord's lips parted and curled painfully upwards as he attempted and failed to smile. 'Why,' he paused, a bewildered look on his face. He was floundering, trying to grasp or recall the appropriate response. 'Why, I will have a half with you.'

The words spilled from his lips like some long-forgotten prayer, and a muted hum of conversation returned as I headed back to our table. I told Sandy about the odd reaction in the tap room.

'You bought Walter a drink? He's an alcoholic for goodness sake.'

'I know, he just looked so unhappy.'

He shook his head and sighed. 'He has always been a misery, never bought a drink for any of the regulars in living memory. Why even when there's a birthday do, he just says it's only another year, only another nail in the coffin.'

' I just thought if I started the ball rolling, he might find that running a boozer can actually be fun sometimes.'

Sandy looked at me with raised eyebrows. 'A few weeks ago, an old chap passed away. He had sat in the same seat in that tap room for as long as anyone can remember. So, naturally they had the wake in here, and Walter laid on sandwiches and pickled eggs. Then at the end of a very pleasant and emotional evening, he presented the widow woman with a bill for two pounds eleven and six.'

'You are joking?'

Sandy shook his head, ' the cost of the spread came to one pound nine and tuppence, but it seemed that the old chap had chalked up a slate, and Walter was determined to collect.'

As we left, Walter looked quickly in my direction, and raised his glass. I faltered, not knowing how to respond. But In the end, I nodded, I couldn't possibly do anything else...that's just the way I am. Sandy was as good as his word, and we returned home with a fish and chip supper.

CHAPTER 10

It was 9 am. There was a scribbled note from Mary, propped against a jar of marmalade.

There is bacon in the meat safe Jimmy, enjoy your day.

I smiled and settled for a cup of tea and a cigarette. My house keys were lying on the table in front of me. One key was obviously for the back door, much larger and fashioned for an older lock. It turned easily with a reassuring solid clunk. I then threw a couple of bolts to the top and bottom of the door, and I was out in the morning sunshine, locking the door behind me.

Stepping down into the yard, I paused to look across the street, to Beatie's house. She would still be in Jamaica of course, and would not arrive until next year. The neighbouring yard was a mirror image of our own. Kitchen window and back door facing ours. I caught a fleeting movement of the net curtains, and then they were still again. It was no time to hang about, it was time to explore.

I turned left at the top of the street, and headed into town. As it was such a fine morning, I wore my light grey summer suite, white shirt and tie, and comfy but somewhat creaky shoes. I stopped to look at an old oak tree in the middle of the road, surrounded by a decorative wrought iron railing. It worked as a traffic island, and an eye-catching reminder of simpler times. A brisk walk on and I approached a row of shops. The first was a second hand bookshop, with trestle tables laid out on the pavement. A hand written sign attached to the trestles proclaimed.

'ANY BOOK IN A BOX 6d!'

Suddenly I was an antique dealer again, my radar telling me that something was hiding there, and I was going to find it. It didn't take long, and soon I had collected a dozen or so. Four first edition hardback 'Just William' novels in pristine dust jackets, two immaculate books from the 'Tintin' series, and several early bloodhound books by James Hadley Chase, complete with original dust jackets, oh and not forgetting three very thin and quite rare wartime volumes of ' Wisden' cricket books. Soon I had as many as I could possibly carry. Digging deep, I counted the change in my pocket, from the ten shilling note I had split in the boozer. I had two half crowns, four sixpences, three threepenny bits, four pennies, one half penny, and a partridge in a pear tree.

'Loads of money Jim boy,' I whispered, and entered the shop, arms laden.

I was immediately struck by the size of the place as I entered. It was much larger than it appeared on the outside. The proprietor sat before an old oak serpentine fronted roll top desk, and rose as I set my selection on the counter.

'There's more,' I said, and retrieved the rest of my purchases. He placed the books into large brown paper bags with string handles, his lips moving silently as he calculated the cost.

'That will be six shillings please.'

'Six shillings,' I echoed, staring at the coins in my hand.

He smiled and misread my hesitance. 'Call it five bob.'

Now I was really confused, and starting to sweat, 'five bobs' I mumbled to myself. I selected the two large silver half crowns. Somehow, I recalled Mary telling me that they represented two shillings and sixpence, so by my calculation, two were five shillings.

He waited patiently, as I dropped them uncertainly into the palm of his hand.

'Thank you sir.'

He appeared not to have noticed the beads of sweat that had formed on my forehead, or perhaps he was quite accustomed to serving strange folk.

'I'm popping into town, I wonder if I can pick them up on my way back.'

'Certainly sir.'

Two doors down, I came across an old gallery. Flaking gilded letters on the window proclaimed that they were frame makers, restorers, gilders, and purveyors of fine art. An elegant 18th century portrait study was displayed in the window, against a screen of green velvet hanging from a brass rail. The old lady stared grimly from the canvas, as if she had just shared some choice words with the artist. The painting was presented within a rather exquisite Florentine gilt frame, and to my mind the frame was worth considerably more than the portrait.

A small brass bell above the door announced my arrival. Like the bookshop, the gallery appeared much larger on the inside. A tall middle aged man emerged through open double doors at the far end of the room.

'May I look around?'

'Absolutely, 'he replied smiling.

The better-quality paintings were displayed at the far end of the room. The majority were English and Italian school landscapes from the early to mid-nineteenth century. With a smattering of Georgian and Victorian portraits, most in elaborate moulded gesso gilt frames.

'You have some very fine paintings here.'

I noticed that he stroked his pencil thin moustache as he smiled and nodded in appreciation.

'Most of our work is supplying framed prints for business premises, hotels and the like bye the bye. However, we do like to stock some paintings for the more discerning buyer.'

'Quite,' I replied, pausing to look closer at some, and then moving on. My shoes creaked, sounding loud on the bare floorboards, and the walls upon which the pictures hung, were brown painted wooden panels of some age. A single four branch brass chandelier hung in the centre of the room, opaque glass shades glowed dully. I detected a soft hiss of gas, like a constant whisper. Some paintings were mounted upon ornate three-legged stands, one of which caught my attention immediately.

‘Have you been here long?'

He stroked his moustache again. 'The business was founded by my grandfather in eighteen seventy two.' He paused and looked around wistfully. 'We have been here ever since. Through two world wars and countless changes of fashion and taste.' The last word dripped off his tongue like bile. It was hard to ascertain which of these events he found more distasteful. The inconvenience of war or the disturbing change in artistic taste. The dealer in me could smell blood in the water. I was a great white shark homing in on the kill. There was something here, floundering and thrashing in the water. Something that said, 'buy me! buy me now and I will show you a handsome profit'. Sadly, I was just a penniless time traveller, passing through. And then I saw it, propped against a wall, an oil painting behind grimy glass. But beneath the grime a quite remarkable painting looked out at me, called out to me.

'Can you see me; do you know who I am?'

I did know, and stepped over to it.

'This is interesting, it looks like an Atkinson Grimshaw.'

The man's demeanour changed immediately as he almost glided silently towards me. It was then that I noticed he was wearing a rather worn pair of tartan slippers.

'I like to work in comfort,' he said, his eyes following mine. 'My feet are on fire today.'

'I'm sorry to hear it,' I replied, ' I too suffer from the occasional corn.'

'Ha!' he declared rather theatrically. 'I would happily adopt a corn or three on these wretched, unfortunate feet of mine, but my condition is much worse sir, much much worse!'

Oh dear, I thought. I'm in the old curiosity shop.

'I have only to glance at a pair of leather shoes, and my feet positively glow and grow with pain, like...like barrage balloons.'

I was lost for words, but heard a voice saying, 'you should see a doctor.' Sadly, it was my voice. He looked at me pitifully, which is all I deserved really. 'Over the years I have seen numerous doctors, and what do they say?'

I shook my head in bewilderment.

'Gout sir, that's what they say. Gout and poor circulation of the blood, and there's nothing to be done.' He shook his head and brushed a finger over his moustache. 'Desist from the demon drink,' they say, 'but what is a man to do when his feet are on fire and about to explode?'

I had no immediate answer, so we simply stood side by side and studied the painting.

'You are indeed correct of course, it is an exceptionally fine nocturnal study of Whitby by John Atkinson Grimshaw, an underrated local artist of some merit.' He glanced at me sideways, 'but of course you know all this, I take it that you are in the trade.?'

'Yes, but paintings are not my field of expertise, however I do know a good one when I see it.'

'You are not local then, I'm sure I would have seen you around?'

I smiled and shook my head. 'Just visiting, catching up with old friends. So, what are you asking for it?'

'Forty five guineas,' he said quickly.

There was a moments silence as we continued to look at the painting.

'I know it sounds like a lot of money, but it is an exceptionally fine painting.' I was aware of his sideways glance, he was studying me, weighing up his options 'However, as you are in the trade, we could offer something of a discount.'

I turned and smiled. I wanted to spit on my palm and shake his hand. To do the deal there and then, but of course I could do nothing of the sort. 'It's a lot of money, but I am here for some time, so let me think about it.'

He lowered his head, anticipation drained from his face. 'Of course, I understand completely, such a large investment has to be considered carefully. Perhaps sir would like a glass of wine?' He produced a bottle of red from behind the shop counter.

That's not going to do your gout any good, I thought. I thanked him, but declined, and stepped out into the street. My head was spinning, I had just been offered a beautiful painting by Grimshaw for forty guineas. I lit a cigarette and frowned...what is a guinea when it's at home? Bob's bigger brother no doubt.

That's when I saw her.

She was alone, strolling on the opposite side of the street. Her head slightly inclined, as if she was lost in thought. A small white leather handbag was strapped over her shoulder, bouncing on her hip as she walked, and she carried a black leather attaché case. My heart almost stopped as I watched her pause before a zebra crossing. I became aware that men and women passed her by without a second glance. I was transfixed and amazed. Why is the traffic still moving, how can anyone pass her by and not pause to stare at such quiet beauty in their midst?

'My god Jimmy,' I whispered, 'she is more than beautiful.'

Then a very familiar voice uttered words that I could have done without at that moment.

'Aye, well her husband certainly thinks so.'

I didn't hang about, ran into the bookshop and picked up my purchases.

'That were a quick trip into town,' he said.

'Change of plan,' I replied, 'I was in the art shop, but I have just seen someone I want to talk to.'

'Here you go then,' he handed over the bags and grinned. 'Did Maurice tell you about his feet?'

'In great detail,' I replied hurriedly.

'Aye, that's Maurice for you, 'him and his feet are well known around here.'

'I'm sure they are, warts and all.'

He was laughing as I hurried out, 'more like corns an' all I'd say.'

She was gone.

As I hurried up the street, I became aware of just how heavy books are when you're in a hurry. I quickened my pace, searching each side of the road. I thought I caught a quick glimpse of her, but then a tram groaned to a halt and obscured my view. People alighted and disembarked, a bell rang, sparks crackled overhead, and it moved on.

Still nothing.

Why was I wearing this ridiculous suite in the midday heat of summer? I started to run then, in an ungainly fashion, my books playfully pulling me backwards. I was vaguely aware of people staring and stepping quickly aside as I ran towards them, the bags trying to pull me to the pavement. I was, in effect, Michael Flatly, doing a Riverdance up the high street. Finally, I came to a halt, I was knackered, disappointed, and gasping for air. My arms belonged to an orang-utan as they seemingly touched the ground. I retreated to a bench and welcome shade, slumped down, beads of sweat running down into my collar.

'By 'eck, you look in a right state young man.'

He sat at the far end of the bench, flat cap pulled over his eyes and swollen knuckles gripping a walking stick with a silver band.

I was really in no mood for polite conversation.

'I've been running.'

'You don't say,' he smiled a toothless smile. 'If you're running from't rozzers, then my lips are sealed lad.'

'What?' I brushed some sweat from my eyes.

'If you're running from't misses then you're lost young man.'

I blinked at him as beads of sweat ran into my eyes.

He rocked in his seat on the bench and pointed the stem of his pipe over my shoulder.

'Hello there, Jimmy isn't it?'

I nodded dumbly as she smiled down at me. I could feel the hump rising like freshly baked bread on my spine.

She smiled sweetly, 'I thought I recognised you, how are you?'

'Very warm,' I said, climbing to my feet and holding out a clammy hand, 'Gwendoline isn't it?'

She nodded quickly as we shook hands, and I noticed a rush of blood to her cheeks, 'you remember my name.'

'He's bin running after thi love, that's why he's leaking like a burst pipe.'

She looked at me, and then the old man questioningly.

I picked up my bags and shook my head. 'He's a bit doolally,' I whispered,' that's what the sun does to some people.'

' I 'eard that, it's thee what's doolally, running around in't sun like a loon.'

We left the old man chuntering, and she fell into step beside me.

'Can I help you with one of those bags?'

I smiled, 'thanks but I'm okay.' I was feeling cooler, and happy that she was suddenly by my side.

'What did he mean, that you were running after me?'

I stopped suddenly, and smiled at her. 'He thought I was running after or away from my wife, and when he saw you he put two and two together and came up with six.'

'He thought I was your wife?' She sounded so incredulous that my heart sank into my size tens.

'He also thought I was running from the rozzers, so I would not pay much attention if I were you.'

Her soft laughter rippled over me.

'You look very beautiful today.' That is what I should have said, but didn't. 'Have you been in town?'

'Yes, sort of,' she answered, but offered up no more, and I felt it prudent to leave it at that.

She paused and gasped, staring at my feet. 'You are not limping, I thought...' Her voice trailed away as she stared at me.

'You thought I was wounded?'

She nodded, confused.

I noticed another unoccupied bench behind us, 'I need to rest a moment.'

'Of course,' she said smiling, ' it's been nice seeing you again.'

'If you would care to share this bench with me for a moment, I could tell you a very funny story, and it concerns my limp.'

She paused, seemingly undecided, I could see she was ready to leave, but a look of curiosity prevented her from doing so. 'A funny story about your limp you say?'

I nodded and beckoned to the seat. Curiosity got the upper hand and we sat. I started with a cock and bull story of my train journey from London to Leeds. And how I discovered that my luggage had disappeared when I returned from the dining car.'

'Stolen, you mean?'

I nodded slowly and offered her a cigarette, but she declined.' Do you mind if I do?'

'No, please, why that is awful.'

I lit a cigarette and shrugged, 'that's life.'

My mind was racing as I formulated my story, and the slow cigarette routine had bought me some valuable thinking time.

'I reported it of course and filled out a form with my details and contact address, but I will not hold my breath. So I arrived at Mary and Sandy's house, without a change of clothes, and stinking of rotten fish.'

I had, I thought, surpassed myself. So much so that even I started to believe it.

She frowned, 'rotten fish?'

I nodded and looked away to some distant horizon, as if the memory was almost too painful to recall. But it was in fact simply another delaying ruse, so I could finely tune my tale of woe. 'I left the station by one of the side exits and immediately slipped on a finny haddock.'

She giggled like a young girl, 'a finny haddock?'

I looked at her sternly, 'excuse me but it was no laughing matter. I slipped and fell amongst a veritable sea of fish and ice, and each time I attempted to stand, I fell again.'

Her eyes were wide as she laughed out loud, and her laughter lifted me to a higher level, a place where music is conversation, and it made me shiver with delight. I was on a roll now.

'It turned out that a fish wagon had left the station fully loaded, and somehow it had shed its load into the street. It was like a scene from a Charlie Chaplin movie.'

She corrected me immediately,' film, not movie, you're not a yank, are you?'

'My apologies, excuse me but this is my story and I would appreciate it if you would stop interrupting me.'

'Sorry Jimmy.'

I drew on my cigarette, and released the smoke in a series of circular clouds, and she clapped her hands. 'You are a man of many talents.'

I did my slow shrug, 'well I'm not one for blowing my own trumpet, but yes, I can't argue with that.' The cogs were still spinning in my bullshit story telling machine. 'So where was I?'

'It was like a scene out of a Charlie Chaplin film,' she reminded me, her voice trembling with laughter.

'Ah yes, I finally skated out of there on the back of a great white...'

'Skate?' she offered.

I looked at her in feigned surprise, ' were you there, among the mocking crowd?'

She raised her hands and shook her head, 'no, but I wish I had been.'

'You're not taking this very seriously are you?'

She reached out for my cigarette, our hands touching. It was, for me, a most intimate of moments. She inhaled just once and handed it back. Her body was trembling, and she wiped away a tear. I was happy to note that it was not a tear of sadness.

'By this time the police had arrived. Some people did step forward to guide me to safety, but sadly the sun was working on me at this point, and they pulled away from me as the stink hit them.'

She laughed aloud again, her silken auburn hair tumbling over her cheeks and shoulders.

'I was, in effect, untouchable, and greeted with odd stares as I walked up from town.'

She dabbed at her eyes with a white cotton handkerchief, 'I can well imagine.'

I ground my spent cigarette underfoot, and shook my head sadly. 'Poor Sandy and Mary, they were so thrilled to see me, but there was no hiding their disappointment at my personal hygiene. I was banished to soak in a hot bath, and armed with a varied assortment of Mary's bath salts.'

Gwen was still wide eyed, 'I imagine that your clothes were beyond redemption.'

I met her sympathetic smile. 'Everything, including my best shoes were consigned to the dustbin, and I spent the rest of that day dressed in a rather fetching Noel Coward type silk dressing gown.'

Her laughter was intoxicating, and I was reeling like a drunk. I was, I must say, quite proud of my story, but not completely convinced that she believed a word of it. I then told her the truth, leaving nothing out. I told her about the mysterious giant's overcoat. The abject failure to fit a man into clothing belonging to a man a good three inches shorter, and the short but painful journey down to uncles.

'You did look a bit distracted and uncomfortable.' She smiled at the memory but I could see that her thoughts had drifted to another place, a place denied to me, and I felt envious. Suddenly she looked down at my carrier bags on the pavement.

'I see you have been to the bookshop?'

'Yes,' I said, pulling out one of the Just William volumes.

She looked at me with a mischievous smile and an arched eyebrow. 'Aren't you a little old for children's books?'

'I am rediscovering my childhood Gwendoline, reading the books that gave me such pleasure as a boy.'

'You tell a good tale Jimmy, but now I must be getting on. We stood and shook hands. 'It was lovely to bump into you again.'

As she walked away I smiled and picked up my bags. Sandy was right of course; her husband is one lucky bugger. It occurred to me that flirting with a woman, even an unobtainable married one, should rack up my guilt. That I would feel I had somehow betrayed Fay, but it did not feel like that at all, it felt like a new beginning, like I was joining the living again and playing the game of life.

That evening we relaxed in the front room. Mary was running up a pair of net curtains on a cast iron floor standing sewing machine. I watched, fascinated as she gently applied pressure on the footplate, and the large drive wheel spun with a light hiss. Sandy was fiddling with the knobs of the wireless, and I picked up a copy of the Yorkshire Evening Post.

'There's a three-bedroomed detached house for sale in here.' I grinned and shook my head. ' Six hundred and fifty quid.'

'I know,' said Sandy absently as he continued to search for a station. 'Houses are so expensive these days.' His fiddling paid off, as laughter entered the room. 'This is really funny Jimmy, you have to listen to this.'

He was not wrong as we all laughed. Of course, it sounded a bit old fashioned and dated to my 'sophisticated' ears. Particularly the odd popular and peculiar catch phrases of the time, but funny is funny, no matter what the year. The sash windows were raised, and a gentle evening breeze rippled at the net curtains. We continued to listen and laugh until the program concluded. Sandy lowered the volume as the show was replaced by a little light music. Mary folded the delicate net curtains and placed them on a small oak occasional table. I then told them of my exploits in the bookshop and gallery.

'Forty guineas for a painting!' he gasped. 'I've never been in there myself, and not likely to do at those prices.'

'In my time Sandy, that painting is worth considerably more.'

'How much more?' said Mary, her eyes widening with curiosity.

'Well, I'm no expert, but I would say in excess of fifty thousand pounds.' You could hear a pin drop then, so complete was the silence.

'Fifty thousand pounds,' she gasped.

'That is only a conservative estimate, it could conceivably make much more in auction.'

She shook her head, 'has the world gone mad?'

'That is just a drop in the ocean Mary, there are some paintings that change hands for many millions in my time.' I soon brought them back down to earth, when I showed them the books I had bought. Sandy glanced amusingly at them. 'Aye, well, they're fine books and that's for sure. But they're no' worth millions of pounds, are they Jimmy?'

'No, but they are still worth considerably more than what I paid for them.'

Mary picked up one of the Tintin volumes. I always loved these stories,' she said.

Sandy looked at me quickly, 'You canna take them back with you Jimmy, I hope you realise that.'

I smiled, waiting for the punch line that never arrived.

'When Mary travelled she was given some keepsakes to bring back, but she returned empty handed, is that no' right darling?'

'It's true,' she said nodding, 'it seems that anything that belongs in that time, stays there. You are the time traveller, and only you.' She seated herself beside me on the settee, and patted my hand consolingly.

'Sorry.' she said.

I sat for a moment in stunned silence. 'Well it's a good thing I didn't have the brass for the painting!'

At this we all laughed.

'And I would'na mind catching up on the adventures of Just William,' said Sandy loudly.

'And I for one,' said Mary laughing, 'will happily say hello to Tintin and Snowy again.'

Suddenly Sandy leapt out of his chair and turned up the volume on the wireless. A lovely big band melody was playing. He stepped over to Mary and held out a hand. 'Would you like to dance lassie?'

She blushed and waved him away, so he turned to me and shrugged his shoulders. 'How's your Fox Trot Jimmy?' I was game for a laugh, and instantly leapt to my feet. 'I thought you'd never ask.'

Mary clapped and roared with laughter as we glided, or rather collided around the room, and it was all over too slowly before it was time for a waltz. This time she graciously accepted Sandy's entreaties, and I fell breathlessly into the settee. It was my time to applaud as I watched them dance together. Not some foolish blokes messing around dance, but a graceful dance of lovers moving together as one. Their intimacy was for me, a joy to behold, and as he led she followed as if they would dance together, just like that, forever. And when it was over, Mary flopped down beside me, laughing and breathless. While Sandy headed for the door.

'Drinks anyone?' he called from the door. We both raised our hands.

There was a moments breathless silence before she spoke. 'So, did you meet anyone on your travels?' I met her look, her simple question.

'Well the bloke in the bookshop was funny, but the chap in the gallery was extremely odd. Oh, and I bumped into that young lady Sandy introduced me to on the way to uncles.'

Sandy entered with the drinks tray, 'Gwen,' he said, 'you met Gwendoline?'

I placed the book back onto the table, 'I've been racking my brains, yes Gwen, lovely lady.'

Sandy poured the drinks and slid the glasses across the table. I thought I detected an atmosphere. Perhaps I imagined the knowing look that passed between them. I told them about our chance meeting and conversation. I told them about my close encounter with the fishes, and they both roared with laughter.

'What else could I say? That I had arrived in your garden from the future, without suitable attire, and you invited me in to stay as your guest without question'.

Mary looked at her husband, 'he has a point.'

He nodded, a perplexed look on his face. 'I agree, but a street of fishes for goodness sake, it sounds almost biblical.'

'Consider the facts Sandy. I have arrived unannounced at your doorstep, minus luggage and even the clothes I am wearing are in effect no longer wearable. How else could you explain my voyage to uncles, wearing an ill-fitting overcoat and wellies at midday in the month of June?' I finished that sentence with a big smile, as they fell about laughing.

It was Mary who composed herself first. 'Well I must say that it is the oddest story that I have ever heard, but I'm glad you told me in case there are any fishy enquiries from Gwen in the future.' She appeared to be on the edge of tears of laughter. 'Do you think she believed you?'

I considered the question for the briefest of moments. 'Not a chance,' I replied. The cool evening breeze from the open windows drifted over me, as I reached for my glass.

'Her husband was badly injured during the war,' she said softly. 'Gwen told me that his injuries healed over time, but the real damage, the damage to his mind was dismissed as 'mild shell shock'. He will snap out of it, she was told, and he did snap, but not out of it.' She sipped her drink. 'He had always been a mild and pleasant man, but on his return, he suffered from frequent, volatile, and sometimes violent mood swings.'

'The police were called out on more than one occasion,' said Sandy.

I felt a sudden rush of blood to my face, and heard a desperate anger in my voice. 'Did he hit her?'

'Never!' said Sandy loudly, ' why he would have pulled out his teeth one by one with a pair of pliers, before he hurt that wee lassie.'

'His anger was turned inwards Jimmy, towards himself, ' said Mary. 'He took to drinking, picking fights with strangers, brick walls or plate glass windows.' She paused, 'but mainly he picked fights with himself. Sometimes they would find him bloodied and swearing in the street. Calling out for his mother or Gwen. He was a man driven to madness by the madness of war and eventually he was admitted to hospital for the umpteenth time, and then transferred to a secure hospital.'

I frowned, 'secure hospital, an asylum?'

She nodded. 'When I spoke to her yesterday, she told me that he was dying. The poor girl had endured years of humiliation and sadness, but still she wept for him.' Mary reached for Sandy' hand, and fell silent. He looked at me as he patted her hand. 'You see Jimmy, although the war ended years ago, for some the horror never ceased, and Gwen's husband was just one of many who continued to battle their demons...it has always been so.'

That night, sleep was a stranger, and I seemed to wake on the hour every hour. Then, as the faint light of dawn coloured the curtains, I found myself walking down a cobbled street. My footsteps loud as broken glass cracked sharply underfoot. It was a full moon, and the light picked out the shards of broken glass in darkened windows. Net curtains billowed out in the soft whisper of a breeze. Lampposts popped and hissed loudly, their flames flickering and exposing more shattered panels. I entered a small square and saw a lone figure, sitting amongst all this destruction, in a rocking chair. He rocked gently, his head bowed, and I announced my arrival with a pistol loud crack beneath my feet. He seemed unaware or dismissive of my presence, and rocked amidst the mayhem in
silence. Then I heard a voice, a desperately sad voice, and realised that it was my own.

'Did you do all this?'

He nodded absently, still staring at the blood drenched cobbles at his feet. 'I have done a good night's work, don't you think?' His laugh was harsh and resonated loudly in the confines of the square, and a faint cloud of crimson blood escaped from his lips. 'They're all out there you know, shivering in their safe and draughty rooms. They are looking at us right now, but dare they show their miserable cowardly faces?' He shook his bloodied face at the cobbles. 'Come, let me see your face.'

I stepped through the moonlit glass that seemed to glisten like wayward fallen stars, as he rocked backwards and forwards in his pool of blood. The breeze increased, and I heard curtains flap and crack. He raised his head then, and stared at me balefully, tear drops of blood spilled into the whites of his eyes. I surprised myself, in that I felt no fear, just sadness and pity.

'Why are you doing this?'

The rocking stopped and he shrugged like a petulant teenager. ' Why not, I want them to feel my horror, my anger, my loss.' He was still for a moment, as if appraising me, studying my face, and then he laughed softly. 'Or maybe it just felt right, like something to do before you die.'

'Are you dying?'

'Oh yes,' he said sharply, I am most definitely dying, I am a dead man rocking.' He began to shake, violently, his body racked in spasms. I stepped forward but he shrank back into his chair, arms raised in a defensive cross. 'Leave me alone!' he screamed, and the scream echoed loudly in the deserted square. Soon the spasms passed, but his breathing was shallow and laboured.

'So, time travelling man, will you look after her?'

I met his crimson clouded eyes that seemed so desperately to search for an answer. 'How do you know I am a time traveller?'

He held out his bloodied arms widely, 'well how the fuck can I answer that? I just know,' he said hoarsely,' maybe it's a special dying trick, who gives a shit.' He raised his head and pointed a bloodied finger at the bay window of a house. The window exploded, sending shards of glass over the neatly manicured lawns. Lobelias cowered and highly perfumed roses swayed in alarm. He tossed his head back and laughed manically. 'Did you see that, did you see what I did, don't you just love the sound of breaking glass?'

I said nothing, but watched as he raised his arms in triumph, seemingly in acknowledgement to an adoring invisible crowd. ‘You want more!' he cried. He pointed at another house, and a second floor window bowed, and then exploded. 'My oh my, life just gets better when you’re dying!'.

I waited for the silent applause to fade, and when it did, his wild eyes focused on me again. 'Well, time travelling man, what do you think of it so far?'

I shrugged, ' I'm impressed, you certainly know how to break windows.'

'I do, don't I,' he said, mouth agape and dripping more blood. 'I've finally found something that I am really good at. Why I've broken promises, bones and wind, but breaking glass is the best thing I have ever done by a long chalk, I am after all a broken man.'

'What about breaking hearts?' I said.

He stared at me unblinking, his bloodied face cocked to one side. He then raised a hand and scratched his chin, his eyes never leaving mine. ' I broke her heart, and that's for sure,' he said softly.' When I came back from the war, I was a changed man. I could see the pain in her eyes every day, as she searched for the man she had once loved, but that man was gone forever.'

The violent tremors returned, and he screamed aloud as his arms flailed and blood bubbled from his lips. This time I stepped forward and held his jerking head in my arms, as his fists beat the air, and my sides. I stayed like that until he was still again, and released my grip.

'Promise me time traveller!'

'I promise, but only if you stop all this nonsense and give these poor people their windows back.' I stepped back as he slumped deeper into the chair. He nodded at the cobbles, and dismissed me with a weary twitch of a hand. 'It's a deal,' he sighed, 'now piss off.'

I turned to leave and was relieved to see that the street was back to normal. Lights glowed behind drawn curtains, and a lively jazz number drifted from a half open window. A final glance back revealed an empty square. And all the fallen broken stars had returned to the night sky.

CHAPTER 11

The dream came back to me as I brushed my teeth. It occurred to me that it was plain silly to make a promise to someone you had just met in a dream, and quite ludicrous when the promise concerned a woman I hardly knew at all...and yet? I spat and rinsed, scratching the bristle on my chin, I needed a shave. A short rummage in the cupboard above the sink, revealed a jar of solid shaving cream and a big bristled brush, but no razor. Then I spotted it, and my heart sank as I unfolded the wicked looking blade of the aptly named 'cut throat' razor. I immediately folded it away. The last thing I needed right now was the sight of yet more blood, especially my own. I was about to leave, when my eye caught a hand-written card propped on the marble shelf above the sink.

JIMMY'S RAZOR! It proclaimed boldly.

It had been placed in such a place of prominence, that only an idiot could possibly miss it. So why, I asked myself, did I almost miss it? The answer was patently obvious, but in my wisdom, I chose to ignore it. I laughed out loud as I lifted the small brown cardboard box. ROLLS RAZOR! it read on the lid, THE FINEST SAFETY RAZOR FOR THE MORE DISCERNING GENTLEMAN.' And fine it was, as my unwanted whiskers whirl pooled down the plug hole. Feeling quite invigorated I headed downstairs, I was hungry. Suddenly Mary appeared in the hallway. She paused to look in the hall stand mirror, unaware of my presence on the stairs.

'Morning Mary, I thought you would be at work?'

She gasped and touched her throat.

'Sorry, did I give you a start?'

She smiled, but her face was pale and drawn.

'I have to go to Gwen,' she said,' her husband died in the early hours.'

The dream came flooding back and I frowned. 'I'm sorry to hear it, give her my condolences.'

My travels that day were fascinating, but tempered by sadness at Gwen's loss. That evening as we gathered in the front room, the wireless playing softly in the background, the mood was more sombre. 'She will be all right,' said Mary, toying with her tea cup. 'It was not unexpected, but it will take time to come to terms.'

'Aye,' said Sandy with a sigh, 'it's a sad day, and that's the truth.'

I almost blurted out my dream, but thought better of it, it was just a dream after all.

'I think I have worked out how you can take your books back to your time Jimmy.'

We looked at him and he coloured slightly as he realised he was the centre of attention.

'Really, tell me more.'

'Well,' he said slowly, 'what if you were to hide them here, in this house. Put them somewhere where they are unlikely to be disturbed.'

I caught Mary's eye and raised my eyebrows, 'I think your old man's onto something.'

She smiled, 'do you mean like under a floorboard for instance?'

He nodded, his eyes bright, 'aye, why not? If it were chosen carefully, say away from any wiring or pipes, where they might be discovered, well, who knows.'

Mary's enthusiasm gathered pace. 'Like buried treasure,' she said dreamily, 'something that remains in its own time, but hidden, waiting to be discovered at some point in the future.'

'Exactly!' He nodded vigorously and then frowned, 'but didn't I just say that?'

'You did,' I said, patting him on the shoulder, ' and most eloquently I must say.'

He nodded appreciatively, 'however, for large items, say like oil paintings for example, well that presents a much bigger challenge.' He was now relishing the moment, ' you canna hide a big oil painting under the floorboards...'

'What about the loft?' Mary added brightly, 'you could hide it in the corner of the loft.'

The pained expression on her husband's face said it all. 'Folk are always messing about in lofts, it would be found in no time.'

'And insulation,' I offered feebly, 'lofts have rolls of insulating material fitted in the future, to stop heat loss.'

It was my turn to blush as they stared at me, but Sandy came to the rescue.

'Well it makes sense I suppose, heat rises so you might want to lay some blankets down to stop some of the warm air escaping through the roof.'

Mary shook her head in exasperation, ' for goodness sake Sandy, do you actually have an answer?'

He grinned, 'I do, but you will both have to follow me.'

We followed, back to the kitchen, and paused as he opened the cellar door. Sandy flicked the light switch, and as they headed down the steps, I hung back.

'Jimmy, are you coming?' said Mary, pausing on the steps.

I nodded silently as a wave of Deja vu swept over me tsunami style. It was cleaner and less cluttered than I recalled, and smelled less fusty too, and I soon realised why when I saw the small open window at the far end of the room directly ahead. A single shaft of evening light gave the room an eerie glow. A quick glance told me that the bread bin and sad one-eyed doll were absent, they would no doubt be consigned there at some later point in time. Sandy flicked an old brass light switch set into the wall, and opened a very familiar narrow door. He looked back, 'watch your heads now.'

We found ourselves standing on an earthen floor, staring at the foundations of the house.

'Is this not the strangest of rooms Jimmy?'

'It is,' I replied, ' but I have seen it before, it is still there in my time.'

Sandy's jaw dropped and he slapped the side of his head. 'Of course it is, how stupid of me.'

'Not at all, this room has no light in my time. I only flashed a torch in here and saw clutter and darkness.'

Mary kicked an old enamel sign leaning against a wall, 'and it's still full of junk.'

'One man's junk is another man's treasure Mary, that old enamel sign for Fry's Chocolate is probably worth a hundred and fifty quid in my time.'

Her infectious laugh bounced off the walls, 'has everyone gone completely mad in the future?'

'Never mind the sign Jimmy,' said Sandy,' look around you, look at the walls.'

The walls were brick and coated in a thick coat of whitewash.

'The wall on your left is a load bearing wall, while here,' he said, stepping up to the wall immediately in front of us. This wall follows the contours of the room above.' He stepped forward and slapped the wall with the palm of his hand. This wall is immediately below the fireplace above, and the recess on either side correspond to the recess on each side of the fireplace.' He paused and looked earnestly at us, 'are you with me so far?'

Mary caught my grin and suppressed a laugh.

'Absolutely,' I said.

He shook his head, 'you's two are becoming a right funny double act.'

'I'm sorry darling, we are not laughing at you, are we Jimmy.'

'Certainly not.'

'Aye, well you'll be laughing on the other side of your face when I'm finished.' Sandy stepped into the alcove, back to the wall. 'Imagine I'm an oil painting.' He raised a hand, ' and before you say anything, I know I'm no oil painting, so we can dispense with the funny stuff. Imagine if you will, that we place the painting in here, and brick it up. Better still, we can use both alcoves, splash on some whitewash, mucky it up a bit, and bobs your uncle. Would that no' be the perfect hiding place for something that belongs in this time, to be discovered sometime in the future?'

I stepped forward. ' A matching pair of time capsules, intriguing.'

Sandy nodded eagerly, ' we could do it in a day, or if you were on your travels, I could do it and Mary could be my labourer. It's no precision brick laying after all, just a dark unused part of a cellar. I could even lay the bricks with just a lick of mortar, so you could open it with a toffee hammer.'

I turned and looked at Mary, 'give that husband of yours a big hug.

I raised my arms and bawled at the top of my voice, 'Sandy is a genius!'

'He is?' said Mary cautiously.

'I am, did you no' hear the man.'

'He is, without question, now are you going to hug him, or shall I?'

They hugged.

Sandy led the way as we headed for the steps, 'so you think it will work then?'

'Oh yes, it will certainly work.'

They chatted like two excited teenagers, but I did not follow. Instead I stepped down the three steps and into the passage that lead to the main cellar. I was standing before that familiar sash window, when suddenly the lights went off, and I imagined a distant rumble of thunder. The naked bulb glowed again and I heard the clatter of their footsteps.

'Jimmy!' Her voice was strident, concerned, and then I felt Sandy's hand on my shoulder.

'Sorry, I thought you were just behind us and I switched the light off without thinking.'

I smiled and put my arms over their shoulders, so that we all faced the window. 'This is where it all began, on this very spot. There was no power and I was standing in darkness. Thunder rumbled some distance away and then I heard the sound. Do you know what I mean Mary?'

She said nothing, but I felt her body tremble as she gripped my waist. 'You must have been so afraid,' she whispered.

'Not at all, the darkness does not spook me and I actually enjoy a good storm. But when the sunlight came, and I saw a bird skimming through a blue sky...then I was afraid.'

When we retired to the front room, Sandy fetched the amber nectar. 'Do you have a large spare suitcase that I could borrow?'

Mary frowned, 'yes of course.'

' Excellent, I will have to pack my shoes and clothing and place them in the time capsule for my return. The suitcase will then be used to bring some cash back.' I raised my glass. ' I must say that I am a lucky bugger to have met you two, I think we are going to have some fun.'

A sudden change of light instantly drew my gaze to the bay window. It was night and it was day in the flicker of an eyelid. A distant sound announced its arrival, like a failing neon tube.

Mary was laughing, 'when he has finished hiding your books, I could put Sandy in the other alcove and do a bit of bricklaying myself.'

The flickering light intensified beyond the net curtains, and the bee in the bottle sounded angrily

'Do you hear that Mary? I think it is time for me to go.'

She was on her feet in an instant, 'you must change into your old clothes Jimmy.'

'What?'

'You must change back into the clothes you arrived in.'

She took my hands as I climbed to my feet, 'don't worry, it will wait!'

Sandy sounded alarmed, 'what is going on?'

'It's time Sandy, time for Jimmy to leave.'

He was in a daze as I hurried to my room. They were waiting for me in the hall when I emerged in my old clothes. Beyond them, light flickered through the textured glass panel of the front door. I placed a hand on Sandy's shoulder.

'Good luck with the bricklaying, and don't forget my clothes in a suit-case.'

'You can count on us Jimmy,' he said, wringing my hand.

I turned to Mary, no words were spoken as we embraced, and then she pushed me away. 'You must go now,' she sobbed.

I turned and looked back at them as I stepped into the garden, but they were gone, and I was back. It was cold and dark, but there was enough yellow street light to pick out the scene of desolation around me. Rubbish spilled from the skip, and I could feel the pull of soft mud as I skirted around planks of wood and sheets of plasterboard offcuts. I felt the nausea then, as I lurched up the steps and tried the handle of the door. It was locked of course, and I leaned against the wall, in the sure and certain knowledge that I was about to throw up, but it never happened. I had imagined that I would feel a sense of triumph on my return, but it didn't feel like that at all. There was a sense of loss, it was like bereavement all over again.

'Jimmy.'

'Fay,' I croaked, 'is that you sweetheart?'

'No, it's me,' she said softly, 'Suzie.'

The warmth of the car revived my flagging spirits, as I watched street lights flash past, and soon became aware of Suzie glancing at me curiously.

'Keep your eyes on the road.'

'I'm keeping my eyes on the road...you look like shit.'

'Thanks, it's a sort of travel sickness, but nothing to worry about.'

She was silent, keeping her eyes on the road.

'Thanks for picking me up, how long have you been sat out there?'

She pulled up at lights and shrugged, 'a couple of hours, we took it in turns, working shifts so to speak.' I felt that something was wrong, and lit a cigarette. The lights changed and the car jerked sharply, forcing me to place my hand on the dash.

'You sound angry,' I said quietly.

'For god's sake Jimmy, we have all been at our wits end!' The car slewed to an abrupt halt, we were parked outside my flat.

I'm sorry, let me make you a cup of coffee.'

She pulled my flat keys from her pocket and shook her head. 'Here, take these and go to bed, you look like you could sleep for a month or two.'

I stepped out into the cold night air, keys in one hand, car door in the other. 'Tomorrow then, I will see you tomorrow.'

She looked across at me, her face stern, but her eyes moist. She nodded and drove away in a milky cloud of diesel fumes.

I felt like a stranger as I let myself in. The message light beckoned on my land line. I passed the open door to my bathroom, a quick shower before sleep perhaps? I passed the bottle of vodka perched seductively on the coffee table. A quick snort or two to help one sleep? I entered the bedroom and decided that it was time to slip off my clothes and slide naked between those welcoming sheets, but in the end, I ignored them all, kicked off my shoes and collapsed on the bed.

As soon as my eyes opened I knew it was going to be a busy day. I showered, shaved, threw on some fresh clothes, and headed for the door. Only pausing to look around for my mobile phone. I snatched up the land line phone and rang myself, but with no success. I guessed that I had left it back at the house.

The local 'tomato dip' café was so close, I could smell it before I could see it. I ordered eggs, soft, runny, and sunny side up, toast done on one side, strong builders tea with two sugars. Breakfast over, I pointed the car towards the lovely town of Harrogate. The road from Leeds to Harrogate is a car driver's dream. A long curving snake of tarmac with hardly a traffic light to halt one's progress. Thirty minutes later I was driving down the Stray, admiring the posh shops, and wide pavements thronged with expensive people. I took a couple of right turns, parked up and dropped a pound coin in the meter. Morphets auction rooms has been around since Dickens was a lad, and the lady I had come to see was the principal picture valuer. I pushed open the half-glazed door and stepped into the elegant passage, leading to the reception desk. Illuminated glass display cases on my right slowed my progress, as I admired some fine examples of porcelain and silver glowing in glazed cabinets beneath the halogen lights.

There were two women sitting beyond the counter, frowning at computer screens. In the foreground a young and very pretty lass, who I had never seen before.

‘Can I help you sir?'

The other lady was older and a good twenty stone heavier. 'Hello Jimmy,' she growled, swivelling in her extra-large chair, 'what can we do you for?' She did not smile, but studied me with bright intelligent eyes. She had a reputation for being something of a misery guts, I had always detected a detached and amused smile, but you had to look for it. Maybe I was mistaken and it was just wind.

'You are looking absolutely gorgeous as usual Elizabeth.'

She nodded slowly, a distant playful glint in her eyes. ' You need to see someone in the spectacle department.'

'Hell no!' I replied with some indignation, 'you know I've always had a thing for fat birds.'

The young thing let out a sharp intake of breath, a look of alarm forming furrows on her brow. 'Excuse me but you can't say that!' She looked at Elizabeth for conformation.

'She's right Jimmy, they call them babes these days, don't you know anything.'

There was a moments silence before the girl caught the drift of the conversation. 'I'll make some tea,' she said.

'Medium brown, two sugars please,' I said.

Her curt nod and frown said it all, I was destined to remain tea- less. In the good old days, when smoking was obligatory in the workplace, a cigarette hung from Elizabeth’s lips permanently. In between puffs she breathed loudly. She still wheezed now, minus the ciggie.

'I'd like to talk to you about a painting.'

'Right, well you're in the right place.'

'I have had the good fortune to acquire a moonlight painting by John Atkinson Grimshaw.'

'So far so good, are you sure it's a Grimshaw?'

'Absolutely.'

'Is it signed?'

'In the lower right corner.'

'And how big is this painting?'

'Roughly five by three feet.'

'Does the frame appear original to the painting?'

'Yes, most definitely.'

She wheezed and nodded, picking up a pencil from her desk. I thought she was going to smoke it, but she let it slide between her fingers instead. The girl returned with the tea, one for her and one for Elizabeth. I didn't mind.

'So what is the subject matter Jimmy?'

'A nocturnal view of Whitby, looking from the west side of the bridge to the houses, church and abbey.'

She simply nodded non- committedly. 'It doesn't sound like a later painting by his son Louis. He was good, but not as good as his dad. He occasionally overpainted his father's work, adding figures and stuff. He was a very naughty boy,' she said dreamily. 'Is there any provenance with this painting?'

'Apparently it was purchased from the artist in Leeds, and remained within the same family until after the second world war. It was then consigned to auction in nineteen fifty-five, and purchased by a local gallery. There is a receipt dated the eleventh of June 1956 when it was then purchased by a Mr T. Traveller, and then the painting was lost for a number of years.'

'Excellent,' she said, still toying with the pencil, 'I would certainly like to see this painting before we consign it to auction. As it happens Grimshaw's work has taken an upturn in recent years. Why even them down south have started to sit up and take notice,' she said with feeling. 'If it is a Grimshaw, in original condition, and it comes with the provenance that you have just stated.' She paused and stared into and beyond my eyes. 'It has to be conservatively estimated at somewhere between one hundred and fifty to two hundred in my opinion.'

'Thousand?'

'Well it's not going to be a hundred and fifty quid now, is it Jimmy boy.'

I slammed the palm of my hand on the counter, and the girl jumped in her seat and spilled her tea. 'Shit! Now look what you made me do', she wailed.

'Oops! Sorry about that. Tell you what, you can have mine.'

She looked at me with deep loathing. If her eyes could have sent me a text message, then it would have probably read 'sexist pig', or much worse.

'Elizabeth,' I said, beaming, 'you are a sweetheart. Got to go, people to see, things to do...we should have sex sometime!'

'Never mind the sex,' she called after me as I headed for the exit.' Just bring me the damn picture.'

CHAPTER 12

Next stop was a rather unassuming red brick two story building. It could have been an old sweat shop or warehouse. The only tell-tale sign that this was a place of business was the high security car park. Admission was by card only, and as I slid mine into the reader, the cast iron ramp slid silently into the ground and the steal barrier reached for the sky. A small brass plaque set into the wall read, M. O' Dwyer and Sons, followed by a couple of telephone numbers. I was about to press the brass buzzer to announce my arrival, but the door buzzed and clicked open. I stepped over the threshold into another world, a world of opulence, wealth and calm beauty.

Alice was sitting at her flame mahogany partners desk as usual. 'Hello Jimmy, how are you?' Alice was the kind of woman who exudes elegance and charm in equal measure. A woman who had reached middle age but seemed to hold back time with aplomb. Always immaculate, calm, charming, and equipped with a smile that made you feel good to be alive. She had worked front of house for Mickey for as long as I could remember.

I smiled, 'hello Alice, is he in?'

'Take a seat Jimmy,' she said, and picked up the phone. I sat, taking a look around at my rarefied surroundings. Deep plush carpets that you could lose your feet in. Air conditioning that smelled of a Caribbean paradise. Large and expensive oil paintings that said, it's okay to look, but do not touch unless you have very deep pockets. adorned the walls, and the lighting was provided by a huge Venetian glass multi drop chandelier.

However, the wall that faced Alice was definitely twenty first century. Security cameras relayed images back to a dozen or more smoked glass screens set into the wall. They showed every angle of the building and car park. Some of them were roving movement cameras that detected passing or pausing cars, logging number plates, and closing in on the drivers and occupants. This was twenty-four-hour cam surveillance. It was in effect Fort Knox, but to the casual observer it was still just another knicker factory.

I had barely settled in the cream leather chesterfield sofa, when the door leading to the inner sanctum clicked open. Ben stepped quickly into the room, hand outstretched. 'Jimmy, lovely to see you.' At six feet he was a couple of inches taller than me. I guessed he was in his early forties, but it was hard to tell as his hair was dyed an improbable shade of black. Quick brown eyes were framed behind thin gold framed spectacles. The hand that shook mine revealed immaculate stiff white cuffs, linked together with sublimely small but quite exquisite gold cuff- link's. I was suddenly reduced to the role of local wino, looking for a hand- out.

It occurred to me that I had been in this situation more than once. Not in this room, but in a bar in Rome or Florence, enjoying a cool beer with Fay. When suddenly some uninvited Italian gigolo would stand beside me, and order a tiny aperitif. He would invariably be astonishingly handsome, with smooth olive skin, and teeth that had their own inbuilt strobe lighting. He would be dressed in a light and immaculate summer suite, probably Armani. Expensive silk shirt and tie, and hand stitched leather shoes.

Yes, it was definitely one of those moments, when I would suggest to Fay that we take a seat at a table. Not because I was desperate for a seat at the table, but simply that I felt somewhat inadequate. Could not bear to stand another moment next to Al Pacino, in my sweaty tea shirt, baggy tourist shorts, plastic flip flops, and shockingly English white legs, that could easily have auditioned for one of the Carry On films

Sean stepped aside and motioned me through the door leading to the inner sanctum. The door closed behind us with a light whisper and loud click of falling tumblers. I could easily have been in the palace of Versailles, as I followed him down the corridor. Rare and extremely expensive old master paintings vied for my attention at every step. Early English and French furniture appeared to shrink before me as I approached, afraid perhaps that I might touch their ancient highly polished patinated surfaces with my warm sticky fingers. I then entered a large room through double arched polished mahogany doors. This was the beating heart of the business. It too was furnished in a manner that said, ' if you have got this far, then you had better be serious'.

A bank of flat screens glowed on one wall, illustrating graphs and numbers that meant absolutely nothing to me. Ben indicated a seat at a superb walnut partners desk, and slid into a chair opposite. He looked across at me and smiled, 'so welcome Jimmy, what do you think of the new office?'

I nodded, 'I noticed you tarted the old place up, its a bit like my office.'

He looked astonished, ‘a bit like your office?'

I looked around lazily, 'mine is a tad smaller than yours, but less tacky if you don't mind me saying.'

I heard a laugh then, loud and hearty, and swivelled my chair to see a larger than life Mickey beaming from a huge screen fixed on the far wall.

'So there you are you old bugger, I knew you wouldn't be far away.'

The single gold tooth burned brightly as he smiled. 'Hello Jimmy, how are you my friend?'

'All the better for seeing you Mickey, where are you anyway?'

'Covent Garden, we have a small establishment here.'

'I'm impressed, you always told me that you specialised in stamps and second-hand furniture.'

He laughed, 'did I? 'I must have forgotten to mention that we are also registered bullion and fine art dealers.'

I looked across at Sean,' he forgot about the fine art and bullion side of the business?'

Sean spread his arms expressively, 'he can be a little forgetful at times.'

I have known Mickey for a number of years. He had served his apprenticeship in Dublin as a young man. Then moved across the pond to England, completing his education with the best that Hatton Garden could provide. Finally, he set up a small shop of his own, under the name of Solomon O’Dwyer. Over a flagon of ale or two he once told me about his childhood. He told me about the abject poverty of life in post- war Limerick, and how he was often the butt of jibes because of his Jewish features. Even his parents were at loss to explain how a normal family of ten (eight surviving) could produce a son who looked like Fagin. He told me that visiting priests to his school would point him out and enquire, 'who is the little Jewish boy?'.

Consequently, he prospered in Hatton Gardens, known by his friends and fellow dealers as 'Mickey the Irish', and to customers as Mr Solomon, a name you can trust. Then he fell madly and deeply in love, and followed his love up north to Leeds, where he continued to prosper, and the rest as they say is history.

'Has Sean ordered your cappuccino?'

Sean reached for the intercom but I raised a hand. 'No really, I want to put a deal to you Mickey, but it comes in several parts.'

His large expressive eyes lit up brightly, 'Sounds intriguing.'

'First, I need to buy some vintage money, pre nineteen fifty-six banknotes. Five pound, one pound, and ten shilling notes.'

Mickey nodded and stroked his goatee beard. 'Not a problem, Sean will be able to sort you out, how much do you want?'

'Five grands worth initially, perhaps more later.'

'No rare dates,' I said. 'I'm only interested in the notes that no one else wants, so long as they predate nineteen fifty six.'

There was a pause as he absorbed my instructions. ‘Do you mind if I talk to my boy for a moment?'

'Not at all, shall I leave the room?'

'Absolutely not, I want you to hear this conversation.'

I settled back in my chair, feeling the urge for my nicotine fix, but there was no ashtray in sight, so I let it pass.

'Sean.'

'Yes daddy?'

'How does Jimmy look to you?'

Sean glanced at me quickly, some colour rising in his cheeks. 'He looks...well, he looks a little pale and unkempt, if you don't mind me saying Jimmy?'

I shrugged and smiled.

'Never mind that, he's always been a scruffy sod, that much I know. 'Does he look like he's been sniffing any solvents, or lines of Charlie, is he sober, compos mentis? that sort of thing.'

Sean shifted uncomfortably in his seat.

'You don't have to answer that,' I said, like a red hot legal eagle. 'Your old man knows I am a drug free zone, and that I only drink in impolite company. He, on the other hand is desperately confused. His old grey marbles are trying to formulate a logical answer to a simple but aggravating question. Why would a seemingly sane antiques dealer want to blow five thousand pounds on virtually worthless vintage confetti. Where, he is asking himself, is the profit in that?'

Mickey's saucer eyes widened to side plates. 'So where is the profit Jimmy? You can tell me I'm an old fart now, I just love to hear a good story.'

I relaxed and relented, 'could I possibly have that coffee now Sean?'

He smiled, and spoke quietly into an intercom.

'Okay, I give in, it's for a film company. They need a close-up scene of some bad boys counting money from a bank heist, you know the sort of thing.'

Mickey folded his hands together, as if in prayer. 'Ah that explains it, I too have hired out antiques for television and films, it can be very lucrative, but these people have no souls for works of art Jimmy, they are so clumsy!' He shook his head sadly, 'you wouldn't believe how many insurance claims I have had to make.'

I smiled, 'you do surprise me, mind you, I have also heard whispers that insurance claims can be quite lucrative.'

The gold tooth showed itself once more as he roared with laughter, tears ran down his cheeks as he fell into a coughing fit.

Sean was on his feet, 'daddy?'

Mickey nodded and held up a hand for silence, while dabbing at his eyes with a large white linen handkerchief.

'Are you okay Mickey?' I said.

He nodded and blew his nose with abandon. 'I'm fine, don't fuss, I am an old man who occasionally coughs when he laughs. My doctor says to me, Mickey you must try not to laugh so much, and then he hands me his invoice, but it is not an invoice as you or would understand it. It is a joke, so I laugh some more.'

Sean grinned at me, 'well it is Harley Street daddy, not benefit street.'

Mickey waved a hand at the screen, like he was swatting a pesky fly. 'So why shouldn't I go to Harley Street? My money is as good as anybody's. Probably better because I have earned it, worked for it, using my talents and brain.'

'Whoa there Mickey!' I said, ' you can spend your money on whatever you like, especially on your health, we were just a little concerned here.'

'Well don't be, I am just fine.' He paused and dabbed at his lips. 'Oddly enough, there was a pretty woman in the waiting room when I called in last week, and she seemed surprised when I struck up a conversation. I asked her what she did for a living and she informed me that she was a socialite. Well I had never heard of such a profession, and she explained that it entailed going to endless parties thrown by very important people. Or occasionally to art galleries and expensive restaurants. Consequently, she was obliged to purchase clothing that befitted the event, and visit Harley Street for what she called female body enhancement surgery.' He frowned then, and tugged at his beard. 'I said this was a good thing, that young people should enjoy themselves before committing to something more useful and challenging, but I repeated my question.

'That's very nice dear, but what do you do for a living?'

It was our time to fall about laughing.

He grinned mischievously, 'she was not pleased, I can tell you.'

Alice entered with the coffee, smiling as she listened to our laughter, 'I hope you boys are not talking dirty.'

'Ah Alice,' said Mickey brightly, ‘how are you my dear?'

'I'm fine Mickey, have you been to see the doctor yet?'

'Yes I have, and I will show you my doctors note when I return.'

'I'll hold you to that,' she said, and glided from the room.

I was somewhat surprised to see that the coffee came in white builder’s mugs. Sean seemed to read my mind. 'The bone china is for the punters, we prefer mugs.'

'Suits me, ‘I said blowing and sipping.

'Is the coffee good Jimmy?'

'Freshly ground and lovely, I replied, 'it certainly beats the instant crap that I poor down my neck.'

'Good, now I on the other hand would like a decent pint of beer.'

' It's a bit rough down there, isn't it.’

'It's like horse’s piss, flat, tepid and lifeless, but that's enough about me, now this deal of several parts, this interests me.'

'Well I may need more of the same for a start.'

He frowned and pulled at his beard. He reminded me of Ron Moody's portrayal of Fagin in the musical 'Oliver'.

'More,' he said, confirming my 'Oliver' connection. 'Let me get this straight, you may need more of...' he tapped the side of his skull, ' What did Jimmy call it Sean?'

'Vintage confetti daddy.'

'Ah yes, vintage confetti, I like that!' He puckered his lips, a questioning look in his eyes, 'how much more?'

'I don't know yet Mickey.'

He shrugged expressively, as if to say, it is none of my business. 'Okay, that is not a problem, Sean, remind me what Jimmy's five grand will buy at today's rate?'

Sean played some keys on the computer, while I sipped my coffee. 'Five thousand pounds will buy three thousand two hundred and seven pounds in pre-1956 banknotes of no collectable value.'

'So, remind me son of mine, how many times have you harangued your father about holding on to vintage confetti?'

Sean looked a little crestfallen, and glanced at me sheepishly. 'More than once daddy.'

'More than once a week I would venture. The notes are dirty and many of them are torn, you said. Who in their right mind would possibly buy them, you said. We should have a clear out and consign the lot to auction, you said.' Mickey was not finished by a long chalk, and turned his attention on me. 'As for your bullshit story about a close up of bad boys counting their loot from a bank job. It just doesn't quite ring true Jimmy. The notes are grubby, crumpled and some torn, as my boy constantly reminds me. Are these the same banknotes that have just been nicked from your local bank, somehow I don't think so.'

Lights sparked in my brain as I attempted to answer a rather tricky question. 'They were old banknotes heading for the destructor, but were intercepted by the bad boys before they reached the mail train,' I answered quickly.

Mickey nodded, his large lazy eyes never leaving mine. 'So, I'm guessing that the title of this film could be, 'The Great Train Robbery That Happened Before The Cash Actually Reached The Train?'

I nodded, 'that sounds like a reasonable working title, yes.'

Mickey smiled, 'I like it, that sounds like my kind of film, and you may require more vintage confetti in the future, presumably for even yet more close ups of bad boys counting their ill-gotten gains?'

The few feeble lights that had charged through my brain, were now spent. 'Okay Mickey, you got me, it was
bullshit, but now I am going to reveal the truth, but before I do, you both have to swear that what I tell you will remain within the confines of these walls.'

The glint of a gold tooth beckoned once more. 'We are all ears Jimmy.'

'You promise not to tell?'

Mickey nodded, 'Cross my heart and hope to die in a cellar full of rats.'

'I have acquired a time machine,' I said, ' and plan to spend the vintage confetti on works of art, and make a whole stash of cash.'

Sean shifted uncomfortably in his chair, while his dad pulled on the beard. ' What a wonderful notion,' he said softly, as though he were talking to himself.

'An antique dealer with cash to splash, and the freedom to travel into the past ,to buy at will and somehow bring it back to the present day. He grinned, ' Do you see me smiling Jimmy?'

'I see you smiling Mickey.'

'Well thank you for giving an old man a reason to dream, and a reason to smile every time he thinks of that dream, he shook his head. 'Now back to business, it is obvious that you are not about to reveal the identity of your client, and why should you? I would have been extremely disappointed if you had done otherwise. Sean, forget about the going exchange rate and give Jimmy five for five.'

' Are you quite sure daddy?'

'He is my friend, and true friends can usually be counted upon the fingers of one hand in this life. Besides it's only lying in my basement earning me absolute zero interest. Does that sound agreeable to you Jimmy?'

'More than agreeable Mickey, thank you.'

'My pleasure. Sean, give Jimmy an ashtray, I suspect that it is way past his cigarette time. '

Sean produced a crystal glass ashtray from a drawer in the desk. I lit

up and proffered him the pack, but he declined.
'My boys do not smoke Jimmy, filthy habit.'
I inhaled deeply, 'quite right too, but as I recall, you were a smoker once.'
'Ah yes, in another life, but I quit for the sake of my wife, my life, my children, and the business.' His expression then changed to one of loss and despair. 'Just blow a little smoke over here for old times' sake.'
I laughed, 'your boys, you say, just how many do you have?'
'Six,' he announced proudly, 'not all working in the business you understand. One is a barrister, another an orthopaedic surgeon, and one who is a member of parliament for Huddersfield. Sean works with me in Leeds, and the other two run our emporium in Covent Garden.'
'You have been a busy man... you never said?'
'Are we married, do I have to tell you everything?'
Suddenly he lowered his head and was silent for a moment, and when he looked up again, there was a suggestion of moisture in his eyes. 'I know you have had a bad year Jimmy. After Fay's funeral, I asked your friend Ammo to keep me informed.' He nodded, 'you are blessed with fine friends, and it makes my old heart sing to see you back in the saddle again.'
I climbed out of my chair and stepped over to the screen, inhaled deeply a blew a blue cloud of smoke. Mickey laughed and inhaled through his considerable nose. 'Ah, thank you my friend.'

CHAPTER 13

The drive home passed in a blizzard of thoughts, I stopped off at Effin Elsie's and ordered a sweet and sour chicken with fried rice. The answer phone was winking at me as I entered the flat. I, ignored it and warmed a plate under the grill, it was 6.15 pm. The phone rang and I picked it up.

'Jimmy boy, where have you been?'

I grinned 'Ammo, how long have I been gone?'

'We followed you out into the garden, and you were burbling how beautiful it all looked, and then you disappeared, it was amazing!'

'I know, I was there.'

'You just dissolved in front of us, like the invisible man.'

'You didn't see the garden, the flowers, the lovely green lawn?'

'Are you kidding, what garden is this then, not that muddy mess out front surely? I will tell you what we did find though.'

'Go on.'

'We found your wallet, your mobile phone, house keys, some loose change and a tissue, unused I am happy to say, lying in the mud, but you were gone my friend.'

Mary's voice came to my assistance then.

'Nothing travels that does not belong in that time Jimmy, you are the time traveller, and nothing else.'

' Jimmy, you still there?'

'Yes, sorry mate, how long have I been gone?'

'What, you don't know?'

'I wouldn't be asking otherwise, would I?'

'Twenty-three days.'

The steel fork slipped from my fingers and clattered onto the table top.

'Each day that passed, Sally chalked it on a board.'

'We must rally the troops Ammo, get them all in the pub tonight, seven thirty sharp.'

'Already done Jim boy, everyone knows you are back. You are on stage at eight sharp, not seven thirty.'

'Good boy! I will see you then.'

I left my meal unfinished and laid on my bed, watching ghostly lights flicker on the ceiling, as traffic ebbed and flowed beneath the window. My thoughts turned to Mary and Sandy, to the boys who collected sterilised milk bottles, and the boxing man from uncle. I thought too of the kindly ex-soldier with the ravaged face, and the loneliness of the hard drinking landlord, who was known by many, and loved by none. I recalled the final curtain of the rocking chair soldier, who had bravely fought a painful and protracted war, only to find his last post sounding many years after the celebrations of V E day had passed into the history books, but most of all, I thought of Gwen.

I must say I do love a busy boozer. All of life is there, and for the price of a pint you can observe and listen to most of the dreams and dramas that we all face in a lifetime, for free. I did not join them immediately, but paused in the shadows and looked on from a distance. It was for me a joy to see my friends again, and to watch their animated conversations and laughter. It was good to see that Tristan had joined our group. He owned the barbers shop next to the pub, and was proud of the fact that he was the only gay in our gathering. He was a lovely bloke and cut hair like Edward Scissorhands. There was one vacant chair with a freshly pulled foaming pint, waiting, and I smiled. It reminded me of the value of true friendship, and I was sure that without them, without their unbridled and unwavering love and support, I would now be a lost soul in a very dark place. Gordon saw me first as I weaved my way between tables, and it was he who started the chant.

'Jimmy! Jimmy! Jimmy!'

Immediately they all joined in, like I was some returning all-conquering hero. Even groups of people sitting at adjoining tables joined in good naturedly. I took my seat quickly, feeling a self-conscious rush of blood to my face, and raised my glass in a toast.

'My people,' I said with pride and some emotion, 'strength and honour!'
They raised their glasses in response and repeated after me, 'strength and honour!' It was an emotional moment. A bit like 'Life of Brian' meets 'Gladiator.' The ritual greeting over, I drank deeply, wiping the impressive walrus moustache of beer foam from my upper lip. I told them everything, and when I finished they were silent. So silent you could hear a cough drop. I took advantage of the silence and popped a cigarette in my mouth, but was prevented from lighting it by a restraining hand from Sally.
'What are you doing Jimmy, you can't smoke in here.'
I realised then that they were all staring at me, and slotted the fag back into its box. I say that I told them everything, but in fact I was a tad more than economical with the truth. I failed to mention Gwen, I'm not sure why, but I did.
'This is fantastic!' said Ammo, ' you did all this in just over three weeks?'
I frowned and shook my head, No, it seems that time does not run parallel, and that is a little confusing. This all took place over four days and yet you say that I have been gone for three weeks, that is interesting.'
'Scary is the word I would use,' said Elvis, 'you must have been scared Jimmy?'
'I was,' I said quickly,' I was like a frightened child lost in a forest of unrecognisable adult legs, but when I discovered that I could travel at will, all that fear melted away like an ice cream cornet in hot seaside sunshine, and I was ready for an adventure.'
I took another sip of beer. 'Not only that but I can prove the truth of my story if Sandy has done his job. My box of books and clothing should be waiting to be retrieved, in the cellar behind a brick whitewashed wall.'
Ammo was staring at me intensely, 'well let's check it out Jimmy.'
'What, now, tonight?' It was my voice but I was surprised at the reluctant tone, a fear perhaps of finding absolutely nothing?
'Would you be able to sleep tonight without knowing,' he said, 'I don't think I would.'
He was right of course, I had to know tonight.
The house seemed so cold and unwelcoming, not at all like Mary and Sandy's lovely home. The naked light bulbs burned into my eyes as I led them down the hallway. We sounded like a herd of wilder beasts as our footfalls fell on bare floorboards, and there was a strong smell of gloss

paint. There was also a lot of giggling and whispering from the ranks, which I chose to ignore, pausing at the cellar door. Crouching, I opened a tool box lying on the floor, and retrieved my torch and a claw hammer.

'Are we all ready? ‘I said rather theatrically.

The rabble murmured in a manner that suggested they had been rather longer in the pub than I was aware of.

I shook my head sadly, 'am I the only one with a torch?'

'Sorry old boy,' said Gordon, 'normally I would not be seen in polite company without my trusty torch, but sadly the battery expired the other day without so much as a by your leave.'

'How sad, my condolences.'

Tristan raised a hand at the back.

'Yes boy?'

'I have my mobile phone,' he replied, waving it above his head, 'it glows quite brightly.'

I dismissed him with a look so severe, that he lowered his head and hand quickly.

'Sir?' Suzie had raised her hand.

'Yes,' I said, with a rather sharp edge to my voice, 'what is your question old hag- like crone?'

'If I had known we were going treasure hunting, I could have brought my big ol' pussy. She 'as bright green eyes wot glow in the dark like.'

'Excellent, well bag -puss will have to wait until our next excursion into the hellish dark place we are about to enter, follow me chaps!'

I noticed that the one-eyed doll occupied the shelf in the room beyond.

'Why do we need torches anyway?' whispered Sally, 'it's pretty well-lit down here.'

'And quite spooky,' added Suzie with feeling, 'don't forget spooky.'

I pointed at the plain narrow door, 'because we are about to enter here. A room below ground level, and darker than a black hole. It is also recognised as the epicentre of even darker supernatural activity, so we must be on our guard.'

I looked at each one of them in turn. 'As soon as I open this door, there is no going back, understood?'

Elvis raised a hand.

'Elvis?'

'Maybe we should leave it until the morning, things always look brighter in the morning.'

'Shame on you Elvis old chum,' said Gordon, 'you whose family tree is steeped in honourable samurai warriors.'

'Not samurai warriors Gordon, but sushi warriors.'

I pointed at the door, ' in there Elvis, natural light has never entered this ancient place. It has always been a place of whispers and malevolent slime oozing through the brick walls, forever searching for an innocent soul to enter and release them from the darkness to enter the world of light and wreck their revenge.'

'Bloody 'ell Jimmy!' said Ammo, 'now you've got me going, can we just get on with it.'

I smiled. 'Sorry Ammo, follow me people.' I lifted the old metal latch and pulled, the door opened reluctantly with an arm shaking judder . The torch light revealed that it was much like it was in Mary and Sandy's day, but more cluttered. There were new additions. An old motorcycle, sprayed silver and in bits. A twin tub washing machine that was so dilapidated it cried out to be in the Leeds City art gallery, and several cabinet television sets which had once transmitted images and sound for our entertainment and education. Now discarded, blank grey screens that seemed to be waiting, watching, rather than been watched.

I almost tripped over an old bicycle frame, and played the torch light onto it. 'Watch your step,' I said, looking over my shoulder. They were all holding mobile phones aloft, as though they were at a rock concert. I felt a hand grab the belt of my jeans as I flashed the torch around. Ammo cursed as he tripped over something. Finally, hand on mouth, I played the light onto the far wall. It was time to breathe again as the light revealed a whitewashed wall with no alcoves. There was more moaning and bitching behind me. 'What's going on back there?'

'Someone grabbed my arse,' whined Tristan.

Ammo snorted in the gloom.

Gordon laughed, 'sorry old thing, thought you were sexy Suzie.'

Now it was Suzie's turn to moan, 'thanks for that love of my life, so you think I have a bloke's arse, very nice!'

'If you have all quite finished acting like a bunch of teenagers who have been told that their mobile phones have been crushed, do you want the good news, or the good news?'

Elvis seemed more confused than usual, 'can we have the good news after the bad news Jimmy, that's how I like to hear the good news.'

'Well I am more than happy to inform you Elvis, that the bad news is good. The walls are solid, minus the alcoves that were there, which means...'

'Buried treasure,' replied an invisible Ammo.

'Precisely.'

I handed my torch to Sally who was still hanging on to my belt. She played the light as I tapped a brick at eye level. I heard the dusty fall of mortar on the other side. Another tap on a neighbouring brick was even more dramatic, as cracks appeared. Sandy had been as good as his word, and had only applied enough mortar to keep the wall upright.

I could hear his words ringing in my ears.

'I can even lay the bricks with just a lick of mortar Jimmy, so you could open it with a toffee hammer.'

Gordon chipped in, 'Don't want to be a party pooper old boy, but shouldn't one start at the top of the wall, otherwise the whole darn thing could come toppling down.'

I paused, feeling the need to explain that I was simply confirming how Sandy had laid the bricks, but I couldn't be arsed. The first brick almost fell into the cavity, but I managed to retrieve it. After that it was child's play, and before long I had created a big enough gap to peer inside. I saw two metal trunks, one on top of the other, covered in dust, and my heart did an Olympic gold double flip and pike.

'What do you see Jimmy?' whispered Sally.

'I see wonderful things,' I answered. It was the defining moment for me, and I knew then that my life would change forever. Not just my life, but this moment would impact on my friends present, and my friends in the past.

Soon I was able to reach the tin trunks, and Ammo was by my side. We lifted the first and carried it out into the light. Leaving the others to carry it upstairs Then we returned for the second and carried it up into the kitchen, placing it gently on the floor.

They were all silent as I dropped to my knees and opened the first trunk. My first reaction was one of frustration and impatience as I lifted out layers of brown wrapping paper, but then I retrieved the first book carefully wrapped in the same strong parcel paper. The thought that Mary (in all likelihood) had carefully wrapped each book before handing it to Sandy to place in the trunk, brought a lump to my throat.

I felt Sally's hand on my arm as I unwrapped the first of the 'Just William' books 'So it's all true then, these are the books you described?'

I simply nodded and handed her the book. I confess that I was close to tears and unable to speak at that moment, so I busied myself, carefully unwrapping each volume and offering it blindly to anyone to anyone who would take it. Soon the trunk was empty and I climbed to my feet. They stood silently around me, each clutching their books.

It was Suzie who spoke first. 'So, Sandy kept his promise.'

I nodded dumbly. 'He bricked up the wall, and they have been hiding here for...?'

'Fifty-nine years,' said Gordon quickly. 'They've been hiding behind that wall for fifty-nine years, waiting for you to return and claim them Jimmy.'

'Amazing isn't it, I said, it opens up all sorts of possibilities.'

I stepped over to the second trunk and threw the lid open. There was more tissue and brown paper, as I recovered my clothes. First my Bogie hat, and then the rest followed. Soon they were all admiring my taste in trousers that had a crouch that reached the lower part of my chest. I snapped on my hat and looked at Sally.

She smiled, 'it suits you, you look very handsome.'

I raised the hat and inclined my head, 'well thank you my dear. What time is it?'

She glanced at her watch, 'quarter to ten.'

'Quarter to ten,' I echoed, 'okay, let's go people.' They all fell in beside and behind me, making an awful racket as we stomped out of the house. Sally linked her arm in mine.

'Where are we going Jimmy?'

'Why back to the pub of course wench, there is much to discuss.' The pub had thinned out, and we claimed our usual table. I watched them as they settled into their seats, looking at their books and then at me.

'The books are yours by the way, a gift from me to you from another time.'

'I'm not sure I want to,' said Suzie with a frown, 'aren't they quite valuable?'

I grinned, 'they are certainly collectable, but probably not worth more than a hundred or two a piece. I really don't know, it's not my area of expertise, but the books you are holding cost me sixpence each.'

She frowned,' sixpence?'

'We are talking about pre- decimal money Suzie. Sixpence was half a shilling, or a Bob, as it was known then. A shilling was worth twelve pennies, and twenty shillings equalled one pound, so if you broke a one-pound note into pennies, you would have a whopping two hundred and forty pennies. The books you are all holding cost me six pennies each.'

'There is a downside of course,' she replied.

I frowned, 'what downside?'

'Well you had to travel a fair distance to buy them Jimmy.'

I laughed out loud then, partly from sheer relief I think, but what he had said was not only amusing, but true. I had indeed travelled far. I headed for the bar, returning with a tray full of drinks. 'The real value of those books, is the fact that they have arrived,' I said, sipping my pint, ' and that I can do it again and again.'

Sally looked at me in alarm. ‘What are you saying, you are going back again?'

'Absolutely!'

'Aren't you scared?' said Elvis, his eyes wide.

'Scared of what exactly?'

'Not coming back springs to mind' said Gordon, 'you could be lost in another time, somewhere where you don't belong.'

'So, what would you do?'

He shrugged and looked to the others for help.

'It doesn't seem to work that way, after listening to Mary and Beatie’s stories, I believe that they are all linked. As far as I am aware, all the people who travelled had one thing in common.' I took a quick slug of beer, and attempted to light a cigarette, but felt Sally's restraining hand on mine.

'Sorry, I keep forgetting.'

'What is it, this thing you have in common?' Her voice was soft, almost a whisper.

'We were all in mourning, we had all lost someone and we were grieving. Sudden loss of someone you love dearly, can lead one into dark places. You all know that I still talk to Fay, even now, as if she were still here. So perhaps this slight unhinging of the mind, opens doors that no one else can see. Certainly, the professor qualifies, having lost his wife and daughter in that terrible fire in Edinburgh. And poor Mary miscarried with twins, and on her own admittance, was completely inconsolable. It was only Sandy's strength and love that pulled her back from the edge. My own loss is well recorded here, so I will say no more.'

The silence was deafening. 'I'm sorry, I didn't mean to depress you, it's just a theory.'

More silence.

'Will somebody say something for goodness sake!'

Suddenly Ammo broke the silence. 'I like it, it's a good theory, the human brain is an immensely powerful organ, capable of things beyond our comprehension. In fact, we only actually use a tiny portion of it, and much of its power is a complete mystery to even the finest minds.' He was in full flow now, and I was reluctant to stop him. 'I remember reading something about poltergeists once, and it said that when sugar bowls and things fly, it was commonly noted that young girls were present. These girls had just reached the age of puberty, a powerful change of body and mind.'

'The butterfly effect,' said Gordon.

Ammo nodded, 'precisely, it suggests that the change within their brain patterns, enables them to move inanimate objects at will, without really knowing, apparently a quite common ability that we have lost over time. Studies of ancient aboriginal tribes also suggest that they could communicate over vast distances, simply by the power of thought.' He paused, a host of wrinkles creasing his brow. 'A sort of email, but minus the laptop.'

More silence.

'Well, thank you for that Ammo,' I said, 'most illuminating, does anyone else have a theory?'

'You mentioned the professor Jimmy,' said Suzie. 'You said that one day he walked out of his home and never came back. As my right honourable friend Elvis remarked, perhaps he was lost in time and unable to return?'

I nodded, 'that is an excellent point. It is however, well past my nicotine fix, so I will adjourn to the smoking room, and consider your questions.'

It was cool outside as I lit my cigarette and inhaled deeply. I was passed by people entering and leaving the pub, some were strangers and some more familiar faces. Occasionally someone would say 'good evening' or goodnight, and I would respond with a smile or a word, or both. I had, in my youth, spent some time living in London, where such events simply did not happen. But this was Yorkshire, a place where greetings from strangers are commonplace, and I would always acknowledge such a greeting, as one should.

I could hardly believe the steps I had taken, the journey that had led me into uncharted territory, but one thing was plain, I could barely wait to return. The pub door opened, as a young couple left. I heard a murmur of voices, felt a waft of warm beer infused air for just a moment, then the door closed and I was left to my thoughts once more. They were my dear friends in there, and I loved them all, but now there was a stronger call, and I felt increasingly drawn to answer it. Suddenly I was joined by Elvis, he lit a cigarette and hugged himself.

'It's cold out here.'

I nodded and smiled. 'So, what do you think, am I just a basket case, am I going completely gaga?'

'Probably, but at least you have us, your friends. 'I'm not sure you should be thinking of going back in your fragile state.

I laughed, and the laughter made me cough. 'Fragile!' I spluttered, I have never felt stronger or fitter in my life.'

He blew a ragged smoke ring, 'you know what I mean.'

I did of course, I knew exactly what he meant, and we finished our cigarettes in the company of silence, as only true friends can.

My fresh pint of beer awaited as I settled into my seat again.

'When Beaty spoke to me about the professor, she said that Cleve watched a man in the depths of despair. That all changed completely as he began to travel. His spirits rose and he spoke of the next journey with increasing excitement and anticipation. It is my firm belief that he made that final journey with a smile on his lips, that he had found, not only peace, but a new life to embrace. I believe that he made that journey with absolutely no intention of returning. Why would he? There was nothing left for him in his own time.'

'Is that allowed?' said Suzie with a frown. 'I mean, if someone decides to relocate to a time where they should not exist, surely that may have some cause and effect on the future?'

I shrugged, 'who knows? Theories abound about trampling through time, but that is all they are, theories. If as you say there is some compelling shift in the future because a time traveller unwittingly puts his size nines on a frog, who got splattered by someone who shouldn't be there...well. I'm not convinced. With what I now know, I believe that there have been time travellers for millennium, and if there has been some compelling shift in the future, it is probably so small, so minuscule, that we see no change, no cataclysmic alteration of the future of mankind.'

When Sally spoke, I could barely look into her eyes. There was only pain and sadness there. 'So, you are definitely going back then?'

I nodded quickly, hoping beyond hope that she could not read the sadness in my curt nod, or notice the barely perceptible tremor in my hand as I raised the glass to my lips.

'I recall reading an article about professor Stephen Hawkins,' said Elvis. 'Apparently, he held a birthday party, but did not post the invites until after the event. Sadly no one turned up. Professor Hawking offered this as experimental evidence that time travel into the past is not possible. 'Although,' he is quoted as saying, 'we secretly hope that by publishing the party's existence, someone in the future may retroactively decide to pay a visit. Hawking said that while Einstein's theories allow for time travel into the past, but that it is likely that warping would trigger a bolt of radiation that would destroy the space ship and maybe the space-time itself.'

'Is that true, or are you winding us all up?' said Ammo.

Elvis shrugged, 'that's what I read, you can google it online if you don't believe me.'

'I believe you,' I said, 'and from the little that I have read about Stephen Hawking, it sounds just like the mischievous and humorous thing he would do to prove a point.' I then told them about my busy day, and my meeting with Mickey and Sean.

'You have been a busy boy,' said Gordon, a note of respect in his voice. 'As Ammo and Elvis described quite eloquently how you disappeared...' He paused, 'in a puff, I think was the term used, then I have to accept that all of this is for real, and you have not been engaged in some secret bricklaying...'

'No secret bricklaying, I promise.'

'Well, then you will need our help Jimmy, I take it that you are moving house?'

'Absolutely,' I smiled and raised my glass, ' I knew I could rely on you all, 'strength and honour!' Time was called as they raised their glasses, 'strength and honour,' they cried. As we headed for the exit, I felt a tug at my sleeve.

'Yes Tristan?' I said, as we all paused to look at him.

'A thought just occurred to me, it may be something and it may be nothing, but shouldn't we have opened the
other alcove, that too was bricked up as well, and you never know...' His voice trailed away as I stared at him, before throwing an arm around his shoulder.

'Well spotted Tristan, I was wondering who would spot the deliberate mistake, you put all the rest to shame.'

He blushed. 'Do I? Oh my, that is nice to hear.'

Ammo and Gordon exchanged knowing glances, that simply read, 'deliberate mistake my arse.'

CHAPTER 14

The following day was bright and breezy. Beaty was hanging washing on the line, with her back to me. 'Woman,' I called in my excellent West Indian accent, 'where can a man get a good cuppa tea around 'ere?' I laughed out loud as she turned, mouth agape and hands on cheeks.

'Jimmy! She cried aloud, and we hugged as I entered the back yard. She looked at me then, a searching look that brought a lump to my throat. 'You make a happy woman very sad when I look at you, why you is all skin an' bone boy.'

She rolled her lovely old eyes and laughed so loud I swear I saw the washing billow on the line. 'If you get any thinner, I'll be using you to prop up this here washing line.' Her smile froze then, and her eyes narrowed as she peered at me intently. 'Have you been travelling Jimmy?' she whispered. I nodded and her eyes grew wide as she covered her mouth with the palm of her hand.

'Back to nineteen fifty-six, a year before you and Cleve arrived.'

She nodded silently, her eyes now moist with tears, and a low gasp escaping through the fingers of her hand.'So, it was you who knock on our door with the pie, all those years ago.'

I said nothing, no words were necessary at that moment.

'Come,' she said, 'you need a proper breakfast inside you.'

'No really, a cup of tea will be just fine,' I protested.

She almost pushed me into the now familiar kitchen, ' a cup of tea will not be fine, what you need is a full Jamaiclish.'

I leaned against the kitchen door frame as she busied herself with cooking. 'Jamaiclish? that is a word I am unfamiliar with Beaty.'

She dropped a couple of sausages into the frying pan, and cut the rind from the bacon with a pair of scissors. 'Me Cleve loved a full English breakfast, but I always add a little West Indian black magic to the mushrooms and tomatoes. He call it a full Jamaiclish, and the silly word had a special meaning to us.'

I told her everything as she busied herself with my breakfast, but I consciously made no mention of Gwen, and she listened, constantly asking questions and nodding at my replies. I was then ordered to sit and eat, which of course I did on the penalty of death should I disobey. There was bacon and egg, sausage and mushrooms, tomatoes, black pudding and a rack of toast, and she watched me eat with a smile on her face.

'I'm getting the Jamaica connection in the tomatoes and mushrooms, they are a little spicier than I expected.'

The questioning look in her eyes said it all. 'Is it good, or is it too hot?'

'It is by far the tastiest breakfast that I have ever had Beatty, I'm with Cleve, and will insist on the full Jamaiclish whenever possible. I sat back with a full belly as she pushed the ash tray across the table.

'You have had quite an adventure Jimmy.' She tapped the table with a finger, her eyes never leaving mine. 'So, you are going back, an' at some point in time you will knock on my door with the pie.'

'Yes,' I said, 'I believe I will.'

She looked troubled, ' there must be many reasons why you are going back?'

I paused and pulled a face, 'well yes, there are lots of reasons. I have a fantastic opportunity to travel back in time, and I can return almost at will, which I think you will agree does not happen to everyone. I must deliver your pie of course, and it's an antique dealers dream Beatty, it promises me riches beyond my wildest dreams.

Her eyes stayed focused on me, 'but you tell me that you is already rich.'

'Ah, yes I did, but I also told you that I could be a womanising cad, remember?'

Her pearly white tombstone teeth made an appearance, as she peeled back her lips with laughter. 'Oh yes, I remember, and I said, 'I should be so lucky.' She dabbed at her eyes with the linen hankie. 'My oh my, what a wonderful thing has happened.'

I smiled, 'and I can probably help some of the people, like Mary and Sandy, times were tough then.'

'I know Jimmy, I was there, remember?' She smiled, 'tell me about the

young lady?' She said it so quickly I was caught off guard,
'Gwen,' I replied.
'Ah, now Gwen is short for Gwendoline, a lovely name, tell me about her.'
I couldn't believe that I had just blurted out her name. 'In the good old days, you would have been tied to the Ducking Stool.'
'Just tell this old witch about Gwen, an' I promise not to put a spell on you.'
It didn't take long to fill in the gaps. 'So you see,' I concluded, ' We have only met a couple of times, we are barely friends and certainly not lovers.'
'But you could be Jimmy, if you went back.'
I laughed and was surprised how hollow it sounded. 'That is a very big 'if' Beaty.'

The weeks that followed kept me very busy, my friends were true to their word, and soon I was the sole occupier of the old house. The front room was now a relatively comfortable bedsit, complete with portable fan heaters. I still had to nip to my friends for a shower, and live on take away food when I was feeling guilty about eating at their homes, but at least I could sleep in a sort of eerie comfort. On the first day I showed them the ancient standing stone, and smiled as they stepped forward to run their hands over its rough surface.
'How old is it Jimmy?' was the first question, and I simply shrugged, 'how old is Stonehenge?'
Ammo was enraptured, 'is that why this place is so special, is there some hidden power within the stone itself do you think?'
Again, I shrugged helplessly. 'I don't think that the stone itself hides hidden powers. It is my belief that it was raised on this spot as a marker. Perhaps travellers and pilgrims recognised these stones way back in the mists of time. It could have been an ancient invitation to rest a while in a special place, somewhere where one could find a welcome shade and an inner peace.'
Gordon touched it tentatively, as if he was half expecting something dramatic to occur. 'It's smaller than I thought it would be.'
'That is because most of it is now buried deep in the earth. When Mary

described it, she was told that it stood taller than a man, in the centre of a gently sloping hollow. At some point in time, this wall was built, and ended here, at the stone. It is my guess that the hollow was filled in and levelled, so as you see it now, it is only marginally taller than the wall.'

Sally was standing by my side, and I felt her hand on my shoulder. So, what you are saying, is that this could have been a special place for thousands of years?'

I nodded, 'yes, why not? It's not inconceivable.

Elvis stamped his foot. 'It's this stuff isn't it, this earth, this small plot of land that the house stands on?'

'Yes, I think it is, I believe the stone marks the spot, and the ground that the house sits on has always been a time portal, but only for those whose brain patterns have been rewired. Those who mourn the loss of a loved one so deeply, that they are on the edge of eternity, just a whisker away from madness and oblivion.'

I smiled as they all shifted on their feet while instinctively looking down at the grass. Then the rain returned and we all retreated back indoors. As I played mother and handed out mugs of instant coffee, a deep rumble of thunder sounded overhead. I noticed that Sally looked a little troubled at the storm, and I pulled up a banana box beside her.

'You okay?'

She blew on her coffee and nodded. 'I just find it all a bit sudden and strange, there is a lot to digest here, and the thought of you rattling about in this big old house, it's a lot to take in Jimmy.'

I slid a comforting arm around her shoulders, ' I know what you mean love, if it makes you feel any better, I still have many more questions than answers.'

Coffee break over, we descended into the black hole once more, and opened the second alcove. It revealed nothing more than an old and battered leather suitcase, and an enamel sign for Fry's chocolate. The murmur of dissent amongst my fellow pirates was music to my ears. Sandy had provided the suitcase I required, and had also sent me the enamel Fry's Five Boy sign, a quite rare and collectable item.

'An empty suitcase and an old sign,' said Ammo, 'not exactly pieces of eight is it?'

I smiled, 'on the contrary, this is just part of the jigsaw to a fortune

Ammo.'

We returned to the kitchen with our haul and I opened the suitcase, there was a strong smell of mothballs. 'Before I left, I asked Sandy to find me an old suitcase, something to carry my vintage money in, and this is perfect.'

Gordon tapped the enamel sign, 'I'm quite taken by this, I should imagine there are collectors for this sort of thing.'

'Absolutely, this one is worth around three hundred.'

'What did you pay for it?'

'Nothing,' I replied, 'it was dumped in the cellar and I remarked that it was worth a bit in my time, and Sandy threw it in for good luck.'

'Good chap,' said Gordon, continuing in fine fellow mode. 'This old suitcase obviously pre-dates nineteen fifty-six, and will carry your dosh back, but remind me again, nothing travels back that does not belong to that time, correct?'

'Correct, and yes I did arrive in clothing that was not the fashion of the day, and no, I did not stumble into the past bollock naked. Don't ask me why because I do not know, perhaps there was a common decency clause added to the time travellers' manual, that states you are allowed to travel in your own clobber once, but only once.'

They all laughed, but in truth I did not have an answer.

'You make it sound almost like a spiritual experience Jimmy,' Suzie chided.

I had to think about that for a moment. I was brought up as a good Catholic boy, who in time became a good lapsed Catholic man, and in the fullness of time became a fully paid up member of the Agnostic club. Convinced that, if there was indeed a god, he was probably quite old, smelled of Vick's vapour rub and said things like. 'Believe me, if you don't believe in me then you're buggered...so think on!'

I shook my head, ' No, I only remember thinking that if I had ever heard of Quantum Physics, then I would have stopped fiddling with myself and paid more attention.'

Almost five weeks passed, and I continued to work on the house with more than a little help from my friends. The subject of time travel had hit the back burner, and I hid the yearning I felt to hear the bee in the bottle calling me back. It surprised and unnerved me that the past meant so much more to me than my own time, with my friends. I was chomping at the bit, wanting so much to be with Sandy and Mary once more, but most of all I thought of Gwen, and the guilt I felt for leaving her without a word, in her time of need.

My change of clothes were laid out in preparation for a quick exit, next to the battered suitcase, now bulging with vintage confetti. Tristan and Gordon were watching an episode of Coronation Street, while I was sitting on the steps, cradling a cup of tea. It was early evening, and the light was fading fast as I stared out at the barren garden.

The return of the angry bee was so loud and sudden, that I released my hold on the cup, as it slid from my fingers and shattered on the concrete step. The garden was smothered in a thick layer of snow. I laughed aloud then, and whooped like a man possessed. I could see the old houses across the street, the soft glow of the gas street light. The bee was buzzing, its wings telling me that it was time, and I was on my feet in an instant. I retreated into the house.

'Time to go boys!' I bellowed. They were on their feet in an instant, rushing out into the hall and gawping like a pair of Kentucky mountain inbreeds at the open door.

'It’s snowing boys!' I cried with glee, 'I do love the snow, don't you? I need to change my clothing fast.'

They were staring at me now, mouth's hanging open. I could almost hear duelling banjo's playing. I grabbed Gordon's arm and dropped the house keys into the palm of his hand. 'Don't forget to lock up, and unplug all the electrics.'

As I threw on my travelling clothes, Gordon appeared in the doorway. He looked pensive and troubled. 'I'm not sure you should be going back so soon Jimmy, and it's not snowing out there at all.'

'It's not snowing now old chum, but it is snowing in nineteen fifty six.' I threw on my overcoat, and set the brim of my bogie hat over my left eye.

'How do I look?'

He clasped his hands together and cocked his head to one side. 'Like Warren Beatty in 'Bonny and Clyde', but minus the dazzling good looks.'

The bee buzzed louder as I picked up my battered suitcase full of vintage confetti. 'So, this is it my friend, I've got the suit and I'm in the money. Don't need a passport where I'm going, wish me luck.'

It was an emotional moment for both of us, as I held out my arms and we hugged, in a manly, fellow rugby player sort of way. Tristan was standing by the door, he glanced nervously out into the garden, and then back at me. I paused, the snowflakes were larger now, drifting silently from a black sky, and creating dreamlike abstract images in the garden.

Tristan reached out and took my hand, I smiled, leaned forward, and kissed him on the cheek.

'Just come back to us Jimmy.'

'Oh, I'll be back,' I said, turning back to look at them. 'Don't forget to lock up.'

Unlike my previous journey, I was back in an instant. I felt the chill of winter immediately, could hear my footsteps crunching in the deepening drifts of snow. I glanced back, the door was closed but light spilled through the upper glazed diamond textured glass.

The nausea came quick and fast, and I was swaying, not sure if it was me or the house that moved, but I staggered sideways, and came to a sudden and painful halt against the old stone wall. I released my grip on the suitcase, and it fell into the snow with a whisper, and I remained still for a moment. I was however, surprised how quickly it passed, no puking or hallucinating. I was back, my breath creating clouds in the cool evening air. I leaned with my back against the ancient standing stone, and looked around in wonder at the snowy

landscape. Then I heard a familiar sound, it was the regular clump of guillotines from the glove factory up the road. If they were still working, then it was obviously still late afternoon. The gas lamp glowed across the street, casting a pool of light over the tiny wet fish shop.

Suddenly I was under attack as a number of snowballs splattered against the red brick wall to my left. One hit the old suitcase, and I grinned as I heard the retreating laughter and the sound of young feet running through a sea of snowflakes, out of sight, beyond the misshapen mounds of Gelato hedges. It brought back fond childhood memories of winters first snowfall. I reached into my suit pocket, searching for a cigarette, but my fingers curled around the house key that Sandy had given me. Yet I paused at the door, feeling shy to just let myself in, so I knocked on the glass panel a couple of times. As expected, they were still out at work, so I let myself in. My room was just the same, everything was as I remembered it, but I had envisaged a right royal welcome on my return, not the silence of an empty house. I sat on the bed and placed my suitcase full of loot on the floor. It was late summer when I left, what had happened in the mangled passage of time since then? I looked up at the wall clock, it was four thirty, suddenly I heard a familiar whirring noise as the hammer rose within the clock's mechanism, followed by a flat clang as hammer struck the coiled gong. So, I knew what time it was, but what month was it, indeed what year?' I opened the suitcase and peeled back some notes, folding them into my inside jacket pocket, and reminded myself that I should buy a wallet as I closed and locked the front door and went for a stroll.

The shop's bell announced my arrival. He was a portly man with pronounced red cheeks, dressed in the traditional grocers brown top coat, with a starched white collar and dung coloured tie. I noticed his twin brother replenishing packets of cereal on a high shelf, and he too was dressed in the same manner as his sibling. I waited as an elderly lady was being served in front of me.

'An' I'll 'ave three rashers of streaky bacon, make 'em thin mind.' This was not a polite request, but a command, and I watched fascinated as he pressed a large piece of pork against the circular blade, he then cranked a handle and the blade spun one revolution. He lowered the slice of bacon onto a sheet of greaseproof paper.

'Is that thin enough for you Mrs Tarpy?'

She leaned forward and peered closely, 'aye, it'll 'ave to do I reckon.'

He sliced two more rashers and wrapped them, placing them in a brown paper bag and sliding it across the white marble topped counter. I grinned as she produced a large earthenware jug from the depths of a very off-white shopping bag and placed it on the counter. Without a word he took hold of the jug and commenced to fill it with ale or beer, from one of three brass and porcelain beer pumps, decorated with hunting scenes. Slowly he levelled the jug as a brown foam emerged and climbed to the rim. She delved once more into the 'seen better days' bag, and produced an old piece of towelling, which she placed over the jug. Then the bacon was pushed in as she rummaged some more, finally retrieving her purse.

He looked at me over her head shawl, and beamed, 'I won’t be a moment sir.'

'Fine, I’m in no rush.'

In fact, it gave me time to look around at my surroundings. From the spring-loaded brass bell fixed above the door, to the bank of glass topped biscuit tins set at a convenient angle for scooping out the required selection. Then there were the tins of 'Whoppa' peas, standing shoulder to shoulder with tins of spinach, sardines, pink salmon, spam and corned beef. More tins of Biles beans, golden syrup, black treacle, Fussels milk (sperm in a can) Boxes of baking soda, baking powder, dried eggs and self raising flour. Huge tins of powdered baby milk, blue bottles of milk of magnesium, cod liver oil, tins of pears or peaches in syrup.

My eyes were drawn to a corner dedicated to keeping the home warm. Stacks of coal in paper sacks, rolls of kindling sticks, and compressed powdered coal bricks stacked neatly. There were colourful enamel and paper signs in abundance, declaring the virtues of syrup of figs, fry's chocolate, black cat tobacco, and 'Three Castle' cigarettes. A whole bank of shelves on my left were filled with glass sweet jars, some with screw on lids and some with glass lids with a clear marble on the top.

There were jelly babies, mint imperials, liquorice all sorts, sherbet limes, flying saucers, liquorice sticks, bonfire toffee, Turkish delight, chocolate drops, the list and lines of jars went on and on, and I felt a childlike urge to try them all.

She paid reluctantly, 'everything’s getting' so dear these days, I don't know.'

I stepped back and opened the door with a tinkle, as she left with her bag hanging from one arm. The jug of ale she cradled in both hands, as if it were the holy grail.

'Thank you young man,' she said gracefully.

The time had arrived for me to buy my cigarettes with my own money, and I must confess that I felt a bit nervous. 'Could I have twenty Senior Service please?'

His initial expression was one of alarm, as if I had asked him for twenty wraps of heroin, and then it softened to one of sorrow. 'I'm so sorry sir but we only have Woodbines or Park Drive.'

I heard Sandy's voice then. 'They keep the better cigarettes under the counter Jimmy, for their regular customers.'

'Oh, that's a shame, I'm staying with Sandy and Mary up the road, and he suggested that you may discover something more acceptable under the counter.'

His grin spread so wide, I was afraid that the top of his head would fall off. He tapped the side of his nose and looked furtively around for invisible customers.

'Now you're talking sir,' he said, reaching under the counter, ' Sandy and Mary, a lovely couple, he is not from these parts you understand, but we forgive him for that.'

He slid a packet of 'Players' across the counter, ' will these do?'

'Absolutely, oh and can I have one of your cheap cigarette lighters?'

His smile slid away to the graveyard of smiles.

Sandy's voice came to me again, sounding more than a little exasperated. 'Think before you speak Jimmy, otherwise folk will think you are a right daft apeth.'

'Sorry, I bought a cheap lighter the other week, and it has packed up on me, I was miles away, must be losing my marbles, could I have a box of matches please?'

He nodded, produced the matches and rang the ornate brass till, but I detected a certain look in his eyes, and suspected that it was a look that was reserved for daft apeth's.

'You're not from these parts then?'

'London,' I lied quickly, 'I'm from London.'

His head splitting smile returned. It was as if my answer explained everything, and the light in his eyes changed to one of sadness. 'Ah, London,' he said, 'very nice.'

It was my moment of absolution, he had forgiven me for my moment of insanity, because I was not a son of god's own county. The fog was a surprise as I stepped into the street, it hung in a thick sickly yellow haze, and I could barely see a few yards in front of me. However, it did not deter me from lighting up one of my newly purchased cigs, consequently I was not paying much attention to where I was going, and we collided shoulder to shoulder.

'I'm so sorry!'

'No really, it's this awful fog.' I recognised her voice immediately.

'I know you. You are Gwen's mum if I am not mistaken. Sandy and Mary introduced us a while back.'

She took a short step back and raised a gloved hand to her lips with a gasp. 'So, you are Jimmy?'

I smiled and nodded.

' I remember you fine, only you looked quite different...'

' I was having a bad day.'

She laughed and held out her hand. ' I know; I heard all about the tale of the fishes.'

I was thankful that the fog hid my blushes. ' She told you.'

'She most certainly did, and we laughed together until we cried.' She must have observed my discomfort then, as I searched for a crack in the pavement; big enough to fall down.

'I'm making a wild guess here,' she said. ' But I feel that as tall tales go, yours was something of a skyscraper.'

I shuffled my feet like an errant schoolboy. ' She looked sad, like she needed cheering up.'

I was more than surprised when she stepped forward and clutched my hand. ' It was the sweetest thing you could possibly have done; it was time she laughed again.'

'So, how is she?'

'She's fine; well as fine as can be expected under the circumstances.'

It was my voice, but it sounded more than a little shaky. ' Be sure to give her my regards.'

She laughed, ' you can tell her yourself, after all she will be dropping by tonight.'

My heart leapt from basement to penthouse.

'They are going to the pictures and decided to call it a foursome.'

'A foursome?' I echoed, and I was instantly bundled back into the elevator and transported back to the basement.

She smiled sweetly. ' Yes, Sandy and Mary and Gwen and Lance. Such a lovely young man, and fine prospects too, he's an accountant you know.'

The warm glow from the shop window illuminated her smile, ' it was nice to finally meet you Jimmy,' she said, and then she was gone in a ring of a doorbell.

My mind was spinning as I made the short journey back up the street. ' Lance for god's sake! She's taken up with someone called Lance, how could she? ' I paused deep in thought. ' So, this is the situation Jimmy boy. Some joker called Lance has steamed in on his white charger and scooped up my Gwendoline while I have been travelling...well, I'm ruddy well not having it!'

The house was still empty when I let myself in, so I busied myself building a decent fire in the kitchen. I screwed up some old newspaper into tight knots, adding some kindling lying in a box beside the coal bucket. Soon the flames were snaking around the wood chips, but when I added the coal it looked like it was in danger of snuffing out. I unfolded a double sheet of newspaper and held it across the fire. This encouraged more up draught, and soon I could hear the spit and crackle as the fire took hold. I released my hold on the paper as it started to glow in the middle, and it disappeared up the chimney like a burning wraith from hell.

The fire set, I checked out the meat safe in the cellar, but found only a couple of rashers of bacon. The walk-in larder proved to be more productive. I found a tin of stewing steak; a tin of processed peas, a small sack of potatoes, an onion, and a bunch of carrots.

I half-filled a pan with water and set it on the gas ring, glancing quickly at the wall clock. It was almost five thirty. I peeled the potatoes and cut them up into quarters. The onion and carrots were peeled and sliced, and set aside. Soon the water had reached boiling point, and I dropped in the spuds, adding a generous sprinkling of salt. Then I turned my attention to the fire, adding a few more lumps of coal. The fireside chair beckoned, and I sat, staring into the flames.

A smile crossed my face as I looked around the room. I was back, and more than ready to grab what time I would have here. The potatoes were now soft enough for me to add the vegetables, and I emptied them into a colander, returning them into the pan of boiling water. I then opened the cans of stewing steak and peas, and stirred them in, adding a sprinkling of pepper. I had already spotted the familiar brown box on the shelf. Illustrated with a boy and a girl; their pointy noses raised as the they followed the delicious aroma of Bisto gravy. I followed the instructions on the pack, and mixed a tablespoon with boiling water; adding the mixture to my stew. The gas ring was then set at its lowest point, and I let it simmer. Okay, I thought, it's not quite fine dining; but you have to work with what you've got, and it should dispel the winter chill outside. I made myself a cup of tea and lit a cigarette. It was almost six fifteen when I heard some fumbling with a key at the front door. The alarm in her voice brought a smile to my lips. ' Sandy, are you cooking?'

I stood too quickly and the chair made a loud scraping noise on the floor. She came to an abrupt halt and instinctively raised a gloved hand to her lips. She stood frozen like that for a second or two, and then rushed into my arms without a word. Emotions were high. I felt like I was home, and said the first words that entered my head.

'There's tea in the pot.'

She sat without removing her coat or gloves, and stared at me as I poured her a cup.

'How are you feeling Jimmy?'

'I'm fine, I said brightly. ' I felt a bit giddy when I arrived, but it soon passed; nothing like the first time.'

Suddenly I heard the front door open, and the sound of stamping boots. I stood and retreated to the wall beside the back door, finger on lips; and she nodded smiling.

'My something smells good.' Sandy glanced at the fire and kissed Mary on the cheek. ' You've been busy darlin', did you knock off early?'

'No darling,' I said, ' I arrived early, so I thought I would make dinner.'

He spun round, face ashen. ' Jesus Christ Jimmy!' he said hoarsely, beating his chest with one hand. ' Don't ever do that.' He stumbled forward, hand outstretched, but it was for me, no time for stiff formalities, and I gave him a hug. Questions rained on me thick and fast, but I was having none of it and ordered them to sit and eat. I ladled my stew onto plates and Mary produced a freshly baked loaf of bread from her shopping bag; cutting three thick slabs for the mopping-up ceremony.

I told them everything as we drank tea and smoked cigarettes.

'My oh my,' said Sandy, his eyes growing wider by the minute. ' So, it worked.'

'Like a dream my friend, everything was there, behind your wall. You did an excellent job!'

He coloured then. ' Away with you, it wasna just me Jimmy.' He reached for Mary's hand. ' It was us, me and my darlin' wife here; she was the brickie's mate.' I raised my teacup and we made a toast. ' To the brickie and his mate!'

Sandy stood and added some more coal to the fire.

'I bumped into Gwen's mum earlier, she said you were planning to go to the pictures tonight.'

'Aye,' he replied, taking his seat; but it's no longer a foursome but a fivesome.'

I shook my head, ' I don't think so, I'm a bit travel weary.'

He patted me on the shoulder, ' of course, we understand.'

I caught Mary looking at me quite intently, she coloured as our eyes met and turned to look at the glowing embers of the fire. Sandy meanwhile was on a high. ' It's fantastic news Jimmy; it looks like you will be able to transport anything back in those alcoves.'

'Well yes, so long as it fits in there.'

'You could even buy that painting,' said Mary, ' the one you saw when you were last here.'

' If it's still there; how long have I been gone?'

'Four and a half months,' said Sandy, ' give or take a day or two.'

' Now that is interesting, just over one month passed in my time.'

'Is that significant?' Mary asked.

'I have absolutely no idea,' I replied.

CHAPTER 15

I was lounging on the settee in the front room, listening to a big band number on the wireless, when I heard a knock at the front door. They were changing upstairs and I heard Sandy bellow from above.

'Get that will you Jimmy!'

I did, but with more than a little trepidation, and a host of golden butterflies were doing the fandango in my stomach. What should I say, would she still remember me after all this time, what if she walked passed me without even a hint of recognition?

I was reduced to Igor once again. Could feel the hump distorting my spine, could hear the bells clanging in the vast emptiness of my skull. At this point I would have loved to report that he was an ugly insignificant boil that I could Lance at will. Sadly, he was quite the opposite. Errol Flynn sprang to mind as he stepped briskly into the hall and handed me his overcoat, without meeting my smile. I was reduced to butler and hung his coat on the hall stand. He was a good two inches taller than me, and elegantly dressed for the evening. His high and haughty cheekbones seemed to have been chiselled from the finest Italian white marble, and he sported a thin moustache hanging over thinner lips.

Gwen paused as I helped her off with her overcoat, her dark brown eyes shone as she smiled up at me, but I detected something else, it was a smile with a question mark. Had I been gone so long, was she asking me why I was not there to comfort her when he died, when she needed my friendship most. Did she feel that I had abandoned her, even though we were just on tentative speaking terms?

'I heard you were back, its lovely to see you again,' she whispered.

I felt a sudden urge to pull her aside, to speak with her alone, as we had done in the heat of a summer's day on a bench in a busy thoroughfare, but

I didn't.

'It's lovely to see you again,' I replied.

Lance appeared at the door of the front room and stared at us. 'Don't hang about old thing, or you'll be catching your death.'

At that precise moment Sandy and Mary trotted down the stairs and ushered us all into the warmth of the front room, Mary closed the door behind her to prevent the loss of heat into the hallway. Lance seemed to remember that wearing your hat indoors is not good form, and handed it to me. I reached out and then let the hat flutter to the floor, I wasn't going to be caught out the second time.

'You've dropped your hat old man,' I said with some relish, and he bent and retrieved it. If looks could kill, then I would be toasting sinners' innards with the devil himself and we would be singing country music to the demented screams of tormented soul singers.

'Lance,' said Mary, 'this is Jimmy, an old friend of ours who will be staying with us for some time.'

He looked at me disdainfully, stroking his worm like moustache, 'my pleasure I'm sure.'

'Lancelot, that is an uncommon name,' I said brightly.

'Just call me Lance,' he hissed between perfectly formed clenched teeth.'

'So, what do you do for a living Lance?'

He lit a cigarette and crossed his legs, 'I'm in the numbers racket.'

I feigned shock and surprise in equal measures, 'so you're a gangster?'

Everyone, including Gwen burst into spontaneous laughter.

'What?' his face was now quite red, 'what on earth makes you think I am a gangster for goodness sake?'

Gwen leaned forward from her chair, a smile playing on her trembling lips, 'Lance is an accountant,' she said.

I slapped my temple with an open palm, 'an accountant, but of course, how silly of me. It's just that when you mentioned the numbers racket, you sounded like Bogart or Jimmy Cagney. Sorry old man, completely got the wrong end of the stick.'

He nodded curtly, 'It's a sort of slang term we use to describe our profession, anyway, apology accepted.' He glanced at his wrist watch, 'shouldn't we be making a move?'

Sandy looked up at the mantle clock, 'it does'na start till seven thirty.'

'So,' I said brightly, 'what's on at the pictures tonight?'

'It's a film called 'High Society,' said Mary, 'a musical I think.'

Sandy pulled a face.

'What's wrong Sandy?' I asked with a grin, 'musicals not to your taste?'

'Not really my wee dram Jimmy.'

'Well believe me this will be your wee dram, it's a film with class, starring Grace Kelly, Bing Crosby, Frank Sinatra and Satchmo himself. I've seen it lots of times and it never fails to entertain, you'll love it.'

I realised my mistake as soon as I saw Sandy position himself behind the settee, waving his arms and shaking his head like a man doing the St Vitus Dance. Mary just stared at me, one hand concealing her mouth, and Gwen appeared to be studying me with a frown, as if she could not quite work out what planet I was on, and who could blame the poor bewildered girl. Lancelot was quickly on my case. 'Really, and here was I thinking it was a new film that has just been released.'

Mary came to my rescue, 'I imagine that it was released earlier in London.'

'Indeed,' I added rather too quickly, 'and I found it so entertaining that I sat through three showings.'

Lancelot lit another cigarette, and blew a curling spiral of smoke dramatically. 'Forgive me for doubting you, but it seems to me that seeing a film three times, does not constitute 'lots of times', he spat contemptuously.

Sandy was in quick as a flash. 'Well it does to me, once I've seen a film then that is it.'

'I'm the same', said Mary. She smiled at me then, rather mischievously I thought.

I detected a flash of annoyance as Lance listened to the lame excuses from my defence team. He stared balefully at me before checking his watch again, 'I think we should be leaving.'

'Aye,' said Sandy, 'I think we should, are you sure you won't come with us Jimmy?'

Lance appeared about to explode, 'he's seen it three times for god's sake!'

I grinned, ' Lancelot is right, you young things go and enjoy yourselves, I'll just sit by the fire on my own and think of you all out there enjoying yourselves.'

Mary reached out an arm, 'oh Jimmy, I can't bear the thought.'

I grinned at her, 'I'm only kidding kid, truth is that I am bushed and looking forward to a bit of peace and quiet, so go.' I saw them to the door, watched as they donned wellies, hats and coats, and then crunched down the garden path, leaning into each other, arms linked for extra support. The gate clicked, the chatter muted but jolly, and I waited. Gwen looked back at me then, just fleetingly, but it was enough.

I was exhausted and retired to my room, lying fully clothed on my bed, arms folded behind my head. But sleep was a stranger. The sound of stamping feet and laughter woke me in an instant. and I swung into a sitting position on the bed. I looked at the wall clock, it was ten thirty-five. I could hear them gather around the hall stand, kicking off snowy boots, and discarding hats, coats and gloves. Suddenly Gwen laughed aloud, and my heart beat a tattoo on my rib cage.

'It was so romantic,' said Gwen with an audible sigh, ' and Grace Kelly is so beautiful, don't you think?'

Aye, she's a bonny lass,' said Sandy, 'but I still would'na swap her for my lassie.'

The girls laughed.

'And I would not swap you for Frank Sinatra darling, unless of course he came calling with flowers and sang below my window, then, well who knows?'

They all laughed then.

'Well there's a fine thing, I pledge my undying love for my wife, and she tells me that she is thinking about running off with a yank.'

I stood and stretched, smiling at the laughter below, and walked out onto the landing, as I heard them disappear into the warmth of the kitchen.

'Jimmy must have gone to bed,' said Sandy, 'but he was right, it was a very classy film.

Lancelot's voice was instantly piercing, acerbic. 'Even so, there is something odd about him, something I can't quite put my finger on yet.'

I took a seat on the top step.

'Mary's voice was calm and soothing, 'Jimmy can be a little eccentric sometimes, but he is a good man with a good heart.'

Lancelot was less than convinced. 'His speech is a bit odd, and he appears to be other worldly, as if he has lost something.'

'He's an acquired taste and that's for sure, but given time I'm sure you would warm to him.' Sandy's voice was warm and placating.

'Well I'm sorry, but I just do not like him, did you see how he made me look a fool by not taking my hat?'

I detected a change of tone in Mary's voice, there was a hint of ice and steel. 'You must remember that Jimmy is a guest in our home Lance, not the butler.'

'Yes,' I whispered from the god's, ' you go girl!'

There was a pause, long enough for me to light a cigarette and lean forward from my perch, I felt that something important was about to occur, something life changing, and I was not disappointed.

I imagined that Lancelot leaned towards Gwen as he spoke. ' Gwen darling, if we have a future together, any chance of tying the old knot. Then I must say to you now, that you must not have any dealings or conversations with that man. When you promise to respect and obey on that happy day, I ask you now to respect and obey this simple request.'

The cigarette stuck to my lips as my fingers slipped down to the glowing tip. I almost cried out in pain, but didn't. I just blew on my finger and licked.

When Gwen started to speak her voice was steady and clear. ' I confess that I have a soft spot for Jimmy.' There was a pause as she seemed to collect her thoughts. 'I know very little about him, but in our brief encounters he has always made me smile. He made me laugh out loud, even on my darkest day.' I raised a triumphant arm in the darkness and pulled an invisible toilet chain, with a silent cry of...yeees!

'When I left the hospital as a widow, I met him by pure accident. In fact, I hardly recognised him at first sight, and he told me a story about his close encounter with fishes.'

My blood ran as cold. ' Not the fish story Gwen,' I pleaded in a whisper as one would whisper a prayer to the giant cod in the sky. I retreated to the toilet and released the stub of my cigarette. If she tells them the fish story then I am deader than a dab hooked on hooks. I was, therefore, more than a little surprised when I heard a ripple of laughter below. I returned to my perch, intrigued.

Sandy was the first to speak, 'that's a fine and funny tale, and that's for sure.'

Lancelot however was less than impressed,' I don't believe it, you're all laughing like it's one big joke, but the man is a liar!'

'Don't you understand Lance?' It was Gwen's voice now, strong and passionate. 'I hardly know you, and yet you are talking about wedding bells.'

There was another moment of silence, and I craned my neck from the perch.

'Let me make something abundantly clear, I thought I liked you, but I was mistaken, and I certainly have no intention of marrying you.'

If I could have craned any more, then I would have been a fully paid up member of the Crane family

'I did not believe his story for one minute,' she continued, 'but it doesn't matter. I was at my lowest ebb when it seemed to me that there was no prospect of a future on this planet, and Jimmy threw me a lifeline.'

'Steady on old girl,' said Lancelot in an almost pleading tone.

She was on a roll. 'I am not an 'old girl'. Her voice was trembling and I felt an urge to vault down the stairs, smack Lancelot in the kisser, and pull her into my arms, but I didn't.

I nodded vigorously in the darkness. 'Good on yer girl,' I whispered, 'you tell the little shit!'

'Gwen,' it was Mary's voice now, soft but urgent, 'before you go love, I have to tell you that when Jimmy arrived at our doorstep, he looked an absolute mess, didn't he Sandy?'

'Aye he did, and he did'na smell too clever either.'

'Indeed, and what was that awful stink husband of mine?'

'Why as I recall, it was a distinctly fishy kind of stink. Not, I hasten to add a salty fresh fish kind of stink, but more like a fish gone orf.'

'It was not very pleasant, was is Sandy?'

'Most unpleasant, in fact we had to run a hot bath with lots of Mary's bath salts, and he soaked in there for a good hour.'

'At least,' Mary replied, 'it could easily have been two hours. His clothes, shoes, socks, everything was beyond redemption.'

'So we burned them,' said Sandy, 'in the dustbin.'

Now if a whole wing of flies had been passing at that moment, I have no doubt that they would have taken refuge in my gaping gob. There was a moments silence, broken sharply by a nasal hoot from Lancelot.

'My god, so it was true, what a sap, I tell you Gwen, you are well rid of that idiot!'

'Yes, I am well rid of that idiot as you say, but the only idiot I see, is the one I am looking at right now.'

'Go for it girl,' I whispered, ' and give him a slap from me.'

Gwen lead the way as they appeared in the hallway, and I slipped back into the shadows of the landing, my back against the wall, but I could still see them through the bannister rails.

'At least let me walk you home, once you've had a good night's sleep, you will realise that I was right all along old thing.'

Gwen threw on her coat and pulled a woollen hat over her long auburn hair, peering into the hall stand mirror and ignoring him completely.

'Once I have had a good night's sleep, I will awake, and you Lancelot will be nothing more than an unpleasant memory.' She then pulled some leather gloves from her pocket and slid them on, sidestepping the idiot, and hugged Mary and Sandy in turn.

Then a strange thing happened; as she turned to face the door. She looked back, up the stairs, where there was only darkness, and me, pressed against a floral papered wall. It was a quick searching look that made the hairs on the back of my neck stand to attention. And then she was gone in a whisper of winter air, and a cotton-picking flurry of snowflakes.

***

It was a new day, Mary and Sandy had gone to work, and I was out the door quicker than a casual winter sneeze, feet crunching on fresh snow. I urgently needed a winter overcoat and headed in the direction of uncles once more. I flipped up the collar of my summer coat, but it was not enough to keep out the winter chill. I was therefore thankful that I had taken time to fill up on some hot porridge that Mary had left for me.

The bell tinkled softly as I entered that familiar place once more. I stamped on the doormat and looked up to see a very thin old lady behind the counter. She was studying a piece of jewellery through a brown Bakelite magnifier, clamped to her left eye. I noticed the swollen arthritic knuckles of her hands, and she had some difficulty keeping hold of the ring. The eyeglass fell expertly into the palm of her right hand, and she looked up, unsmiling. 'Buying or selling?'

'Oh buying, definitely buying.'

She nodded, stepped off the stool, and completely disappeared. 'Gentlemen's overcoats are over 'ere,' said a disembodied voice. Dispensing with the need to raise the counter flap, she emerged through the open counter door like a hobbit.

'It was that obvious?' I said, attempting to make some light conversation.

'Oh yes,' she replied without a backward glance. 'Anyone who steps out in this weather without a good winter coat is either on hard times, or a barmpot waiting for the men in't white coats.' She stopped and looked up at me quizzically, 'so which one are you?'

'Oh a barmpot,' I replied with a smile, 'definitely a barmpot.'

She cocked her head back and gave me a quizzical glance. 'Well tha's got a sense of humour, I'll give thee that.'

Her ancient smile told me everything I needed to know, it was honest, down to earth and frank. It was also obvious that she had never darkened a dentist's doorstep in her long life. The doorbell tinkled and she looked back. 'Well there you are, 'ave a look through 'em, and I'll be back in a tick.'

I flicked through the various coats of ages. Some appeared to have survived the battle of Waterloo, and others radiated a distinctive unwholesome smell. Mothballs seemed to be the weapon of choice, but it didn't really help. It may have deterred the moths, but the combined smells of mothballs and rank body odour, were less than appealing. I came across a navy-blue serge number, with big brass buttons and a gale force wind high collar, minus the aforementioned stink, and it fitted fine. I stepped back to admire myself in an elaborate Victorian mahogany cheval mirror, and caught a women in my reflected image of splendour, engaged in conversation with the hobbit, a man's suite laid out on the counter.

She glanced quickly in my direction and then appeared to relax. 'Now I'll be back Friday for it, otherwise there will be hell to pay if he finds it missing for the weekend.'

'That's fine missus,' the hobbit replied. She pinned a large cardboard label on the sleeve of the jacket and hung it on a low rail behind her. The woman scowled at me and hurried out into the snow. I must have looked perplexed, because the hobbit breathed a low laugh and resumed her perch on the high stool. 'Her husband works hard and drinks even harder,' she said quickly, in reply to my unspoken question. She gets what money she can on Friday, but come Monday and there's not a coin left.' She toyed with the eyeglass on the counter, 'you're not from around these parts, are you?'

'I am, but not for a long time,' I answered truthfully.

'They've got hungry mouths to feed, so they pawn their old man's suite. She knows he'll not miss it 'til Sunday, when it's time to dust it down and go to chapel an' pray for a better life. And then he will head for the pub and drink with his mates like he doesn't have a care in the world. He knows that when he gets home, 'is dinner will be on the table as usual. He doesn't care how it got there or how it was paid for, but woe betide the woman who fails to conjure up those magical meals.'

There was a fleeting moment of silence, as she looked me up and down. 'Coat fits well, tha looks reet dapper!'

I found it hard to smile in such dingy surroundings, especially after listening to her a tale of woe, but smile I did.

'It's fine, how much?'

She paused, her eyes doubled as a cash register, as she tried to place me in a basket. 'Ten bob', she said rather too quickly, it wasn't really a statement of fact, but more like a sounding board. I was supposed to barter, or better still to pull the coat from my back and cast in on the floor. 'Have you completely taken leave of your senses woman? Ten bob for a second hand moth eaten old coat, you must be mad!'

That is what I should have said. 'Fine, I'll take it.'

Her startled demeanour was reward enough for me. I pulled out the roll of notes in my inner breast pocket and peeled off a red ten-shilling note. Sandy's warning came to me a bit too late, ' for god's sake don't flash the cash around Jimmy. These are hard times and you have to be careful.'

The roll of one hundred pounds was pocketed instantly, but I was far too late.

'You'll be needing some winter boots,' she said quickly, the shoes you are wearing won't last five minutes in this weather.'

I had no intention of wearing dead man's shoes, shirts or long Johns thank you very much. 'Thank you but no, the overcoat's fine.' I made it to the door, pulled, and heard the tinkle of the bell.

Round one.

She made one final wistful plea to my departing roll of money. 'You should visit our shop next door sir, where there are fine examples of gold and silver jewellery.'

I stepped out and pulled the door behind me, fully intending to make my way into town. I paused, lit a cigarette and walked back around the corner. The shop was double fronted, with large display windows to left and right. An old Edwardian wooden porch jutted out onto the pavement, framing the main half glazed door.

The moment I stared at the array of jewellery on display, I was hooked. Sure, there were the usual suspects, poorly made 9ct gold rings and chains, boxed garish paste jewellery and knackered wrist watches, but there was treasure hiding amongst the dross.

My eyes were instantly drawn to a nineteenth century French carriage clock. I could see that it was fine quality, with beautiful enamelled decoration, and the brass button on the top told me that it was a quarter repeater. In other words, that it chimed on a gong every quarter. My eyes then rested on two gold pocket watches. One, a half hunter, and the other a larger and earlier Fusee movement example.

The bell announced my arrival.

Round two.

She appeared through a connecting glass panelled door, and seemed much taller then I recalled, as she beamed down at me. Obviously, the area behind the counter was raised, but it did the trick and took me completely by surprise. 'Hello again,' she said. ‘Welcome to our humble emporium.'

'I would like to see the carriage clock and the two gold pocket watches please.'

She nodded smartly and stepped from the counter, sliding back the rear access door to the window display, and retrieving the items for inspection.

'Could I have an eyeglass please?'

She reached under the counter and handed me a large magnifying glass. Now I am no expert on jewellery, but the enamel work on the carriage clock was quite exquisite. It was ticking away and when I pressed the brass button, the gong sounded sonorously. The price tag read eighteen guineas, and my heart missed a beat. The gold watches also passed inspection with flying colours. Both were fully marked 18ct and the half hunter also had a heavy fob and chain, and that too was stamped 18ct. The retail price for these three lovelies came to the princely sum of thirty-eight guineas.

'I like them, so what's the trade price? and I mean the very death.'

She slammed the counter with the palm of her hand, it made me and the clock jump. 'I knew it, as soon as I clapped eyes on thee I said to me sen, he's a dealer or I'm a fishmonger's wife!'

'Very perceptive of you.' I said with a smile.

'Coming in 'ere, buying second hand coats, clever, very clever, I like the cut of tha jib.'

'No, I did actually need a coat,' I protested.

She ignored my comments completely and tapped the side of her nose with a talon like forefinger. 'I've seen it all in 'ere over the years tha knows, but no matter. I'm 'appy to do business with the devil 'isself if it means the difference between running this place, or selling matches on Briggate.' She shook her head and peered at the items on the counter. 'Now let me see,' she squinted at the label on the clock first, emitting a deep sigh followed by an odd clucking sound. The process was then repeated with the watches, with much sighing and clucking as she scribbled on a note pad. 'These are all unredeemed pledges you understand, folk brings stuff in an' we give them a generous loan against the perceived value of the said item. Then we give them a more than generous amount of time to buy them back.'

I nodded, 'precisely, 'I added helpfully.

'An' when folk don't bother to reclaim their goods, then we are obliged to sell them on to cover our initial outlay, plus a modest profit.'

I smiled and nodded again, but this time I added some gravitas to my nod by sucking in my cheeks and exhaling meaningfully.

She peered at me then, possibly recalling the wad of notes that appeared and disappeared so quickly, that she questioned her own sanity. 'The pitiful mark up price,' she declared, consulting her scribbled notes, 'is forty one guineas.'

I feigned surprise, 'really, I made it thirty eight?'

She frowned and consulted her notes once more, then she slapped the table again and the clock rang out in protest. 'Why you are quite right young man, please forgive an old lady's oversight. Sums get 'arder when you're getting on in years.'

I smiled, ' not at all, I understand perfectly.'

'For the sake of a quick sale, I am of a mind to let you have them for...' She paused, her furrowed brow adding multiple wrinkles to established wrinkles, and I detected a clash of
forces working here. Too little trade discount and I could be walking out of the door. Too much...well, where's the profit in that?

'I can let you have them for thirty two guineas.' The words spilled from her lips like water gushing through a fissure in rocks, and then hung, suspended in the air, twisting into the form of a question mark. I realised that I held the upper hand, and could easily have played the hard man, but I didn't have the heart. I held out my hand with a grin. 'Excellent, we have a deal!'

She looked flabbergasted, her mouth opening and closing, like the sad old goldfish who leapt from a bowl into a brave new world, and cried hoorah! Only to discover his quite lamentable mistake as he breathed his last and thought, ' now that wasn't very clever old son.'

She nodded, wrapping my goods in sheets of thick brown paper, and placing them in a brown carrier bag with string handles. The bag had the name of the pawnbrokers printed on each side in Victorian style blue letters, along with the address and telephone number.

'When I was last here I was served by a gentleman.'

'Billy,' she said, 'he's at the gym.'

I paid her, 'the boxing gym?'

'Aye, is there any other kind of gym?'

I realised my error immediately. This was post war Britain, and people had more important things to occupy their time. Popping down the gym with the obligatory bottle of water, and paying a king's ransom to run on a running machine, wearing the latest 'designer' gym kit, was yet to come.

Her teeth glowered at me like ancient breakwater stumps on a stormy beach, when she smiled. 'So, I take it that you are a dealer in jewellery, on a buying trip like.'

'Not at all, these just caught my eye, I'm really a picture man, I buy and sell paintings.'

'Do you now? Well this could be your lucky day young man, as it so 'appens we 'ave a few pictures in't back room, if tha would care to 'ave a gander.'

'Absolutely.'

She headed for the far end of the long counter and once again disappeared from view, emerging beneath the fold up section and reaching for a large bunch of keys hanging from a broad leather belt. She then locked the shop door and turned a card that now read 'closed'.

'Can't be too careful tha knows,' she said, ' turn yer back an' thieves will pounce.'

'Very wise,' what about the other door?'

'Already locked,' she said over her shoulder, 'follow me.'

It was a large and dingy room, lit only by a solitary naked bulb. I almost walked into a full sized stuffed grizzly bear, and immediately apologised.

She cackled like one of the witches in Macbeth.

'Winston we call 'im,' she said, 'sometimes we chain 'im up outside when the weather is fine; to drum up trade like. The youngsters round 'ere love Winston.'

'I'm sure they do,' I replied, looking at the extended arms, and huge razor like claws. His bearing was almost regal, as he stared off into the distance with a frown, and for a moment I could see a bit of Winnie in there.

'Pictures are over 'ere.'

They were stacked against the wall, and I crouched and flicked through them. I was disappointed, half of them were prints or oleographs, and the rest fell into the category of pot boiler paintings. Original and old, just not very good.

I heard my knees crack as I stood, ' sorry, but there is nothing for me here.'

'Aye well, it's just as I thought, they came in with other stuff an' don't stand us at nowt. There's not a big demand for art round these parts.'

I was about to leave when I noticed a rather beautiful lady peering at me from the far end of the room. I knelt before her and gazed into her rather aloof blue eyes. It was a rather superb Regency portrait painting, and quite took my breath away. The old varnish had crackled and darkened the painting over the years, but it could not completely hide the breath-taking skill of the artist.

'There's five of 'em in total as I recall, all pictures of posh folk. They came as a job lot from one of the big 'ouses up in Headingley. We were called in to empty the attics.' She laughed, 'even the posh folk sometimes run out of brass tha knows.'

I said nothing as I studied the other four portraits stacked behind the lovely lady. Two were of gentlemen dating from the eighteenth century, wearing their finest silks, and one appeared to be a century earlier, and had a distinctly Italian School look about it.

'We send 'em off to auction eventually, an' sometimes they make good money, for the frames like.'

I nodded, scratching my chin, deep in thought. ' I must say I do like the frames, but I also like the portraits.'

She appeared taken aback, 'you do?'

I laughed, 'I know, who in their right mind would want to buy a painting of a complete stranger. Call me eccentric if you will, I just like them, so how much?'

I caught her on the back foot and she looked surprised. 'What, for all of them?'

I nodded and added my winning smile.

'Well now, let me see, as I said before the frames alone are very popular in the auctions like, so I couldn't let them go for less than...' I could almost see the pound notes registering in her eyes,' and I would expect that lot to fetch...what?'

She appeared to be appealing to me for some guidance.

'Absolutely,' I said. ' Three guineas if I'm not mistaken.'

Her poker-faced demeanour was quite admirable, but there was something in her body movement that told me, if she were alone she would now be doing a very lively jig.

'Delivered of course.' I added, explaining that I was staying just up the road. She spat on the palm of her hand and held it out for me to shake, which I did quite willingly. This was nineteen fifty six after all, a long time before 'elf an' safety had deemed that sharing spittle was somehow unhygienic I said goodbye to Winston, and we returned to the shop. I then wrote down my address on a piece of paper. She in turn filled out a bill of sale, only pausing to ask my name.

'Mr T. Traveller,' I answered.

CHAPTER 16

I left the gold watches and clock at home, it occurred to me that I had thought of my friend’s house as 'home'. It was a strong and contradictory notion, but that is how it felt, I could come and go as I pleased and it felt like home to me in this time.

Another bell announced my arrival and I was alarmed to see that the Atkinson Grimshaw was nowhere to be seen. He glided silently from the back workshop in his moonwalk slippers.

'Good morning sir, how may I help you?'

'Hello, I was in here a few weeks ago, and....'

He raised a hand, 'and you were looking at the Atkinson Grimshaw as I recall.' He offered a thin smile, ' I am blessed or some may say cursed with a photographic memory sir.' His deep piercing china blue eyes searching my face. 'It has been more than a few weeks I would venture.'

I felt a rush of blood to my face, ' yes you are probably right, how time flies.'

The corners of his mouth twitched, and then curled upwards, but the smile took a little longer to arrive. It was almost like witnessing someone who had forgotten how to laugh or smile, so painfully slow was the process.

He fixed me with an uncomfortable gaze, frowned and raised a finger to his cheek. He was so close now that I could smell stale red wine and something else, something almost herb like. I could only deduce that it was snuff, when I saw that his nostrils and moustache were stained a bright, almost luminous yellow.

To my relief he turned his back on me and glided towards the rear workshop, but not before indicating with one raised finger that I should follow, which I did, but with some feelings of trepidation. Then I saw it, the frame had been repaired and re-gilded, and it almost took my breath away.

'We have restored the frame in your absence.'

I smiled, running my fingers over the new gilding. ' You have done well; the gold leaf work is quite exceptional.'

'We only use the finest gold leaf, have done since father's day.'

I looked at him curiously, 'I'm sorry but I thought you were the sole proprietor here, but you said 'we'?'

He smiled the thinnest of smiles, not at me, but at the painting. 'I am not alone you know, far from it. I look after the gallery in the daylight hours, and Harry, my brother, maintains the restoration while the world sleeps. We meet of course, at breakfast time, to discuss matters appertaining to the business, and then he sleeps while I work, and I sleep when he works.'

'It sounds like a partnership made in heaven.'

'It has worked well enough since father passed on.'

Suddenly a telephone trilled on the shop counter. 'Damnation! He hissed, a look of contempt and annoyance on his face.

'My apologies sir.'

'Not at all, you must answer it.'

He looked at me then, with a haunted almost pleading question in his eyes. 'Must I, must I really? I think not, not today, or any other day come to think of it.' He glided away from the telephone at a fair rate of knots, but the black Bakelite telephone almost rocked in its cradle.

'Should I answer it?'

'Would you?' he whispered.

'What is the name of this establishment?'

'What?'

'The name of the gallery?'

He thought about it and slapped his forehead, 'Pearson and Sons.'

I picked up, 'Good morning Pearson and Sons, how may I help you?'

There was a pause as I nodded and smiled. 'Certainly sir, we have the finest selection of frames to suit your purpose, our business hours are eight thirty to five.' I paused and nodded, 'absolutely, we look forward to meeting you, goodbye.'

I placed the telephone back in its cradle, he looked astonished. 'That was a gentleman enquiring about a frame for a family portrait.'

He said nothing, his clenched hands still raised to his lips.

'They also wanted to know the hours of business, fortunately I had seen them on the door when I entered.'

He glided slowly towards me, 'you were magnificent sir, magnificent I say!'

'Thank you, but it's only a telephone, it's very easy really.'

'Yet you spoke so naturally, as if the gentleman was in this very room, so eloquent.'

I leaned on the counter. 'What is your name?'

'Walter,' he said.

'And how long have you had the telephone Walter?'

He looked at me defensively, 'a while, it was Harry's idea. We should modernise he said, we should move with the times.' He looked at the telephone with undisguised loathing and pent up anger. 'It was alright for him, working nights when the beast is silent, but I had to suffer its shrill cry all day every day, today I forgot to leave it off the hook as I usually do.'

'Have you ever attempted to pick it up and answer?'

He nodded, 'I did once out of curiosity and a ghostly voice whispered 'hello' in my ear, most unnerving.'

'Did you answer?'

'I did not!' he said heatedly, 'I had no desire to speak with the devil.'

'Well I answered your phone and it was not Satan looking for someone to frame, but one of the potential customers you have lost because of your refusal to talk to them.'

He stood like an errant schoolboy, but I could see that he was still not convinced.

'Surely you used the public telephone boxes at some time?'

He shook his head, 'father forbade it, he said that all conversation should be done face to face, or if that were not possible, then write a letter, and in times of urgency one should send a telegram.' He paused, 'father was very strict, but he was still a good and god-fearing man, and we mourned his passing deeply. He told us that the new-fangled telephone was in fact a curse and not a boon, and that we should avoid it at all cost, as there was medical evidence that proved it could melt the brain over time.'

'When did your father die?'

He frowned for a moment, ' the third of August nineteen thirty nine.'

'Well things have moved on since then Walter, I could teach you, I can show you how to use the telephone. Or better still, let's wake Harry up and explain the situation?'

He stared at me, unblinking, 'I'm sorry, but that is out of the question, Harry is sleeping now and must not be disturbed.'

'Well then, I will teach you, Harry is quite correct, you must pick up the telephone, otherwise all that you and your brother and father have worked so hard to establish over the years could be lost. Do you understand?'

He appeared to relax a little, and nodded.

'So, I will be the customer and you will pick up the phone and talk to me, agreed?'

I was proud at the way he stood to attention and puffed out his chest. 'Very well, I am ready.'

There was a pause as I looked at him and inclined my head to the phone. 'Is that the telephone ringing?'

He appeared startled and stared at me with a combination of surprise and sheer panic. 'I hear nothing?'

I released a deeply audible sigh, ' I cannot teach you if you refuse to play, we are just pretending Walter.'

He produced a white linen handkerchief from his pocket and mopped his leaking brow.

'So, shall we try again?'

He nodded nervously.

'Why is that the telephone I hear ringing?'

The corner of his mouth twitched as he reached out, but failed to connect, and his hand began to shake. I snatched up the phone and put it to my ear. 'It's for you.'

'Me?' he replied faintly, 'are you quite sure?'

'Absolutely,' I thrust the phone into his hand, and he tentatively placed it to his ear.

'Yes,' he said, with a trembling voice, 'who is this?'

'Hello,' I said loudly, 'is that Pearson and Sons?'

He clutched the phone like his life depended upon it, and in a way, it did. ' Yes, it is.'

'Excellent, I was admiring a fine Scottish landscape painting displayed in your window last week, and I was wondering if it was still for sale?'

I watched as he visibly relaxed, and his fingers lost their tortuous grip on the phone. He was now a man in his own element. 'We have several Scottish landscapes sir, but I believe that the one you refer to has a group of highland cattle grazing in the foreground. The painting is signed with a monogram in the lower right corner and dated 1864. It is without doubt a fine original oil painting on canvas, and is presented within its original ornate gesso gilt frame.'

'Couldn't have put it better myself, yes that's the one. Would you be so kind as to arrange a viewing for myself and my good lady wife?'

'That will be my pleasure sir, may I take your name please?'

I clapped my hands crying bravo as he placed the phone back in its cradle. He looked flushed, the rising blood painting his cheeks pink in an instant.

'Well done Walter, just try to remember where you are when someone comes calling. Why this is Pearson and Sons! I cried rather theatrically, so your opening greeting must always be.

Good morning or afternoon, Pearson and Sons, how may I help you? Announce the name proudly, it is after all a successful business established by your father, from humble beginnings if I'm not mistaken.'

'You are not mistaken sir, my parents arrived on these shores with just the clothes on their backs. Diligent hard work and a determination to succeed was all they had to offer, but it was more than enough. Sadly, mother died when we were still children, and it was left to father to bring us up on his own.'

He paused for a moment of reflection, 'he was a strong man, a spiritual man, a man of energy and ambition. Traits that he instilled in his two sons, with love, tempered on occasions by a fist of iron.'

The telephone rang.

He stared at it mutely.

It rang again.

'You should answer that Walter.'

'Should I?'

I nodded as his hand hovered, beads of sweat bursting from his forehead as he picked up. 'Good morning, Pearson and Sons, how may I help you?'

His voice was steady and confident, and I sat on a stool, otherwise I could easily have fallen over.

'Certainly sir, we stock a fine selection of readymade frames for the discerning buyer, or you can choose from our extensive stock of mouldings and timbers.'

He paused and smiled, ' a portrait photograph of your son in uniform, why of course, it would not only be an honour, but we also offer a discount service for portraits in military attire.' He paused and listened, 'it is my pleasure sir, we are happy to be of service, good morning.' He set the telephone down, a slow smile rising and setting as he stared at me, eyes widening in disbelief.

I clapped my hands, 'by George you did it Walter!'

He mopped his forehead with the linen handkerchief, ' I did, didn't I.'

I laughed, ' you most certainly did.'

He stepped back then, his eyes never leaving mine. 'Who are you really sir, are you an angel sent among us?'

'Sorry to disappoint you but I am just a mere mortal, here to buy a painting.'

‘ Oh, the painting is yours’, he said quickly, 'how could I charge you a farthing when you have greatly improved my life in an instant?'

I shook my head, ' I am here to buy the Grimshaw at your full asking price, plus the cost of the excellent restoration work on the frame.' I pulled out the roll of notes and counted out forty two pounds, placing them on the counter. ' These are lean times Walter, and you and your brother have a living to make.'

I helped myself to a sheet of paper from a steel ringed pad on the counter, and wrote down my details. 'I will require you to deliver the painting to this address, plus any paperwork of how you acquired the painting, and any information you may possess as to the provenance.'

As I finished writing and looked up he was still studying me silently. 'Now,' I said brusquely, 'as to the cost of the frame restoration and delivery...'

He stopped me right there, arms outstretched, as if he were defending himself from a rogue assailant. 'No, please, I will not hear of it, the restoration and delivery are free, upon this at least I do insist.'

And so the deal was done.

'Who shall I make your receipt out to sir?'

'Mr T. Traveller,' I replied.

I watched as he filled out the bill of sale in elegant copper script with a blue steel nib pen. He dipped the pen into a cut glass inkwell on the counter, and completed the task by applying a sheet of blotting paper to his finished work.

'There is something I wish to confess before you leave,' he said without looking up. He then folded the bill of sale carefully and slid it across the counter. 'My brother is not sleeping,' he said softly, 'he died during the war...he was only seventeen. I am completely alone Mr Traveller, and anything I may have said to the contrary is a complete fabrication, a lie, for which I apologise.'

Our eyes met, and for the briefest of moments I sensed his loss, almost felt his pain.

'You must have been very close.'

'We were inseparable,' he sighed wistfully, 'and even joined up together on the same day. I was a lucky bugger and caught some shrapnel in my legs, so the war was over for me.'

I felt so moved and completely inadequate at that moment. Here was a very private man telling me, a stranger, about momentous events in his past, that he had probably kept locked away in a box for many years.

'Sometimes I feel that he is still here with me, I can hear his giddy laughter as we larked about in the workshop, placing our heads in picture frames and pulling daft faces, much to fathers utter dismay.' He seemed to search and then find some composure, and gave me a shy wintery smile. 'I'm sorry, I should not have burdened you with my troubled thoughts.'

'Oh yes you should Walter, and if I were a betting man, which I am, then I would wager that you feel a little better for it.'

He nodded quickly and turned his head to look away. A moment passed before he found his voice and spoke again. 'I have never spoken out like this to another soul, and now here I am blubbering away to a complete stranger, whatever must you think of me?'

'I think you should get yourself out of here Walter, for one or two evenings a week at least, put on your best bib and tucker and go dancing.'

He stepped back and stared at me in alarm. 'Dancing?' he shook his head and retreated to the safety of the workshop. 'Dancing indeed, what with my feet? why I have never heard such a thing.'

'Do you ever venture outside, see what's going on in the world?'

He fidgeted, 'of course I do, why I go to the shops to buy groceries and other necessary provisions.' There was a pause as he looked wistfully towards the shop window. 'I confess that I have never danced Mr Traveller. Our parents were strict Presbyterian's who viewed all public entertainment as coarse, frivolous and downright sinful.'

'Do you believe that?'

He looked down at the floor and shook his head slightly. 'I do remember a time when I bunked off with my best friend Albert, and we saw a show at the City Varieties...it was bloody marvellous!' he raised a hand to his mouth, 'forgive my French.'

I shrugged, 'consider yourself forgiven, I've heard worse at a nun's convention.'

He looked shocked, 'you have?'

'No, not really.'

He ignored the interruption and continued on his journey down memory lane. 'It was so funny that we almost split our sides with laughter, it was quite magical.'

'When did all this happen?' I said, sounding like a poor man's shrink.

'I was sixteen, did I tell you that I went with my best friend Albert?' He smiled fondly at the memory, but the smile lingered in the sunshine for the briefest of moments and then froze in an icy wasteland.

'Father overheard our conversation, as we laughed and giggled like boys do.'

'What did he do Walter, did he punish you?'

'Yes,' he said, and sighed. He beat me with a broad leather belt that was kept in the kitchen cupboard for such a purpose, but I was the wrongdoer and therefore I was punished, it was only right.'

'What of your best friend, did you ever see him again?'

'I was working in the gallery, and the time for childish play had passed, there was no time for such frippery and foolishness anymore.' He was silent then, head bowed, cheeks flushed, avoiding eye contact.

'In your own words you are now alone, your parents and your brother Harry are gone, so perhaps it is now time for some frippery and foolishness.'

He stole a look at me, 'do you think so?'

'We only pass this way once my friend, and it's an interesting world out there. It would be a shame to watch it all pass by without actually taking part, don't you think?'

'I'm not dancing,' he said defensively.

'Forget dancing, go to the theatre instead, take in a film at the cinema, visit the art gallery, the parks with their glorious flowers and towering trees, and the City Varieties is still a place of magic, you should try it.'

'Do you really think so?'

'Absolutely, you don't have to decide right now, but I will be checking in from time to time to see how you progress.'

The tiny bell rang overhead as I made my exit.

'Just think about it, think of the possibilities.' Then I was gone before he could respond, but I imagined that I had planted a seed. Whether that seed would grow and flourish, rested on the tired and slender shoulders of a very lonely man.

CHAPTER 17

Finally, I ventured into the town centre, and I was suddenly thrust into a merry go round of surprises and pleasure. The first surprise occurred when I slipped in the snow and landed ignominiously on my arse. It seemed that the witch had been right after all, and my first port of call was a shoe shop, where I purchased a sturdy pair of winter boots. Crunching through the snow with confidence was quite exhilarating and brought a smile to my face. It was far busier and certainly much noisier than I had imagined, and as I stood and stared, I immediately realised that the closure of certain roads to make way for pedestrian precincts, and the introduction of 'one way' streets, had calmed things down in my time. Now it was just ordered chaos.

Trams sparked and groaned, vintage cars of every description blew horns at every opportunity, coughing and spluttering at traffic lights. They vied with horse and carts, from magnificent drays pulling colourful open carts loaded with huge barrels of Tetley's beer, to the more humble milk carts, delivery men and flat open rag and bone carts, pulled by a single horse and loaded with junk. I stood and watched as people picked their way through this mad traffic with casual aplomb, my open mouth was in fly catching mode once more.

Most of the buildings were familiar to me, but the goods in the shop windows were less so. One such shop had a fine display in wooden cased wireless and television sets. I admired an array of huge television cabinets, in assorted shiny veneers, topped with tiny grey blank screens. Wireless sets of every shape and form, with large dials and decorative screens inviting me to Luxembourg and other exotic destinations.

Tea rooms also seemed to be the order of the day, a popular destination for gentlemen in starched collars and ties, and ladies wearing large hats, some festooned with exotic feathered plumage, or assorted fruit, the latter of which I presumed was not freshly picked. I was however ill prepared to see just how many lovely old theatres had disappeared over the years. I counted three in my short sojourn of the centre, and not one of them had survived.

I paused at a large gent's outfitters called Montague Burton's, and peered at what the man about town was wearing. Certainly, the mannequins were interesting. Humphrey Bogart absent in the line-up, but there was a David Niven lookalike alongside a smart and exceedingly handsome chap who looked suspiciously like his chum Errol Flynn. The clothes were dull and conservative, but hey, this is the nineteen fifties, I reminded myself.

I bought several of everything, the complete ensemble for the cad about town. I had the hard cash and felt a need to cast off the dead man's clothing purchased at uncles. I did have personal issues with two items, the underpants were seriously big, and the trousers even more so. The underpants I could live with, as they could possibly double as a 'hammock' in the garden when I returned to my own time. The trousers however were more of a challenge. They seemed so big and baggy, with a crutch that appeared to start just above the knees and end in the mid chest area, consequently there was also an annoying number of buttons. I could only assume that the waistcoat was invented to cover up the cavernous crutch.

I had intended a languid liquid lunch and a little more time tourist sightseeing, but I was now so overburdened with baggage that I decided to head for home. That's when I saw him, his dirty grey matted long hair framing a flaming ruby red face. He sat on a bench, clutching a half empty bottle of cider, and trembling beneath a paper-thin blazer that had seen better days. I was wearing my brand new Burton's winter coat, and placed my shopping beneath the snow laden trees. I fished out the coat I had bought that very morning from Uncle's.

'Here, try this on.'

He peered up at me, his deeply veined and mottled bulbous nose twitching. Sad, red, piggy eyes tried to focus but failed. He then slid his bottle out of my reach, like a mother protecting a baby. 'Fuck off!' he growled. I shrugged and pulled it away but he reached out surprisingly

quickly and touched the coat tenderly.
'Try it on.'
He lurched to his feet, swaying like a sailor after consuming an incoming tide of ale., and grabbed the coat. He was far too gone to place his arms into the sleeves, so elected to throw it over his shoulders, and collapse back upon the bench once more, pulling the coat around him. It seemed to do the trick as his shivering abated. I picked up my shopping and looked down at him.
'Merry Christmas!'
He peered up at me again, and for just a moment I imagined that I saw the individual who once upon a time had lived a life. Someone who had once loved and been loved, had laughed and cried with family and friends, and who had once stood proudly as a man. But sadly that person had now gone, and there was no going back from the chasm of despair lurking within a half empty bottle of cider.
'Fuck off!' he said.
I did, with a grin and salutary shake of the head, 'charmed I'm sure.'

The garden gate clicked behind me; I paused and looked up at the house. There was a thaw in the air, crooked finger- like icicles hung from the gutters of the bay window, now dripping and dissolving the wet snow beneath. I placed my bags in the porch, stepping back into the winter wonderland, and found myself staring at the ancient standing stone again. The urge to walk over and run my hands over its rough surface proved irresistible.
'Hello.'
The voice was soft but loud enough to pull me away from the stone. I looked quickly down at the gate and the street beyond, but saw nothing.
'Hello there.' It was a whisper from the snow laden hedge dividing our two gardens.
It was now late afternoon, daylight was fading fast and the gas lamp outside the fishmonger's shop popped into life. I stepped into the garden and peered through the dividing hedge. Suddenly I detected some movement through the tangled leaves and dripping snow.
His piercing blue eyes studied me, like I was a marginally interesting passing butterfly.

'Hello there.' I raised my voice, thinking the old duffer might be a little deaf. 'My name is Jimmy, I'm a friend of Mary and Sandy, your neighbours,' I added slowly.

'No need to shout young man, I'm not deef tha knows.'

I was instantly put in my place.

'Smashing couple, couldn't wish for better neighbours, an' I've seen a fair few come an' go over't years.'

'I'll bet, and you have,' I said, 'so, how are you?'

'Cold young un, an' getting colder, time I was back indoors.'

'Of course, it was nice meeting you.'

'Aye, well never mind all that bollocks, I should like to have some words with thee, does dinnertime tomorrow suite thee?'

I nodded dumbly, 'dinnertime is good for me,' but then I frowned, 'what time is dinnertime exactly?'

I detected a look of alarm and then pity in those sad old eyes, 'Twelve O' clock sharp young man'

'In the afternoon?'

'Aye, in the afternoon', he frowned at me, 'tha's not the sharpest tool in't box, if tha' dunt mind me saying like.'

I smiled, ' I don't mind at all, it wouldn't be the first time, and I'm sure it won't be the last.'

He retreated in the gathering gloom, 'aye well, think on young man.'

'But I'm not sure what we have to discuss?'

I heard the door open with a judder, ' time travel, we are going to talk about time travel,' he said, and then I heard the door close and a key turn in the lock.

That evening we sampled the delights from the local chippie, care of yours truly, cod, chips and mushy peas, and later we relaxed in the front room, before a coal fire, listening to soft music on the radio, a new-fangled name for the wireless I learned from Sandy.

'So,' I said casually, 'did you enjoy the film?'

Mary laughed softly, 'it was a real treat Jimmy, you should have come with us.'

Sandy nodded, 'while I'm not a man for musicals I must say it was a fine film.'

I nodded, looking into the heart of the flames, 'and Gwen and what's-his-name, did they enjoy it?'

There was a pause long enough to become an Elephants pregnancy., I heard everything actually.'

Mary's eyes widened in alarm.

'I heard you all return, and fully intended to join you, but then I heard that I was the subject of your conversation, so I held back and took a seat on the stairs.'

'So, you heard everything?' said Sandy.

I smiled and nodded into the flames, 'I did, is that man a complete arsehole or what.'

Suddenly they burst out laughing, Mary instinctively raised a hand to her mouth and rocked back in the chair. While Sandy's shoulders shook so violently I thought he was going to have a fit.

'A complete arsehole,' he spluttered, 'now that is what I would call a perfect description.'

I sat grinning into the fire as they tried and failed to compose themselves.

'For goodness sake you two, it was not that funny.'

Sandy slapped me on the shoulder and produced a hankie to dab away his tears of laughter. 'It is when I tell you that his name is not Lance at all.'

'Really?'

'His real name is Wilfred Higginbottom,' Sandy wept, dabbing at his eyes,' everybody knows it, except you and Gwen. He just likes to be called Lance.'

I looked at Mary and she nodded in confirmation. 'So when you insisted on calling him Lancelot,' she said between giggles, 'he was less than pleased.'

I stood and headed for my room, with a purpose. Listening to their spluttered laughter brought a smile to my face as I climbed the stairs. When I returned with the suitcase it became suspiciously quiet. They fidgeted in their seats, and there was a moments silence before Mary raised a finger and pointed at the case.

'He's not in there is he Jimmy?'

They both fell into hysterical laughter once more.

'Sadly not.' I snapped the suitcase open. 'Nope, he is not in here, however I do spy with my little eye a suitcase full of money.'

Mary hiccupped but still managed a singularly simple question, 'money?'

I tipped the contents onto the table, and they fell like neat paper bricks. Each brick represented one hundred pounds. The larger bricks were the red ten shilling notes, then the pound notes followed by the five pound notes. As the bundles dropped onto the table top, they both rose to their feet and stared. Sandy reached out and touched one of the bricks. 'May I?'

I smiled, 'surely, be my guest'.

He picked up a bundle of the ten shilling notes. 'So how much am I holding Jimmy?'

'One hundred pounds.'

Mary gasped, 'how much is on my table?'

'Five thousand pounds, give or take. I spent some today.'

Wrinkles formed on her forehead as she attempted to absorb the figure, looking to Sandy for help. Sandy placed the bundle back on the table, 'Jesus Jimmy, I've never seen so much money.'

I grinned, 'this is nothing, a drop in the ocean, this is just the beginning.' I dropped the money back into the suitcase, leaving three remaining bundles as I snapped the suitcase shut.

'Those three are for you, for my food and lodgings, not forgetting the lashes of eight-year-old Babycham.'

Immediately they both physically shrank away from me, like I was a visiting madman from a leper colony.

'No Jimmy, we canna take your money!'

Mary nodded in agreement, 'It's too much, far too much.'

'It's only three hundred quid for goodness sake, in my time the well-heeled spend that on lunch.'

Sandy shook his head, 'aye, well that may be so, but in the here and now three hundred pounds is an awful lot of money.'

I looked at them in silence for the briefest of moments. ' I bought that painting today, along with some others. They will swell my bank account by several thousand pounds when I sell them in my time.' Of course, that would not be possible without the bricklaying skills of your good selves. In fact, I would go as far as to say that as you are willing partners in this enterprise, and as such, you should also reap the rewards.'

I leaned forward and pushed the cash across the table, ' you must understand that this is not a gift, this is payment for services rendered.'

Sandy scratched at a day's stubble on his chin, 'services rendered?'

'As the paintings are delivered they will have to be placed in the time capsules. I may or may not be here to help you, but when I do leave, I will count on your bricklaying skills once more.'

Sandy lit a cigarette and nodded, 'that's nothing, I can do that in a day.'

'Then we slap on the whitewash,' said Mary.

He grinned, 'and she does a grand job make no mistake, considering that she ends up wearing most of it.'

'Then of course I have to mention the mere fact that you literally pulled me in off the street, and gave me sanctuary when I was sick, and a stranger in a strange land. You allowed me to come and go as I please in your own home. You made me more than welcome, so much so, that I feel like part of the family; and that my friends is something that money just can't buy.'

Suddenly Mary rushed around the table, throwing her arms around me and placing a big smacker on my cheek. 'You are a member of our family,' she said. Then Sandy came over all weepy and blew his nose loudly into a man sized off white linen handkerchief. Suddenly aware that he was the focus of attention as we smiled at him, he changed tack in an effort to divert any impression that he had become quite emotional. 'I think I might be coming down with a wee cold,' he said.

We celebrated in style, by gathering around the open fire, and drinking tea. Sandy then discovered another bottle of malt Babycham, which was added to the tea as a healthy alternative to sugar.

I told them about my day, showing them the watches and clock from uncles, and then the story of my time at the art gallery. Mary laughed softly, her hazel brown eyes wide in the reflection of the dancing flames. 'He sounds like a rather eccentric character.'

Sandy agreed as he swirled his scotch tea, 'he sounds like a man uncomfortable in his own time.'

I looked at him quickly, ' do you know Sandy, you have an uncanny gift for putting your finger on the button.' It could have been the heat from the fire, but I thought that he blushed, an awkward almost

embarrassed look on his face.
Mary sat back in her chair and reached out until their fingers entwined. 'He has always had the gift for seeing folk the way they are.'

He shook his head and smiled sheepishly, 'away with your blethering woman.'

CHAPTER 18

It was just after 9am, I had worked up a decent lather and slid the safety razor down my cheek when the doorbell rang. My head jerked and I nicked myself, swearing softly. A small mushroom of dark red blood appeared and blossomed in the foam. I took the stairs two at a time and threw the front door open. The two young men wore brown linen coats, one looking at a clipboard in his hand, and the other staring at me, mouth agape.

'Good morning sir, we have a painting for Mr T. Traveller...' He looked up from the clipboard then, and fell silent.

'Excellent,' I said, and stepped aside as they carried the painting into the hallway. I was pleased to see that the painting was tied between two sheets of plywood as they rested it against the wall.

He held out the clipboard and pen, 'if you will just sign here sir.'

I signed.

'We are also here to assist with the hanging of the painting if that is required?'

'Thank you but that will not be necessary,' I replied, and closed the door as they walked down the garden path. I heard some banter and laughter as the gate clicked behind them.

The doorbell rang again and a thought suddenly occurred to me, did I sign my own name, or Mr Travellers? The part of my brain that controls bullshit was now in overdrive.

She looked absolutely gorgeous. Her long auburn hair was tucked under a colourful woollen hat, as she looked at me with those mesmerising bright blue eyes. I was startled, she was more than startled and took a step back. She looked shocked and I was equally shocked at how shocked she looked. Then she laughed, and for the briefest of moments I was Julie Andrews, dancing in an alpine wonderland and singing 'The Hills are Alive.'

'Gwen, how lovely to see you again, please come in.'

She pointed a finger at her chin. 'You look like you have just survived a visit to Sweeney Todd's.'

I stepped back then and caught my reflection in the hall stand mirror. The shaving foam was beginning to dissolve, it now resembled a dripping beard of ice cream. On one side, vanilla, and on the other, raspberry ripple. I felt a rush of blood to my face and groaned. 'Sorry, I was shaving when the delivery men called with the painting, and I nicked myself.'

She raised an inquisitive arched eyebrow, 'you bought a painting?'

I nodded like the village idiot, 'an Atkinson Grimshaw no less, it is a very fine work.'

She smiled vaguely and followed my glance to the plywood parcel leaning against the wall.

'It sounds...' she struggled to find the right word, 'it sounds lovely, and quite expensive.'

I shook my head and sprayed vanilla and raspberry ripple in every direction. She stepped back, but too late to avoid looking like a paint ball victim. She retrieved a small blue linen handkerchief from her handbag and dabbed at the spots on her frock. I could have quite happily died then, should have died then, should have collapsed at her exquisite feet and drowned in my own shaving cream.

'Sorry, maybe now is not a good time, I should finish shaving.'

'No,' she replied firmly, 'now is the perfect time, and yes you should shave, and in the meantime, I will make us both a cup of tea.'

A clown stared back at me in the steamy bathroom mirror, all that was missing was the classic pronounced tear drop hanging on my cheek. Once again, I had made a complete fool of myself in front of the woman I was slowly learning to love and loose.

It was time to step up the ante. I shaved so close that I was in a whisker of never having shaved before. I was the teenage virgin shaver, you could have brushed my manly jaw with a silk stocking and it would have slid to the floor with a whisper. I then removed the brand new white shirt from its box, and carefully removed the numerous steel pins hidden within. Some so hard to find, that I assumed it was packed by someone who probably had more than a passing interest in watching men bleed. The suite and new shoes completed my ensemble, and I entered the kitchen a new more confident man.

'My oh my,' she said, pouring the tea, 'you look quite the man about town now.'

I smiled and sat, 'I needed some new clothes, the stuff from uncles was fine for a while, but wearing dead man's shoes has never really appealed to me.'

She said nothing and slid the cup and saucer across the table. I drank deeply, aware that she was studying the new me. I must have coloured and looked quickly at my new attire. 'You disapprove,' I said. 'Have I chosen badly? This is the latest fashion,' I burbled, 'the correct style of clothing for this time.'

The cup had almost reached her blood red full lips, 'for this time?' she echoed with a curious smile.

I reached for the sugar bowl as a delaying tactic, while I collected my thoughts from my scrambled egg of a brain. Normally I took two, but these were exceptional circumstances, and I counted six before I was back on track. 'of my life,' I said too quickly,

She threw back her head and laughed softly, 'why you sound so old Jimmy.'

'I've had a hard life, on the outside I may appear to be a man in his prime, but on the inside, there is a pensioner trying to remember where his dentures are.'

I offered her a cigarette but she declined with a shake of her head.

'Do you mind?'

'Not at all, I love the smell of tobacco, it always takes me back to a time when I was a child, and my dad would cradle me in his arms when I cried. The smell of his nicotine stained fingers was a comfort to me, a place of refuge and safety.' She pulled a face and still managed to look like a goddess, ' but I could never bear the taste, it left me feeling quite dizzy and quite sick.'

I nodded in agreement, 'me too, I remember the nausea and dizzy spells. But if you are really determined to pick up an unhealthy, expensive and absolutely filthy habit, then one has to persevere.' I realised then that her laughter was more intoxicating than a whole bottle of ten-year-old Babycham. I sipped my honey sweet tea. 'Did you enjoy the movie last night?'

Again, she looked at me oddly, ' movie?'

I instantly corrected myself, but was way too slow. ' Sorry, I spend too much time in London and they are going all Yankee down there, calling films Movies and the like...tch!' I shook my head in despair and slapped my wrist playfully, 'sorry about that.'

I had a feeling, deep in my waters that she did not buy my story, but her smile was broad as she toyed with her teacup. 'It was just as you had said, a lovely and immensely entertaining musical, though I'm not sure the boys were so enthralled. You should have come with us but of course you had seen it before, more than once as I recall.'

I nodded, ' in London.'

'Quite so,' she replied, ' more tea?'

I shook my head and inhaled deeply on my cigarette. The subject of Lancelot Pratt was stirring in my curious mind, but I let it stir. If she decided to broach the subject, then fine, but I was happy to let sleeping dog's breaths lie.

'So, how long are you here for this time?' The question was innocent enough, but I was instantly transported back, racked by a feeling of deep sadness and guilt that I had abandoned her at such a desperate time. But I cast aside the melancholy and stubbed out my cigarette.

'So what's going on Jimmy?'

Her question was delivered quietly, but quickly, and to the point. It caught me off balance and I realised that bullshit and lies were no longer acceptable. I yearned to hold her close and dance with her, not dance around her.

'I'm not a fool, I can see how Mary and Sandy try to protect you, and you say so many strange things, and then attempt to charm your way out of a corner. You are all hiding something from me and I feel hurt and left out, the charm offensive has run its course and I need you to be honest with me.'

I reached across the table and took her hand, it was time for some home truth's. 'I'm sorry, we were just trying to protect you from the truth, what I have to tell you will be more than a little hard to believe, and I cannot say anything without Sandy and Mary present.'

'I don't understand Jimmy?'

I paused and gazed into the bright pools of her anxious eyes. ' I have decided to make dinner tonight, will you come?'

She looked confused, ' you're making dinner?'

'Is that so odd?'
'It is around these parts.'
'So, will you come?'
She nodded, but a frown lingered, 'it all sounds very mysterious, but I must go to work now.' I walked her to the front door and watched as she tentatively made her way down the snow laden garden path. The gate clicked and she looked back, giving me a cheery smile and a wave.
A bacon sandwich and a cup of tea later, and I was out the door, stepping into a winter wonderland. Sharp sunlight made me blink as I pulled the gate behind me. I could hear the guillotines biting through leather from the factory up the road, and the harsh scrape of shovels scraping against stone steps and pathways. I inhaled deeply, it felt like a good day to be alive.
Suddenly I became aware of curious eyes studying me, and raised a hand to shield my eyes from the morning winter sun. She was a big lady, completely filling the doorway of the tiny shop across the street. She lifted a large wooden crate lying by the door, nodded curtly in my direction and disappeared into the interior. Intrigued I stepped across and entered. She occupied one half and I the other, in between there was a large slab of white marble supported on whitewashed stone pillars, which seemed to act as both shop counter and preparation area. On my left there was an ancient pair of cast iron pillar scales, and numerous wooden crates filled with ice and fish balanced precariously on small wooden shelving.
'Good morning.'
She nodded, ' aye, if you say so mister, not much good for trade tha knows.'
'No, I suppose not, but it does look pretty.'
'Aye, it's pretty enough, I'll give you that, but when it turns to slush, folk'll be moaning, like they've never seen slush before. Or their galoshes will be leaking or gout playing up.' Her chins wobbled independently as she shook her head, 'but there you go, folk rattle away like dustbin lids, 'specially 'bout the weather.'
I nodded like I understood what she was saying, 'so what do you have today?'
She pointed a bloodied filleting knife at the various crates. 'Ah've got cod, 'addok, finny 'addok, kippers, an' some fresh cow 'eel.'

The cow heel appeared to stir when its name was mentioned. The pale glistening flesh was to me, utterly repulsive to behold. I heard a voice then, almost fearful and slightly squeaky. It was my voice as I said, ' that is nothing like any fish that I have ever seen.'

Her voluminous body shook as she laughed so violently that globules of fish gut slid from her shiny apron to escape.

'Nay, it’s not fish lad, 'as thee nivver seen tripe before?'

I shook my head, and prayed and hoped that I would never see it again.

'Here,' she said, slicing a portion and placing it on the marble slab 'Try a bit, its reet popular round these parts, and cheap.'

I almost gagged and was about to decline her offer for a tasting, when I noticed the bloodied filleting knife nestled in her right hand. It seemed to me at that moment, that it resembled a samurai sword, capable of removing a man's head in one casual sweep, so I picked up. It was in fact the fastest fast food that has ever passed my lips. It lingered in my mouth for just a nano- second, just long enough to say, 'you'll be sorry sucker', and slide down my throat at an immeasurable speed of knots. I fully expected it to fly out of my arse and a bell to ring, but it didn't.

'Well?' she said, as her chins wobbled like an aftershock that probably would rate more than six on the Richter scale.

I licked my lips and concentrated, trying and failing to conjure up a recognisable after taste. I shrugged, 'I'm sorry but there is no taste, it has no flavour whatsoever.' A sudden chill breeze blew up my trouser leg, as I realised that the truth was sometimes best left in its box. I saw alarming images of the samurai 'addock sword removing my head, and joining the finny 'addock in a box.

She raised her considerable arms in the air and grinned. 'Well hallelujah and praise the lord!'

I only had eyes for the sword and took a step back.

'Is that good?'

'Oh aye,' she replied, as her chins continued to mime amongst themselves.

'If it's fresh like, then it tastes of nowt, but if its orf it leaves a gammy sticky taste in't mouth.'

'I don't get it, I mean if it is completely tasteless then what is the point of eating it in the first place?'

'Well you 'ave to put plenty of malt vinegar on it, that's the secret. You can boil it, fry it, or eat it just as it is, so long as it's got plenty of vinegar.'

'I'm glad you cleared that up, so now it is transformed from tasteless to vinegar flavoured.'

'Exactly.'

'A bit like pork scratchings.'

'Aye,' she paused and scratched one of her chins, 'can't say I've ever 'eared of pork scratchings mind.'

'I think I will stick with the fish, the finny haddock looks good.'

'Good? Why this fish is so fresh you could put it back in't sea an' it would swim away, 'appy as an 'addock, 'cept its dead now of course.'

'I'll take three, I'm staying across the road with Mary and Sandy. So, I thought as they are both working it would be nice to cook dinner.'

'I thought as much when I saw you come out the gate, I was on me way back out the shop to ask thi business, but thee followed me in 'ere.'

She wrapped the fish in newspaper. 'Well it goes without saying that you could 'ave bin up to no good. We 'ave to look after our own round 'ere, cos the rozzers are only good for blowing whistles, if tha gets me meaning.'

I got her meaning in an instant, the image of her considerable presence, complete with a blood and gore stained apron, carrying an 'adduck samurai sword, brought a whole new meaning to neighbourhood watch. Suddenly my attention was drawn to a horse and cart across the street. It came to an abrupt halt, and the portly driver peered into our garden, a greasy flat cap was pulled down over his eyes. The lovely old horse brasses glowed like burnished gold as the horse tossed its mane in the sunlight, snorting a light winter cloud like a safety valve on a steam engine. She followed my gaze, peering through the rusted ancient tin lined window.

'That's old Ben,' she replied to my unspoken question, 'rag an' bone man.'

'He seems to be looking for something?'

'It's a funny story, apparently he was passing one morning, when all of a sudden like, a madman pops up from behind the 'edge, foaming at the mouth an' eyes rolling in an alarming manner. The 'orse was spooked an' they shot off around the corner. 'e's bin looking' for't madman ever since.'

The story sounded familiar to me, and as horse and cart moved on, I stepped out of the shadows.

'How much do I owe you?'

'That'll be one and seven.'

I gave her two shillings and she rattled coins in a hidden box beneath the counter.

'That's fine,' I said shaking my head, 'keep the change.'

She looked at me in alarm and shook her head. 'Nay, I can't be doing with that, thi pays for what thi sees an' buys, no more, no less,' and she dropped five pennies into my hand. I smiled and turned to leave, but she had no intention of letting me step out of her shop so easily 'So you're cookin' dinner for Mary and Sandy, very nice.'

I smiled and attempted to step out of the door, but my retreat was halted.

'An' you're cooking dinner for them tonight?'

'Well they are busy people, I have the time,' I held up my parcel of haddock, 'and the fishes, so why not.'

'Aye why not,' she answered absently. The samurai sword was raised, and in one fell swoop another cod lost its head.

I assumed this was the moment I made my bid for freedom, but I was wrong.

'I've never 'ad dinner cooked for me tha knows.'

My left foot almost made contact with the outside world. 'What?'

She smiled wistfully and wiped the blood from her knife tenderly, 'it must be a wonderful thing, 'aving a man cook a meal for thi.'

I frowned, ' you must have had a meal cooked for you at some time?'

'Oh aye, when I was little me mam cooked for me all the time, but never since. I sometimes think me old man believed that dinner cooked itsen.'

With one small step for mankind I made it out into the bright sunlit snow, when a thought occurred to me, and I stepped back in. 'Why don't you come to dinner tonight?'

She was engrossed in carving up a large quivering portion of Satan's snot. Her formidable eyebrows arched and her mouth fell open like an unhinged trapdoor.

'What, me come to dinner at Mary an' Sandys 'cross the road? I don't think so.'

'Why ever not, you would be my guest.'

She leaned on the marble counter and peered at me with deep suspicion. I became momentarily uncomfortable, even though she had laid her sword on the slab.

'You could bring your husband along too.'

'Aye, well that would be a challenge, as 'e's bin dead this past seven year.'

'I'm sorry.'

'Nay, there's nowt to be sorry about, one minute he was moaning about lumps in't porridge, an' next he had his head in it, dead as a dodo.'

'That must have been quite a shock.'

'Oh aye, there were no lumps in't porridge and that's for sure.'

I informed her that dinner was at seven sharp if she had a change of mind, and bought another fish just in case.

CHAPTER 19

It was lunchtime when I walked down the neighbours' path. There were only two steps up into the porch, rather than the three next door, and the garden was marginally smaller. Dark green paint peeled from the front door, and two narrow Victorian coloured leaded light panels occupied the upper half. I knocked and waited, stamping my feet to keep warm. I noticed an old metal door bell grip set within the centre of the door at chest height, and twisted it to the right. A short sharp bell announced my arrival, but to no avail.

Reluctantly I turned and headed back down the path, only to be halted by the sound of a bolt been drawn. Not once, but three times, followed by the sound of a chain dragged against metal that would not have sounded out of place in a Hammer Horror film. The door juddered open a fraction, and a disembodied voice said, 'well come in if you're coming in.'

He was halfway down the hall when I entered, his old body bent and leaning on a silver topped walking stick. He paused and turned to look at me. ' Shut blooming door, was tha born in a barn.' I was suitably chastised and shut the blooming door, and I was immediately transported to an earlier time in an instant. Sunlight filtered through the leaded light panels in the door, and a cascade of colour spilled onto the narrow carpet. The walls were smothered to the ceiling with old paintings, portraits and sepia studio photographs of family groups. Huge Scottish highland deer antlers hung from dark shadowy nooks and crannies. The layout of the house was a mirror image of next door. With the stairs on the right, and the two ground floor rooms on my left. A large ornate Burmantofts art pottery jardinière and stand, bearing an aspidistra stood at the foot of the stairs. its long elegant leaves wilting under a fine film of dust. My footsteps disturbed more fine dust, as it rose and swirled, caught in the multi-coloured shafts of sunlight, like a much older winter. The house was cold and had an unwholesome smell of damp, decay, and urine. I followed him into the kitchen where a poor fire barely glowed in the Yorkshire range and he stood with his back to it and motioned me to a chair at the table. I sat, my left arm resting on the edge of the table, the surface was covered by an adhesive plastic cover. In another time it had been brightly decorated with scenes from a children's fairy tale, but now it was faded dirty and damaged with cigarette burns and ring marks from how many cups of tea. I raised my elbow slightly and felt some resistance, it was the Velcro effect.

'Tea?' he said.

I looked at the discoloured moulded glass sugar bowl, the sugar stained brown and lumpy, and the pint pot mug stained with years of tanning.

'No thanks, I'm fine.'

He nodded curtly and remained standing, leaning on his cane. 'Well I'll not beat about the bush, you're a time travelling man are you not?'

'Yes I am,' I replied without hesitation, there appeared after all no point in denying it. I noticed his body sway slightly as he moved from the range and sat at the other side of the table. 'What time do you come from?'

I pulled out my cigarettes, 'may I?'

He nodded absently

'Twenty nineteen,' I replied.

I watched his lips move silently, forming the words twenty nineteen, and pushed my pack of cigarettes across the sticky table top, but he shook his head. 'I've always favoured the snuff,' he said, and reached into his waistcoat pocket, placing a small antique silver snuff box on the table. It was shaped in the form of a Scottish thistle, with a glistening emerald adorning the top. He tapped it absently with his forefinger. 'It's one of the few pleasures I have left.'

'How long have you lived here?'

He toyed with the snuff box, spinning it around in circles with his index finger. 'Well now, there's a question,.a long time. Long enough to see time travellers appear and disappear in the garden. Oh aye, I saw your arrival, staggering and swaying and puking on the lawn...not a pretty sight.'

I smiled, 'it's a sort of travel sickness, but it soon wears off.'

'I know that lad; as I said you're not the first traveller I've met tha knows.' I stood and walked over to the smouldering excuse of a fire, flicking cigarette ash into the embers. I noticed an old brass helmet shaped coal bucket on the tiled hearth, it was empty. 'You need to keep warm,' I said turning, but he was no longer with me. He was shaking a crooked forefinger at the far wall, engaged in an intense but silent debate. 'You need some coal,' I said, raising my voice, but he ignored me, his lips working furiously, spittle forming at the corners of his mouth. I looked down at him sadly and then picked up the bucket. I was never one to come between a man and his wall, so I left them to it.

The cellar was a familiar place, but with everything on the wrong side. Fortunately, the electrics worked, and I shovelled coal. I was disappointed that such a house of clutter should have a remarkably clean and empty cellar, and headed for the stairs, but for some inexplicable reason I could not pass the narrow door without taking a peek inside. It too was completely devoid of clutter, and it occurred to me that he must have been a man with few hobbies over the years. I was about to close the door when the outline of a lone picture caught my attention in the gloom, leaning against the wall to my left. I stepped sideways through the narrow gap, my head bent, and fetched the picture out for inspection. My quickly beating heart almost stalled in disappointment. It was a bog-standard Victorian studio portrait of a rather grim looking middle aged woman. She was standing before a studio back-drop depicting a romantic Italian garden overlooking one of the famous lakes. Ancient Corinthian columns forming a gateway on either side. A place, one would imagine, that would bring a smile to one's lips, but this lady was not for smiling. Her pursed lips and bored demeanour suggested that she would rather be in Italy than a studio in grim and grimy Leeds. I grinned, and it occurred to me that there is no pleasing some people. She held a dog lead with a remarkably ugly bunch of fur seated at the other end. I confess that I am no expert on dog breeds, but this particular mutt had a certain something. I think it was all in the eyes and short snotty snout, there was a suggestion that if you had the effrontery to stroke it, then it would either bite one of your fingers clean off, or shit in your hand. Or on a good day, it would do both, and then suggest that fried chicken would be a good choice for dinner. I put it back where I had found it and closed the door.

When I returned to the kitchen with my bucket of coal, I was unsure of the reception I would get. Would he remember who I was, or what I was doing in his home, or would he still be away with the fairies? He beamed as I entered, 'ah, good lad, wondered where you'd got to, stoke fire up will you.'

It was good to see him back, he was smiling, animated, and I could only assume that the wall had lost the argument. So I did what I was told and stoked up the fire, finding a sheet of old newspaper to create an up draught. Soon the paper browned as I listened to the roar, and I released it as it dissolved into flames and disappeared up the chimney. He stared at the flames and smiled, 'that's grand, my name's Donald by the way,' he said, reaching a deeply veined and wasted arm across the table, and we shook hands.

'Jimmy,' I replied.

He arched his eyebrows, 'Jimmy, that's a good name.'

I sat and lit another cigarette, staring into the flames. No questions, no prompt, I let him speak when he was good and ready.

'We moved here in the summer,' he said wistfully,' August I think it was, in the year 1902. I remember it well, as that was the year my mother died. We worked hard as everyone did in those days, and life it seemed was a constant struggle .'He snapped open the lid of his snuff box, but then seemed to have a change of heart as he closed the lid with a finger. 'Everything changed when Lydia died.'

My lazily slumped spine straightened in an instant, I was on familiar ground as a wave of Deja vu almost swept me off my feet.

'Agnes, my wife, doted on Lydia, and nothing was the same after that.' It was becoming a familiar story and a pattern was emerging, of love, loss, and new beginnings, but I must say that I was ill prepared for what he said next.

'Personally, I couldn't stand the bitch, but I put up with 'er for the sake of some peace.' This time he opened the box with purpose and sprinkled a mere suggestion of snuff onto the base of his bent forefinger. He sniffed once and it was gone. It left a pungent and quite aromatic smell in the air, which was not unpleasant in the least. He surprised me then, by suddenly standing and reaching for his cane. 'All will be explained Jimmy,' he said, and followed his cane out of the kitchen and into the dusty depths of the hall. I followed as he paused at the front room, leaning on his cane. He then made a rather theatrical sweep of one arm, and I stepped through the open doorway.

On a day like today it would have been a welcoming place, with bright low winter sunlight pouring through the large bay window, but heavy brocade drawn curtains forbade the sunlight to enter. Instead, he switched on the light and an elegant brass and etched glass chandelier banished the shadows to alcoves. It was to me a delightful clutter of fine watercolour paintings and antique furniture. On the wall to my right stood a tall bow fronted mahogany china cabinet, finely inlaid with floral swags. It was crammed with porcelain and silver objects of vertu. A fine nineteenth century walnut Davenport desk occupied the recess next to the fireplace. Pens lying in a cradle and a sheet of blotting paper encased within a leather holder revealed past use.

'I don't come in 'ere much now,' he said, leaning on his cane. 'No point really, it's not like I'm expecting guests. He pointed his cane at the fireplace, 'there she is,'

I looked, my eager eyes trying to pick out what I was supposed to be looking at. Was it a portrait painting, some photographs perhaps? Then my eyes alighted upon the tiled hearth, and I gasped, stepping forward for a closer inspection.

'Is that her?'

'Aye, she loved the misses an' the misses loved 'er, but she loathed me an' the feeling was mutual. I would 'ave 'appily kicked 'er sorry arse out of the door. I actually love all of God's creatures, except that one.'

I knelt on the rug for a closer inspection, 'so this is Lydia?'

'Aye, the bitch from hell.'

It was the dog in the photograph, 'She certainly looks a bit battered and cross.'

'A bit cross? He hissed with some feeling, 'she caught me in the crotch once, an' I almost ended up like Hitler.' Overcome with emotion he lowered himself into a handsome red leather armchair. 'She could shit for England when the missus was out, an' seemed to look at me in a frowning sort of menacing way. As if to say, I've finished now, so clean it up and be quick about it.'

I climbed to my feet with a smile.

'It's all right for you with that big fat grin on yer mush.'

I looked down at him, clasping his cane and staring angrily at the stuffed dog.

'So why is she still here Donald?'

'Aye well, I did think about chucking 'er in't bin, but then I had a better idea.' He looked up at me with his watery blue eyes and tapped the side of his nose with an index finger. 'When I were a lad I liked nothing better than a game of footie. I even 'ad scouts sniffing' round, but it never came to nowt. They said I was too small and too physical, can you imagine that? I was a defender an' not many wingers got past me tha knows, and when they did they'd be limping for a week at least.' He smiled fondly at the memory, ' I might 'ave been small but I knew how to hang onto a pair of bollocks in front of goalmouth.'

It was my turn to take a seat on the red leather settee, and I laughed out loud. Donald stared at me for a moment, like a man who had forgotten how to laugh. But the memory resurfaced and we laughed together in that dusty mausoleum of a room. Finally, we composed ourselves, I dabbed at my eyes while he chose a linen handkerchief stained with snuff and goodness knows what else.

'Anyway,' he wheezed, eyes bright and body shaking with laughter. 'Even now I still fancy the occasional kick about.' He then pointed his cane at the stuffed Lydia.

I was a little slow on uptake, 'what, you play football with a dead dog?'

He shook his head in exasperation, 'can you hear yourself Jimmy?'

Dawn arrived just in the nick of time, and I looked at him in mock dismay, 'you don't?

'I do, he said, a light bright smile playing on his old cracked lips. ' She gave me nothing but hell in life, so in return I use her for the football, I get my kicks and she gets what she deserves.' He looked to me for approval and all I could do was shrug my shoulders. 'Well, so long as it keeps you fit, I do believe that the modern term is anger management.'

I realised then that he was no longer with me, but shaking an angry fist at his left foot, miming some form of admonishment.

'Donald?'

No response.

'Donald?' louder this time.

He suddenly looked up from his slipper and grinned like an errant schoolboy, 'did I do wrong?'

I shook my head, 'not at all.'

He seemed to take some comfort in that and relaxed into the chair, his pliant fingers playing on the silver top of his cane.

'So how did Agnes change when Lydia died?'

He frowned at the carpet. 'Well it's hard to describe like, she went into a sort of terminal wilt.'

'Terminal wilt?'

'She even smiled sometimes, an' that took a bit of getting used to. Then one day I woke up and she was gone, no note, no explanation, nothing!'

'How long Donald, how long was she gone for?'

His cracked old lips worked furiously and in silence, and then, 'I never saw her again, she never came back to me. I had to report her as missing to the rozzers, an' whispers began to circulate, that some foul play had taken place and I had been instrumental in her disappearance.' He looked at me sadly, 'if you know what I mean?'

I knew in an instant, but simply nodded.

'Well the coppers came an' took down details an' such like. They searched the house, even prodding around in the garden.' His voice faded and cracked. 'They dug up some of my prize roses would you believe, they thought that I had done her in an' laid her to rest in me garden.'

For a moment I thought that I had lost him again, as he stared at the wall, his busy lips working but failing to form words of any meaning. Then suddenly he was back.

'Bear in mind that all this happened in nineteen twenty.' His sad old eyes seemed to mist over as he leaned on his cane.

In the time it took me to reach for the ashtray, he was picking a fight again. His lips working silently and furiously, eyes wide and fearsome, his trembling hand pointing accusingly at Lydia.

'Donald, come back to me Donald.'

Spittle bubbled from between thinly drawn lips, as he continued his silent tirade at the one eyed kicked about bitch of a stuffed dog. Then quite suddenly and rather alarmingly, his anger was no longer silent.

'You dirty fucking bitch!'

His pale contorted face turned a florid red as he shook a fist and attempted to rise from the settee. But he fell back, breathing heavily. 'Shit on my carpet again you fucking dirty little cunt and I'll kick your bastard stinking shity arse to kingdom come.' His whole body was shaking now and his sad old eyes seemed to be hanging on stalks. 'What, what was that? You think I'm joking you useless bag of puss, you fucking bastard bitch of a stinking cunt, you shity arsed fucker, I'll 'ave you!'

Again, he tried to rise from the sofa, but fell back exhausted. I stubbed out my cigarette and waited for him to return. Then I heard the front door judder open, and heard Mary's warm and welcoming voice, 'it's only me,' she said, and stopped abruptly, framed in the doorway. Her eyebrows were raised as she saw us together in the front room. 'I'm surprised to see you in here Jimmy, how are you two getting on?'

'We're fine Mary, but Donald here has just taken a turn for the worst.'

I was amazed how the sound of a friendly familiar voice, could ease the agony of his tortured mind. He was back, eyes alert and smiling, 'Is that you Mary?'

She stepped into the room and laid a hand on his shoulder, 'well who were you expecting, the queen of Sheba?'

The look of delight on his face was sublime, 'Well hello Mary.' He looked at me then, his face a picture of serenity. 'This is Mary,' he confided, 'and I wouldn't swap her for all the tea in china.' He looked at me, a wide-eyed pool of delight. 'You've got a good one there Sandy.'

Mary smiled and produced a small flannelette from her handbag, dabbing gently at his eyes and chin. 'I've brought you some roast chicken Donald, do you want anything from the shop?'

His brow furrowed, 'an Alfie apple would be nice.'

She nodded, and then smiled at my mystified expression. 'It's an apple pie Jimmy, don't you know anything?'

'Of course it is,' I said, climbing to my feet, 'how silly of me. Perhaps it is time to let Donald rest for a while.'

He reached out, gripping my wrist with surprising strength. ' Don't go yet Jimmy, you have to hear the whole story.' There was an urgency in his voice that I could not ignore. I sat back in my chair and glanced up at Mary. She smiled at me, and then she was gone, to meet a certain Alfie apple. When I looked back at Donald, I found that he was leaning on his stick, a gentle smile playing on his cracked old lips, and then a nod of the head and raising of the eyebrows as some distant memory ushered in a moment of joy.

'What is it Donald, what is it that makes you smile so?'

His eyes were wide and full of childlike wonder. 'That's when I saw the only woman that I have ever truly loved, that's when I saw my very first time traveller.'

CHAPTER 20

He was silent for a moment, tapping the snuff box with his index finger.' It was August nineteen twenty eight, and I was sitting at the upstairs window. I smoked a pipe in those days and opened the window. It was late afternoon, a warm day as I recall. Children were playing in the street and couples sauntered passed arm in arm. When a sudden movement caught my attention in next doors garden. I could feel a cool breath of air, as a swirling vortex of light shimmered in the grass, and she emerged wraith like from nowhere. Suddenly she was standing there in the middle of the lawn, very still, shielding her eyes from the light. She was very beautiful, with high cheekbones, a pale complexion, and long auburn hair. She wore a knee length figure hugging summer dress, printed in small multi coloured flowers. When suddenly she dropped to her knees and was violently sick. I'm ashamed to say that I was shocked, mesmerised, and glued to the seat of my chair. I could not comprehend the scene that was unfolding before my very eyes. The hairs on the back of my neck shivered to attention, and I recall feeling very frightened. She knelt in the grass for some time, in a prayer like posture, and then climbed unsteadily to her feet. Her slim body swaying like a flower caught in the gentle whisper of a summer breeze.'

He seemed to look at me with a chilly air of despair, his pale blue sad old eyes. Recalling a moment in his past life, a moment of such importance that he had kept it under lock and key, buried deep within the rose garden of his mind, until now.

'I was slow to react, but when I did race down the stairs three at a time, out of the door and into the street, I reached Sandy's gate quite breathless, and stared at an empty patch of lawn, she was gone, disappeared into thin air.'

Donald stared wistfully at his feet, and for a moment I thought I had lost him again, but then he tapped his snuff box and sighed. 'The house was occupied by a Doctor and his wife at that time. I was in a bit of a panic as I'm sure you would expect, and ran up the drive, hammering on the door. I could hear music from the wireless. It was the doctor who answered, his shirt collar removed and braces hanging by his side. I remember feeling a touch of guilt at disturbing him. I remember that he smiled at me, but then the smile turned to a look of concern.'

He shook his head, 'I must have looked a right apeth, standing there babbling like a baboon, but finally I told him what I had just witnessed in his garden. His reaction quite startled me. He caught me by the arm and stared at me intensely.

'Did you see which way she left Donald?'

I shook my head and he darted back inside, emerging a moment later wearing his walking shoes, and braces strapped over his shoulders. 'We must find her Donald,' There was a note of urgency in his voice, as we hurried down the path. I was, as you might expect, more than a little confused at this point. 'Do you know this lady?'

He shook his head impatiently, 'no time for explanations old chap, we must find her quickly.'

' I looked quickly in both directions.'

'Do you see her?'

I shook my head as a motor car passed, honking its horn at a group of children playing football.

'Well it makes no sense our looking together,' he said quickly, 'what does she look like?'

I had no difficulty in describing her appearance.

'Excellent, you take the high road and I'll take the low road, and hopefully one of us will be lucky.'

' I hurried through side streets, stopping folk on my travels and describing her appearance, but I was always rewarded with a frustrating shake of the head. I reached Woodhouse Lane, and dithered. Should I follow the road into town or head up to Hyde Park corner? In fact, I did both at a smart run, only turning back when logic told me that she could not possibly have come this far. Street lights popped as dusk turned to darkness and I returned defeated and with a heavy heart. The doctors garden was well lit as lights burned from almost every room. I was feeling very tired as I rang the bell. Maud, the doctor's wife answered and she beamed at me broadly, ushering me into the front room where the doctor was listening to some jazz music on the wireless. He was on his feet in an instant, pummelling my hand in a hearty handshake, his grip was firm and sure.

I take it you found her then? I said quickly.

He smiled and gestured for me to sit, while he poured two glasses of whisky from a cut glass decanter on the sideboard. He handed me a glass and settled into the armchair opposite. 'She was wandering down a side street in a distressed state,' he said, 'we found her just in time Donald.'
I watched as he struggled to recall important moments in his past, frowning at the carpet, lips moving silently. So his next utterance was painful to hear.

'Am I going mad Sandy?'

I almost corrected him, but thought better of it. It took me by surprise, didn't sound like a question at all, but more a statement of fact. It threw me and I responded in the only way I knew how.

'Absolutely.'

His jaw dropped at my rapid diagnosis.

'Mad as a hatter,' I added for good measure, 'so join the club because it's a mad old world out there.'

He surprised me again by bursting into laughter, rocking in his chair. He pulled his stained handkerchief from his pocket, dabbing at his eyes, and fought to contain the second wave of laughter, but failed dismally. It was quite contagious and I succumbed, laughing along with him.

'That was the right answer, spoken like a true Yorkshireman,' he spluttered, dabbing at his eyes. I waited, impatient for the next instalment of his tale, but he just looked at me, his eyes wide, searching for the next sentence.

'So, the doctor had found her,' I said, trying to jog his memory, ' and you were drinking whisky?'

His gaze drifted to the damaged dog, and then to the shafts of light that pierced the gaps in the curtains. A mantle clock chimed and suddenly he was back like a damaged prize fighter alerted by the ringing of a bell. 'Oh aye, doctor found her, and I said, where is she now?

'Resting my friend, she is unwell at the moment. Nothing life threatening you understand, she just needs to rest for a while.'

Donald fixed me with his unblinking eyes, ' I remember that the doctor toyed with his glass, staring into the glowing embers of the coal fire. 'We have lived here for seven years now,' he said slowly.' Very happily I may add, but when we bought the house and received the deeds and such like, we were also handed a sealed envelope.'

He rose from his chair and retrieved the said envelope from a drawer in the writing bureau. He placed it into my hand and sat without a word, sipping at his whiskey. It was a letter from the previous occupant explaining the special nature of the house they had purchased, and advising them that a room should always be set aside for the occasional traveller. When I looked up after reading the letter, he appeared embarrassed. 'I know, it sounds like the ramblings of a simple mind, and I was all for casting it into the fire, but Maud stayed my hand. She has always been the gentle and more thoughtful of our union I'm glad to say, and convinced me that it would do no harm to set a room aside. She has cleaned and dusted that room along with the rest of the house ever since. I confess that I gently chided her on occasions as we never experienced anything untoward in the house, but she would simply shrug and change the sheets once more. All the doubt disappeared in an instant when you came knocking at our door, I knew she was a time traveller when you clearly described what you had witnessed.'

A single shaft of sunlight settled on Donald, his pale head bowed as he leaned on his cane. He looked drawn and exhausted, and I decided it was time to leave him in peace, but his head rose sharply as I stood.

'Please don't go,' he whispered, his eyes bright and shimmering with tears, 'just let me finish my tale Jimmy.'

I sat and watched as he tapped at the snuff box.

'She was the only woman I ever truly loved,' he said quickly, and then looked away, as if it were a declaration of weakness.

I said nothing, but simply observed as his pinched lips worked silently, I found it upsetting and moving to watch. Then he was back again, eyes bright and focused, a look of childlike innocence and wonder smoothing the craggy contours of his smiling face.

'It were Saturday morning', he said suddenly. 'I was out fetching bread and milk from't corner shop, an' there she was sitting in the garden, looking pretty as a picture. I stopped at the gate with me gob wide open, catching' flies. 'It's a grand day', I said, and she smiled the sweetest of smiles. Then Maud emerged from the porch, carrying a tea tray.

'Donald, come and meet our guest.'

He went silent for a moment, and then looked at me. 'Well I can tell thee I was more than willing, and before you could say Jack Rabbit I had joined them at the table, and Maud formerly introduced us.

'Imogen, this is Donald, our good neighbour, and Donald this is Imogen, our time travelling friend.'

'I remember that I held out my hand across the table, which she duly ignored, and suddenly she was on her feet and by my side.' The snuff box made an appearance again, and he flipped the lid, sprinkling a little on the side of his left hand, and it was gone in a sniff. He then blinked once and looked at me with a watery eyed lopsided grin. 'Do you know what she did? She took my hand, leaned down and kissed me on the cheek.'

'Thank you,' she said, 'for rescuing me in my hour of need.'

In the time it took to light a cigarette he had lurched to his feet, snatching up Lydia and booting her across the room. I had no time to react but secretly admired his shooting skills. She flew through the air, bounced off the curtains in the bay window and dropped out of sight behind an American rocking chair. He then raised his hands in a silent display of utter joy. 'Did you see that Jimmy, was that a goal or was that a goal.'

I was on my feet as he swayed in celebration, afraid that he might fall over, I caught him by the arm, but he shrugged me away. I let him sway on the spot, no doubt listening to the rapturous applause from the fans, and then he allowed me to guide him back to his chair.

Suddenly several clocks chimed throughout the house, and he paused and listened closely. Confusingly not all of the clocks agreed upon the appointed hour, which left us both a little lost in time.

'What time is it Jimmy'?

I automatically glanced at the space on my wrist where my watch should have been, and mindfully added 'must buy a watch' to my list of things to do. I glanced at the French Ormolu mantle clock ticking away on the mantelpiece. It had chimed just once on a bell, and I felt in my waters that it was probably one of the few clocks in Donald's home that told the truth.

'It's one o'clock in the afternoon on a bright and sunny day Donald, may I open the curtains?'

His pale eyes searched my face, confusion reigned as he seemed to consider my request, and then dismiss it with an almost regal wave of the hand. 'The curtains are fine where they are,' he replied in a voice that was surprisingly calm and contained. He snapped open his snuff box and appeared to study its contents before closing it again.

'She was a very special person in my life. The good doctor and his wife were busy people you understand, so it fell to me to show her the new old world as we called it, and I have to say it was the most joyful task that I have ever performed in my long life.'

'Did you become lovers?'

He leaned on his cane and appeared to contemplate the question. 'We kissed once, an' I would say that I loved her and she had become fond of me...'

He shook his head slowly, 'not quite lovers...but almost. When she was here, by my side, it was like all the roses in't garden had blossomed at once, but it couldn't last of course. She was after all a time traveller, someone passing through, she had to return to her own time. We talked an' cried, an' held onto one another, scared to let go, but letting go we had to do.'

He fixed me with a sad old smile, 'I never saw her again.'

His head dropped and I watched as his hand gripped the cane, his swollen knuckles ivory white. I felt he must have sensed that I was about to leave him in peace then.

'Two months later I received a letter from the wife, asking me for a divorce.'

'What?'

'Aye, it were a bit of a shock I can tell thee. Turns out that she ran off with a traveling salesman, she was living over the brush with 'er fancy man.'

He caught me unawares as he lifted his head, a slow soft smile emerging. He then nodded at me and I saw a change of pallor in his skin. It seemed to change Chameleon like, from a deathly white to a hearty and healthy pink. An uneven hissing sound escaped from his lips, followed by a rumble of low distant laughter.

I confess that I was alarmed at this point, thinking that he was having some sort of a fit. Then the laughter proper arrived, it was so sudden that it forced him back in his chair, head tilted to the ceiling. I stared as he coughed and spluttered, but still failed to stem the laughter. It was infectious, and when Mary returned with the Alfie apple, she simply stared, as we roared with eye watering and uncontrollable fits of laughter.

CHAPTER 21

I peeled potatoes as they sat on opposite sides of the fire, Mary was telling Sandy about my encounter with Donald. He looked up, 'Well there's not many folk round here who can say that.'

I paused in my peeling duties and frowned at him, 'I don't get it, what is so unusual about talking to your neighbour?'

Sandy lit his cigarette and stroked his chin thoughtfully, 'well, when you put it like that, nothing. It's just that Donald is something of a recluse, has been for years. Only Mary and I see him regularly these days, to do his shopping, and help pay his bills and suchlike.'

'You saw how he was Jimmy,' said Mary softly. 'One moment he is polite and pleasant, and the next he can be abusive and extremely angry.'

'Dementia,' I replied, the poor man is suffering from dementia...I take it that he has a doctor?'

Sandy nodded, 'he has now.'

'What does that mean?'

Sandy coloured, shifting uncomfortably in his chair. 'We learned that his old doctor was more interested in one of his paintings, constantly reminding him to leave it to him in his will. But then he suddenly died of a heart attack at a Halloween ball in Batley before he could collect.'

'So it's not all bad news,' I muttered. 'Whatever happened to care in the community?

Their bewildered and bemused expressions lassoed me back to 'real time'. 'Forget I said that, so if he is such a reclusive person, who looks after the garden? His garden is a picture, I remember seeing it in summer and it was very beautiful.'

Sandy smiled, 'well the old man who tends the rose garden, can only be seen in the wee small hours. If you step into the garden around midnight, you may see some movement, as he tends lovingly to his blooms.'

Mary nodded, a soft smile playing on her lips, 'folk round here call him the midnight gardener.'

I emptied a can of' whoppa peas into a pan and added the sliced carrots. The spuds were boiling when I laid the finny haddock on the grill tray. I was really cooking, nineteen fifties style. I remembered to season everything with plenty of salt, because salt was good for you in those far flung care free who gives a toss anyway days after the war. I imagined that during the war itself, the same meal may have been cooked between a bit of shagging and puffs on a Wills Woodbine while singing 'There'll always be an England.'

'I invited a guest to dinner,' I said, looking over my shoulder. I saw Mary kick Sandy fondly on the shins, a smile on her lips, and a grimace from him. 'I hope you don't mind?'

Mary smiled at me sweetly, 'our home is your home when you are here, you can invite whoever you please.'

'Oh, it's only Gwen,' I remarked a tad too casually, and caught Mary silently mouthing the words 'it's only Gwen', with a big smile on her face to Sandy.

'Actually, I have invited two ladies to dinner, sorry I almost forgot.' It was almost a surreal moment as I witnessed the lowering of Mary's eyebrows in a frown, and the raising of Sandy's as he looked at me in surprise.

'Two ladies,' he murmured, 'you are becoming quite the ladies' man Jimmy.'

Mary's response was less convivial, in fact she sounded quite tense. 'And who may I ask is the other lucky lady?'

I paused for dramatic effect, drying my hands on the tea towel. 'The lady with the shop across the street, the fish lady.'

The silence that followed was almost complete, except for the sound of Sandy drowning in his teacup. 'You invited dab hand Dolly to dinner? 'he managed to splutter.

I grinned, 'is that what you call her, 'dab hand Dolly?'

'Her name is Dolly Maguire', said Mary with a sigh.,' as you well know husband of mine.'

We were both instantly chastised.

'I mentioned that I was cooking dinner and she said....'

I got no further as they burst into laughter, I had to smile, but my obvious look of bemusement seemed to make matters worse.

'What?'

Mary produced a white linen hankie and dabbed at her eyes. 'She said that no one had cooked her a meal since she was knee high to a grasshopper?'

I nodded like an imbecile, 'it's not quite the truth, is it?'

Sandy lit his cigarette, grinning at me, 'it's nowhere near the truth more like. Why that women has had more free dinners than a school dinner lady with a tapeworm.'

Gwen was the first of our guests to arrive, the sonorous sound of the doorbell was still ringing in my ears as I opened the front door. Only her bewitching hazel eyes were visible, her hair hidden beneath a brightly coloured woollen hat. The lower half of her face was concealed beneath a thick scarf, and the collar of her long winter coat was pulled up around her neck. A flurry of snowflakes followed her into the hall, and I closed the door quickly.

'You must be absolutely frozen.'

She laughed, shaking off her mittens and unbuttoning her coat, I slid the coat from her shoulders, hanging it on the hall stand. She sat on a chair and kicked off her boots, retrieving a pair of light blue high heel shoes from a carpet bag, now lying at her feet. She stood then, discarding the hat and scarf, running her fingers through long shiny auburn locks, as she studied her face in the hall stand mirror.

'I must look a frightful mess.'

'You are looking absolutely beautiful...' is what I should have said. Not, 'you are looking just fine,' which I did. She wore a slightly flared knee length blue dress, with a narrow white leather belt accentuating her wasp like waist. A fine gold chain adorned with a simple gold cross, shimmered at the porcelain whiteness of her swan like throat, and small diamond and gold earrings sparkled fleetingly through her hair.

She looked up at me, a playful glint in her eyes, 'will I do?'

I placed my hands on her shoulders, and inspected her like a soldier on parade. And finally, I untied my tongue and said what I should have said all along. 'You madam, look absolutely gorgeous.' I leaned forward and kissed her on the cheek, 'come, were eating in the kitchen as it is the warmest room in the house.'

Dolly arrived at the appointed hour, wearing a hat adorned with more fruit than your average market stall. She looked even larger when she was not wearing fish guts and blood. She wore a huge hooped silken frock that could easily have housed a giggle of girl guides.

'You're very welcome Dolly,' Said Mary warmly, and gesticulated to one of the chairs at the kitchen table. She sat and nodded affably, and the fruit laden hat rocked drunkenly from side to side. 'I must say that it is a pleasure and an honour to be 'ere. To be asked to dinner as a dinner guest by your guest is just lovely, and ah've not come empty 'anded tha knows.' She snapped open a large worn and cracked pure plastic crocodile skin handbag. A bottle appeared, which she proudly thumped upon the table. 'Sloe gin!' she announced with feeling. 'Ah mek it missen, an' tha'll go a long ways to find a better brew, even if I say so.'

I caught Sandy's eye, and we silently agreed that she had already indulged in more than a few nips. The meal went down well, but the sloe gin less so. I have never actually been called upon to drink cats piss, I imagine that if I had done so, then it would no doubt taste like this brew from hell. Consequently, the rest of us stuck with the wine I had bought that day. That did not deter 'dab hand', who kept her bottle close at hand. She beamed broadly, her fulsome cheeks glowing like polished cox's apples.

'Well I must say that my fishes 'ave never tasted so good, that were a reet good meal young man.' She raised her glass and tossed back her head to swallow what remained of pussy's piss. In doing so, her fruity hat flew from her head and clattered softly to the floor. She appeared not to notice, but looked at each one of us in turn, with a large flushed and benign grin. It was at that moment that the wall clock drifted into her double vision, and a look of alarm appeared in her ever so slightly bloodshot eyes. 'By 'eck!' she cried, and lurched quickly to her feet in a gravity defying swaying motion, 'is that the time?'

Her chair somehow remained upright, but shot across the floor, coming to an abrupt halt against the wall with a dull clatter. I was on my feet in an instant, retrieving her hat of many fruits, and offering her my arm for support.

'Are you alright Dolly?'

'Oh aye, never been better young man.' The sloe gin entered my bloodstream through the close proximity of her breath. 'Ah've 'ad a reet champion time thanks to thee, but now I 'ave to get back to me babbies.'

'Your babies?' I must have looked alarmed as Sandy took her other arm, and he shook his head and mouthed the word 'cats'.

'Aye,' she continued to mumble, 'Sooty an' Smokey, they'll be sulking, mek no mistake.'

We led her down to the garden gate. The snow lay thick as our crunching footfalls came to an abrupt halt, when suddenly the voice of a chivalrous lunatic offered to walk her home, and I realised with some alarm that the voice was my own.

'Nay, I'll be reight lad, why I only live roun't corner, an' if any man wants to tek advantage of a tipsy olé' woman, then he's more than welcome.'

She roared with laughter at her own good humour, and then suddenly embraced me. I felt like Popeye gripped by a playful Bluto, and then she was gone. Forging her way through the snow, her powerful piston like arms working like a paralytic rugby league prop forward on a promise.

There was much banter and laughter as we adjourned to the warmth of the kitchen, and it was my turn to produce a bottle of twelve-year-old malt Babycham. I poured the drinks, listening to their laughter and exchanging quick coy smiles with Gwen. It seemed to me then, that I could not possibly return to my own time. Yes, I had friends, but when my darling wife died, part of me also died that morning, and I had become resigned to accept that I would never find that hunger for life or love again, but I was wrong. I had another chance to live a life as it should be lived. All I had to do now, was win her heart.

I raised my glass, and in my mind we toasted the fact that we were alive among people we loved in a world that was so beautiful it took my breath away. But I was also aware that others, less fortunate than myself occupied the same world, and it was a place so bereft of beauty and humanity, that they were more than happy to die. So that they could enter a better place in another life, it was simply another reason to grasp what I had.

I stood then, tapping my glass with a teaspoon, like the best man at a wedding, and silence was restored. 'I invited Dolly to dinner because I mistakenly believed that she had never been invited to dinner, and I was wrong. However, she seemed to have enjoyed herself, so where's the harm?' I looked down at Gwen and smiled, ' I invited Gwen because I think it is time to tell her the truth, the whole truth, and nothing but the truth.'

I sat in a silent room and studiously ignored my open-mouthed hosts, focusing my attention on Gwen. I told her everything, leaving nothing out, from the death of my wife, to the present. She stared at me then, turning to look at her friends for some affirmation that I was indeed a complete basket case, but none was forthcoming.

She smiled and nodded at me, 'well this even beats the tale of the fishes I must say.' She quickly gathered her things and seemed on the point of leaving, when Mary reached across and took her hand. 'Jimmy is not the only traveller Gwen, I too have travelled back to another time, is that not so Sandy?'

He nodded quickly and brushed a stray tear from his cheek, ' this is no' a joke Gwendoline, and if you will stay awhile and listen to Mary's story, you will understand why we have all kept the truth from you.'

She paused with a frown, and then sat and listened, and we talked late into the night. It was snowing again as she took my arm and we crunched down the garden path and out into the street. She leaned into me for fear of slipping, and I silently said a prayer of thanks to the god of snow. 'So when I first saw you and you appeared to be in pain, it was because you were wearing Sandy's wellies, which were too small?'

'Not just his wellies, but it's best that we don't delve too deep into my deportment.'

She laughed aloud, 'and the fishes' story?'

I shrugged, 'how else could I explain my lack of suitable clothing?'

Suddenly she slipped, and as she fell I followed as she held my arm tightly. We lay laughing in the empty snow caked street, I sat upright brushing the snow from my sleeves, as she smiled up at me, and then I leaned down and kissed her. Tentatively at first, but her response was immediate and full of hungry repressed passion. I almost believed that the snow must melt around us, as we held one another in a tight embrace. I felt her warm gasps of breath on my face, her body arched hard against me, as I kissed the nape of her neck. Suddenly a car horn sounded on the opposite side of the street. I looked up and waved as it slowly crunched past, and Gwen cupped her hands to her face. I stood and held out my hands. 'Come on, it would be a shame if we were to be run over just as we were getting to know one another.'

She had both arms looped through mine as we approached her house, 'does this mean we are engaged?' I said. She placed a finger on my lips, 'shush, you'll wake mother.'

I made a zipping motion across my lips, and she frowned, 'what was that?'

'What was what?'

She mimicked my zipping motion, and I laughed. 'It means that my lips are sealed.'

She cupped my face in the palms of her hands, 'you do say some strange things Jimmy, but now at least I know why. It's going to take some time to sink in, but after hearing both of your stories, it all seems to make sense somehow.'

I grinned, 'does that mean you will come dancing with me?' Her eyes widened and she covered her mouth to suppress a laugh, 'dancing...you like to dance?'

'Absolutely, but I must warn you that I am not very good, probably somewhere between Fred Astaire, Gene Kelly and Mr Bean.'

'Mr Bean?'

'Forget I said that.'

She blew me a kiss as the door closed, and I was dancing and singing in the snow.

The house was shrouded in darkness as I let myself in. Dying embers of coal shifted as I sat in the kitchen, and I poured myself a drink. I was about to retire when the bee in a bottle returned, and silent flashes of bright light flickered beyond the net curtains. I was on my feet in an instant and rushed into the front room, pushing curtains aside. The garden flickered, a seasonal snow-covered landscape gave way to a more depressing muddy dawn. It called me, beckoned me, it was time it said, but I ignored it, now most certainly was not the time. The angry bee was insistent, and there seemed to be a subconscious warning. I could not put it into words, but it seemed to suggest, ignore me now and you may not have this opportunity to travel again, but ignore it I did. Beads of sweat forming and running into my eyes, but I was determined that I would not travel, now was certainly not the time.

After what seemed like an age, the call ceased and I stumbled into my room. Seeking the solace of sleep, which finally came as a dawn chorus of birdsong swept away any doubts that I should have travelled. I felt that I had unfinished business, but became suddenly and acutely aware that my options were becoming increasingly thin, and I was fast approaching a moment when such decisions would no longer be mine to make.

We did dance, and I soon discovered that I was quite light on my feet and mastered the fox trot, and the waltz without falling over or treading on too many toes. We also took in a show at the Empire theatre, the day after bonfire night. I was pleased and surprised in equal measures that it was Britain's first ever 'rock 'n' roll' show. Presented by Bernard Delfont, and featuring the likes of Tony Crombie and his Rock and Roll Rockets, Andy Stewart...television comedian, and the dancing McKenna's. It goes without saying that I was completely charmed by the experience.

We were in the money and decided to head into town for a meal one evening. Sandy led us to a large hotel in city square, and the food was surprisingly better than average. We linked arms as we stepped out into wet soft snow, Mary and Sandy on my left and Gwen on my right, I was in heaven. There were many nights like that and we became quite inseparable. As they each worked during the day, I spent my time seeking out more treasures in auction houses and antique shops, until the alcoves became quite full.

Then one particularly grey day, I passed the Graveyard pub and decided to pop in for a pint. The narrow tap room on my left was sparsely occupied with flat capped old men, there seemed to be a lively game of dominoes taking place at one table, as the laughter was muted but good natured in a fog of pipe smoke. The gargoyle glanced in my direction as the door clattered behind me. The snug was silent, only two tables occupied. One near the serving hatch by two old biddies who appeared to have left their teeth at home, a solitary man at a corner table, his head bowed as if in deep thought, and two younger men, standing near the door, deep in conversation.

The gargoyle more than filled the serving hatch, and placed a foaming pint on the beermat. I grinned and pulled out my roll of notes, 'now that's what I call service.'

He beamed at me, and the overall effect was probably more frightening than his scowl. 'Nay lad, your money's no good in here, why your simple Christian act changed my life, an' I joined the human race again because of you. I have found friendship and kindness once more, thank you sir. Whenever you enter these premises, there will always be a pint waiting for you, on the house.'

I smiled, 'it's good that you have turned your life around,' I replied, and raised my glass, 'cheers.'

The roll of notes were placed back into my jacket pocket, I was pleased and happy, but sadly unaware that other watchful eyes had studied our exchange with more than a passing interest. So I sat and sipped my beer, my buying trip complete, the alcoves full. I lit a cigarette and smiled to myself as I recalled the previous night. Gwen's mother was called away, visiting friends, and we took the opportunity to cement our relationship, becoming lovers in the true sense of the term.

As we lay naked, our bodies coiled together, she spoke softly.

'I know that you must inevitably return to your own time, but I will live with this moment for the rest of my life.'

I pulled her close, feeling her heartbeat on my chest. 'Why must I return?'

She tapped me playfully on the chest, 'because you belong there silly, that is where your family and friends are.'

I smiled at her and brushed a lock of hair away from her eyes. 'It's true, I do have some very dear friends, but no family.'

She frowned, raising her body on one arm to look down at me, 'no family?'

I shrugged, reaching for the pack of cigarettes, and lit one. 'A fisherman found me, wrapped in swaddling clothes bobbing around in a reed basket on the river Aire apparently.'

She gasped, raising a hand to her lips, as I blew smoke rings, and then the truth kicked in and she beat me within an inch of my life. 'For goodness sake Jimmy!'

I fended her off laughing, 'okay, I'm sorry, please don't hurt me.'

'Are you a man or a mouse?'

I raised an eyebrow, 'cheese on toast would be nice.'

She laughed. 'I was found in the accident and emergency department of Leeds General Infirmary. Seemingly well dressed and nurtured and in a brand-new baby carrier. There was a note saying when I was born, my Christian name, and a few desperate lines from my mother describing how she just could not cope any more. And how she hoped and prayed that I would find people who could love me and bring me up as one of their own.'

She laid her head on my chest and sighed, 'that is so sad, but you must have found adoptive parents?'

I ground out the cigarette in the ashtray, a lump in my throat. 'Yes, yes I did, and they were the most wonderful people in the whole wide world, but they died in a road traffic accident when I was nineteen.'

'What about your Aunties and Uncles?'

I smiled grimly in the darkened room, 'they never really cared for me, not being one of their own, and made it clear that I was no longer a member of the family. It never bothered me really, they were just a sad middle- aged pack of shit heads as far as I was concerned, and I was better off without them.'

We dressed in silence, neither of us broaching the subject of a permanent return. I could not possibly make a promise that I might be unable to keep, and I suspect she thought the same.

I finished my pint and headed for the door, pulling my coat collar up as a chill wind caught my breath. The blow to the back of my head sent me sprawling and I felt rough hands rolling me onto my back. He was straddled over me, his hands tearing at my coat. In fear and desperation, I reached up gripping his crutch, and heard a sound like walnuts cracking. He roared like a wounded bull and rolled onto the pavement. His accomplice was about to play football with my head, and I closed my eyes, waiting for the boot that would obliterate my face. Instead I heard a muffled series of thuds, and when I opened my eyes they were both writhing in the blood-stained snow.

He stood over me and reached out a hand, 'are you okay soldier,' he said with a grin. I recognised him immediately, his burned ravaged face was one that remained with me for the rest of my life. I reached out and he pulled me to my feet. I nodded and stared down at the two puking bodies in the snow.

'I know you, we have met before.'

He grinned as we shook hands, 'we have, and you owe me a pint I think.'

I smiled, 'shouldn't we call an ambulance or something.'

He looked at me in surprise, 'what for? they've just had a good bashing, nothing more. They will wake up tomorrow with sore heads and bollocks, and no doubt some lingering regrets, but they will live to fight another day.'

The gargoyle still refused my money, and nodded over to the solitary figure lighting a pipe in the corner. 'So you know Jack?'

I nodded, even though the name was new to me.

'He's a good man with a fearsome reputation.'

'So I have discovered,' I replied, and returned to the table with our beers.

'Cheers,' I said, raising my glass, and he smiled as we clinked glasses through an aromatic cloud of pipe smoke, his pale blue eyes almost piercing.

'You saved my bacon today, my name is Jimmy by the way,' and we shook hands.

'Jack,' he replied, and offered nothing more.

I lit a cigarette, 'how did you know...?'

He grinned, 'that the brothers Grimm would follow you when you flashed the cash? Well I saw it, they saw it, and the rest was a robbing waiting to happen.'

I stared at my beer and shook my head, 'I was warned about that by wiser folk than me, but forgot.'

He laughed and sipped his beer. 'These are lean times Jimmy, if you have money it is best to keep it well out of view.'

I nodded, 'so you know these men?'

His winter smile returned, 'aye, I know them well, we fought together in the same battalion, they are good lads.'

I frowned, ' I don't understand, you have just knocked the seven bells out of a couple of friends of yours?'

He smiled, 'I had a strict Christian upbringing and don't approve of violence or theft. They deserved a good bashing and will be better men tomorrow, they know it, I know it. One will have a sore head in the morning and the other a swollen pair of knackers that will hurt like billio, but that aside they will be wiser, and less inclined to avarice and violence with a bit of luck.'

' I wouldn't like to get on the wrong side of you.'

He laughed softly, 'you've got a strong grip yourself soldier, it fair made my eyes water when I heard his nuts crack.'

I sipped my beer, my mind working quickly. 'Actually, I am not a soldier, never have been, I was in a reserved occupation during the war,' I lied. He never asked and I in turn never implied what that occupation was. He simply shrugged his shoulders and sipped his beer.

'Fair enough, you were still working for the common good, fighting the fight in your own way, and that's good enough for me.' He struck a match and relit his pipe, a thin snake of smoke emerging from his thin lips. 'I was one of the lucky ones and came back in one piece.'

I looked at him with some surprise, 'you still paid a price Jack.'

'Oh you mean this?' he said with a sad wry smile, pointing a finger at his face. 'No, this happened when I was a nipper. My old man came home drunk as usual one evening, and threw me across the kitchen, and I ended up face down in the coal fire.' I sat back and stared at him in horror, lost for words.

'It was the end of my childhood. I only have nightmare memories of indescribable pain, endless visits to the hospital, and bullying. Kids called me Frankenstein and the bogey man...children can be very cruel sometimes.'

He paused to take a drink of beer.

'What of your dad, did he go to prison?'

'No, I never let on, I told them that I had been larking about and tripped. Mam pleaded with me to give him another chance, and I could never refuse her, and deep down I still loved my dad. He never touched a drop after that, but turned to God for redemption. He even became a church warden, and we would often sit by the fire and listen as he read passages from the good book. Whenever I woke up bathed in sweat and screaming at the world, which was frequent, he was always there, cradling me in his arms. Many years later mam told me that when they finally returned from the hospital, she reached for a carving knife and raised it high, ready to plunge into father's chest, and he ripped open his shirt and closed his eyes. She was incapable of course and fell to her knees in tears, and they cried and prayed all through the night.'

I noticed my hand was trembling as I lit a cigarette, and slid the packet across the table, but he declined with a shake of the head. 'I take it that the bullying continued.'

'Oh yes, but I soon learned that there was a pathway I could follow to bring it to an end.'

'Let me guess, you turned the other cheek.'

It was the only Christian course of action I could think of...'

He lifted his pint and drank deeply, collecting his thoughts. 'Then I bashed them, I broke noses, split lips, and spilt blood on a regular basis.' He looked at me sadly, ' I was not proud of these acts you understand, but I was a very angry young man and it simply had to stop. It didn't matter if they were older or bigger boys, the rage inside me was all consuming and I retaliated with such power, they staggered back in shock and fear, and in the end, it worked to a certain degree, and I was befriended by the sort of weak moronic cowards who always bray for violence, whilst hiding behind a bully. It continued to a lesser degree by the girls, simply because they were safe in the knowledge that I wouldn't and couldn't hand out the same punishment. But that did not concern me so much, as I was aware that I would always be a bit of a joke and quite repulsive to the opposite sex.'

A quick smile lit up his tortured face, as he reached a hand to an inside breast pocket, and slid a small photo from his wallet, placing it on the table. I picked it up and studied the sepia formal studio image of a young women.

'She is lovely.'

'Aye, she is at that, her name is Clara and I am proud to say that she is my wife and mother of our two happy and healthy bairns.'

'So you were wrong after all.'

He returned my smile and the photo to a pocket next to his heart. 'I was wrong, though what she ever saw in me is a mystery, and I count my blessings every day that I awake with her by my side.'

I watched as he weaved between tables, heading to the gents. The landlord was busy in the tap room, and this time I checked for prying eyes, but we were alone. He was a proud man and I instinctively knew that he would not accept my money, so I snatched the only available moment open to me, and slipped my roll of notes into the breast pocket of his winter coat draped over the chair. We shook hands in the thaw, the only evidence of our earlier skirmish lay in a rippling tide of watery brown slush, mixed with thin traces of pale pink blood dissipating through cracks in the pavement.

We parted as friends...I never saw him again.

CHAPTER 22

Now we were four, discussing time travel like it was a walk in the park. I told them about my refusal to travel back, and Gwen squeezed my hand, but I left out my encounter with the muggers, and my new found friend. We were sitting around the fire in the front room, drinking tea and simply enjoying one another's company, it was early evening and we had planned to catch a show at the City Varieties.

Sandy lit a cigarette, a troubled look on his face. 'So, because you refused to travel, the signal is becoming weaker?'

'I think so...but I could be wrong.'

A sharp flicker of light drew my attention to the net curtains of the bay window, and my heart missed a beat or three. Then the angry bee returned, loud and insistent, and I smiled.

'Fortunately, it seems that I was wrong,' I said standing.

They stared at me, and Mary was the first to realise what was happening. She too stood and clasped my hand, as Sandy looked on, a look of wonder and awe in his face.

'It is time,' I said, and Gwen stared open eyed at the three of us in alarm. 'What is happening, please tell me what is happening?' She leapt to her feet and placed a protective arm around my waist.

I pulled her to me and kissed her gently on the forehead, 'it is time for me to go sweetheart,' I whispered.

'You must change Jimmy,' said Mary urgently and I nodded, reluctantly unravelling Gwen's arms from my waist. I dressed slowly, even as the angry bee urged me to hurry, and looked around my bedroom fondly as I packed the battered old suitcase with my return travelling clothes. My remaining money was stacked neatly on a shelf in the wardrobe. It seemed silly to hide it in a time when most left their doors unlocked, because we were all in the same boat and there was nothing of value to steal.

Light flickered through the upper glass panel of the front door, as I descended the stairs. They were waiting in the hall, and Gwen swayed when she saw me in my future attire. She would have collapsed had it not been for the supportive arms of our friends.

Mary hugged me tightly, 'please come back to me,' she whispered in my ear. I placed the suitcase on the floor, 'these are my clothes for the return journey Mary, they must be placed in the cavities before they are sealed.' She nodded and hugged me one more time before letting go. Sandy almost broke my spine and I looked at him sternly, 'I am relying on you to finish the brickwork downstairs,' I said.

He nodded vigorously and brushed away a tear. 'Away with you Jimmy, the time capsules will be sealed until you return to your own time, make no mistake.'

Finally, I took Gwen into my arms and we held onto one another until I felt that my heart would break, and when that moment arrived, I pulled away from her and opened the door. She cried out and lunged forward, and I looked back briefly, witnessed my friends desperately holding on to her arms as she attempted to break free and follow in my footsteps.

I was back, standing in a barren muddy wasteland and staring at a door, now firmly closed. There was no nausea this time and I felt fine, but the scream that followed was loud and piercing. She was framed in the gap between overgrown tangled hedges where a gate had once been, her eyes wide open, staring at me in alarm. I guessed that she was no more than five or six years of age, very pretty, and pretty frightened. Her mother appeared, dragging a dog on a lead, 'any more screaming from you madam and it's early to bed.'

The girl pointed a chubby little finger, 'bogey man.'

Her mother's gaze followed the pointing finger. Her eyes widened quickly in surprise and then narrowed as her expression changed to one of disdain and contempt. She snatched the girl's hand and pulled her away, I could hear the squeals of protest as they hurried away into the night. I must say that I was more than pleased to see my car parked on the street, complete with driver. Admittedly the chauffeur was deep in the land of nod, but it was common knowledge that Elvis could cat nap at the drop of a hat, and my heart rejoiced to see him once more.

I rapped on the passenger window, no response, so I decided with a smile that a more radical approach was called for. I gripped the roof bars, flexing the weight on my feet. The car rocked and the alarm kicked in. Sadly, Elvis was forever a bit of a cool dude. I was hoping for a little bit more than a lazy opening of his eyes, the quick toothy grin, and the sigh of the window as it slid down.

He fobbed the alarm, 'Hi Jimmy, you look like shit.'

'Cheers, do you have the house keys?'

He reached inside a pocket and handed them to me.

'I'll just be a minute, there's something I have to check.'

My footfalls echoed loudly as I headed for the cellar, picking up my torch in the kitchen. The narrow door juddered open reluctantly, and I played the beam on the far walls.

They had done a sterling job, the grubby whitewashed walls were undisturbed. No one would ever have guessed that there had once been two alcoves there. Sandy had even removed the light switch and wiring.

'Well done you,' I whispered.

I let Elvis drive, unsure if the sickness would belatedly have me puking, but we arrived at my flat completely puke- less.

'How long have I been gone Elvis?'

'Five days almost,' he replied.

'Anything happened in my absence?'

'Not really, we just talk about you and wonder what is happening. You're the only time travelling friend that we have right now.'

I looked at the clock on the dashboard, it was just after eight.

'So what's it to be Jimmy, an early night, or the pub?'

'Oh the pub,' I replied, 'most definitely the pub.,

It was quiet as we slid onto the bar stools, I ordered a couple of beers.

'What day is it Elvis?'

'It's Thursday, welcome back my friend.' he threw an arm over my shoulder and almost pulled me off the stool. The beers arrived and I peeled off a ten-bob note. The almost comatose youth stared lazily at the note and shook his head. 'Sorry mate, can't take no foreign currency, 'has to be coin of the realm like.'

I stared for a moment at the red note in my hand and started to laugh. Somehow this ten shilling note had travelled back with me, but how? Then I recalled the moment I had inspected my loot before closing the suitcase. I had peeled off a note and folded it into my inside pocket, and it was now a note that belonged to the past, but had come from the future. Consequently, it was free to travel each way.

Elvis was quick on the uptake and shook his head. 'You trying to pass off some mickey mouse money boy,' he said in his excellent imitation of Tommy Lee Jones. ' Why you should be ashamed of yourself.' He reached for his wallet and handed the kid a ten pound note, and now we were both laughing.

The kid frowned, absently scratching at a newly acquired tattoo on his neck, that probably translated into ' I am a knob head' in oriental script. His dull listless eyes were less than amused at our mutual amusement. 'Did I say something funny?'

I laid the note on the bar, 'now pay attention 007, the queens head on the note indicates that this is indeed 'coin of the realm' to quote your words, but a bit before your time.'

He picked it up and studied it. 'It's a ten shilling note,' I explained slowly, 'a vintage coin of the realm note, no longer in circulation.'

'So how old is it?'

'Well, ten shilling notes were withdrawn in 1970.'

'So what's it worth?'

'Fifty pence in today's money,' replied Elvis quickly.

The kid laughed and dropped the note on the counter, 'fifty pence for two beers, are you having a laugh?'

'However, now it is a collector's item, and...'

I reigned Elvis in. 'Let's leave it,' I said, and pulled the note toward me, but still left it on display. I could see the kids' brain was working overtime.

'So, it's a vintage note, that could be worth something.?' he said, scratching his neck.

I shook my head, ' I wouldn't think so.' I looked at Elvis for confirmation, and he shook his head lazily. 'There's probably hundreds of them out there, maybe thousands.'

The kid stared as I scooped the note up and folded it into my top pocket.

'Well I've never seen one before, let me take it off your hands for a couple of beers.' The kid was good, I liked him.

'To tell you the truth,' I said, 'I never thought of it as a collector's item, but now...?'

Elvis cut in sharply, 'give the kid a break Jimmy, make it two beers apiece and the note is yours.'

He beamed so brightly, I almost felt guilty.

I frowned and pulled the note from my pocket reluctantly, it could be worth something 'are you quite sure about this, the kid might be right.'

Elvis scolded me, ' you've been carrying that old note around as long as I have known you Jimmy boy, now is the time to let go, do the deal.'

I did as I was told and slid the note across the counter. The kid snatched it up and slid it into his pocket.

'Why do I feel that I have just made a big mistake?'

The kid grinned smugly, 'don't worry about it mister, if it turns out to be worth a fortune, then I will be sure to let you know.'

I smiled into the dead pools of his vacuous eyes. 'Well thank you, that is most reassuring.'

We drank our beers and Elvis flipped his mobile phone, 'do I call in the troops?'

I shook my head, 'not tonight, I'm all done in.'

He nodded at the barman, talking incessantly into his mobile phone, 'at least you made his night.'

'It is nice to bring a little joy into a stranger's life,' I replied, 'even if it is a bit short lived.'

***

I slept well, awoke refreshed, showered and nuked a bowl of instant porridge. It was a grey and sombre morning, but I felt neither, and was more than glad to be alive. The morning air was cool and crisp as I walked briskly to the house. I then did a detour and headed for Beatie's house instead, but my repeated knocks on the door went unanswered, and I headed for the back door of my house.

It was then that I saw an old woman pulling a shopping trolley down the street. She leaned forward as if a wild wind was impeding her progress, and her eyes were on the pavement, studying her slow but methodical and painful progress. I waited as she approached, but she trundled past without so much as a glance. I fell into step beside her. 'Woman, is you so old you can pass a friend without so much as a smile?'

She stopped and raised her head, frowning as she peered down the street. Then she turned and looked up at me, and my heart almost stalled as that big Beaty smile emerged. 'Jimmy,' she whispered, a pool of tears gathering in those lovely old eyes. She reached up and brushed my cheek with the back of her hand, 'is it really you boy?'

I had to swallow hard, and just nodded dumbly as I gave her a hug. Her white linen hankie appeared magically from a sleeve and she dabbed her eyes. I took control of her trolley, and looped my arm through hers.

'A cup of tea would be nice.'

She said nothing as I led her home, aware that she constantly looked up at when she wasn't studying the cracks in the pavement. It seemed to me that in a short passage of time, she had become much frailer, less steady on her feet. I helped her with the keys and unlocked the door, leading her to a winged armchair by the fire. Her eyes followed me as I slipped in and out of the kitchen.

The kettle was on the boil and I busied myself filling the milk jug and rattling tea cups. I swilled some hot water around the tea pot and emptied it into the sink, before adding four tea spoons of loose tea. I then added the boiling water, and stirred before replacing the lid. The chrome tea strainer was placed over each cup as I poured, and she followed my movements in silence.

Then she discovered her voice again, 'you have bin a time traveling haven't you, she said softly,

'Yes I have,' I answered quickly.

She raised a hand and beat her chest softly, 'oh my oh my!'

I placed her tea on a small occasional table beside her chair. 'Drink your tea woman, you look like you've seen a ghost.'

'Did you bring us the pie Jimmy?'

Her question tugged at my heartstrings, 'not yet.'

She smiled and sipped her tea, ‘but you will knock on our door an' bring us the pie.' It was not a question but a statement of fact, and I had nowhere to hide any more.

'Yes,' I said, 'I am the pie man.'

She cried softly for a while, and I reached out and held her hand. Soon the tears passed, and she smiled again, looking more like the formidable Beatie of old.

'You must think I'm just a silly old woman.'

I nodded, patting her frail old hand, 'absolutely, but less of the 'old'.

She laughed, and it was her old laugh, so loud that I swear my day-old emerging whiskers returned from whence they came, and I was clean shaven again. She insisted that I tell all about my adventures, listening with the intensity of a child at bedtime, sometimes roaring with laughter, and occasionally rolling her eyes in wonder. I completed my tale by saying, 'and here I am again, come to see me Beaty on me first day back.'

She smiled, patting the back of my hand, a slight frown and questioning look in her eyes. 'What about the girl, the lovely Gwen, you don't say nothing about her?'

I must have coloured then, as I bought time by fumbling for my cigarettes. 'There's no future in it Beaty, she cannot travel with me to my time, and I can't stay with her in her time.'

She looked troubled and continued to absently tap the back of my hand. 'You love her, don't you?'

'Yes, yes I do.'

'And by all accounts the feeling is mutual?'

'Yes, but there are problems, insurmountable problems.'

'Who says so?'

'The law of physics says so, if I went back and stayed for good, then I would reach a point in time when I was born. We simply cannot co-exist together in the same time and space.'

'Who says so?'

I paused and stared at her, it was a good question. 'Well, some of the brightest minds on the planet springs to mind, after all Quantum Physics is not a subject favoured by your average spotty student.'

She shook her head sadly, 'well you got me there Jimmy.' She worked her dentures furiously, 'I'm a simple woman who has led a simple life, an' I never had no need for the law of feesiks I must say.' Suddenly she slammed her hand on the arm of her chair. 'Now the law of god I understand, an' believe me he knows a thing or two about the law of love. And there ain't no barrier that hasn't bin broken by the law of love...praise the lord!'

I was suddenly transported back to a gospel meeting in the deep south of America. The urge to raise the palms of my hands as I heard a joyful chorus of black gospel singing was almost irresistible. But resist I did. My love and respect for this old woman forbade me from such a childish and adolescent display.

She smiled, ' so if you did go back to her, and you said sod it to the law of feesiks, you could possibly live with the woman you love for years, before whatever happens happens.'

I inhaled and blew a smoke ring. ' And I would die at the grand old age of fifty three.

She shrugged, 'but you don't know that, none of us know when the Lord will come calling.' Suddenly she was leaking sweat, her eyes wide in a trance like state and her hand gripped mine with surprising strength. 'You must go back Jimmy, she needs you by her side.' Then suddenly she was back, and seemed to nod at some unseen messenger.

'You will go back Jimmy.'

'I will?'

'Oh yes, you were always destined to be with her, from the day you was born.'

'How do you know these things Beaty?'

'Me talk to Cleve 'bout such things.' Bout the house an' the travellers, an' why such things should happen to some folk an' not to others. 'She tilted her head back and laughed the Beaty laugh. 'He say to me, don't meddle woman, don't question why some folk travel an' some don't. It's a special place for folk who is in pain, who have lost someone an' had their hearts broken. It seems to me that sorrow is the passport to that magical garden, it takes them to a place where they can heal their pain an' mend their broken hearts, an' where they can help other lost souls with their sorrows on the journey.' She paused and looked at me searchingly, 'does that ring any bells Jimmy?'

'Oh yes,' I replied, 'it rings a whole host of bells, an ear popping great big Ben clatter of bells.'

***

Elvis had rallied the troops, and they were chatting amongst themselves when I took my seat and raised a glass of beer. 'Strength and honour,' I said, and they responded in kind. I then outlined my adventures to a totally captive audience, but without any reference to Gwen, I don't know why, but I didn't. It was Gordon who spoke first. 'So, let me get this right Jimmy, you have an untouched time capsule of art work to open in the cellar, right?'

I nodded, 'that is correct.'

'Fantastic, we must film it of course and put it on U tube,' his eyes were bright as he raised his pint. 'Imagine the massive international response as we filmed the opening of the time capsule. The first man to travel through time and return with booty to prove it.' He slapped me on the back, 'you will be the most famous man on the planet.'

My flock were silent as I looked at him in surprise. 'What in heavens name are you talking about Gordon?'

The quick look of a startled deer appeared in his eyes, but he play punched me on the arm, 'you nearly got me then Jimmy.'

'No, I am really serious Gordon, this must never be leaked to the media. This is not a story for Twatspeak or Mushbook. This has to remain here, with us...do you understand?' My voice was raised and I checked myself, aware that other people were glancing in our direction. I was also surprised at the anger in my voice, edged with something akin to panic.

'Easy Jimmy.' Sally frowned at me and threw a protective arm across Gordon's slumped shoulders. 'Gordon is wrong to suggest we tell the world about your travels, but he is right to say that these are extraordinary circumstances. For goodness sake, we all worry shit loads when you are gone, and whether you will make it back, did you ever think of that?' There was a flash of anger in her eyes, and a still shimmering pool of tears, held back by a firewall of willpower.

My anger ebbed away like a retreating tide, 'you are right Sal, my apologies Gordon.'

He smiled thinly, but still avoided any eye contact.

'It's just the very thought of the media camped outside the house, is the stuff of nightmares, and besides, what does a stack of paintings behind a brick wall prove? I could easily have bought them in the here and now and bricked them up myself.'

Ammo grinned across the table, 'hey I never thought about that, you could have set all this up yourself and be just stringing us all along.'

His smile faded in an instant, replaced by a serious searching look. I stared back at him, unable to comprehend what he had just said. I looked at all their familiar faces, and I could see that they looked troubled, as if they were looking for answers to unspoken questions. 'Why this is preposterous, you cannot possibly believe that this is some kind of hoax on my part?'

Ammo shrugged and toyed with his beer glass, but not for long. His shoulders started to shake, and a sound escaped through his lips, like gas escaping from a fizzy drinks bottle. Then he was joined by the rest of my motley crew as they could suppress their laughter no longer.

'You 'orrible bunch of bastards,' I said with feeling.

CHAPTER 23

Tristan patted Gordon's hand, 'So,' he said, 'we are all agreed that Jimmy's travels go no further than this table.' We looked at one another, and then raised our glasses as one. Sally seemed to distance herself, and appeared detached and troubled.

'What's up Sal', I said, 'you look like a banker who suddenly realises she has to pay tax on her billion-pound bonus?'

Tristan chirped in, 'she's got a new boyfriend Jimmy, and doesn't know how to tell you that she don't love you no more.'

'Tristan.'

'Yes Jimmy.'

'Shut the fuck up.'

'Yes Jimmy, 'I'm shutting the fuck up right now.'

Sally looked into my eyes then, and I saw pain there. 'I'm so sorry.'

I reached across the table and took her hand, 'What's all this,' I said softly, 'what in heavens name do you have to apologise for?'

She gripped my hand and shook her head sadly, 'you don't understand Jimmy,' she whispered. ' I posted a message on facebook and twitter.'

A silence followed, Ammo was visibly shaking like a balloon who had just had bad words with a drawing pin.

'I am so sorry,' she pleaded, gripping my hands with both of hers. 'I thought it was a good idea at the time. I thought that the world should know that time travel is possible. It is the story of the century Jimmy, and would make you, and, well all of us very famous and possibly rich even'

I stared at her and withdrew my hands. 'Okay, we have a situation people, I need constructive ideas, and I need them now.'

Suzie raised a hand, 'that was a line from one of the Bourne films.'

I nodded grimly, 'well spotted, go to the top of the class, but I am still waiting people, and the clock is ticking.'

Tristan fluttered his eyelash extensions at me. 'Well I think we should just come out and tell them the truth, after all it didn't do me any harm.'

I dismissed the idea immediately. 'I imagine that declaring that you are glad to be gay to your parents can be somewhat daunting. But to declare to the world that you are the first time traveler to return and appear on telly, is, I suspect, a tad more challenging.'

Sally raised her hand and I just pointed at her and barked, 'yes?' because I was still miffed with her.

'I could go back online and tell the world I was somewhat economical with the truth?'

Ammo laughed and slapped his knee pantomime style, 'a lying toe rag you mean.'

'That's not fair.'

'This is really not helping, the media are going to descend on the house tomorrow morning, like flies on a freshly laid steaming turd.'

Sally caught my eye by raising both of her arms.

I smiled, 'you are not under arrest, and I am unarmed, so shoot.'

'Facebook is knee deep in knob heads with conspiracy theories and alien abductions, so the fact is that this story will just go down the plug hole with all the rest.'

'Good point,' I said with a measure of relief, 'Sally's probably right, but I need someone to get over to the house and scout around.'

Sally stood and looked at me, ' I created this mess...'

'I'll go with her,' said Tristan, 'but we may be gone sometime.'

They were in fact gone for a remarkably short time, with Tristan leading the charge, breathless and flushed, while Sally hung back, staring at her shoes.

Somehow, I knew that it was not good news.

'The house is lit up like a Christmas tree,' he gasped, 'there's media all over the shop. High tech TV. vans with rooftop antennae, animated reporters talking to camera, talking to neighbors, even interviewing each other, it's really scary.' He gulped and almost paused for breath, 'what do we do Jimmy? Why the cops have even cordoned off the road.'

I frowned at the news, 'but it's a cul -de- sac.'

He pulled a face, 'they've cordoned it off anyway.'

'Well we can't hang around here.'

'But I just got a round in,' said Elvis with a look of alarm.

I raised my glass, ' down in one people, we may be in a hurry but I hate to see waste.'

All in all, they did well, and I was impressed. There was some snorting and gagging, and a little coughing, but the glasses were mostly empty when we slammed them down onto the table. We hurried out in a rather disorderly fashion, and bodily collisions were inevitable, accompanied by curses and some laughter. The timing was perfect as we passed a gossip of reporters and a camera crew heading in the other direction. We adjourned to Gordons flat, a five minute walk away, and I stared out of the window to the street below. Beer cans cracked like muted assassin's gunfire behind me, and there was the comforting sound of chatter and laughter. Someone handed me a beer, it was Ammo standing beside me, following my gaze into the street.

'So what do we do now Ammo?'

He shrugged, 'we drink.'

'Thanks, but I was looking for something a little more constructive than that.'

'Elmer Gantry,' whispered a voice behind me, and I turned and smiled at Suzie.

'Explain?'

She grinned, 'Elmer Gantry was the title of a movie starring Burt Lancaster...'

'Film darling,' Tristan corrected, 'we are after all English, so do try to speak like one.'

'And Jean Simmons,' she said, ignoring him completely.

'Great movie,' said Elvis, and then immediately corrected himself, 'sorry, film.'

I stepped away from the window and started to pace the room. 'I remember it well, ol' Burt was a quick thinking fast talking preacher man. Who fell for the obvious charms of the lovely Jean, but he loved the dollar value of being a dodgy preacher more as I recall.'

I stopped my pacing and looked to Susie for more.

'So how does that help our present situation?'

'Well, you could be Elmer.'

I lit a cigarette, inhaled, exhaled, and considered.

'I like it Susie, I like it a lot.'

'You do?'

'I most certainly do.'

I paced some more, 'let me get this straight, you want me to step into the lion's den, and tell the world that I am a time travelling man. You want me to lead my flock into the cellar as I tap my toffee hammer on solid brick walls. Is that what you are suggesting?'

Suzie nodded, her perfectly formed ruby red lips parting in a smile, 'do you think you can pull it off Jimmy?'

I frowned, 'well to tell the truth I don't rightly know. I mean I am just a quintessentially shy and reserved English bloke, what do you think?'

She laughed out loud, 'you could do it with your eyes wide shut.'

'Yes, I think I could, but a preacher man is not enough. I would also have to be a bit of a nutter, a crank, an unwashed waste of space on planet Earth...I need more people?'

Elvis raised a hand nervously.

'Yes Elvis.'

'Gween men from Mars, alien abductions, that sort of thing maybe?'

Suddenly Tristan burst into laughter, 'it's raining gween men halleluiah!' I frowned and pointed the black fingernail at him, and the affect was immediate.

'Sorry Jimmy.'

I pursed and tapped my lips, studying his eager upturned face thoughtfully.

'I like it Elvis, tell me more.'

He blushed, 'well, you could perhaps explain that you were abducted by aliens in the same garden before you became a time traveller.'

'Cranking up the crank, I like it, good thinking Elvis.'

He grinned broadly as Gordon slapped him on the back.

'You'll need some really nerdy spectacles,' added Ammo, 'something that marks you out as a bit of a twat.'

Elvis raised his arm again, ' I have a pair of very large glasses with thick lenses that belonged to a half blind cousin of my uncles.'

I was half tempted to inquire why he held on to such a remarkable pair of specs, but time was short.

'Goofy teeth,' offered Ammo, 'I got some from the joke shop once and

I can highly recommend them.'

I grinned, 'the teeth sound good, I will trust you with that purchase. I will also require some second-hand clothing, an ensemble that does not quite fit, but I will source that myself...anything else?'

'You'll need to carry a shopping bag,' said Sally.

I frowned, 'will I?'

'You will,' she replied.

'I've got a bag for life from Waitrose,' said Gordon helpfully.'

Sally frowned, 'no, it has to be something vintage, something cheap and nasty.'

'Me Nan's got one of those old string bags,' offered Susie.

'Excellent,' I replied, 'it will be perfect for showing off copies of 'The Bus' magazine.'

She looked puzzled, 'I never realised you were such a big fan?'

We all groaned her into submission.

I looked at each one of them in turn. 'So, who is going to accompany me into the lion's den?'

'Personally, I can feel some root canal work coming on at the dentist,' replied Sally sadly.

Elvis shifted uncomfortably in his chair, 'piles,' he replied, 'I believe I have an urgent doctor's appointment so we can get to the bottom of it.'

Gordon shook his head sadly, ' got to take the dog to the vets, we think he's got rabies.'

I cocked an eyebrow.

'Well, maybe not rabies, but he is not well and is in urgent need of a pedicure.'

'I'm confused Gordon, I didn't know you had a dog?'

'Oh yes,' he replied confidently, we bought a rescue dog about....' He glanced at his watch, 'about three hours ago, from adogisforchristmas.com. It was recommended to us by friends. They even show you pictures of mam and dad, but as they were like people, and he is a dog, I never saw the connection. He is quite aggressive to goggles our goldfish, but we reckon that is because he was probably abused by a goldfish when he was a pup.'

I turned to Ammo, who was texting someone.

'Ammo?'

He looked up from his mobile phone and shook his head. 'Sorry mate, it's my flower arranging class. If I miss it now then I can kiss goodbye to my diploma.' He met my perplexed stare and pocketed the phone, his round face cracking into a grin. 'I was joking man, I'll be there.'

I looked at Tristan, but he beat me to it. 'We'll all be with you Jimmy, wouldn't miss it for the world. I have some stuff in the salon that may come in useful.'

'Stuff?'

Sally chipped in, 'he used to work at the YTV studios, didn't you love.'

Tristan nodded demurely, 'I was in 'make up.' He paused and frowned at a chipped fingernail. 'Honestly, the things I could tell you about telly land would make your ears bleed...'

'I'm sure it's very fascinating, but could you fast forward please.'

'Sorry Jimmy, the point is that we were there to make people look good on camera, or to make them look somewhat less than glamorous, are you with me so far?'

I was fast losing the will to live.

'I can make you look unwashed, unkempt, pale and spotty. In fact, I would go so far as to say that you will be transformed into the nerd of the year.'

And so it came to pass, that Jimmy the bespectacled spotty and hygienically challenged time traveller emerged into a world that waited with bated breath.

I must confess that I was quite unprepared for the scene that unfolded before me. The crowd were loud and animated, some craning their necks hoping to see something interesting. Children screamed, ran in circles screaming, and screamed at their parents. Or remained still as they texted, then screamed 'oh my god!' when someone replied with mundane regularity. There were hippies in abundance of course, banging on drums, playing tortuous tin whistles and throwing clubs and balls into the air, as they do.

I turned to my team, 'how do I look?'

'You look like Mr Beans ugly brother.' said Suzie.

'Excellent, let's go.'

It took us some time to struggle through the crowd. I had to resort to bawling at people. 'Excuse me, we live here! Thank you we live here! Can we get through to our house please!'. Pockets of the crowd resisted until they looked upon my toothy pale and spotty countenance, and then they shrank away in fear and dismay that I had not rung a bell and cried 'unclean'.

When we reached the police tape a child copper held out his hand and stared at us sternly.' 'Sorry sir, but you must remain behind the tape.'

I pulled the house keys from my pocket and rattled them in his face. 'Well I'm sorry too officer, but that is my house,' I said pointing theatrically, ‘and if I am not mistaken this is not a crime scene, and we would like to enter and have a cup of tea.'

He raised a hand and brushed the faint suggestion of a man 'tache with his index finger, before taking a step back. Perhaps fearing that his taser gun would be no match against my halitosis. The constable paled, his eyes flickering over boils made more puss like by the unnatural sickly pale pallor of my skin. The huge spectacles, my ill-fitting clothes and ancient string shopping bag, displaying a rusted tartan tea flask and a copy of a 'Short History of the Bus.' Supplied, I was surprised to find by Elvis, who when questioned simply shrugged and replied, 'buses are big in China.'

There really was no answer to that, but I was grateful.

Meanwhile the child community officer was speaking into his radio. ‘Sarge, he’s here, Doctor Who has arrived.’ He coloured as I stared at him through my magnificently magnified, and changed tack .‘The key holder of the said property has arrived sir,' he corrected himself.

He listened and nodded, 'Sarge is on his way,' he said.

'That's nice,' I replied.

As we patiently waited for Sarge I lowered the glasses to the end of my nose, to relieve the double vision and peer at the plod. 'Is that what they are calling me, Doctor Who?'

He looked down at his boots and said nothing.

My eyes flickered over the mob, when suddenly I spotted a familiar face and sidled over. 'What ya doing here woman? You should be 'ome making me jerk chicken.'

The big Beatie smile appeared as she looked up at me, but it was soon replaced by a sudden quick frown eclipsing the sunshine of her smile in a heartbeat. 'You ain't Jimmy,' she cried accusingly and pointing an angry shaking finger. 'Why do you want to go confusing an old confused woman like me for?' she said. You should be ashamed of yourself boy.'

I raised my specs and winked at her, 'it really is me Beaty, I just need to be in disguise today.'

The phrase 'eye popping' had to have been formed by someone, and I reckon that someone had to be someone very like Beatie. As she stared up at me and her eyes grew larger and larger, until she clamped a hand over her mouth and slowly released what sounded like a slither of hissing snakes.

'Is that you in there Jimmy?'

I smiled down at her, 'I am in disguise for a reason, do you understand woman?'

She nodded her head vigorously, her eyes wide open with laughter and delight.

I heard Gordon call for me then and touched her gently on the cheek, before returning to the business of the day.

Sarge had seen it all before, his eyes were painted dull and lackluster, and they told me that he really would rather be somewhere else. Perhaps at home, or a rugby match or a pint or two with the lads, but certainly not here, in the valley of the cranks.

His eyes revealed neither surprise or revulsion when he looked at me. 'Are you the key holder to this house sir?'

I nodded and he raised the tape for us to enter.

The camera crews were having lunch, the TV presenters were bitching amongst themselves, as make-up girls fluttered between them, applying a comb here and a puff of powder there, and occasionally pausing to hug one another as they tend to do in telly land. We were completely ignored until we passed the policemen posted at the gap in the hedges. Suddenly there was a shout and all hell broke loose. I retreated behind my Praetorian guard as planned, and more police arrived to hold back the hoard of invading hacks, as everyone seemed to be shouting at once.

'Are you the time traveller?'

'Tell us about time travelling Jimmy?'

'It is said that you have evidence, conclusive proof that you have traveled through time Jimmy, is that true?'

'Is time travel really possible?'
'Where's your proof Jimmy?'
'Come on, don't be shy, the world is waiting Jimmy.'
'Is time travel bad for your health?'

The questions came thick and fast, but the questioners were confused as to who they should be addressing these questions too. Consequently, Ammo and Gordon shared the burden, until they stepped aside and I assumed my position as leader of the pack. It became instantly obvious by the groans in the crowd, that they were less than impressed by my appearance, and my heart soared to new heights.

Accustomed as I am to public speaking, the joke teeth had proved something of a challenge, mainly because they kept falling out. We solved the problem by using denture glue, but my speech and delivery sounded a bit on the odd side, which was perfect from my point of view. I pulled a sheet of paper from my pocket, and unfolded it ceremoniously. Their eager upturned faces were to me, a joy to behold. TV camera lights glowed, and as the noise subsided, I looked down at the blank sheet of paper in my hand. I could see it all unfolding before me. The BBC newsreader looking earnestly on the telly, as she warned, 'this report contains some flash photography.'

It was time, time for Elmer Gantry's smarter brother to take a bow.

CHAPTER 24

I set my nerd bag on the path, gleefully aware that a host of telephoto camera lens had focused on the bag and contents, and in a number of happy snappy clicks the images would be relayed to a waiting world faster than a sneeze in a pepper factory.

It was playtime. I stared solemnly at my blank sheet of paper, and then crumpled it up, tossing it aside like an old sweaty sock, and holding my arms aloft I swayed slightly, ushering in the widest beaming smile that I could possibly muster.

'Welcome brothers and sisters, welcome to a special place. A place where I have found peace and journeyed into the past. A place where I have journeyed through time itself and emerged wiser and unharmed. A place where I sought and received the protection of the Lord and his son Jesus Christ.'

I heard a voice in the distance cry, 'praise the lord,' and I was pleased, even though it sounded suspiciously like Beatty. I saw some camera lights pop off, and media folk lighting cigarettes and talking among themselves.

I was encouraged, this was a promising start.

'When I bought this old house, I just knew it was special because the lord had guided me here. I raised my voice a couple of octaves, 'he took me by the hand and raised it high until the auctioneers hammer of destiny fell with a thunderous crash and I was suddenly the proud owner of a sanctuary for troubled souls.'

I paused for breath, the natives were getting restless, and I was just getting into my stride. I was verbally walking among them, only pausing fleetingly so that they could touch or kiss the hem of my robe.

'Praise the lord!' I cried, arms outstretched.

Suddenly a small voice sounded from the heaving throng. 'That's all very well Jimmy, but we were led to believe that you have definitive evidence that you have traveled back in time?'

'Indeed I do sister, I have hidden items behind the walls of this very house, that have remained undiscovered since the year of our lord nineteen fifty six.'

Another impatient voice came from the crowd. 'Well in your own time Jimmy, me dinners on the table and it's getting cold.'

The aggressive and impatient laughter that followed was music to my ears.

'Soon brother, very soon,' I turned and looked at my followers solemnly. 'Do we go in now,' I cried, projecting my voice over the gathered gawping mob, 'or should I tell them?'

'You gotta tell 'em Jimmy!' cried Ammo with gusto, and I nodded slowly.

'Is that how y'all feel?'

'Yes!' they cried as one, ‘and may the lord be praised.'

At this point there was activity around the media vans, as they loaded cameras and lighting equipment.

'When I bought this house, I was standing in that very room,' I pointed at the bay window. 'When suddenly a bright blue beam of light flooded the lawn,' I cried, pointing at the mud.

'Is that the first time you traveled into the past Jimmy?'

'No brother,' I replied, my arms reaching skywards once more. 'It was the first and only time that I was transported into a Martian spaceship.'

I detected a collective groan, and felt my spirits soar. It was time to lay it on thick. 'All I remember brothers and sisters is a feeling of pain and revulsion, as I was exposed to a series of probes assaulting my mind. I recall seeing shadowy sinewy silent creatures with bloated spider like limbs and large oval heads...'

'I know what you mean, I've been there myself after a few pints of snakebite,' said a welcome wag from the crowd. There was a ripple of laughter as some of the media vans slid away in a soft toxic cloud of diesel fumes. Their rooftop antenna pointing to the stars, searching perhaps for E.T. or the meaning of life.

'Then I was returned to that very spot,' I cried, pointing to what had once been the green green grass of home. 'I was a wandering confused and lost soul, until I was found.' I looked at my followers, 'is that not so brothers and sisters?'

'It is so!' they cried as one, and I was pleased.

People started to drift away, some laughing, others complaining loudly, until the mob became a thin curious collection of people with nothing better to do. It was time, and I signaled to the bored cops on the gate, 'pray let them enter.'

I had assumed that at this point most of the media would have made up their minds that I was a lost cause, and simply barking mad. However, I was also aware that some would stay the course, for a variety of reasons. Page five, 'let's all have a laugh at this nutter,' was one. Or perhaps a light hearted and extremely cheap TV show called 'Losers or Loonies? You decide.' Or even an end of news light bite, 'and finally, a chance to get up close and personal with Jimmy, the time travelling, ghost encountering, and god-fearing alien abductee, is he simply unlucky or just plain crazy?...you make up your own mind.'

As I turned the key in the lock, I felt a sharp dig in the ribs. 'You haven't mentioned the spooks,' hissed Ammo. I turned and smiled my big Burt smile. 'Before we enter this special place, please be aware that it is occupied by others, by mischievous spirits, some of you will know of them as poltergeists.'

I looked back at the patient spill of bodies behind me, disappointed to see no looks of alarm, and could only conclude that they were experiencing some difficulty in absorbing even more exciting revelations. 'Anyway, should you feel a tug on your hair or a nip in your tuck, then I can tell you right now that it wasn't me.' This at least was followed by some banter and laughter.

I could easily have been in London, Rome or New York as I raised my arm and they filed eagerly behind me, jostling for the best position. I paused then in the main cellar, a place where sunlight had spilled on a dark and stormy night, so many seasons ago it seemed. I picked up a hammer placed there by one of my advanced guard, and tapped the old brickwork an either side of the fireplace. I frowned and crossed the room, turning my attention to a wall beside the window.

' That's an outside wall Jimmy,' said a voice from the crowd that had now become merely a group. I chose to ignore him, entering a recess under the stairs, tapping as I went.

'Are you sure it was down here Jimmy?'

'Absolutely,' I replied, tapping away and listening to the echoing footfalls of people retreating.

'The man's a loony,' I heard.

'A total basket case if you ask me.'

'He's off his rocker.'

'Well...you only have to look at him.'

'I'd bet that if you tapped that hammer on his head, there would be an echo.'

A ripple of receding laughter brought a smile to my face, but I wiped the smile and emerged to find three people still hoping for an exclusive.

I looked suitably perplexed and stepped past them to the long narrow room, with its assortment of junk on a shelf, and the poor one-eyed doll, staring into oblivion, tapping my hammer with some anticipation on the way. But Soon I had run out of walls to tap.

'You sir, are a scoundrel and a bounder!' It was Ammo's voice, low but tinged with laughter. It was then that I felt the first pat on my back, and a hug from one of the girls. We gathered in a sort of rugby scrum of relief. 'I can't believe that we have pulled it off, well done team Jimmy!'

I looked fondly at each of my friends, but paused when I looked upon a pensive Elvis.

'Why the long face Elvis?'

'We should get out of here Jimmy, it's spooky.'

I slung an arm over his shoulder, 'don't you worry me old mate, any ghost daft enough to mess with you, will have to answer to big bad Jimmy, the ghost busting basher.' We emerged into daylight, relieved to see that everyone had magically disappeared, and I breathed deeply, content that everything was back as it should be. That was until Ammo appeared, his face pale and sweating, and wheezing like a sixty fags a day bloke. 'There's someone or something down in the cellar Jimmy.'

I looked at him sharply. 'Are you sure?'

He nodded and patted his chest, as if doing so would slow his quickly beating heart. 'I heard a tapping sound, like someone or something was trying to break out of a wall. His eyes rolled wildly, 'it fair gave me the heeby jeebys I can tell you.'

Suddenly an alarmed Elvis had not only left the building, but was headed down the path at a rapid rate of knots.

'Where are you going?'

He paused and looked back at me. 'Sorry Jimmy, time travel I can handle, playing mind games with the media is fun...but.' He shook his head, wide eyes staring past me at the open door. 'Spooks just spook me man, always have done, even now I sleep with a light on and the bedroom door open and a whole bulb of garlic within easy reach.'

I smiled, ' you soft sod, you never said.'

He blushed a crimson tide, 'well I'm telling you now.'

'What if I told you that I plan to go back into the cellar alone, to find out who is tapping on my walls, would you desert me then?'

His normally cool calm and collective demeanor deserted him as he stared at me with owl like eyes. 'You shouldn't do that, someone has to come with you.' He stared despairingly at the girls, but they were already clinging onto one another for support. The boys were no better, as they avoided eye contact and stared at their mobile phones or absently kicked mud.

'Someone has to go back in there with Jimmy,' he pleaded, but sadly volunteers were notably absent.

I smiled, 'don't worry about it Elvis, they are my walls and I really need to know who is knocking on them,' and I turned to enter the door.

'Then I will come with you,' he said quickly

I turned and looked at him with a frown, 'are you sure?'

He gulped and nodded furiously, ' I am sure.'

I turned once to look at my friends as we stepped through the door, and the smiles and thumbs up were a pleasure to behold.

Needless to say, I led the way, we paused for a moment at the top of the stairs and there was indeed a tapping noise below.

'What is it Jimmy?' whispered Elvis, 'is it the polterghosts?'

I frowned, 'can't really say, why don't you go down and check it out for me.'

He stepped away and looked like he was about to wet his pants, his eyes took on a saucer like appearance as he stared at me in disbelief. 'Me...are you a madman?'

I grinned, ' I was kidding Elvis, look there seems little point in us both going down there, so I am going alone.'
He brightened, 'well only if you are quite sure.'
I patted him on the shoulder, 'if I need assistance then I will call.'
'What will you call Jimmy?'
'Help, ' I replied tersely, 'I will call help in my loudest voice, you got that?'
He got it and I stepped down into the unknown.
The narrow door was open and I could see a faint glow of light within. 'Hello, is there anybody in there?' I shone my torch as he turned and raised a hand to his eyes.
'Oh, hi Jimmy, I think you got the wrong room.' The light from his mobile phone glowed dully as he stood before the right alcove, and I was shocked to see that he was holding my hammer. He was a small and wiry young man, with quick eyes working behind thin wire spectacles. I strode quickly to where he was standing and played a beam of light on the wall. 'No, it definitely was not in here.'
But he was like a dog with a bone, 'this wall sounds hollow, listen!' He tapped the bricks with my hammer and soft shuffle of falling mortar followed.'
'See,' he whispered', the brick moved.'
Now I have to say, hand on heart, that what followed was not my finest hour. As he raised my hammer again I slapped him hard on the back of the head, and the rustle of mortar was even more pronounced as his head cracked into the wall. He then uttered a low soft cry that sounded like 'ow!', and the mobile phone and hammer fell to the earthen floor.
'What's going on...you hit me!'
'What are you saying,' I bellowed. 'I hit you, why should I hit you, are you mad?'
He stumbled away from me, "you hit me, why would you do that?'
He almost fell through the narrow door as I followed. We now had an audience as my gallant troops were gathered outside, staring at us in silence. His body was shaking as he raised a hand to his forehead. 'I'm bleeding,' he moaned, staring at a slight smear of the red stuff on his fingers. I felt bad, he was only slightly bruised, but I still felt sick in my stomach. Then I was back in Burt mode, arms outstretched and a wide

engaging toothy grin.

'It was not my hand that chastised you brother, but the playful and mischievous spirits that dwell in this dark place.' I took a step forward and he a step back, and I was suddenly alarmed as my praetorian guard gathered around him. He was then gently led up into the kitchen by the girls, with words of encouragement, like 'there there,' and 'I think I have some ointment I can dab on that.'

'What were you thinking Jimmy?' said Gordon with a hiss in his voice.

I raised my hands defensively, 'I know I know, let me think.'

'He's a reporter from the 'Yorkshire Evening Post' for goodness sake, this could be very bad, he could call the cops.'

'Yes I do realize that, but he was knocking down my wall with my hammer, what was I supposed to do?'

I inhaled the dreaded leaf once more as Ammo slung an arm over my shoulder. 'What's the worst that can happen?'

'He could report you for assault,' said Elvis, 'you could even go to prison.'

Ammo sighed deeply, 'well thank you mate but we were looking for something a bit more optimistic than that.'

Elvis stared nervously around. 'Sorry Jimmy, can we get out of here now, this place gives me the willies'. We filed up into the kitchen as the girls completed their first aid on the ace reporter. I felt uncomfortable as he seemed to shrink in his chair when I appeared. 'I did warn all of you about the poltergeists,' I said, looking at him sternly. 'We have all experienced strange things occurring in this house, especially in the cellar.'

'Jimmy's right,' added Ammo, 'this is one very spooky house.'

Suddenly and rather surprisingly the diminutive reporter leapt out of the chair and stared up at me with some disdain. 'Ghost's and ghouls, is that the best you can do?'

He grew in my estimation at that moment, he was like a magnificent miniaturized version of Russel Crowe, minus the gladiatorial body Armour, the handsome profile, the sweaty rippling torso, and menacing presence.

'You're having a laugh,' he cried mockingly, turning on his heels and heading down the hall to the open door, 'you are facing an assault charge mister.'

It was time for my last cast.

'Fair enough,' I called after him, 'it's a shame though, you being a reporter for the Yorkshire Evening Post, and missing a story that would have the worlds media eating out of your hand.'

He paused at the door and looked back at me with a frown, the invisible fly dangling before his open mouth. 'What story?'

He was hooked, he was mine, and I started to reel him in.

'You saw how many of the press and TV were out there today, but where are they now?'

My mind was racing as I attempted to formulate a feasible story.

'Well there's a surprise,' he said. 'They have all gone because they think you are a weird nutter, and who can blame them, count me in.'

'Precisely, 'but all they have is a page three or four single column piece about Jimmy the nutter, whereas you, you have an inside story that has legs and will run and run.'

He pulled at his lower lip petulantly, 'what story?'

I couldn't help but raise my Burt like arms again. 'Why, don't you remember how you were the only remaining reporter to enter the evil portals hidden in that dark place, a place where you stood side by side with crazy Jimmy?'

He nodded, stroking his chin, 'I remember it well.'

'The place where you were physically assaulted by evil forces?'

His eyes opened wide at the memory. 'One minute I was standing there, next to crazy Jimmy, when I heard this sound.'

I raised my arms again, and raised my voice even higher, 'what kind of sound brother?'

'A sort of whoosh!'

'That is the sound brother! Why I couldn't have put it better myself. That is what you hear when they come a slapping, or a pinching, or a pulling of hair.'

He nodded as the memories came flooding back. 'I looked behind me for an instant I thought I saw...?'

'Tell me brother, what did you see?'

'I saw a wraith like figure snake between me and the light from beyond the door, and then I felt an unearthly powerful blow to the back of my head.'

'Halleluiah brother! why I saw you rise into the air, your poor body brutally smashed into the wall.'

'It's true!' he cried back, 'I was propelled into the wall with incredible violence, as Jimmy is my witness.' He stared at me from the doorway, eyes bright with hunger for a headline story. Then, as I approached him, he hung his head for a moment, and when he looked at me again, the fierce light that had momentarily burned in his eyes was extinguished.

'Sorry, I can't do it, I didn’t come into journalism to tell lies.'

I laughed a hollow laugh, 'lies...what lies? You were assaulted before my very eyes. All you need to do is spice it up a little for your readers. They will thank you for it, believe me.'

He shook his head and I could see that he was faltering. 'I'm not sure Jimmy, to be a journalist you have to be true to your heart, you must seek out the truth and inform your readers without prejudice, rancor or malice.'

I stared at him, mouth agog. ' But times have changed. The news is at our fingertips twenty-four seven now, people don't buy newspapers for the news anymore...they buy them to be entertained for God's sake.'

'Don't blaspheme,' he said quickly, 'there is no need to take the name of our lord God in vain,' he chastised.

'I'm sorry, I really am, and I apologize.'

A moment passed when we faced each other like verbal prizefighters.

'What’s your name?'

He looked confused. 'My name? my name is Robert.'

'Robert, you are a cub reporter for the Yorkshire Evening Post, yes?'

He nodded, blinking through black broad rimmed glasses. ‘They don't call them 'cubs' anymore.'

'Whatever, now I am sure that you are an ambitious man, and don't plan to work for a local rag forever?' As soon as his eyes narrowed and he placed his hands on his hips I intuitively knew that I had said the wrong thing.

'I am proud to work for a regional newspaper that is respected internationally.' He replied, blinking through his Woody Allen’s.

I shrugged, 'that's all very well Robert, but my guess is that you harbor dreams of working for the more serious press, like The Sun or the Daily Star.'

He shrugged, his posture coolly dismissive.

'But believe me Robert, if you ever stepped into their lair, and uttered the admirable sentence that you have said to me...' I paused and scratched my head, sighing deeply for dramatic effect. 'They would laugh at you like the sad pack of hyenas they are. They would form a vicious circle around you, and take turns to yelp and snap.' It was a moment to savour as he shrugged off the invisible manacles, I could almost hear them clatter to the floor as he held out his hand. 'You are right of course, to hell with them, when do we start?'

I had won the battle, but any feelings of triumph lay at my feet, beside the invisible manacles. I felt like the snake in the garden of Eden.

'Go on son, take a bite...I won’t let on.'

CHAPTER 25

Robert's front page exclusive brought renewed interest in the 'Crazy Jimmy' story. Consequently, I kept a low profile, and bunked up with whoever could offer me a bed for the night. It was a difficult time as the media turned up at my friend's doorsteps at all hours. I took time out to visit Beatie on one occasion, always checking my rear-view mirror in case I was being followed, Philip Marlowe style.

A week passed and Gordon volunteered to mingle among them, gathering intelligence. It reminded me of the young buck in 'The Magnificent Seven,' who mingled with the naughty bandits, and returned to tell the tale. I was relieved to hear that real reporters were now thin on the ground, and that most of the curious consisted mainly of anarchic tree huggers and earnest bible bashers. I was more than glad that I had kept my distance.

One week rolled into two and I was getting restless. At the start of the third week I had to take a look for myself. The car purred to the top of the street, and I found to my utmost relief that they had all disappeared, save for one ancient VW camper van, draped in a 'Jesus Saves' banner. It was time to start knocking down walls.

That night, I dreamt I was standing on the brow of a hill. Below me a deep forest stretched to the horizon, a place bereft of birdsong. A caravan of travellers followed an ancient track, all dressed in long robes, faces hidden beneath hooded cowls. Some rode on horseback, others were carried in rough open carts, but most walked. My eyes were drawn to a still figure, a hand shading eyes from the glare of the sun, as she looked up at me. My mobile phone rang and I pulled it out of my pocket.

'Hi Jimmy darling!'

Even in a dream I found it hard to articulate the words.
'Is it really you?'
She removed the cowl, shaking her long golden hair, her mobile phone raised to her ear. I swayed, and then my legs buckled as I fell to my knees. 'I'm coming down,' I said, my voice breaking.
'Sorry sweetie, but I am going where you cannot follow.'
'Where...where are you going?'
She raised an arm and pointed up the ancient track, where I saw people disappearing beneath the arched canopy of ancient and gnarled oak trees.
'Is that the path to heaven?'
She laughed that oh so familiar Fay laugh. 'It's the path to peace Jimmy.'
She raised her cowl, and even from that distance I saw her blow me a kiss. She turned her back on me then, and approached the ancient arch of mighty oak trees, still holding her mobile phone.
'I love you darling,' I said, 'I have always loved you, even before we met.'
'I know, but now your heart belongs to another.'
'No, no please don't leave me!'
She paused, 'You must go back Jimmy, she needs you,' she said softly. 'Goodbye my love,' and then she was gone and all I could hear was static.

***

The retrieval of the paintings had to be a quick and covert operation. I hired a swat -like black van, and team Jimmy spilled out of the back like a well drilled special forces crew, or perhaps a special needs crew? Sally agreed to keep an eye on the individual who believed that Jesus was no spendthrift, while we sneaked through the back door like thieves in the night

I started at the top, tapping gently and listening as mortar fell on the other side of the wall. The first brick was the most challenging as it inched away from me and threatened to fall onto my treasure, but I carefully removed any loose surrounding mortar and worked the brick back with the tips of my fingers. After that it became child's play as I handed each brick to the chain gang behind me, and soon I had created a hole large enough to shine a light.

'What do you see Jimmy?' said Ammo.

'I see wonderful things,' I answered.

We worked methodically, passing each plywood panelled painting from hand to hand, and stacking them in the kitchen above, until finally I retrieved the large biscuit tin, containing the jewellery that I bought from uncles so many years ago, and followed them up the stairs. The room was eerily silent as they stared at my loot. I could only hazard a guess as to what each of them were thinking, they were, I imagined, simply coming to terms that all this time travelling lark was no longer a dream.

Ammo reached for one of the boxed paintings and looked at me quizzically 'May I?'

'Absolutely, help yourself.'

He pulled at the string holding the plywood boards together, and held up a lovely old painting, and then emitting a low whistle. 'I like this, she's a real cracker.'

'Good choice, it is a painting from the pre- Raphaelites and is quite remarkable...it needs further research and a good clean.'

'So, what's it worth Jimmy boy, a king's ransom?'

'Not quite sure yet, but several thousand without a doubt, in fact there are no paintings here that would fetch less than five grand in auction, and some that are worth considerably more.'

'Wow!', said Suzie, scratching her head and staring at the stack of paintings, 'that's a lot of thousands.'

'Correct, and the sooner we get them in the van and away from here, the better.' I glanced at my watch, it was eight thirty. 'Anyone fancy a celebratory beer when we're done?'

'Sorry mate,' said Ammo with an expressive shrug, ' I'm washing my wig tonight.'

'Me too, said Elvis, before frowning, ' I didn't know you wore a wig?'

'Only on bad hair days Elvis,' replied Ammo laconically.

'Me and Sal are going to a late show at the Grand,' offered Suzie.' It's the return of 'Poetry of the Penis,' absolutely unmissable.'

I nodded with a grin, 'Alright you clowns, I'm in the chair.'

'Ah well, that casts a different light on the matter, said Ammo brightly, 'the wig can wait, but only on conditioner that I can wash it tomorrow'.

His pun was met with a collective groan, and we got to work.

It was just after 9 am when I leaned out of the driver's window and swiped my card on the screen, watching as one barrier reached for the sky and the larger curved lump of metal slid silently into the ground. I pulled the swat van into the car park, killed the engine and lit a cigarette. I was aware that I was on candid camera again, as several security cameras swivelled and focused on me, staring passively at my nicotine addiction, and recording every puff I made. I pressed the buzzer and was about to announce my presence when the intercom crackled and a familiar voice greeted me. 'Hi Jimmy, please pull your van around to the rear of the building.'

I stubbed the fag out on a wall mounted ash tray, and did as I was told. The smooth tarmac drive curved in a gentle arc, and I passed a solid green wall of leylandii on my right, interspersed with holly and other spiky plants, and realised that this was natures answer to razor wire and keep out signs. Simple but clever, the tall leylandii were obviously managed and kept under control, concealing all activity to the rear of the building, and the extra layer of shrubs armed with cruel barbs made it completely impenetrable.

I swung the van around the final curve and the tarmac dipped down into the bowls of the building, as steel shutters rose with a clatter and bright neon lights flickered into life.

It was more like a huge underground bunker than a mere warehouse. I blinked, adjusting my eyes to the bright lights as the shutters clattered to a close behind me. I saw half a dozen top of the range cars, nothing too flash or ostentatious, but very expensive nevertheless, and four navy blue vans, all bright, brand new, and unlettered.

It occurred to me that emblazoning the company name, and adding fine art and bullion dealers may tempt the criminally curious to want to take a closer look. Perhaps a sign on the back doors proclaiming 'No Kruger Rand's or Gold Sovereigns Are kept in this Van Overnight,' may deter some, but not many, in fact on further thought, not any.

Benjamin entered through a steel door, and was by my side as I stepped from the van.

'Jimmy!' he said, his hand outstretched, his voice echoing loudly in that vast space, and we shook hands. He was dressed immaculately of course, a solitary diamond winked at me from his white shirt cuff, showing an inch below the sleeve of a perfectly tailored jacket. I was suddenly transported back to an 'all inclusive' sweaty Brit tourist again. In my cheap shapeless shorts adorned with numerous Velcro pockets, and plastic flip flops barely concealing feet that had swollen in the sun like ripe tomatoes with toes on.

As we shook hands his grip felt firm and cool, and I had no doubt that mine felt clammy and warm, and no doubt he would retreat to the men's room at the earliest opportunity and wash all contact away.

He talked as we walked into the inner sanctum. 'So, did you have a good trip Jimmy?'

A good trip...is that all it was? It felt like a bit more than that to me. A good trip is a relaxing drive over the moors to Whitby, or a meandering drive through the Yorkshire Dales.

'Yes,' I replied a bit belatedly, 'it was a good trip.'

I paused and Ben looked at me, a small smile playing on his lips.

'There's something you are not telling me,' I said guardedly. 'I need to speak to your dad, but I don't want to be waking the old bugger up if he's having a bit of a nap'

He threw back his head and laughed, shamelessly displaying two rows of dentist's dream teeth. 'No chance of that happening Jimmy, the old buggers here and waiting to see you.'

My jaw dropped, 'he's here?'

He smiled and ushered me through another door, gently closing it behind me. The old man was out of his chair with an agility that belied his advancing years. His eyes were quick warm and appraising as we shook hands and he ushered me to a sofa. If anything, the father was even more immaculately attired than the son.

'So, what's your poison Jimmy.'

I smiled, 'it's a little early for me.'

'Ah now, and it's a little late for me.' He retrieved a bottle and two glasses from a dazzling array of drinks, displayed on a very fine Regency walnut sideboard. He then sat in a red leather deep buttoned winged armchair facing me, and poured our drinks.

It was time, time to ask the silliest of questions. I picked up the glass, swirling the amber nectar as he studied me in silence. I sniffed and feigned a look of doubt.

'Scotch or Irish?'

His eyes rolled wildly as he visibly shrank away from me in his chair. 'My boy,' he whispered hoarsely, ' if you ever see a bottle of Scotch under my roof, then you have my permission to order me to bend over, and shove it where the sun don't shine.'

We burst into laughter and touched glasses before savouring the contents. Suddenly the phone on his desk buzzed and he crossed the room and snapped it up. He said nothing, but nodded a couple of times and glanced at me smiling. 'Aha,' he said, nodding into the phone, 'well now, that is very interesting, good boy, keep up the good work. Me and Jimmy are not to be disturbed for a while, you understand?'

He nodded as if he was actually talking to the phone, 'that's grand, we'll talk to you's later.' He gently replaced the phone back into its cradle and raised his glass, 'to absent friends Jimmy!'

I raised my glass, catching a curious look in his eyes. I wanted to ask him what Ben had said, wanted him to explain the curious almost desperate look he gave me, but I didn't.

Mickey took his seat again, 'so, I must say you're looking well Jimmy,' his voice fading, 'all things considered...'He stared intently at his glass, 'it broke my old heart to hear of Fay's death.' He sipped slowly and blinked quickly, 'she was such a vibrant fun-loving lady.' He smiled at distant memories and I let him travel back without interruption. 'I would be there in the auction house, and suddenly she would be by my side. Mesmerising me with her knowledge, humour and beauty, and then, within the blink of an eye, a lot that I had been waiting for was knocked down for a song to you.'

He pointed a slightly arthritic finger at me accusingly, and then burst into laughter. ' 'What a partnership, you two made a considerable antiques dealer!'

I laughed, ' as I recall we were not quite in the same league, you bought from the top of the tree, while we generally bought the crab apples that lay in the grass.'

He chose to ignore me, recalling happier times.

'She would always give me that sweet smile, that mocked me and at the same time seemed to say, 'you fell for it again you daft old sod, will you never learn?'

He shook his head and sighed, 'and you know what? I never did.'

Then suddenly he was back, daydreams cast aside like an empty whiskey bottle, and a frown creasing the careworn skin around his troubled eyes. 'I'm sorry Jimmy, please ignore the ramblings of an old man.'

I raised a hand and smiled, 'there's no need to apologise Mickey, it's been over a year now and it is nice to hear someone speak of her like this.'

'Really?'

'Absolutely, I love my friends to bits, but hate the nudges and soft whispers whenever her name is mentioned. I have to confess that we did continue to chat from time to time after she died...'

'You talked with your dead wife?'

'It seemed like the most natural thing in the world, suddenly she was by my side, in my head, talking the talk, and I answered. I know it sounds a bit mad, but there we have it. I've said it and you can ring a bell, dust me down and call me crazy Jimmy.'

The words had tumbled from my lips so quickly, that I panicked and wanted to snatch them up and swallow them again.

'Don't ever say that, sure we have seen the media circus on TV, and read the stories in the press about crazy Jimmy, but you have to rise above all that nonsense.'

He sipped his whiskey again, and I thought I saw a tremor in his hand. It could have been the drink or something else. I felt that it was something else. 'You don't get to my age without feeling the kind of loss that you described so eloquently.'

I looked at him questioningly, 'but your wife is still alive?'

He responded with the most withering of smiles, 'must you remind me.'

In truth Mickey adored Freda, I knew it, he knew it, and most importantly, she knew it.

'How is she?'

'Ah she's grand, not so quick on her pins these days, but still fast enough to spend me money on lost cats and stray people.' He leaned forward and opened a large silver cigarette box on the table. 'I take it that you are still a smoking man Jimmy?'

'I am, but you are not, I can wait.'

'Ah go on, I still love the smell, you would be doing me a favour.'

I obliged, ignited, and inhaled, as he raised his considerable nose and sniffed. Then the phone buzzed again and he rose and stepped over to his desk. 'I believe that I said we were not to be...'He came to a grinding halt mid-sentence. 'My apologies Jimmy, please give me a couple of minutes,' and he left like a man in a hurry.

A cigarette later, Mickey and Sean entered the room, and I could see by the look on their faces that the time for bullshit had passed. I looked at my watch.

'Anyone for lunch?', I said.

Mickey smiled, 'already sorted, Benjamin has booked a table for two at a nice little Italian restaurant we favour.'

His son nodded, but his eyes betrayed him, he looked distracted and sad. I made up my mind and took control of what could have been an awkward situation. 'Call them again and make it a table for three, we need to talk.'

Ben visibly perked up and looked quickly at his dad.'

Mickey shrugged, 'so who minds the shop? Forget I said that, a table for three it is.'

We occupied a window seat, enjoying the finest Italian cuisine in a leafy suburb of Leeds. I rolled spaghetti on a fork as the waiter faded discreetly into the general buzz of ladies who do lunch.

'So, let's cut to the chase,' I said,' how are the paintings looking Ben?'

The glass of house red had almost reached his lips when he set it back down onto the table. 'Interesting,' he said slowly, his fingers toying with the wine glass. 'You have brought us an eclectic selection of art, and the accompanying sales documents are in my opinion, completely authentic. Such provenance adds to the sale of a work of art enormously...'

'I think I detect a 'but', I said.

Mickey speared a meat ball and chewed with relish. A casual observer would possibly observe that he was more enamoured with his food than the conversation, but they of course, would be completely mistaken.

'Well, the thing is Jimmy, all the bills of sale are made out to the same person. A certain Mr T. Traveller would you believe,' said Mickey, pointing a blood red tomato dipped fork at me. Which can only mean that you bought these paintings from a single collector,' he added, 'is that right?'.

I skewered a brace of mussels and rolled them in a coating of garlic spaghetti. 'Ah yes, I should have been a tad more imaginative with the name.'

Mickey frowned, and his beard twitched so violently that I half expected obscure foreign life forms to emerge and make a hasty bid for freedom. 'For god's sake Jimmy, what are you up to, are these paintings kosha or not?'

I paused, staring at my wine glass as if it was a crystal ball, took a very deep breath, and then told them absolutely everything. A silence followed, it was so complete that all the convivial chatter in the restaurant was suddenly placed on 'mute', no clatter of cutlery, no laughter. Special effects even lowered the lighting, so that it appeared we were alone, in a box, them staring and me stared at. Even the delicious and decidedly dead mussels fell from my fork in disbelief and alarm.

Ben was the first to speak, he removed his fine silver rimmed spectacles and polished the lens with his napkin.

'So what are you saying Jimmy, that all the speculative nonsense in the newspapers is true?'

'Yes,' I replied quickly.

He placed the glasses back onto the hump back bridge of his nose. His expression said it all, and I was convinced that if the restaurant had served strait jackets, he would have ordered one on the spot.

Mickey rapped the table with his knuckles, and let out a laugh so loud it made me jump. 'Jesus wept, will you listen to the man, is that not a fine tale Benjamin?'

His son nodded uncertainly, losing his calm and collective urban accent on the way. 'Aye, it's a fine enough tale as you say daddy...' Blood levels rose and painted his cheeks bright red, 'but...'

Mickey raised a hand, ' I will hear no buts my boy, because I believe Jimmy's story to be true.'

'You can't be serious?'

Mickey stroked his considerable beard. 'Consider the facts, Jimmy recently bought a stack of notes from us, remember?'

'Of course.'

'So tell me why he bought the...' He paused and looked at me for assistance.

'Vintage confetti.'

'Exactly, the vintage confetti, the common old scruffy notes that even we can't shift?'

Ben stared at the two of us, 'well let me see, so that he could travel back in time and purchase valuable works of art for peanuts? Yes of course, why didn't I see that immediately? What a blind idiot I have been, I promise to thrash myself with split cane later on as a penance.'

I had to laugh then, ' I know it all sounds a bit fantastic and mad, and believe me, I have had more than one passing moment when I thought I was going doolally, but I have witnesses now, friends who saw me disappear into the garden.' I took a sip of wine, 'but really, the truth lies with the paintings I have brought you. I am sure that you will do all the necessary checks to ensure they do not appear on police stolen files, but I can tell you now that they will all come up clean, because they were all bought in the year nineteen fifty six, by me, Mr Time Traveller.'

Mickey raised his glass and drank, 'ah well now, it's only a sane man who thinks he's mad as a mad man's madder mother, whereas if you are indeed a complete basket case, more often than not you will believe that you are the sanest soul on planet earth.'

I wiped my plate clean with a ragged piece of garlic bread and chewed thoughtfully, 'your dad is speaking a lot of sense Ben… I think.'

Ben slid a hand through his immaculate but casually tousled lock of hair, ' I would love to believe it.'

'Then believe,' I said, 'what do you want me to say to convince you. Do you want me to swear an oath?’

Mickey's eyes shone brightly as he absently stroked his beard. 'It is every antique dealer’s wet dream. To travel back and buy works of art at post war prices. Just imagine, one could catch a lovely old steam train down to London, and bid at one of the world’s great auction houses. Why you could buy just one important painting that would set you up for life. Just think about it Jimmy, is that not a wonderful dream?'

I looked into his bright old eyes, wide with wonder, and nodded smiling, 'yes, I admit it is indeed a wonderful dream.'

He reached quickly across the table and gripped my hand, it was a surprisingly powerful grip for a man of his advanced years. He laughed then, 'and you can do it Jimmy, why with our resources we could send you back with more than enough money.' His grip tightened, 'why you could buy a Van Gough or a Matisse, a Turner or two perhaps...'

I patted the back of his gnarled old hand gently, 'sadly it will have to remain just that, a wonderful dream.'

I saw the light waver and flicker like candlelight caught in a sudden whisper of air. 'But why, why must it remain a dream?'

I looked outside through the plate glass window, watched as golden autumnal leaves fell and gathered to form a moving living carpet. The Americans have a wonderful name for Autumn, they call it 'The Fall', and to me that said it all. It conjured up images of burnished copper and blood red leaves falling into fading green grass in New England.

CHAPTER 26

I told them about my dream; about my final words with Fay before she disappeared beneath the ancient oak trees, and the stark message on my mobile phone, 'no signal.' A double decker bus caught my eye as it sighed to a halt at a stop outside; its windows all steamed up. Some travellers had wiped the glass, and I could see blurred faces that appeared to be weeping as condensation ran down the glass. But most were content to leave the panes of glass alone and remain anonymous, like Georgian silhouettes locked in another time.

'So you had a dream,' said Mickey earnestly, ' so what, it was just a dream.'

Ben looked at his father. ' I think I know what Jimmy is saying.'

'Well please do tell son of mine, because I'm fucked if I know.'

' I think if I have got this right, the house that Jimmy bought is a very special place. But in order to open the door to another time requires a rather singular key, am I right so far?'

'You're doing just fine.'

Ben nodded and then continued. ' Your sad loss took you to the edge of reason, and if I am not mistaken, that was the key to the door.'

' Mickey, your boy's a genius.'

He did his exaggerated Fagin shrug. ' I know it, he's a chip off the old block, what do you expect.'

'It is my belief,' I said, ' that this condition creates a profound chemical change within the human brain. Awakening electrical impulses lying dormant and unused. It goes without saying that one needs to be in the right place at the right time; and as it happened, I was.'

Mickey frowned, ' then answer me this if you will, why does the dream mean that the door is now closing.'

'Because I have said goodbye, and now I know that I will never see or hear Fay again.'

'Then by all accounts the door may never open again.'

I shook my head. ' It must, I have a pie to deliver.'

Mickey stared, ' a pie?'

' Of course,' said Ben with a gasp. ' The old West Indian woman you spoke of in your story. She recognised you as the boy who delivered the pie.'

A glance at Mickey brought a lazy smile to his lips. ' I know, I know, he is a damn sight brighter than his old man.'

' Beaty and Cleve will not arrive until March 21st 1957, but yes, I will return. Of that I have no doubt.'

Mickey sipped his wine, his bright old eyes locked on mine. 'We would dearly love to see this magic house of yours, but when you do go back it could easily be a one-way ticket. Have you thought about that.'?

'Yes I have, and even if I was offered a first class return on the Orient Express, with free vintage champagne and a bucket of caviar served by a gaggle of nubile nymphs; I would still decline.' I paused and smiled at them. ' Because I have no intention of returning.'

The silence was complete as they exchanged bewildered glances, and it was Ben who recovered first. ' You would abandon this life for an uncertain future in the past. Leave your friends and deny any life you have in the here and now?'

I smiled, ' I will of course sorely miss my friends, even you two rogues, and all the people I should have met but didn't. I will miss my mobile phone, but not the internet. I will miss my Chinese takeaway and cold beer in a can, but not those people who desire fame for doing absolutely nothing with their lives. I will miss trousers that fit properly and ten disposable cigarette lighters for a quid. But most of all I will miss my lovely wife, forever, and the life I should have had, had I remained.'

The bill arrived, and the waiter hovered. The ladies who do lunch had long gone, and I realised that we were the last occupied table. But one dismissive glance from Mickey, was enough to remind the waiter that he had other duties, and we were left alone.

Ben shook his head. ' So why do it Jimmy, why would you contemplate leaving all this behind.'

I was about to explain, when Mickey beat me to it. ' You have found someone else.' He looked quickly at his son and beamed. ' Jimmy has found love again.'

I looked at Ben and smiled.

' I know,' he said, ' my dad is very quick and bright.'

' Yes, I have found someone else, and yes she has stolen my heart, and yes I do have to go back and retrieve it and her.'

Mickey sighed, ' ah well that's grand, amour vincit omnia.'

I grinned, ' it does indeed.'

'Then we must all get to work,' he said, rapping the table top with his knuckles. I summoned the waiter over and reached for my wallet, but Benjamin raised his manicured hand. ' This is a business lunch Jimmy, and the company always pays for lunch. We do pay our taxes after all, so, when we can legitimately claw something back to feed ourselves and our clients, then all the better.'

Mickey nodded, ' if we didn't claim our lunch expenses then the tax man would assume we were all robots who require no sustenance, and they would take the money anyway. This way is best.'

The following day I kept a pre-arranged appointment with my solicitor. Finalising my financial arrangements. It felt strange explaining why I was leaving the house to my friends before I had actually died.

'I'm going away,' I replied to his unspoken question, 'and will not be coming back '

' Ah,' he replied knowingly. Probably assuming that I was about to become a long-term guest in her majesty's hotel. ' When would you wish the transfer of
ownership to commence.?'

I thought about it for a moment, ' one month from today.'

He nodded and keyed in the information on his computer. ' This is most unusual if you don't mind me saying so.' He looked at me with world weary eyes. ' Is it a terminal illness?'

I laughed out loud, 'good god no, nothing like that.'

He honestly appeared relieved that I was not expecting a visit from the grim reaper any time soon. 'Well, there is always some hope that you will be released early for good behaviour.'

I stared, and then realised it was my get out of jail card, and I must say that I played it with some aplomb. Shaking my head sadly and gazing

probably a touch too theatrically into the distance. 'That, I am convinced, will not be the case. I'm afraid when that door is closed behind me, there will be no coming back.'
His saucer round eyes were magnified behind steel rimmed spectacles. ' I am sorry to hear it,' he said, eyes darting furtively for the nearest exit as he pushed paper across the desk. ' If you will just sign here, here, and here.'

I did as instructed, and signed my life away in the present, in exchange for an uncertain future in the past, to quote Ben.

That evening I ate king prawn chow mien, courtesy of effing elsies, and joined my crew at the usual table. I listened with a smile as they still talked about the crazy Jimmy incident. I resorted to the tried and tested method of doing nothing, and saying less. Soon the laughter abated, squabbles ceased, and eyes turned in my direction.

'The first thing I have to say, is that when I go back, I will be travelling with a very large suitcase full of cash.' The announcement was met with loud cheers.

'The second thing I have to say, is that I will not be coming back.'

This declaration was met with stunned silence.

Sally reached across the table and took my hand. ' You can't do that Jimmy. Just up sticks and leave us for good, we won't have it.'

I looked into her lovely eyes and squeezed her hand. 'I have met someone there, someone very special, someone I have learned to love, and she needs me by her side.'

'So let me get this right,' said Ammo. ' You're going back for good because you've met some bird.'

Sally's rebuke was as swift and silent as an Exocet missile, as she slapped him on the back of the head. ' For goodness sake, will you listen to yourself you great lummox.'

All eyes were on me as I sipped my beer. ' The signal is getting weaker, so I will need all of your support in the time remaining.' I looked at each one of them until I saw Elvis shaking his head.

' What's up Elvis?'

' You can't do it Jimmy, you belong here, in this time and space, you should think very carefully about this.'

' I've thought of little else since all this started, but I now believe that I was meant to go back.' I have never seen Elvis lose his temper. He always was and still is the mister cool of our gang. So when he slammed the palm of his hand on the table, making the glasses rattle, we all jumped.

' That's bullshit; you still don't get it do you,' he said in a raised and trembling voice. ' If you go back for good you will still be a relatively young man when Jimmy the baby is born. What happens then, when Jimmy Junior and Jimmy senior occupy the same time and space?'

I looked at him sadly. ' I have absolutely no idea my friend, no one does, but I suspect it will all end in tears.'

'Well there you are then,' he replied, avoiding my eyes. ' It is madness to even think of going back for good.'

Suzie slipped an arm around his shoulders. ' I'm thinking that Elvis might be right, this all sounds a bit dangerous. Maybe it is time to think again Jimmy.'

I tried to light a cigarette but Gordon stayed my hand, and I slid it back into the packet. 'I read the same article as you Elvis, and you may recall that it also concluded that time travel into the past is not possible, so bang goes the theory. Besides it's too late for second thoughts; if I did decide to call it off, who in heavens name delivered Beatie's pie.'? I scraped back my chair and moved to where Elvis was sitting. He looked up as I held out my arms, and we hugged.

‘ I will miss you too,' I said hoarsely.

More chairs scraped back as we formed a scrum-like hug- in. ' I will miss you all I said. 'Now whose round is it?'

As I waited at the bar, I looked back at them and I am not ashamed to say a painful lump formed in my throat, and tears momentarily blurred my vision. My life in this time was coming to an end, and I will miss it and them.

Glasses were clinked as I took my seat. ' Tomorrow I will collect my vintage dosh, and after that I will remain indoors. From now on, when we share a beer or six, it will have to be at the house, and not here. I dare not miss the call you understand.'

Gordon still looked confused, ' but what about the house?'

'I was just coming to that,' I said, reaching into my inside pocket and producing a bunch of business cards, flicking them around the table like seasoned croupier. 'This is my solicitor's business card, and you should each make an appointment to see him. You must bring some form of I.D. A passport, drivers licence, something with your mug shot on. You will then answer some simple formal questions, and then sign an acceptance of ownership' form.

Tristan, who had been almost invisible until now, held his hand up. ' I don't have a driving licence Jimmy, or a passport.'

I smiled, ' I'm surprised, nay shocked at you Tristan, not having a passport.'

' Well I do have a passport as such, but it is out of date. I keep meaning to renew it, but what, with one thing and another, I never got around to it.' He was the centre of attention again and blushed. ' I do have a Waitrose card...'

'Fuck the bloody passport fiasco,' said Ammo, ' what is all this about Jimmy?'

'The house,' I replied. ' I have left each of you equal shares in the house, and you must all work together to complete the restoration. What you do when the house is complete is entirely up to you.'

They were silent, but not for long.

'When the house is complete it will be worth three hundred and fifty grand or more,' said Suzie. She slid the card back across the table. ' That's too much Jimmy; generous though it is I cannot possibly accept it.'

There was a general murmur amongst the ranks as they followed suite, and slid the cards back. I shrugged, '

'That is a very fine gesture, but as the old saying goes, ' you can't take it with you. And where I am going that is certainly the case. I will travel back a wealthy man for that time, and I can't possibly hang around waiting for completion day. However, if I hear of any falling out or dissent amongst the ranks, then I might possibly make a special trip back, and issue new instructions that all proceeds from the sale should be evenly distributed to various cat charities.'

Gordon's hand was raised.

'Yes Gordon.'

'I think the first suggestion was the best.'

I nodded solemnly. ' and is that the wish of you all?'

The vote was unanimous.

It was chucking out time, and we gathered outside the pub, cracked jokes, and hugged until only Sally remained by my side. She seemed uncomfortable and flicked her hair nervously to one side. ' I just wanted to say something.' She looked away and composed herself before delivering one of her lovely smiles. 'You must know that I have always had a soft spot for you.'

Suddenly I felt miserable and thoughtless. ' I'm sorry, I didn't think...'

She stepped forward and placed a finger on my lips. 'I have met someone else,' she said quickly, 'someone very special.'

I pulled her into my arms and held her for some time, then cupped her face in my hands and looked into her tear stained eyes.

'Is it serious?'

She nodded, ' I thought I should tell you before you go.'

I smiled and kissed her on the forehead. ' I just hope he is good enough for you.'

She pulled away then and took my hands. ' That doesn't mean I won't cry when you are gone, because I will, we all will.'

***

It was raining when I knocked at Beatie's door the following morning, but there was no answer. When I stepped out of the yard, I saw 'two barrels' waving at me as he hurried down his steps. ' Jimmy,' he called, and my heart sank at the look of panic in his eyes. ' Beaty collapsed in the yard this morning, we think she had a heart attack.'

My own heart beat an erratic tattoo at the news, ' where is she?'

'The Infirmary, but they won't let you see her unless you are family.'

I was already running, cursing the god of speed bumps as I drove. I was breathless when I arrived at the reception desk.

'You have an old west Indian woman here,' I wheezed, ' she was admitted this morning with a possible heart attack.'

'Name.?'

'Jimmy,' I replied.

'The patients name sir.'

'Oh, of course, sorry, her name is Beaty.'

'Surname.?'

I floundered, cold sweat running into my eyes. ' I only know her as Beaty, she is a dear friend of mine.' She looked up from her computer screen and her expression softened. ' I'm sorry, but only next of kin are allowed.'

I frowned, ' she never told me her full name, but there is no next of kin that I'm aware of. Just friends like me, who would dearly love to comfort and reassure her. She is quite alone now, and probably very frightened.' I watched her wilt before my emotional onslaught. Saw her melt like a Mr Whippy in a tropical climate, and she keyed in 'admissions' on her computer. 'Beatrice Veronica St Claire, aged 84, and currently residing at number seven...'

'That's her.'

'She is in ward twelve, the Becket wing,' and she gave me directions.

I glanced back and blew her a kiss, and she blushed, smiled, and waved me away. She was sound asleep, and somehow looked small and fragile, half hidden by the raised bars either side of the bed. It was like looking at her familiar face; but with some of the essential Beaty leaking from her body and disappearing into the ether, leaving a ragged, depleted image of the woman I had grown to love. I pulled up a chair and took her hand, and it was cool and limp. I must have nodded-off, but I was soon pulled from my slumbers by the sound of a very welcome and familiar voice.

'Jimmy, you come to see ol' Beaty, that's nice.'

I was amazed how the helium gas of life had inflated the old girl. She almost looked like the Beaty of old.

'How do you feel,' I said as she gripped my hand.

'Oh I feel just dandy, a little tired maybe, but sometimes I forget that I am just a knackered old woman. But enough about me boy, why you is all skin an' bone. What you need is a big bowl of Beatie's surprise.'

I smiled and stroked her hand, ' sounds lovely, what is it exactly.'

'Can't tell you Jimmy, it's a surprise.' Her booming laughter made my heart soar almost as high as the graphs on the monitor she was connected to.

'Seriously Beatie, you are going to have to stop rushing around with that tartan trolley of yours.'

'I know,' she answered, a wide-eyed penitent look on her face. But sometimes I feel like a younger woman on good days, even though I really know I'm just an ol' bag deep down.'

I tapped the back of her hand, ' behave yourself, you will always be the youngest old bag that I ever met.'

She looked at me all coy and then giggled in a girlish manner. ' You have a gift Jimmy, a refreshing turn of phrase. You belong to a rare breed, who can deliver an insult and a compliment in a single sentence.'

I pulled a face,' Is that a good thing?'

'It is better than good, you speak your mind an' tell it as it is, like all true Yorkshire folk should. You put folk down an' then raise them up again and they is better for it. Too many people hide their thoughts these days because they are afraid to offend. There is a whole generation of thought police growing up in our midst. Prepared to be offended at the most innocent and innocuous remarks an' scream sexism or racism an' such stuff an' nonsense.'

She stroked my hand gently. ' If it is my time, then I am glad an' I will be reunited with my Cleveland.' Then she closed her eyes and her grip on my hand relaxed. A light tap on my shoulder and I was awake in an instant. ' She is asleep,' said the nurse softly, ' you should follow her example and get some rest.'

I looked down at her, and she seemed small and fragile again, but I nodded and slid my hand from hers. 'Tell her I will be back in the morning, she is an extraordinary women, look after her.'

CHAPTER 27

The following morning, I was as good as my word, buying flowers and chocolates on the way. I swept past the reception desk and waited impatiently for the elevator, along with a small group of people. Some who had surely been here many times before, their sadness etched in lines upon their faces, and others with troubled puckered brows, who were possibly visiting for the first time.

The empty bed came as a shock. It was so neat and tidy one could imagine that it had never been occupied, but it had, and my blood ran cold.

'Hello, can I help you?'

I turned so quickly that she stepped back and frowned. 'I am visiting Beaty, she was in that bed last night. Do you know if she has been moved to another ward?'

She glanced at the newly made bed and then back at me. 'You should have spoken to reception.' She paused and looked embarrassed.' I'm afraid Beaty has gone.'

'Gone?' I was teetering on the edge of a total meltdown.

She nodded, a concerned look in her eyes. 'She resisted all our attempts to keep her in for observation, I'm sorry but you have had a wasted journey. She was quite insistent, and said that she had things to do, and something about collecting a pie.'

My look of relief alarmed her, and she raised a hand to her lips. 'I am so sorry, did you think..?'

I smiled and shook my head, glancing at her security name tag. 'Sophie, now that is a lovely name. Do you like chocolates and flowers Sophie?'

She frowned with a small smile playing on her lips, 'of course I do, but...?

I handed her the chocolates and flowers, and she accepted them in a confused state.

I was running again. She answered the door and gave me that toothy beaming Beaty smile.

'You should be in hospital!' I gasped, with a hint of admonishment, suppressed anger, and relief.

She pulled a face, looking all coy and guilty. 'I know, but I feel fine Jimmy, I just had a queer turn. They say they want to keep me in for observation, but I know that they really want to see if I can catch something interesting, something challenging that may call for major surgery. Hospitals are such unhealthy places Jimmy. If you can walk the walk then walk,' she said.

I tried and failed to argue against such sensible logic, and entered her parlour. 'My, something smells good.' She chuckled and entered the tiny kitchen, the bead curtain clattering behind her. 'It's Beatie's surprise, she called back. 'Now you take a seat, light a cigarette, an' relax.'

I did as I was told.

Soon she emerged with a tray containing two large steaming bowls, and we ate in silence. I pushed my empty bowl away and involuntarily emitted a loud burp.

'Sorry,' I said, patting my chest as if it was to blame for the escaping wind.

She looked surprised, 'why should you apologise because you burp?'

I smiled meekly, 'well it's not the done thing in polite circles.'

She laughed the laugh that could make roof tiles clap. 'My Cleveland, why he could burp and fart for England. But he always explain that they is just a symphony of appreciation after a fine meal.'

I grinned and lit a cigarette. 'I think me and Cleve would have been very good friends.'

She patted my hand across the table. ' I think he would have been more than that Jimmy. I think he would have loved you as the son we never had.'

I felt warm stinging tears accumulating in my eyes, but blinked them back into oblivion. And then I told her about my travels and she listened in mesmerised silence.

'You make a good preacher man,' she said with a smile. It was so funny that I laugh myself to sleep.'

'It had to be done Beaty, someone had let the cat out of the bag.'

She nodded, a great big smile on her face, and then she was silent for a moment. 'So, when you go back again, this time you go for good.'

I gripped her hand, 'the door is closing, but I will deliver your pie.'

She smiled, 'I know you will boy, I was there, remember? But will she still be waiting for you?'

It was a good question, a question that remained unanswered, and then finally I left Beatie's house for the last time. After a prolonged hug, I turned to leave, but paused. She seemed agitated, wringing her hankie in knots.

'What is it Beaty?'

Her lips trembled, 'It's nothing, you'll just think that I am just a silly ol' ninny woman.'

I smiled, ' well I ain't going no where's woman, 'till you tell me what's on your mind.'

She smiled at my dubious but otherwise excellent delivery of a West Indian accent.

'Well, I was in church the other day, jus' minding my own business an' talking to the lord. When the priest stop an' look down at me. He says what he always say. 'I hope you are saying a prayer for me Beaty?' She blinked back tears and looked up at me like a naughty child. 'I say, not this time father, this time I say a prayer for the time traveller.'

***

We continued to work on the house, everyone mucking in without exception, it was after all their house now. Then I got the call from Mickey. 'We have found buyers for all your items Jimmy.'

My heart raced, 'excellent, shall I call round?'

'We would prefer to meet you at this mystery house of yours, if you don't mind.'

I didn't, and they did, that very evening. Elvis and Ammo were still working when I ushered them in. I gave them the grand tour and left the cellar until last. 'These are the alcoves where the paintings were stored.'

They stared, and Mickey even stood in one and stroked his Fagin beard. 'Very clever,' he said with the widest of smiles. Ben meanwhile was unusually silent, looking nervously into the shadows.

I laughed, 'don't worry Ben, the ghost story has been wildly exaggerated I'm ashamed to say.' And we all laughed, possibly louder than was necessary.

When we entered the front room, Elvis had brewed some tea. We sat and Ben snapped open a smart leather briefcase, and produced a number of stapled papers, which he handed to me. 'As you can see, some of the sales are in American dollars, and others in Euros. Although some of your paintings sold for less than expected, others far exceeded our valuation. We hope that you will be happy with the final figure.'

Mickey nodded smiling, 'We are all aware of great paintings making eye watering sums in the news. But mid-range art work goes generally unreported, so no surprise there. Consequently, what Joe public does not see, are the number of paintings consigned to auction that do not sell. They may take several months to appear at auction, and then simply fail to meet the reserve and go unsold. However, the auction house still charges a more than generous fee for not selling your painting.'

'That's why I brought them to you,' I said.

Benjamin smiled and nodded. 'Quite so, and the Atkinson Grimshaw aside,
you bought a number of fine eighteenth century portrait paintings, and three French Impressionist oils on canvas. Plus, some assorted jewellery.'

I nodded impatiently, 'and...?'

'And your net total comes to the sum of five hundred and eighty thousand pounds.'

I stared at him in silence.

Benjamin raised a hand. 'However, before you get carried away, there were costs involved. We could not convert that sum into pre- nineteen fifty-six confetti. So, we had to use our International contacts, and they in turn were generally more than happy to offload their duff notes. But some could smell the dead fish in the water, and did what shark's do, and charged a higher rate. We in turn penalised the sharks and only paid the going rate on the five-pound notes. If they wished to offload the lower denomination confetti, then they
would have to pay our offer price. Are you with me so far Jimmy?'

I nodded, even though he had lost me a couple of sentences ago.

'It was quite impossible for us to purchase Stirling alone, so we took the liberty of buying US dollars, Swiss francs, and some other currencies that were more stable in the years after the war. We assumed you would not immediately blow the lot on your return. But open several bank accounts, and we would strongly suggest that at least one of those accounts should be offshore. But we made it Jimmy,' said Ben with a smile. 'We converted all your money into pre- nineteen fifty-six currencies.'

Now I was completely lost. 'How could you possibly change that volume of notes into vintage confetti?'

'Ah well now,' said Mickey proudly, 'here's the trick. As a forward-thinking company, we always keep abreast of the latest technology. We have a computerised box of tricks, that not only counts notes, but also grades their quality, authenticity, and year of manufacture, faster than you can say 'fake off'. Any questionable notes are then rejected and returned to source in the blink of an eye, and replacement notes demanded even faster. In short Jimmy, we can guarantee that the notes you receive will be one hundred per cent kosha. Some may look a bit sad

and wilted, or grubby and crumpled, but they will be the real thing, and certainly legal tender in nineteen fifty six.'

'This means,' said Ben, 'that your total was reduced by three thousand, four hundred, and seventy two pounds, because of the exchange rate charged by those heartless and greedy traders.'

I frowned, 'what about your fee?'

Mickey shook his head, 'there is no fee Jimmy, why the journey alone was worth more than that.'

'Sorry,' I said quickly, 'but this is not going to happen, I insist you take your fee.'

'Why?'

'Because you are my friends, and I love you all dearly, and I want you all to rejoice in my new-found fortune.'

Mickey pulled at his beard, 'it's a handy sum of money Jimmy, but not a fortune by any stretch of the imagination.'

I laughed, 'where I am going it is a fortune, think about it?'

Mickey pulled a face and looked at his son for ideas, and Ben came to the rescue. 'What if we agree to accept our fees and donate them to good causes?'

I looked at Mickey and smiled. 'I know already,' he said, 'he is a very smart boy.'

The following day I cleared my bank account, and placed the money into a large brown buff envelope. I held on to a few quid to tide me over, not knowing how long I would be here.

The last time I spent away from the house, was as a guest at Mickeys luxurious home. We sat in the orangery, in modern cushioned Lloyd loom chairs and gazed out across a huge immaculate lawn, bordered by woodland. I watched as a Robin alighted on a nearby balustrade, puffing out its considerable prize fighters' breast. Shaking droplets of water from its fragile and colourful feathers.

Freda entered with a tray of hot coffee and fresh croissants. 'It's a bit chilly in here boys, are you sure you don't want this indoors?'

'No, we'll be just fine darling,' said Mickey. 'We're just taking in some air.'

She glanced at my cigarette and pulled a face. 'It's lovely to see you Jimmy, but sad to see that you are still puffing on the cancer sticks.'

'This could possibly be the last one Freda, I'm becoming more health conscious these days.'

'Really?' she replied with an edge of scepticism in her voice, hands on hips.

I smiled up at her and nodded. 'I take fresh orange juice with my vodka these days, rather than cola.'

She tutted and turned to leave us. 'Now don't you be giving Michael a puff, or you will almost certainly be in my bad books.'

I played mother, pouring the freshly ground coffee into fine china cups. Mickey stared over my shoulder, and then looked at me pleadingly.

'Give us a fag Jimmy.'

I feigned shock and shook my head.' Certainly not, Freda would have my manhood spitting on the barbecue, besides, I always took you as a fine cigar smoker?'

He stared over my shoulder and pulled a face. 'That's just image, it's good for business, but I would still prefer a cigarette.'

I relented as he stared at me with his bright hound- dog eyes, and he inhaled deeply. Releasing the smoke only when it could not be held captive any longer, and his eyes were closed when he spoke. 'Jesus wept,' he whispered, 'that is more than good'. Then he opened his eyes and was on Freda high alert. 'Have you ever asked yourself Jimmy, why all the good things in life are bad for you?'

I nodded, 'Absolutely, it is a question that troubles me even before I eat my cereal laced with mountains of sugar in the morning.'

He leaned forward and looked me in the eye. 'I have a theory.'

I sipped my coffee and smiled, 'I like it already.'

He beamed at me, 'I thought you might. My theory is that all of the world's lonely, sad, smug and sanctimonious individuals formed a sort of secret society. Bent on making the more optimistic members of society to wilt under their thin lipped and humourless doctrine of 'how to live a life.' So now the delicious bacon sandwich is frowned upon. But boiled broccoli is deemed good. Booze is the blood of Satan, but designer spring water has become the piss of the gods. Smoking is deemed a horror, not only to the smoker, but to anyone who passes within a fifteen-mile radius of a smoker. The real problem as I see it is that if passive smokers kicked the habit, then we, the impassive smokers could peacefully pursue our filthy and quite curious addiction.'

He inhaled, coughed, and looked at me for support.

'Absolutely, I couldn't agree more, and if more passive smokers stopped, then it is reasonable to assume that more impassive smokers would follow suite.'

Mickey smiled at me with a mischievous glint in his eyes. 'Ah now, this is grand. Having a good old smoke and putting the world to rights.'

I slid my pack of cigarettes across the table.

'Ah no,' he replied, staring over my shoulder.

'Ah you will, you know you want to.'

His hand shot out and the cigarette pack disappeared into his inside pocket. 'Jeez, I'm going to miss you Jimmy boy.'

***

It felt so strange when I sold my car. The dealer got a bit of a bargain, but I had insisted on cash. Then I entered unknown territory as I searched for a bus to take me home. I passed an old Catholic church I had been familiar with in another life, and I stopped and entered. Don't ask me why, because I was the ultimate lapsed catholic. The bible to me was a book of hope for people who had experienced only hunger and pain in this life. It offered the possibility of an afterlife full of promise. But I had been lucky, born into a part of our planet that was green and pleasant. It was to me a wonderful world.

Therefore, I really didn't need a fairy story, that said if I was a good boy, then I would be allowed to enter heaven. The miracle to me, was that I had been born in the first place. That I had seen this wonderful planet, with all of its diverse life forms and beauty. That I had met so many people on the way that I had learned to respect and sometimes loved.

If I had been unfortunate enough to emerge from my mother's womb in that other place. Where drought and famine is rife, where disease and violence reign supreme. Then I think my perceptions would have been entirely different, and I would have clung to the good book in hope and desperation.

It was quiet and calm and strangely soothing when I entered, and smelled the incense and candle wax. I heard Beatie's voice then. 'I'm saying a prayer for the time traveller.'

My eyes strayed to the marble bowl on my right, half filled with holy water. I would have dipped my fingers in there when I was a believer, and made the sign of the cross, but I didn't. I looked for the offertory box, and it was not hard to find. There was a slot for coins and a slot for notes, but no slot for the wad of notes from the sale of my car. So I fed them in until my envelope was empty. I was certain that I had not been observed, but I was wrong. A soft rustle made me turn. He was a young man with thin steel rimmed spectacles that framed smiling blue eyes. 'Thank you for your donation,' he said softly.

I don't know why, but I felt a rush of blood to my face. As if I had been caught red handed pilfering from the box, rather than the opposite. I felt that I was ten years old again, caught dipping my sherbet lemon lollipop in the baptismal font.

' I haven't seen you here before, are you local?'

I should have told him that I had been an altar boy here in another life, but I shook my head. 'I was just passing father, I had a bit of luck at the bookies, and thought 'why not'. It was a lie of course, and once upon a prayer I would have had to say three hail Mary's and four our fathers'. But that time was long gone.

He smiled, his eyes unwavering. 'Why not indeed, I will pray that your next lucky wager is on a one hundred to one outsider.'

CHAPTER 28

The flat presented less of a problem. All of my possessions had been moved to the house. There was still five months lease to run, and I would have given them notice and paid up in advance. However, the letting agents had been so grasping for money, it had almost equalled their reluctance to resolve problems and repairs. Therefore, I decided that the only decent course of action, was to say nothing and pay nothing. They could of course pursue me in a small claims court, but, well, good luck with that I thought.

I was resigned for the long haul, I thought that I would have to be patient before the call came to signal my departure, but I was wrong. I suppose it was inevitable, but when the final call arrived two days later, it was in the small dark hours. I was sleeping and awoke with a start.

The room was dark, with just a dull glow through the curtains from the street lights beyond. My eyes closed as I returned to sleep, but snapped open again as a flash of light penetrated my eyelids, and I was wide awake. Sliding from between the sheets, I padded over to the window and peered through the curtains. Everything was as it should be, until a very familiar sound reached my ears. It was the return of the neon tube, firing and failing to ignite. My heartbeat hit the big drum roll, as a flash of light revealed a quite different view
from my window. I was looking at a shiny cobbled street, bathed in moonlight. The gas lamp glowed and everything was cloaked in a misty cloud of fog.

It was time.

I changed into my travelling clothes, and carried my suitcases into the hall. The angry bee returned, louder, more insistent. I laughed aloud then, 'I can hear you!' I called aloud, 'but you'll just have to wait a moment.'

I returned to my bedroom for the last time, and threw my mobile phone onto the bed. The lights in the front room almost blinded me as I searched for pen and paper, and the message was brief and simple. 'Goodbye my friends...have a good life.' I placed the note within the large buff envelope containing the cash withdrawn from my bank account, and added a footnote. ' This will help you finish the restoration of the house...good luck!'

I double checked my clothing before placing my Bogie hat on. 'Well this is it Jimmy boy,' I whispered. ' Let's face the music and dance.'

A cold blast of air greeted me as I stepped out into the porch, placing the suitcases at my feet. I then locked the door and fed the keys through the letterbox, having given Ammo the spare set. The faint light of dawn approached as I waited, pulling the collar of my overcoat up. And there was a fleeting moment of unease as I stared at the barren mud before me. The first dawn chorus arrived, and I stamped my feet impatiently...had I been too casual and missed the boat?

Then it returned, and the angry bee was louder than ever. The garden flickered before me, like images from an old cine camera. Before it settled and I was looking at a very familiar place. There was the white picket fence, and matching garden gate. The dark patches of lawn to left and right, and the gas lamp glowing across the street.

Wasting no time, I picked up my cases and stepped down the three steps. There was no nausea to greet me, but simply a feeling of joy and relief that I had made the return journey. Walking down the path, I could hear the guillotine's chomping at leather from the glove factory, so it was still a working day.

Suddenly an old shooting brake trundled past, parping its horn at a mongrel dog sniffing at something in the gutter. I grinned and turned on my heels. The house was in darkness, but I knocked on the door anyway. The key turned easily in the lock, and I felt that I was home at last. My room was just as I had left it, but somewhat tidier. The soft quilted eiderdown beckoned, and I stretched out, resting my eyes.

The first to enter was firm of foot, it had to be Sandy. Smiling, I closed my eyes again and listened to the clattering of plates and a whistle from the kettle. Then I heard Mary arrive. 'Have you got the kettle on Sandy?' she called, pausing by the hall stand. 'Because I'm gagging for a cuppa.'

The conversation in the kitchen was muted as I swung my legs from the bed. Sandy saw me first as the biscuit in his hand fell back onto the plate. But Mary was faster, as she turned, knocked back her chair and rushed into my arms. I embraced them both but was instantly aware that there was a third person present.

'Why Mary, is that a baby in your belly or have you just been overdoing it on the milk chocolate biscuits?'

She laughed, 'It's almost five months gone now Jimmy.' I gave her another hug and a thumbs up to dad. 'This is fantastic news,' I then looked at Sandy sternly, ' she has to take things easy in the final months.'

He nodded, 'well maybe she will listen to you Jimmy, because she sure as hell won't listen to her old man.'

'She has got a name,' said Mary with a glint in her eyes, 'besides, I feel just fine.'

I took her hands and stared, ' you look better than fine, you look absolutely radiant.' She smiled and indicated to a chair at the table. 'Sit yourself down Jimmy, you look like you could do with a cup of tea.'

'Tea?' I said with a shake of the head,' I think I may need something stronger.'

Sandy rose from his seat with a wide grin, ' Aye well that is easily arranged.'

'Tea is fine Sandy, we can toast your good news later.' I lit a cigarette as Mary pushed a cup my way. ' Have I really been gone that long, five months?'

Sandy nodded, ' A wee bit longer, Mary only found out that she was pregnant about two weeks after you had gone.'

'How odd,' I replied sipping my favourite builders brew, ' time seems to pass on a different level. I feel like I have only been away for a couple of weeks.'

There was a moments silence before I blurted it out. 'How is she?'

Mary reached across the table and laid her hand on mine, and I panicked. 'What's wrong, has something happened?'

'She's fine Jimmy, but Gwen has not had the easiest of times recently. When you do see her, please try not to look too shocked at her appearance,' she urged.

I was on the ropes now, reeling from one punch too many.

Sandy's calm voice came to my rescue. ' The wee lassie is no' ill or anything like that. In fact, quite the opposite was true in the weeks after you left. She was after all in love, and when she found that she was three weeks gone, why, she was the happiest woman on the planet.'

My eyes widened, 'Gwen is pregnant?'

He shook his head. 'She was Jimmy, she was having your bairn. But she took a tumble on the stairs at home and...'

His voice failed him and he lowered his head.

'She lost the baby,' whispered Mary softly, ' and as the months passed she became convinced that you were gone for good. She became agitated and suffered from awful mood swings. She ate like a bird whenever she would eat at all, and the flesh fell away from her.'

'Aye, she's a shadow of her former self, and it does'na help when that creepy fellow comes a calling and bothering her.'

My eyes narrowed, ' what, Lancelot Sprat is back?'

'He is,' replied Mary angrily, ' he is like a bad smell that will just not go away. Gwen has made it plain enough that she is just not interested, and we have made it quite clear that he is not welcome in this house, but will he listen?'

I was angry now, ' I must go to her!'

Mary continued to grip my hand. 'There's no need Jimmy, she will be here any minute now. She has called here every day after work, hoping that you will have returned, and when she sees that you are not here, a little bit of her seems to die. She is still waiting for you.'

My heart was breaking when I heard the front door open. 'It's only me,' she called in that oh so familiar voice, and I was on my feet in an instant.

She smiled, gasped, staggered back and shopping bags fell as her left shoulder shuddered into the door frame.

'Jimmy?' she called.

Tears burned in my eyes, she looked so thin and fragile, like she might shatter in pieces if she fell.

A few steps and I scooped her up in my arms, and we held on to one another like we would never let go. We remained like that for some time, as I listened to her desperate crying. She touched my face, her hands moving over my forehead, eyes and cheeks. As if to confirm that it was really me, and when she was sure, a squeal of laughter followed. It was a sound of pure joy escaping from her lips, and we kissed, oblivious of present company.

Sandy reached into his cupboard and produced a bottle of champagne. 'This was bought in anticipation of our own wee bairn been born, but I can always buy another.'

We sat around the kitchen table with the crackling fire projecting our joyful silhouettes on the wall and toasted the future. I told them about my travels, about the final farewell to my friends, and the short but frustrating journey back. We drank champagne and smoked cigarettes and they laughed out loud when I recalled the crazy Jimmy yarn, and gasped when I told them how much cash was in the suitcases.

'So, when you go back again, you could buy even more important works of art,' said Mary.

I shrugged, 'I would if I could but I can't. My time travelling days are over, I am here for good.' Gwen squeezed my hand as they stared, and Sandy raised his glass.

'Why that is fantastic news,' she said.

'There is something else,' I said, placing my glass on the table. I scraped back my chair and went down on bended knee, looking up at her lovely smiling pain ravaged face.

'I have loved you ever since I saw you emerge from the bakers' shop, arm in arm with your mum, and me, cunningly disguised as the hunchback of Notre Dame.'

She blushed, and laughed out loud at the memory.

'Would you please do me the honour of becoming my wife?'

She puckered up her lips as if in deep thought, 'I really don't know what to say?'

'Say yes,' I pleaded.

She looked at Mary, who nodded furiously, and then Sandy, who grinned like the village idiot. Finally, she relented and dragged me to my feet. 'Yes, of course I will. I have loved you ever since you told me the story about the fishes. How could I possibly refuse?'

We embraced, and I swung her off her feet to enthusiastic applause and whistling from our dear friends. Suddenly there was a knock at the front door, and Sandy headed down the hall. The voice was familiar to all of us.

'Is Gwen here?'

Sandy's response was terse, 'aye she is, but she does not want to see you ever, and neither do we.'

'Let him in Sandy,' I called, and the girls looked at me with raised eyebrows.

His footfalls were loud as he stamped down the hall, entering the kitchen like he owned the place, a sad wilting bunch of flowers in his right hand.

I stood and faced him, 'you brought me flowers, how kind.'

He stared at me, his lips working furiously. 'You?'

I smiled, ' indeed it is.'

His face turned a rather unhealthy mottled red. 'So what fishy place have you returned from?'

'Not fishy at all Maurice, I have been interred in her majesty's hotel for some months. I was accused of bashing a man over the head, and then plucking out his eyeballs as he still writhed screaming on the ground. It was said that I ate them accompanied with a fine bottle of nut-brown ale.' I stepped forward with a smile, and he took several steps backward, without one. 'The case was thrown out of court, due to a lack of evidence.' I continued my advance as he in turn retreated nervously. 'Justice can be so blind don't you think Maurice? But back to you, why in hells name are you stealing graveyard flowers to give to my fiancé?'

He was sweating now, his poor excuse of a brain attempting to formulate a response.

'You are barking mad.'

'Absolutely, why don't you join us for dinner Maurice? You are more than welcome. I believe that we are having meat balls in a delicious Italian blood red sauce.'

The next step I took was too much for the poor man, and he fled down the hall and disappeared into the night.

They stared at me.

'Now you have scared all of us Jimmy,' said Mary in awe.

I shrugged, 'it was nothing, I was just misquoting a certain Doctor Hannibal Lecter.'

'Well whoever he is,' she answered, ' I would not like to meet him on a dark night, or any other night come to think of it.'

We returned to our champagne. 'How is old Donald next door? I must pop in and see him tomorrow.' The quick exchange of looks between them told me everything.

'He's dead, isn't he.'

'Aye,' said Sandy, ' he passed on about a week after you left.'

'I'm sorry to hear it.' I raised my glass and they followed suite. 'To Donald,' and we touched glasses, toasting the life of a man who had seen not just one, but two world wars. A man who had lost a wife, but had honed the fine art of how to kick a stuffed dog, without actually hurting the loathed snapper.

The following morning, I dressed quickly, frowning at the trousers. The crutch seemed to start well below the point that it should start, and ended just below my chest. I was now completely sold on the purpose of a waistcoat, it was there to hide the crutch that appeared to suggest that it was concealing the presence of a giant anaconda. The aroma of sizzling bacon beckoned and I took the stairs two by two.

Mary smiled, ' did you sleep well.'

'I did, I slept so well that I don't remember sleeping, never mind dreaming.

'Well sit yourself down, there's tea in the pot. Sandy has nipped out for a paper.'

I pulled aside the net curtains and grinned, it was snowing again.

' What date is it Mary?'

She smiled, 'it is March the fifteenth, nineteen fifty-seven.'

This was music to my ears, Beaty and Cleve had arrived, they were now neighbours of mine, living just across the road.

Mary cracked some eggs into the frying pan and laughed softly.

'What?' I said.

She flicked sizzling lard over the eggs and shook her head. ' That stunt you pulled with Maurice last night was so funny.'

'It did have the desired effect though.'

She nodded and scooped the eggs onto a plate in the oven. ' Oh yes, if I didn't know you better, then I too would have run a mile.'

Sandy returned with his newspaper, and we ate a hearty breakfast of bacon, fried eggs, fried tomatoes, mushrooms, black pudding, and crisp fried bread. In my time it would have been denounced as a killer breakfast.

But in my chosen time it was simply delicious, and we didn't give a shit. People still remembered rationing, when one egg was expected to last a week. So, a full English breakfast was now a celebration of better times to come. I cleaned my plate with remnants of fried bread.

'Have you any plans today Jimmy,' said Mary as she cleared away the plates.

I accepted a cigarette from Sandy and smiled. ' I am meeting my fiancé and we are heading into town to buy an engagement ring. Although she doesn't know it yet.'

Mary looked at her husband, who in turn started to laugh. 'Why that is a very romantic notion, but why do you think we are all sitting here having breakfast together.'

I frowned, and then the penny dropped, ' it's Sunday isn't it.'

'No Jimmy, it's Saturday, but look at all the snow out there, the buses will no' be running an' that's for sure.'

I frowned, ' where am I, the Darby and Joan club, where's your spirit of adventure.'

Returning to my room, I pulled out one of my suitcases and counted out a wad of notes, placing them in a canvas bag. I then returned to the welcome warmth of the kitchen and placed the bag on the table. 'There's five thousand pounds in there, your payment for helping me to become a wealthy man in this time.'

They shrank away as if I had placed the head of John the Baptist before them. Mary shook her head, ' we cannot possibly accept that Jimmy, why it is a King's ransom!'

' It's just too much Jimmy,' cried Sandy. 'Mary is right, we don't need lots of money to be happy.'

I picked up the bag and carried it over to the fire, 'Well I have money to burn,' I threatened, holding it towards the flames. ' But it is not just for you,' I said, pointing at Mary, ' it is also for the bump, and his or her future security.'

They relented, and we ended up in a sort of emotional hug-in. Then Gwen arrived, eyes bright and cheeks flushed red, and we headed into town, playing in the snow like children. Running and kicking clouds of snowflakes, throwing snowballs and full of the joys of life. Our quick laughter creating clouds of mist in the crisp cool air.

We stopped at the gallery and Gwen looked at me, eyes wide. 'Is this the shop you told us about?' I nodded and entered, the tiny brass bell announcing our arrival. He stepped through the door of his workshop, a much more confident man than the one I had encountered first time round.

'Why Mr Traveller, what a pleasure it is to see you sir.'

I introduced my fiancé and friends, and they shook hands.

'So, how is business?'

'Absolutely splendid sir, and it's all due to your kindness and guidance.'

'Nonsense, I merely suggested some changes and you did the rest. Your parents and brother would be immensely proud of you.'

Colour rose to his cheeks as my companions moved away to study the paintings on display.

'Are you dancing,' I whispered.

'I discovered that I have two left feet,' he said with a smile and a shake of the head. 'I am not a dancing man, but I do attend interesting lectures at the town hall and other venues. And I have become acquainted with several likeminded individuals.' He paused and looked furtively around, as if his next sentence might possibly compromise the security of the nation. 'We have formed a supper club.'

I raised my eyebrows, 'a supper club indeed.'

He nodded, 'and Elspeth, who is one of my companions, shares my interest in early Roman architecture.'

I felt a gag coming on, but suppressed it. He was living a life again, he was happy and fulfilled, and I was glad.

The bell tinkled as we said our goodbyes, and crunched out into the snow. We men watched as the girls tried on different items of clothing, and we applauded as they strutted their stuff. They watched as I modelled a smart double-breasted navy winter coat with matching Bogie. We watched as Sandy chose a pair of splendid tiny gold cuff links, and held out his arm as if he was holding a sophisticated cocktail.

We dined on mixed grill, in a restaurant that surprisingly seemed to specialise in mixed grill. We were greeted by a lively cockatoo on a stand, who screeched 'hallo' on our arrival, and 'goodbye my darlings', as we left.

The walk home was an exhausting experience, but we were more than happy.

***

The following day I bought a car. Not just any old car, but an Alvis TC 108/G Super Cabriolet, and she handled well in the snow as I slewed to a halt. The large steak pie was double wrapped in brown paper bags, and still felt warm to the touch. Beatie's street was like something out of a Christmas Carol. Snow smothered everything, from washing lines to rooftops. Huge icicles dripped like daggers from gutters, and all was silent. I ploughed my way through the snow, aware that I was being watched. He was standing on the top step, before a half open door, smoking a cigarette. His frame was almost as thin as the loose strands of hair scraped over his skull. It seemed to me that he braved the cold in a stained white vest, to tell the world that he was a real man. Braces hung loosely from his sides as he peered at me through thin wire spectacles, as I struggled through the snowdrift. Suddenly he was there, standing in a gateless gap between high red brick walls, as I turned to enter Beatie's yard.

'You don't want to go in there mate,' he said, 'there's niggers in that house.'

I paused and looked at him, placing the pie on the snow topped wall.

'Is that a fact,' I replied, approaching him with an outstretched hand, and he grinned the grin of an idiot. I have always had a strong grip, and the hand in my grasp was weak and bony. I smiled at him and increased the pressure. He said nothing, but his head jerked to one side, sending his spectacles into a lopsided nose dive. I increased the pressure, feeling the bones in his hand compress, causing him to groan.

He retreated back into his yard until he could retreat no more. Soft snow fell from the branches of an overhanging bush onto his bare shoulders, and he shivered

Then I heard the voice from hell calling. ' What are you doing out there, are them niggers playing up again?'.

'Beaty and Cleve are friends of mine,' I said softly. 'I heard that they were getting some grief from a neighbour, and it has to stop now. I was willing to let you remain living here, but then I just heard the voice of the bitch from hell, so I have decided that you must leave, do you understand?'

He nodded silently, and I stepped back as the snow turned yellow at his feet. He was shaking when I left, but I was shaking more. Violence of any kind is abhorrent to me, but there are moments in life when there is little or no alternative.

I knocked on the door, and smiled at the flattened snow in the yard. It looked like someone had been dancing. A much younger Beaty answered, but the confidence and celebration of life was not quite there yet. She seemed shy and apprehensive.

'Sorry to bother you, but I was visiting me mam in the next street, and she told me that you had just moved in.' I held out the pie and smiled, ' I'm under strict instructions to give you this pie, as a sort of welcome to the neighbourhood.'

Her eyes widened, moving quickly to the pie, and then back to me again.

'Cleveland!' she bellowed, sounding more like the Beaty I had learned to know and love.

He was a tall man, with a small goatee beard and large luminous eyes. Beaty stepped aside and I repeated my message. He looked at me slowly, from the tip of my boots to the top of my head.

I held out the pie. 'Mam said that some local idiots were giving you a hard time, because of the colour of your skin. She said good folk are in charge around these parts, and we should not be judged by the actions of a few inbred loons.'

He accepted the pie graciously. ' What is your name?'

'James,' I said, and then corrected myself, 'Jimmy.'

His sad eyes softened and crinkled into a smile. ' You go an' tell your momma thank you. You go an' tell her that she is welcome in our home come rain or shine.' He held out his hand and we shook, and I saw a glimmer of tears as he closed the door.

The car came to a crunching halt at the bottom of the street, and I killed the engine, adjusting the rear-view mirror. Sure enough, Cleveland appeared, ploughing through the snow, his arms akimbo. He stared down the street, ignoring the parked car, and then rushed up the hill, disappearing around the corner. I smiled and gunned the engine. Beaty was right, he was completely hatless.

CHAPTER 29

July 21st, 1980.

If you ever point your car over the North Yorkshire moors, and head for the coastal town of Whitby, spare a thought for the time traveller and his wife. Ignore the undoubted charms of ancient Whitby, and follow the signs to the tiny village of Sandsend instead.

As the road snakes down, with the sea on your right, leave the car in the long parking strip overlooking the beach and rolling waves, and walk. Your path will curve to the left and you will enter the village proper, passing 'The Hart' pub on your left. An old stone bridge beckons, but do not cross it. Take time out to pause and look at the geese and the ducks in the water below. Listen to them call with their deep throaty laughs and watch as children play with bucket and spade. See dogs run, wet coats matted in sand, wet snouts sniffing a myriad of strange scents. People calling after their pets, their children, their loved ones. Take a glance at the old folk, sitting on benches, leaning on canes, chewing the fat and generally enjoying the Autumn of their days. Listen to the younger generation in their cars, slowing to cross the bridge. Music pumped up, 'look at me' loud, eyes not surfing the surf or the lovely gentle landscape of life around them, but surfing their mobile phones like their lives depended upon it. Lean on the handrail and look up. You will see several houses perched on the hill, surrounded by dense woodland. Look closer and you may see a house that almost seems to hang in the tree tops. That house is called Tanglewood, and it is and has been our home for many years. It was here that we sat in the garden on a balmy July morning. Balloons still fluttered from garden seats and tables, a reminder of a birthday bash that happened a day earlier than it should have done.

Sandy and Mary stepped through the patio doors, and Gwen rose to her feet. The women embraced, and Sandy took a seat and stared at me.

'It was a smashing party Jimmy.'

'It was wasn't it,' I said smiling, ' A grand send off.'

He frowned, 'we don't know that, why we could be worrying ourselves mad for nothing.'

'We both know that is not true, but I am glad you enjoyed the party. You two would have been top of our list anyway, but I needed you both here for Gwen you understand.'

He nodded, 'aye, and we wouldn't have it any other way. If anything happens we will be there for the lassie.'

'Thank you Sandy, that is all I ask.'

The girls joined us, and Gwen slid her hand into mine. We watched the sun rise higher in a deep blue sky. Watched as day trippers arrived in cars and camper vans below. It was low tide and the beach came alive, as families settled behind windbreaks, joggers jogged, dogs barked, children screamed and shouted. And in the distance Whitby abbey glowed on the headland, in the bright brittle light of a summer's morning.

Gwen lowered her head into my chest and started to cry softly. I wrapped her in my arms and held her until it passed. We had been here many times before She looked up at me and brushed away tears. ' I know we have prepared for this day from the start...' Her voice faltered, and she buried her head in my chest once more. ' I can't bear it Jimmy; please tell me this is not happening?'

I stroked her forehead and kissed some of the salty tears from her cheeks, and soon she was calm again. 'I remember you telling me that you were abandoned as a baby. That you were found well-nourished in a lady's loo at the hospital, but you never said at what time you were born.'

I continued to stroke her hair and smiled. ' My mum and dad told me all they knew. They said that I was found bawling my head off on a nappy changing table, by an old lady. There was a quickly scribbled note pinned to my sleeve. It was apparently desperately short. Giving the date of my birth, my name, and a plea to find someone to take me in and love me as their own.'

'But no time,' she whispered, ' she didn't say what time you were born?'

I shook my head, 'no, there was no time.'

We fell silent for a time, listening to the joyful sounds of life drifting up from the beach. Then another sound caught my attention, it was the gentle flapping of wings as a large seagull alighted on the fence at the gardens edge.

Gwen pulled away and peered up at me like a startled Doe. 'We could be wrong of course, have you ever thought of that?'

'We could indeed be wrong, but if I were to leave you now, would you have any regrets?'

She pulled me to her and kissed me with a passion, ' no regrets Jimmy, I just want a few more years...is that too much to ask.'

Two more seagulls settled on the fence, all three were strangely still. Their wings folded, beaks lowered to the lawn, and I knew it was time. A darkness came, even though there were no clouds in the sky, and I saw a flash of lightening far out to sea. I stood and pulled Gwen into my arms, 'It's time for me to go darling.'

She screamed then, and I looked at my friends, 'you must take her into the house now.'

They gently prised her from my arms and stumbled away from me over the lawn. Somehow, she managed to pull free and ran to me with a scream so desperate, that I raised my arms, expecting that she would be there, where she belonged. But she was gone, they were all gone, and I was plunged into darkness.

The sound of the sea beckoned, and lightening flickered over the dark surface. I closed my eyes and started to count. Then my eyes snapped open, and the look of surprise quickly softened into a smile of recognition. For it was not the crack of thunder that rumbled over that black sea, but the sound of a new born baby boy, crying.

THE END

Printed in Great Britain
by Amazon

63714096R00175